Crawlerz
Book 1

"Red Sky in the Morning"

R S Merritt

Text Copyright © 2020 Randall Scott Merritt

All Rights Reserved

This series is dedicated to my beautiful wife and family.

**Cover Design By:
Harry Lamb**

Table of Contents

Prologue: As Long as you Both Shall Live

Chapter 1: Forever Family

Chapter 2: Denial is a River in Egypt

Chapter 3: Stocking Up

Chapter 4: Preparing for the Worst

Chapter 5: Crisis at the Border

Chapter 6: A Rude Awakening

Chapter 7: Another Day in Paradise

Chapter 8: The Greater Good

Chapter 9: Lessons Learned

Chapter 10: A Looting We Will Go

Chapter 11: Lights Out

Chapter 12: Pancakes to Piracy

Chapter 13: Fort Russel

Chapter 14: The Surge

Chapter 15: The First Night

Chapter 16: Hump Day

Chapter 17: A Time to Panic

Chapter 18: Are We There Yet?

Chapter 19: North

Chapter 20: That New Car Smell

Chapter 21: Death by the Dashboard Lights

Chapter 22: Ghetto Tank

Chapter 23: Don't be a Hero

Chapter 24: Go Gators!

Chapter 25: The Hell Out of Florida

Chapter 26: Orphaned Again

Chapter 27: A Dark Cloud

Chapter 28: A New Day

Chapter 29: Cut Bait

Chapter 30: Saying Goodbye

Chapter 31: All for One

Chapter 32: Step Right Up

Chapter 33: Story Time

Chapter 34: Canaries

Chapter 35: The Man in the Suit

Chapter 36: The Gift Horse was a Trojan

Authors Note:

Other Books by RS Merritt

Prologue: As Long as You Both Shall Live

"Hurry up or we're going to miss our ride!" John yelled into the steam filled bathroom of an executive suite in the Cairo Marriott. The tour company had emphasized that if they didn't get to the pyramids on time, they could end up missing out on getting to go inside.

"I'm hurrying!" Desiree said tersely emerging out of the steam wearing one of the fancy hotel robes with a towel wrapped around her head. She made a beeline for the balcony to crack open the door and get rid of the steam from the shower. Opening the curtain covering the glass door to the balcony revealed a gorgeous view of the old city. You could also see a small patch of the Nile. Just enough for the hotel to justify calling it a river view upgrade. She plopped down in the chair at the desk and pulled up a mirror to start working on her make-up. To keep himself from saying anything he may regret John walked out on the balcony to take in the view for the umpteenth time.

The hotel had drained the last of the Marriott Reward points he'd accumulated over the past year of business travel. Between the hotel rewards, rental car points and the sky miles the honeymoon was already over halfway paid for. Which was a good thing since they were planning on house hunting as soon as they got back home. Neither of them could pinpoint the exact time they'd started watching HGTV excessively but they'd both formed some pretty strong opinions on what they wanted in a home. That happens after a few months of falling asleep with terms like 'city living' and 'open floorplan' serving as your lullaby.

Tempers were a little frayed since the flight hadn't been the best experience ever. They'd been able to bump up to business class using points, but first class had been ridiculously expensive. It hadn't seemed like a big deal until they actually had to spend fifteen hours stuck on a plane together. Halfway through the flight the extra fifteen grand for those extra inches of legroom began to seem much more reasonable. Having to wake up at three in the morning to get to the airport in time for the flight had also seemed like a good idea when they were planning it.

In retrospect they should've given themselves more time to relax when they arrived. The jet lag might not kill them, but it may cause them to kill each other. He would've just rescheduled the pyramid tour but only a certain number of visitors were allowed in per day. If you didn't get in one day, it wasn't like they gave you front of the line privileges the next day. He supposed with enough money anything was possible but despite the fact they were staying in a gorgeous hotel on an exotic international honeymoon they weren't exactly flush with cash. Weddings weren't cheap.

John and Desiree both wanted to travel before settling down. They'd gone on some pretty awesome vacations while they were dating and continued the practice into their engagement. When they were coming up with honeymoon ideas John had thrown out Egypt as an option. On their first date they'd ridden the Mummy ride at Universal Studios. The ride had broken down halfway through leaving them sitting awkwardly in the small seat with their legs touching. John had leaned over to whisper a joke in her ear at the same time as she'd turned to tell him something. The result had been a painful head butt that'd led to an embarrassingly passionate first kiss. They would've toned it down if they'd noticed the car right behind them was full of little kids riding with their grandma.

Desiree loved the idea of going to Egypt for their honeymoon. She was confident as she did her makeup that once they'd both slept for around twelve hours the vacation would become much more enjoyable. She was excited to go check out the pyramids. She just wished she could nap for a day or so first. It didn't help that she felt a pounding headache coming on thanks to the arid climate and lack of sleep.

She slapped her makeup on ignoring the obvious signals to hurry up she was getting from John. He kept opening the curtains leading out to the balcony to see if she was done yet. He'd literally rolled out of bed, brushed his teeth, splashed water on his head and announced he was ready to go. He was thinking about finally getting to see the pyramids after all the research he'd done on visiting them. He was thinking about their schedule. Having seen the extensive work that he'd put into their itinerary Desiree had joked he'd missed his calling. He should've been a travel planner for AAA.

Desiree wasn't about to be rushed. They were going to be taking pictures in front of the pyramids of Giza. They'd be knocking out selfies in front of the last remaining wonder of the ancient world. They'd most likely never be back here again. John had emphasized they basically had one shot at getting inside the pyramids according to the tour company. All of that added up to her needing to look good in the pictures they took today. They'd be popping up on social media for who knew how long. John would inevitably order one of the pictures as a canvas print to put in the house they'd eventually get.

John may not care if he looked like a hobo in the pictures, but she did. She'd put at least as much thought and planning into the outfits she'd brought with her as he had into their itinerary. Looking in the mirror she saw a need for some serious work on her face. She looked as jet lagged and tired as she felt. Once she got through the makeup and hair portion of getting ready everything else went fast. A mere fifty minutes after emerging from the bathroom they were walking through the ritzy hotel lobby on the way to meet their ride.

Originally built as a palace for royal guests the hotel was a place worth exploring all on its own. The history of the ancient city they were in was something that was hard to grasp for most Americans. To most of them the American Civil War was history and Columbus discovering North America was ancient history. The city they were staying in was founded 3,500 years before Columbus was able to talk the queen of Spain into lending him some money to go off exploring.

The bellman met them in the lobby to let them know their driver was waiting for them. John handed the bellman a couple of dollars in the funny looking currency they'd gotten from the currency exchange at the airport. Desiree had already slid some into the back of her wallet as a souvenir. She'd tried to do it sneakily knowing that otherwise John was bound to run out and need to borrow some from her for tipping people.

Driving through the tiny streets of Cairo reminded them both of other wild car rides they'd taken outside the states. The horn was used just as frequently as the turn signals. There was a lot of yelling in a language that neither Desiree nor John had the slightest ability to understand. John had tried learning to speak some of the common phrases but given up on that part of his trip preparation when Desiree had shown zero enthusiasm for it. Plus, the guidebooks all said English was commonly spoken in the tourist sections of Egypt.

The thirty-minute drive from the hotel took about an hour. The finale being a yelling match between their driver and the ticket agent at the parking lot outside of the pyramids. In broken English an apologetic driver had told them that because they'd arrived late their tickets had been sold to another couple. The guard happened to have another set he could sell them though. Their driver let them know that they were being screwed but there was nothing he could do about it. John pulled out the wad of funny money and watched as the guard and driver made most of it disappear.

Twenty minutes later him and Desiree were standing in line on the side of the pyramid waiting to go inside. It was hot and miserable. They were both sucking down overpriced bottles of water and had swallowed fistfuls of Tylenol. The jet lag catching up to them right as they were reaching the exact spot that they'd been talking about for the last four months.

"What's that over there?" Desiree asked looking out across the rocky desert towards a huge tarp that'd been setup to cover an excavation site. The tarp was surrounded by a broadcast crew with professional looking cameras. Several large vehicles were parked around the site. One of them was sporting a large satellite dish on top of it.

"Beats me. Probably something for the Discovery channel or something. Hurry up. It's almost our turn and I want to get out of this sun." John said after a quick glance across the lot towards the film crew in question.

After all the money and time spent getting there, they were slightly underwhelmed by the actual experience. The main pyramid needed an escalator. You had to climb along this board with ridges in it for what felt like forever. It was hell on your calves. Once you made it to the top you were rewarded with the view of a much larger opening in the middle of the pyramid. They did their time walking and climbing around sneaking the occasional obligatory selfie in defiance of the no photography signs.

The exercise helped with the jet lag and headaches. Walking out the entrance to the pyramids once they were done Desiree pointed out the camera crew were still doing their thing. Deciding it may be more interesting to check that out than to walk around inside the other pyramid they headed in the general direction of the tarps. The tarps looked a lot closer than they really were. They gave up when they saw they'd have to exit the area they'd paid to get into if they kept going and went to explore the other pyramid instead. After a long day they headed for the parking lot and the welcome ride back to the hotel.

Back in the room John told Desiree to wait up so he could go grab a coffee from the lobby. He hit the elevator and rode it down to the gift shop where he was able to get a tray put together with chocolates and strawberries. He was also able to add a couple of miniature bottles of champagne at an exorbitant price. He was happy to have gotten them at all. He'd read differing messaging about buying alcohol in the highly Islamic country. Once he had everything together one of the bellhops insisted on carrying it all up the room for him.

His beautiful bride was passed out under the covers with drool leaking out the side of her mouth. The bellhop struggled to hide a grin as he wheeled the pricey fruit tray into the room. John tipped him and sent him on his way. He sat down hard on the side of the bed hoping to 'accidentally' wake Desiree up. This was not how he'd pictured their first night in Egypt on their honeymoon. He finally gave up on her after shifting around a bunch and coughing and generally trying to wake her up without being obvious about trying to wake her up.

He was exhausted himself but decided to indulge in some of the champagne and fruit before crawling into bed with his lawfully wedded wife. He considered taking a short video of her to prove that she snored but decided against it. She was very much against having pictures or videos like that floating around out in cyberspace. It didn't help that he'd absolutely bring pictures like that up any time he did a slide show in front of their friends.

He flipped the TV on and scrolled through the channels once he figured out how to use the remote. He was hoping for a channel with some English subtitles. He was thrilled when he found some news channels with English speaking reporters. He was munching on some expensive cheese and downing the extremely dry champagne in big gulps when he heard the sound of sirens outside. The hotel they were staying in was on an island in the Nile, so you had to cross a bridge to get to it. Their room faced the city across the narrow gap of water that made it an island. John walked out on the balcony to check if he could see what was happening.

He saw the bright lights of the flashers on top of a few emergency vehicles as they headed down the main road. The lights disappeared quickly into the labyrinth of the millennia old city. John chugged the rest of the very dry champagne grimacing a bit at the taste of it before making his way back into the room. He shut the door and locked it before closing the curtain. Climbing into bed beside Desiree he tried to turn the TV off. The remote stubbornly resisted his buzzed efforts to find the right button. He finally figured out he was holding it upside down.

Turning the remote around the other way he started to click the power button when he noticed the images on the TV. It was the tarped off area they'd seen earlier that day from the pyramid. The camera focused on an Egyptian archeologist who was explaining that they'd discovered the ancient crypt by using some kind of new particle seismic X-ray machine. John adjusted his head on the pillows waiting to see if they showed what was in the crypt. Instead, the TV flashed to a drawing of the site. There was a tunnel that went down about a hundred feet before opening up into an underground cavern. The tunnel zig zagged back and forth as it descended into the earth. The archeologist was describing how massive stones had been placed at every turn to block off access to the site. The assumption was the huge carved out space below must be hugely important.

John sat up watching the TV with interest. The excavation had been going on for several weeks now and this was the day they'd be doing the reveal to the world. Now that the announcer mentioned it John remembered having heard something about it on the Discovery channel. It hadn't been about Shark week, so he hadn't paid that much attention to it. It was getting to the exciting part of the live broadcast so of course the show went to commercial. John put his head back and closed his eyes for a second. By the time the show came back on he was fast asleep.

What was revealed on the screen was a massive underground cavern as expected. A huge open space with some sort of bright green mold growing all over the walls. The archeologists all had breathing masks on while they were slowly lowered the thirty feet down to the floor. The camera showed the tomb raiders looking around at piles of broken vases covered in the green mold. A small underground stream trickled through the cavern. That discovery caused a ton of rapid-fire commentary as more explorers were carefully lowered down.

In the eerie landscape the cameras showed the large group of scientists slowly fanning out. Their cameras panning everywhere as they sought to capture what they were seeing and broadcast it to the world above. The bright lights on the cameras revealing more and more of the site. Bones began to be uncovered. The cameramen finally realized they were standing in piles of ancient human bones. One zoomed in on a mold covered skull that he then carefully avoided stepping on. The commentators were busy discussing if it was a mass burial site or if maybe human sacrifice had been involved.

The screaming was the first indication something was wrong. Captured in a live broadcast for the world to see the scientists began screaming to be pulled up to the surface. The camera streaming via satellite to the world swung around wildly as the videographer was yanked off his feet. The light from his camera revealing dark human shapes scattering on the cavern floor to get back out of the light. Then the feed was cut.

"Wake up!" Desiree said loudly poking John in the side hard enough to make him grunt with pain. He tried to go back to sleep but something in her voice told him that'd be a bad idea. He opened his eyes and saw the clock beside the bed showed they'd slept the morning away. So much for his itinerary.

"Good morning beautiful. Do you – " He started to ask her if she wanted some breakfast. He was trying to remember if he'd drank all the champagne the night before or if maybe they had enough for him to whip up some mimosas.

"Shut up. I think we're under attack or something." Desiree said pointing at the TV. A well-rested John rubbed the last bit of sleep out of his eyes and stared at the TV. It was showing aerial views of chaos in the streets. A commentator was saying that there must've been some sort of biological weapon unleashed on the city. Desiree grabbed John by the shirt and pointed him at the balcony.

John walked with Desiree over to the balcony where the curtain had been shut tight. He slid it to the side and looked out in horror at the city burning unchecked across the river. Here and there firetrucks and police cars moved along the street but other than that there didn't seem to be a lot of motion. The TV was blaring an emergency signal now with a message in a foreign language scrolling along the bottom. Much to his wife's amusement John squealed like a scared little girl when someone knocked on their door.

Feeling a bit silly John went to the door and opened it. The hotel employee on the other side told them that it appeared the city may have suffered a terrorist incident of some sort. Officials were working on an appropriate response but for now all citizens and tourists were ordered to shelter in place and keep their windows and doors tightly closed. The bellhop pulled out a roll of duct tape and quickly sealed up the slider going to the balcony.

"That's supposed to protect us from biological weapons?" Desiree asked the man in a panicked voice.

"It will ma'am and sir. You will be fine here. Just don't leave the room. You're very safe here. If there any other orders, we'll ring your phone and let you know. Is there anything else I can get you?" The man asked.

They asked for some bottled water and food to be sent up and the man assured them it'd be on the way soon. Once the bellhop left the room, they worked on getting their phones connected to the hotel WIFI. They immediately began searching the headlines on Google and Yahoo to see what was going on. The searches didn't help to calm their nerves. Raw video uploaded to different social media sites showed scenes of chaos in the streets. People were being attacked in broad daylight for no apparent reason.

"Can we get to the airport?" Desiree asked.

"I doubt it. Not if we're on lockdown. We'd have to cross the bridge and drive through all that mess to get to the airport. I doubt they're even flying right now with all this going on." John replied scrolling through a long list of videos that'd just been uploaded. He clicked and watched multiple scenes of rioters breaking windows to get into buildings. The people going in the buildings had no regard for their own skin. They leapt headfirst through windows with jagged pieces of sharp glass still sticking out in every direction. Videos showed bodies lying in the street. One video showed a little girl with her face covered in blood chewing on the arm of an old man lying face down in the street.

"That one's got to be fake." Desiree pronounced with a shaky voice.

"Agreed. Someone's trying to make this look like Dawn of the Dead. I guess we can't really expect a ton of truth from the internet." John answered. His words didn't come out sounding as confident as he'd wanted them to.

Desiree walked over to the balcony and began peeling back the tape holding the curtain to the window. The bellhop had run tape all over the parts of the door that gas could leak in then taped the curtains to the walls for good measure. John stopped her saying that might let in the gas. They sat down in the bed to watch the TV while constantly checking their cell phones. They sent texts back and forth with their parents and friends back in the US. All of them were freaking out and telling them to get out of Egypt the first chance they got. The worldwide news coverage was leaning towards some sort of terrorist attack. The videos being posted hinted at something even more sinister.

One of John's friends texted him to get the hell out of there no matter what it took. John picked up the hotel phone and hit zero to speak to the front desk. The calm voice on the other end of the line assured him the hotel was safe.

Automatic weapons fire could be clearly heard less than an hour later. They sat on the bed with the lights turned off and the TV volume turned all the way down lost as to what they should do next. A call to the receptionist downstairs reassured them that rioters hadn't been able to get on the island. They should remain in their rooms and refreshments would be sent up for them.

When no food or anything showed up and they'd eaten everything they had in the room John made another call. This time he wasn't able to get ahold of anyone. Not knowing what else to do he popped open the door and left to go get them some food from the lobby. He spotted another man at the end of the hallway standing in front of the elevator and hurried to catch up.

They spoke briefly confirming that neither of them knew what the hell was going on. The lobby was deserted. They gathered some snacks and drinks from the sundries shop and began walking back for the elevator. A soldier walked into the building from the other side and yelled at them to put their hands up. The soldier started walking towards them then got distracted by the sounds of gunfire coming from a nearby street and ran off in that direction. The man John had ridden the elevator with pointed out a woman splayed out on one of the chairs in the lobby. She was moaning oddly while rocking back and forth.

Walking over to check on her they noticed the front of her shirt was covered in blood. When they got directly in front of her, she snapped. Letting out a low guttural growl she leapt straight out of the chair onto the guy next to John. She bit deeply into the side of his neck. John watched in horror for a second before turning and sprinting for the elevator. He pressed the button multiple times while staring across the lobby at the friendly receptionist who was now eating the guy who'd walked to the lobby with him.

Her neck snapped up and she suddenly focused in on John right as the elevator door opened. He jumped in and slammed the shut door button with his finger. The doors almost closed in time. The bloody woman tried to beat her way into the small elevator. She was halfway through the door when John punched her hard in the mouth. Her teeth cut deep into his knuckles. He swung at her face again with his other hand and knocked her out of the elevator. She tripped over her long skirt falling backwards on the cold marble floor. John frantically pressed the button on the door until it finally slid shut.

Walking down the hallway back to the room the lights in the sconces started to blend together into one long light. John stopped and looked at the carpeted hallway. It was gently rising and falling like a lake on a breezy day. A surge of energy jolted through him. Shaking his head to try and clear it he looked down at his bloody knuckles. He couldn't quite remember why they were bleeding. He'd forgotten his room number but was pretty sure he was in front of his door. He rapped on the door a few times until it opened. The sound of a woman's voice sent him into a rage fueled attack on the door.

He rebounded off the door when he charged it. The lock had been engaged so that it would only open partially. Before he could attack the door again it was slammed in his face. Rational thought eluded John as he descended into madness. His heart sped up as adrenaline surged through his system. Rage and fear warred within him as he battered the door with his body to get at the prey he knew to be inside. The door flashed and pulsated hypnotically drawing him to it. He screamed in frustration as he kept smashing into it trying to force it open. All logical thought eradicated in a surge of rage and adrenaline and hunger.

Desiree took a few steps back from the door. She'd seen John in the hallway when she'd opened the door. She'd been about to close it and move the lock out of the way to let him in when he'd gone all insane berserker on the door. She'd gotten it closed and fearfully backed away from it. He was slamming into it hard. She didn't know long it'd last. The whole frame around the door was vibrating every time John hit it.

She grabbed her phone off the bed and stared at it. She wanted to call for help but she didn't know who to call. Something in the door frame made a loud cracking noise. She shuddered and grabbed a knife off the remains of the breakfast tray. The door made that cracking noise again the next two times John rammed it then finally flew open on the third strike. Desiree stood up with the knife in her hand wishing they'd stayed at a modern hotel with better doors. She wished they'd never come to Egypt. She wished she could talk to her mom. She saw her death in John's red eyes.

There was no mercy in the beast bearing down on her. There was no recognition. It wasn't John anymore. When he was close enough, she stabbed him. She kept stabbing him as he bore her down to the ground. He ignored the knife plunging repetitively into his stomach. His mind now that of an unfeeling predator. He ripped into his prey and drank the blood that flowed out. He was gnawing at her shoulder when something in her demeanor shifted. He recognized she was no longer prey.

John stood up dripping with blood. Pieces of her hair and skin stuck in his blood-stained teeth. Without sparing his blood covered bride another glance he turned and rushed out of the room in search of his next victim. On the ground Desiree writhed around like a double-jointed break dancer in the middle of a seizure. A massive surge of adrenaline flowed through her body. The room spun and light came at her from every direction. Her heart was pounding. She leapt to her feet and rushed after what used to be her husband to join in the search for the next victim.

Chapter 1: Forever Family

Drew shook the judge's hand and smiled for some quick pictures with Yue, LeBron and the beaming older couple who were now his legal parents. The judge happily giving them the time to take all the pictures they wanted before shaking their hands one final time and sending them on their way.

"You totally cried." His older sister joked punching him in the arm. Yue was a tall girl of Asian descent. She'd been adopted at an early age. She'd never known any parents other than Mr. and Mrs. Russel. Having heard some of the horror stories of what Drew and LeBron had experienced in foster homes she knew how lucky she was to have been adopted right out of the gate.

"It's easier when they can just pick you up at the post office." Drew shot back at her with a goofy grin.

"I think that just works for brides." LeBron chimed in. He was the most precocious of the three of them. He'd endured plenty of jokes about his name from Drew over the years. Unlike his namesake he was absolutely horrible at basketball along with basically every other sport. Instead of spending his time outside playing sports he spent it inside with his face in a book. He may be the youngest, but he was the one they all relied on when they needed help with their homework.

"Zip it. Time to go get a nice dinner." Mr. Russel shot back over his shoulder as they walked towards the parking lot. His expression softened considerably when he happened to glance over at his wife of thirty years. "Nancy please. It was an adoption not a funeral."

Yue walked faster to take over the task of consoling their mom. Their dad was pretty much useless at that sort of thing. Drew and LeBron crowded around her too. By the time they got to the car she was laughing through her tears and playfully swiping at Drew. She was on the opposite end of the spectrum from her husband when it came to emotional displays. She'd been out of control pretty much all morning. She loved her children deeply. Adopting Drew meant more to her than she could ever explain. He'd been the missing puzzle piece in their family portrait.

The three adoptions had been spread out over the years. Their first child had died from leukemia before she turned two. That'd crushed both of them. Nancy had insisted they keep trying to have a family though. Three miscarriages later it'd been Bart who brought up the idea of adoption. They'd waited for him to complete his final tour of duty overseas then started doing the paperwork. Yue had entered their lives two years after they'd first sat down together to fill out the required forms.

LeBron and Drew had been adopted much later in life than Yue. Over the years the couple had fostered dozens of kids. Bart's time as a deputy and then as the sheriff of a small county in upstate New York had motivated him to want to take in at risk kids and help them turn their lives around. He felt like he was honoring the memory of the daughter he'd only been able to hold for such a short amount of time.

Drew and LeBron had been different from the other foster kids. They'd both asked Nancy at different times how come she'd chosen them to be a part of her family. Nancy told them both that it'd just felt right. They were meant to be a family. God had sent them to their home for a reason. Bart agreed wholeheartedly with that sentiment. Not that anyone bothered to ask him as there was no way he'd be able to express it. You'd be as likely to hear the truth from a politician as you'd be to hear Bart talk about his feelings.

Drew and LeBron each carried around a significant amount of baggage from their formative years. It'd taken so long for them to adopt Drew because his drugged out and frequently incarcerated parents hadn't been willing to sign the papers to give him up. Not because they loved him. They'd wanted to be able to get money out of it. They'd wanted to be able to use Drew to get them released from prison earlier. They'd fought the adoption but with Drew getting close to aging out of the system his social worker had finally been able to get a judge's approval that it was in Drew's best interests to be adopted.

LeBron's story was similar to Drews except that his biological parents had died in a car crash. A car crash caused by overindulgence in multiple illegal substances. LeBron was the acknowledged geek in their trio. Drew was the jock. He'd wound up with the Russels because all the other foster families he was sent to live with kicked him out for fighting too much. Bart got him some boxing gloves and a gym membership. He encouraged him to sign up for football and wrestling at the local high school he attended. He helped Drew learn to channel that pent-up anger constructively.

Yue was the politician. She could pretty much talk anybody into anything. She had Bart wrapped around her finger. She used her powers for good most of the time. The exception being if there was some new purse or makeup she wanted. Then she could be ruthless.

The celebratory dinner was held at Drew's favorite restaurant. They looked a bit out of place walking into an Outback on a Tuesday afternoon dressed for court. The boys had made their outfits a little more casual by the gradual loss of inessential accessories such as ties, buttons, and jackets. Yue and Nancy were pretty much stuck looking like they were ready to attend a homecoming dance. They got a big table by the bar area and an order of waters all around while they waited for the bread to show up.

LeBron was drinking his water while everyone else was still busy studying the menu. He'd already googled the menu on the way over and decided on the burger he wanted. He liked to plan ahead. In this case all it'd bought him was a few seconds to lean back in the booth and stare at the TVs on the wall behind the bar. There was some sort of crisis happening in the Middle East again. If he'd been home, he'd have switched the channel. Crises in the Middle East had become so common they were barely newsworthy anymore.

Something about this one seemed different though. Noticing the bartender and a few of the early crowd at the bar were staring with interest LeBron stayed tuned in as well. The scenes being shown included video footage of the streets of Cairo. The footage sources included everything from people recording out of their hotel windows to footage from actual helicopters swooping around. Someone had even gotten some drone footage of the streets that they'd uploaded.

The method of recording wasn't half as interesting as the subject. In the streets people were running in packs at a breakneck pace then leaping onto other people. They'd bear them down to the ground and attack them. After attacking them for a minute or two they'd get up and start running around again. The footage from the drone showed a couple of people sprint across a parking lot to throw themselves through a big picture window in the front of a small shop. One of them fell to the ground bleeding and didn't get back up but the other one wiggled into the store. More people jumped through the hole they'd made to enter the store after them.

"Woah. Somebody better call Brad Pitt." Yue joked. She'd caught him staring at the TVs and looked over to see what he was watching. Once she'd said it out loud it clicked for LeBron. The people running around in the streets did look like something out of a zombie movie.

"What the hell's going on over there?" Bart asked. He'd put on his glasses to better see the TVs.

Before they could get into it the waitress showed up and they went through the standard meal ordering ritual with her. Yue and LeBron both got burgers while Drew went big and ordered a steak. It was his day after all so why not splurge a little.

"Enjoy that steak. Dad doesn't get paid to watch you anymore." LeBron joked. It wasn't like anyone was going to get rich off what the foster system could afford to pay for people to take kids in.

Drew worked on chewing the massive wad of buttered bread in his mouth before replying. Before he could come up with a good comeback, he got distracted by the TV again. There was a close up of a group of people on a cobbled street in a courtyard working together to rip a person apart. The live feed ended abruptly as the producers belatedly realized this wasn't suitable for an afternoon broadcast. At least not without some sort of warning language.

"Why are they showing that horrible stuff on the TV in a restaurant? People are trying to eat. Drew, can you please ask them to change the channel." Nancy looked a little pale as she slid a small sliver of butter around on the slice of the bread that she'd claimed for herself.

Drew dutifully walked over to the bar and asked if they could change the channel. The bartender looked like he might protest at first then went ahead and flipped over to a golf tournament instead. The people eating at the bar didn't seem too bothered. Most of them either started watching the golf tournament while they ate or continued to stare mindlessly at whatever was on their smart phones.

"Thank you." Nancy told Drew as he got back to the table and sat back down.

The rest of the meal was just food and family. Nancy felt like her heart may break she loved them all so much. It made her sad how old they all were. They'd raised them right, so they'd be leaving the nest pretty soon. All three of them were college bound. Yue was starting on a business degree at the local community college while Drew was hoping to play either baseball or football for whatever college would have him. LeBron should be able to get into any college he wanted with the grades he pulled in.

While they were busy eating the bartender flipped the channel back to the news. It was playing the same scenes in a small box in the corner while talking heads debated whether it was a gas leak or an act of terrorism. None of the news people seemed concerned that it was a problem that may affect more than a small part of northern Africa. The journalists were discussing how quickly the phenomena appeared to be spreading. LeBron and Drew were both watching the graphic violence unfold on CNN when Bart paid the check.

They rode home with the typical school night family chatter. Questions got tossed around about what they needed to get done for school the next day. They all had extra homework since they'd planned on missing their afternoon classes today to attend the adoption hearing. Yue had a waitress job starting the following weekend so that monopolized most of the conversation. Drew logged some time cruising social media. He was proudly updating his various profile info with his new legal name.

LeBron focused on trying to find out more about what they'd seen on the TV at the restaurant. It seemed like a massive bioweapon fueled riot tearing apart an entire city would be frontpage news. He had to scroll past a ton of other garbage before he saw the first mention of the issues over in Africa. He shook his head wondering why reality stars getting new tattoos and politicians getting caught with their pants down was more important than an article about thousands feared dead in Cairo.

The first articles he found were basically just a rehash of what they'd already seen on the news earlier. He kept digging until he found some new information. He stumbled across unedited videos being uploaded onto different social media platforms. The bulk of the time he clicked on the links the videos weren't able to be played. Based on the popup messages the images were too graphic or violent in nature and were being barred from the platform. Occasionally he was successful at getting one to play and it became apparent why the different platforms were rushing to ban them. The ones he was able to get to play were beyond graphic.

"Dude. Quit sending me broken links." Drew said looking over at him. He'd clicked on one of the videos LeBron had just watched maybe a minute ago.

"The videos are getting blocked. The government or the streaming sites or someone's blocking them. The one I just tried to send you showed a little girl attacking a man who keeps smashing her down to the ground. It was bad." LeBron said busily trying to find the video again.

"Do you want to lose your phone?" Nancy asked in her mom voice.

"No ma'am." LeBron said.

"Then stop looking at videos like that or I'll take it." Nancy said with finality. When she used that tone of voice the argument was over. LeBron sulkily shoved his phone in his pocket. He knew from experience that she didn't make idle threats where losing his phone was concerned.

Drew punched him in the arm and Yue told them both to grow up. Bart grumbled at them to all settle down from up in the driver's seat. They semi-settled down for the rest of the short ride. Back at home they continued the celebration with a few friends and family members who came over for cake.

The TV was on in the background the entire time, but it was just sports and a Hallmark movie. Nancy and Yue were currently hooked on binge watching Hallmark movies together. The horrific images from the news they'd seen earlier were soon as forgotten as the thousand other tragedies people see every day on the news. The forgetfulness amplified by the fact that it'd all happened a few thousand miles away on another continent. Something happening that far away didn't feel real to them. It might as well be happening on Mars.

Chapter 2: Denial is a River in Egypt

"Wake up!" Drew yelled over at LeBron for like the fifth time.

"I'm up." LeBron muttered from underneath his pillow.

"Get dressed. You've got like a minute before we're going to be late. Maybe try not staying up all night staring at your phone." Drew said. The sad thing was he knew LeBron had probably been doing actual research the entire night. Not exactly what most teen boys stayed up all night staring at on the internet.

"Something's going on in Egypt. Something pretty bad." LeBron said finally sitting up. He was looking on the floor around his bed to find a clean looking shirt to wear.

"There's always something bad going on over there. You really spend way too much time worrying about the wrong things." Drew said exasperatedly. He loved his brother but there was seriously something a little off with him. The kid had stayed up all night staring at videos of people rioting in Egypt.

LeBron and Drew grabbed their lunches from out of the refrigerator and headed out to get in Drew's old pickup truck. One of the ways Bart worked on turning his boys into contributing members of society was instilling a strong work ethic in them. They'd had chores up to the age of fifteen then been sent out into the world to get real jobs as soon as they were legally eligible. The real jobs didn't excuse them from their chores at home either. The two young men maintained a very healthy schedule between school, their extracurricular activities and working.

'Idle hands being the devil's playthings' was a commonly held belief in the Russel household. None of the kids liked the old adage since it was typically followed by them being given some new chore. You'd think they lived on a farm instead of a four-bedroom bungalow in the suburbs. The bungalow was nice. It was in an affluent neighborhood in the suburbs of Orlando in the small city of Winter Springs. The kind of neighborhood that has a resort style community pool, official dog parks and other amenities. The high school they attended was literally right down the street. They could easily walk to school if for some weird reason they ever felt the urge to do that. Florida was way too hot most of the year to be walking around outside if you didn't have to. Plus, they'd lose the coolness of rolling into the parking lot in a rusty pickup truck.

LeBron kept expecting someone at school to mention the riots happening over in Egypt. No one did though. He supposed everyone had grown used to the atrocities on the nightly news. Every night the media reported shootings and genocide and droned on and on about the worst of humanity. After a while people tended to tune all that stuff out. There was only so much negativity a person could take.

After school LeBron walked to his job in the plaza beside the school. He'd gotten a job at the Publix supermarket as a bagger on his fifteenth birthday. It was mind numbingly boring, but it was close to the house and school. Unlike Drew he didn't see a need to have his own car quite yet. He was busy saving his money. He wanted to go to a real college and study hard core math and science. He'd need money for that. His ultimate goal was to be an astronaut even though he wasn't a fan of roller coasters. When he'd mentioned his dream of becoming an astronaut to Drew, he'd been immediately reminded of his inability to read in a moving vehicle without getting carsick. In a rare fit of thoughtfulness Drew had told him he'd probably be a lot better at designing the rockets than driving them.

    Other than videos on the internet he didn't hear much about the troubles over in Egypt for the rest of the week. Like most people he didn't have the time to spend worrying about the troubles of people living across the ocean. When he did happen to glance at the news most of it focused on how the politicians were arguing over banning all travel to and from Egypt. Especially since it appeared some sort of biological weapon was in play. No one wanted to be responsible for that mess showing up on the shores of the good old USA.

    They were sitting down for dinner on Saturday when the topic reared its head back up. LeBron was late to the table and when Bart sent Yue to get him, she found him in the loft upstairs staring at the TV.

    "It's gotten worse." LeBron said staring at the news. Yue glanced at the screen seeing yet another overhead shot of large crowds of people rioting in a run-down looking city in the desert.

"What's gotten a lot worse? Is this that Egypt thing?" Yue asked. She was still wearing the striped shirt she'd worn for her first shift at IHOP. The name tag on the shirt indicating she was in training.

"It's spreading. This is a city in the Sudan. They were showing scenes from Tel Aviv and the Gaza Strip earlier." LeBron said.

"Ok. Come eat and we can watch the news later and see what's up. There's always some kind of scary stuff going on over there. You know how the news is." Yue said reaching over to turn off the TV. They headed downstairs to join the family for dinner. Yue instantly putting the news out of her mind while LeBron kept turning everything he'd seen so far over and over in his head.

At the dinner table LeBron couldn't help bringing up everything he'd seen on the news and asking what everyone else thought about it. He was frustrated that everyone seemed to be a million times more interested in how much Yue had liked slinging pancakes around all day. Finally getting the hint that talking about people killing each other may not be the best dinner topic he sulkily gulped down his food. Once he was done, he sat there impatiently waiting for them to finish so he could flip on the TV and show them all what he was trying to tell them.

After dinner he was doing the dishes with Drew when Yue yelled out from the living room that there was something they should come see. Putting down the dishes they were working on Drew and LeBron walked over to see what was up. Yue and their parents were all sitting around on the large sectional watching some HGTV show about fixing up houses. One of the fifty shows like that that came on daily.

"You think that's about the Egypt stuff?" Yue asked LeBron pointing at the message scrolling across the bottom of the screen. It said the President would be addressing the nation and had a countdown timer showing about twenty minutes left. LeBron nodded and started to sit down.

"Dishes." Nancy said without even turning her neck to look back at them.

LeBron and Drew hurried back into the kitchen to wrap up the dishes. Knocking them out in record time they rejoined the family out on the couch with five minutes to spare according to the scrolling timer.

"I don't ever remember seeing a news update on this channel." Yue commented.

"Normally they just have them on the main channels." Bart agreed. He sounded vaguely concerned. His years in the special forces back before he settled into a career in law enforcement coming back to him. He knew an announcement like this from the President frequently meant that somewhere in the world operators were either walking away from a mission or getting into position to carry one out. Not that the world would necessarily ever know what'd been done.

They all grew silent as the countdown ended and a message came on saying the President would be addressing the nation momentarily. Drew was wondering if he had time to go grab a soda from the fridge when the President suddenly materialized sitting at his desk in the oval office. The man didn't look healthy. No amount of makeup could conceal the fact that he was completely exhausted. Sleep deprived or not he had a job to do. It wasn't like just anybody could read a speech off a teleprompter after all.

"My fellow Americans. By now many of you have no doubt seen the news broadcasts and videos on social media channels showing the conditions in Northern Africa and the Middle East. A contagion has infected large numbers of people causing subsequent rioting. We have investigators in the region seeking to learn more and have already offered our services via the UN to assist with peacekeeping efforts." The President paused theatrically. More than likely the teleprompter had <*Pause Theatrically*> displayed on it. After an acceptable number of seconds, he continued.

"I have issued orders that flights and any other form of travel to and from the affected regions be immediately halted. Our embassies are assisting US citizens abroad who may be impacted by this travel ban. We will be setting up processes and procedures to enable our citizens abroad to make their way back home once medically cleared." He paused again.

"Make no mistake. This is a very serious crisis. We will assist the stricken countries in their recovery. We will offer our assistance via the UN and the WHO to contain this outbreak. I would implore you not to make the mistake of believing everything you see and hear on social media or the more sensational media outlets. We'll provide official updates on a regular basis as to the situation in these regions. Please go to the website shown below to check on the status of any of your family or colleagues who may be traveling in the impacted zones. God bless you all and god bless the United States of America." The image of the President faded out. The Oval Office replaced by a burly guy in coveralls beating the hell out of a kitchen counter with a sledgehammer.

"Can we switch to a news channel?" LeBron asked.

Nancy and Yue looked like they might rebel for a second. They were thinking that if they flipped the channel, they'd never find out which of the three houses the couple from Idaho ended up picking. Drew snagged the remote and flipped to CNN. Noticing his mom and Yue staring daggers at him he tossed the remote down on the couch and stared right back.

"You both know they'll rerun this same episode twenty times this year. There's no way you won't see it again at some point." He said defensively. His mom wasn't one to just let someone walk in and change the channel on the show she was in the middle of. She let it slide when she saw what was being shown on the TV. The news was showing some graphic video with warnings plastered all over the screen that viewers should be cautioned.

The images were of a street at dawn. The correspondent was describing a night of insanity. The man had spent the evening in Tel Aviv in a hotel reserved for the news media. He'd been given a room with a small balcony. He'd spent the night wrapped in a comforter lying on his balcony when he started hearing people rioting in the hallway of the hotel. The street below had a few people stumbling around drunkenly. Bodies were spread out in various poses. It looked like a truckload of mannequins had been dumped off the top of the hotel.

"That's awful. I just hope they keep that mess over there. We don't want any. Now give me back the remote." Nancy said stretching her hand out towards Drew. Knowing he wasn't going to be able to dissuade her he handed it back to her and hopped up to follow LeBron upstairs to the loft. Situated around the couch Yue, Bart and Nancy immersed themselves once again in HGTV.

Occasionally over the week they heard more about the illness raging through Africa and the Middle East. Most Americans tended to ignore it. They'd grown desensitized thanks to the twenty-four hours a day of doom and gloom they were constantly bombarded with. Jerusalem burned while millions of Americans were focused on perfecting the latest dance to upload to see how many likes they could get. Images of decimated African villages were lower on the webpage than the story about the latest celebrity DUI.

It was like the USA had ADD. The story failed to hold anyone's interest after the first wave of outrage over the videos had receded. Stories concerning massive riots in foreign countries didn't rate too many news cycles. The common man on the streets may not have realized it but in the upper echelons of the government protocols were being activated that no one had ever before taken seriously. The signs were all indicating that the storm that'd started in Cairo could grow large enough to ravage the globe.

Chapter 3: Stocking Up

"My fellow Americans. Today I have issued executive orders blocking all travel into or out of the United States effective immediately. This includes travel to either Canada or Mexico. The state of affairs in the world is such that we need to keep our country clean of the disease currently spreading across all of Africa, Europe, and Asia. We will establish blockades and militarize the borders. States of emergency have been declared in each state to allow all governors to request whatever additional aid is needed from the federal government to ensure this disease doesn't cross our borders. An effective national quarantine is the best defense."

Bart muted the TV before the President got the opportunity to do his standard spiel blessing everyone and everything. He sat there for a moment rubbing his temples. He knew what was coming next. He may not know what was going to happen once the sickness made it over here, but he knew what the fear of those monsters was going to do. He knew why the government was working so hard to keep everyone in the dark. If it hadn't been for social media, the government may have been able to keep everything hidden a little longer. The citizens of China would probably all die completely ignorant of what was going on thanks to the superior level of government censorship available there.

"This is going to be bad." Bart said loudly. Looking around the couch he made sure he had everyone's attention. He had to stare at the kids and cough a couple of times to get them to put their phones down.

"Sorry dad. What do you think's going to happen?" Yue asked.

"There's going to be a run on supplies. First thing we need to do is figure out what we need and go buy a ton of it. People are going to be civilized at first but pretty soon the supplies are going to run low. There's probably enough on the shelves at any given time to support everyone living around here for a couple of weeks. That's assuming they have plenty of stuff sitting in their pantries already. People are going to buy everything they can once the panic sets in. Hoarding is going to be in fashion."

"Like when a hurricane's coming." Drew said.

"Except hurricanes are just going to impact the coast of Florida or wherever. This is going to impact everywhere. They won't have more supplies to send us because the whole country's going to need them." LeBron added. Bart listened to his boys and nodded. They were getting it, but he didn't think anyone besides him realized yet how bad this could really get.

"This isn't just a hurricane coming. This is a nightmare everyone's been watching on TV. This is biblical. This is end of times kind of stuff. I'd say let's make a run for it, but I don't know that anywhere is going to be any safer than right here. At least for the time being. A week ago, this was a blip and now half the world's gone dark and the other half isn't going to make it much longer. Once this hits us, I don't see it ending any differently here than it is in Europe."

They were each assigned different missions. The seriousness of the situation setting in for Drew when their dad had each of them hide a pistol in their cars before letting them leave. He told them he didn't think it'd come to that yet but better safe than sorry. Yue and LeBron headed for the Publix by the house. Their job was to buy as much food as they could get in their cart. Drew and Nancy had been sent to hit up Loews and Home Depot. They were in charge of buying enough wood to barricade all the windows. Bart had headed for the gun store to stock up on everything he could get his hands on there. Everyone was handed a credit card and told to max them out.

 Yue had a compact car. It was pretty tiny, but they should be able to shove a bunch of groceries in it by completely sacrificing their comfort. Considering how close they lived to the store they may be able to just fill up some carts and walk home. He could always return them later. A perk of being a trusted employee. The drive should have only taken a couple of minutes. They turned out of their neighborhood and got stuck in traffic. Everyone was waiting to turn into the parking lot of the plaza the grocery store was in. Yue noticed some people letting their passengers out to head towards the store ahead of them.

 "I could run ahead and start shopping while you wait to park." LeBron said hesitantly. He could feel Yue's eyes on him. It'd be in direct defiance of being told by their dad less than ten minutes prior to make sure they didn't split up for any reason whatsoever.

"Ok cool. Just keep your phone on so I can call you. I might just text you. Not like I'm going to be driving very fast." Yue answered him. She'd decided to disregard the warning from their dad as well. No way people around here were going to go that crazy that fast. She was super nervous about the pistol under her seat and really just wanted to get this over with. She was well aware the concealed pistol was a one-way ticket to jail if a cop caught her with it. She was trained on the weapon. All three of them could shoot. Their dad had made sure of it. If she were old enough, he'd have already made her get a concealed carry permit. She was still three years away from that though.

LeBron got out of the car and walked up the sidewalk to the turn into the plaza. Looking around the corner he reconsidered this shopping excursion. There was a large crowd in front of the doors to the store. The employees were trying to get people to enter in an orderly fashion and stick to the quantities of items they were allowed to buy. LeBron strode right up to the crowd and started working his way into where he thought the line was.

"How long do we have to wait out here?" A man asked the manager standing at the door. She was a petite woman who looked overwhelmed at being responsible for telling people when they could go in.

"Not much longer. We're just trying to keep everyone safe." The manager said politely. LeBron felt sorry for her. What a thankless job. An older woman walked out of the store through the exit doors cussing and yelling loudly that the store was pretty much out of everything.

The manager opened the door to let the next few people into the store. Instead of a few people politely sliding past her so she could shut the door again a steady stampede rolled in. Everyone ignored her asking them to stop. She was unceremoniously pushed to the side by the flood of people desperate to get supplies before they ran out. She pulled herself together and tried again to stop the flood of people. A man shoved her backwards hard enough to knock her over. When she looked up LeBron was standing over her protectively with his hand held out to help her up. She took his hand and let him pull her to her feet.

"Thanks. It's good to see you here. These people are all going nuts. Are you working today or just picking up supplies?" She asked him.

"Stocking up. My dad's worried this may get bad." LeBron said. He was staring at the naked shelves. People were basically just raking everything left into shopping carts then getting in the enormous lines at the checkout lanes.

"Your dad's a smart man. Take a cart to the back. Don't let any of these crazy people see you going back there. You can load up whatever you need from back there. You can come in early tomorrow for more. We should be getting some shipments tonight." The manager wished him luck then waded out to do battle with the volatile crowd waiting impatiently to pay for whatever they'd managed to get in their carts.

LeBron grabbed a cart full of roses and emptied the roses back into the flower case. He casually walked around the perimeter of the store to get to the door leading to the back. He rapped on the door until someone looked out at him through the windows cut into the door. The doors opened and he pushed his cart through.

"Hey man. If you're loading up back here, you just got to be careful when you walk back out into the store. Those people are going to freak out if you have the stuff they're looking for." The stock boy who'd opened the door for him gave him the warning then went back to stacking boxes full of toilet paper on a pallet.

LeBron walked around grabbing the items his parents had told him to focus on. Basically, anything that didn't go bad quickly. Lots of pasta, canned food, and the obligatory huge package of toilet paper. They had plenty of drinking water stored in their garage already so that wasn't a priority. Feeling his phone vibrate LeBron pulled it out and saw it was his mom group texting to see how everyone was doing. He replied the shopping was fine, but the lines were insane. Done texting he headed for the door leading back into the store. As he was struggling to open the doors so he could push the cart out he got another text from his sister. She was letting him know she'd parked up on the median and was headed his way.

A group of men standing around the back of the store staring at the empty shelves saw him coming out of the back with his full grocery cart. LeBron recognized the man who'd shoved the manager out of his way.

"Hey. Hold that door!" The man yelled at him as he rushed towards LeBron.

LeBron pushed his cart out into the store and let the door shut behind him. He ignored the man shouting at him and hurriedly pushed his cart over to one of the checkout lines.

"What if I just take your cart?" The man he'd just blocked from getting in the back had sidled up next to LeBron in line. Another man was with him. They looked like they may be brothers.

"Yeah. Why'd you shut the door so we couldn't get back in the stock room? You special or something? Why do you get a full cart?" LeBron could smell the man's nicotine fueled breath. He didn't know what to do. These guys were easily in their thirties and considerably bigger than him.

"Why don't you just give us this cart and you go get another one for yourself?" The original man suggested as he nudged LeBron away from the cart. All around him people were studiously ignoring the exchange. No one wanted to get involved and risk losing their place in lines or whatever supplies they'd been able to grab. More than a few of them were just as ticked as the two guys bullying LeBron that he'd been able to get special attention. LeBron fought back the tears welling up in his eyes.

"Hey LeBron. Is that your cart?" Yue asked loudly from where she was walking towards him from the front of the store. She was radiating righteous anger.

"This is our cart. The boy here was just leaving to go get himself another one. You should go with him." The man stepped firmly behind the cart knocking LeBron completely out of the way. He stood there smiling at the tall Asian girl who'd made her way close enough to get in his face.

"Let's just go." LeBron said. Yue looked over at him then at the two grown men standing there staring back at her. Neither of the dirtbags looked like they were going to give an inch. She scanned the crowd around her but didn't see where anyone looked like they were willing to step in and help. Everyone had their own problems.

Yue stuck her middle finger in the guy's face. He reached across the cart and tried to grab her. Laughing she backed away from him with both middle fingers up in the air. The guy shoved the cart full of food at her trying to jam her up against the empty shelves. She grabbed the front of the cart and pulled hard enough on it that the cart flew over landing on its side. The extremely pissed off pair of brothers both started cussing at her. One got close enough to grab her. He was pushed back by a uniformed policeman who appeared out of nowhere. LeBron casually dropped the can of beans he'd been about to brain the guy with.

Seeing the manager that he'd helped up earlier standing beside the cop told LeBron who the hero in this story was. He mouthed a big thank you to her as the cop walked the two troublemakers out of the store. LeBron and Yue heaved the cart back up and worked on picking up everything with some help from the manager. After waiting in line for what seemed like forever, they checked out and headed into the parking lot.

"I let everybody know we're on the way." Yue said sliding her phone back into her pocket.

LeBron nodded absently. He was staring all around to make sure the guys from the store weren't going to jump out from behind a car and attack them. He was pretty sure the cop probably had better things to focus on than attempted grand theft cart. The parking lot was less crazy now. Probably because the store had been pretty much cleaned out. Yue had parked up on a median on the far side of the lot. LeBron breathed easier as they got closer to her car.

A rusty mud-covered pickup truck pulled up as they were loading the groceries into the car. The two guys from the store got out and walked threateningly over towards them. Yue threw the rest of the groceries in on her side and told LeBron to get in the car. She jumped in the car herself but one of the men had stepped in between the car door and the seat she was in. She'd have to reach in between his legs to even grab the door handle to pull the door closed. LeBron had his phone out on the other side of the car.

"Leave right now or I'm calling the cops!" He yelled at the guy. He gulped as his own door was yanked open by the other guy who'd walked around to the passenger side. The man grabbed LeBron by the throat and shoved him back against the seat then forcefully took his phone away from him. On the other side of the car the man was telling Yue to give him her phone.

"Bite me!" Yue said.

"You really want us to hurt your little boyfriend? Just give us the groceries and we'll leave. You really want to get hurt over a few cans of beans and some toilet paper? The way you two acted was wrong and we're not going to let you get away with it." The man was squatting down on his knees now looking directly at Yue.

"You two get back in your truck right now and I won't hurt you." An authoritative voice rang out from behind them.

"What the hell you going to do old man? This little bi – " The man started saying as he stood up. He never finished his sentence since Bart slammed an asp into his face before he got a chance. He'd be spitting out pieces of his teeth for the next few days.

Bart stepped into the man and grabbed him by the back of his head tossing him to the pavement. The guy on the other side of the car ran around to the opposite side of his truck and started fumbling around looking for something. Bart pulled a pistol out of his waistband and stepped over to the truck. He flung the door open on the other side right as the guy pulled a pistol out from under the seat.

"I will shoot you! Drop the weapon and step away from the truck!" Bart roared out in his best sheriff voice. The warrior buried in him wanted to just ice the guy and move on. This was a Publix parking lot in the middle of the day though. Not some jungle in the middle of nowhere.

Yue freaked as three gunshots rang out. She kicked at the man trying to get up off the ground. She yelled for LeBron to grab the other gun. LeBron started digging around under the seat.

"Yue. Get out of the car!" Bart yelled. Yue stepped out of the car. She was shaking all over. The man she'd kicked on the ground had rolled away and was standing beside the truck now with his hands up. He didn't look scary anymore. He just looked scared.

Bart was walking around the truck shoving the other guy in front of him. He made them both lie down on the ground face first then spread their arms and legs like they were making snow angels. Yue was so happy to see her dad alive and see that he hadn't killed anybody that she could barely stand up.

"You shot my truck man. You'll be paying for that." One of the men said from his position down on the ground. Bart calmly walked up and kicked the guy hard in the crotch. That shut him up. He'd put three bullets into the roof of the truck instead of into the guy's head. He should be thanking him not looking to sue for damages. If the guy hadn't thrown his pistol down on the bench seat the fourth bullet would've been in his skull. It was a nice nine-millimeter berretta that Bart now had shoved in the back of his pants.

"I should've just dropped you but that would've created a ton of paperwork and honestly I think we're all going to be pretty busy the next few days. Me with putting together supplies and you two losers with pulling together money for bail and trading cigarettes for favors down at the pen. Yue do me a favor and call 911."

Yue did. It was busy. It was still busy fifteen minutes later after they'd tried multiple times. Bart was wondering if maybe he should just give up and let the two morons go when a cop pulled up with his flashers on. The cop got out and had Bart put his weapons down. Yue sighed in relief when she recognized the cop as the same one who'd walked the two men out of the store earlier. After talking to Bart for a few minutes the cop told them to head home. He handcuffed the two men and shoved them in the back of his car. The cop nodded at them as they drove past him out of the parking lot.

"It's just going to keep getting worse." Bart intoned. Neither Yue nor LeBron had any doubts now that he was right.

Chapter 4: Preparing for the Worst

The hardest part for Yue of almost being killed in the parking lot over two hundred bucks' worth of groceries was Bart ordering them not to tell their mom. That was no big deal for LeBron, but Yue told her mom everything. There was no way she was going to be able to keep such a big secret. She understood why she shouldn't tell her mom. If Nancy found out what'd happened, then none of them would ever be allowed out of the house again until everything blew over. Everything blowing over wasn't likely to happen any time in the near future.

It was getting worse. Videos that were posted to public sites were still being censored but not before they were downloaded and shared via e-mail. The flood of videos and messages on every conceivable platform was too much to block without completely shutting down the internet. Humanity was dying and the internet echoed it's screams.

The origins and effects of the disease itself were less of a mystery now. The video of the archeologists descending into the tomb in Egypt provided multiple clues. It had now been played and analyzed more thoroughly than any other video clip in the history of video clips. It'd been viewed exponentially more times than the clip of JFK being assassinated. That short video clip launched a thousand conspiracy theories. Aliens, mummies, zombies, Pharaoh's curses, and the wrath of multiple gods were all thrown out as viable causes of the pandemic sweeping the globe clean of humanity.

One of the saner reasons being considered for the insanity was that it all had something to do with the strange green mold growing inside the cavernous space. The date of the entry into the tomb aligned with when the infections had begun. The tomb itself was at the nexus of all of the events that were cascading across the globe. If there was a patient zero, then the smart money was on one of the people who'd gone down into that darkness.

The mold spore theory held up well. It'd been tested numerous times by both professionals and amateurs cutting into the dead bodies of the infected. None of the archeologists had been wearing any sort of advanced air filtration systems or anything when they descended into the tomb. Not only could they have become infected but anyone from the film or support crew in the tunnel could've also been exposed to the spores. None of the film or dig crew had made it out of Egypt so there weren't any witnesses who could be interviewed or examined.

Even if the cause for the disease hadn't been one hundred percent nailed down yet the actual phases of it had been observed and documented countless times. An exchange of bodily fluids seemed to be the main way to catch the disease. Nine times out of ten this happened when one of the infected individuals caught and bit a non-infected victim. At some point during the attack the victim would flip from being a victim to being one of the infected. Once that flip occurred the attacker somehow sensed it and immediately lost interest in attacking the former victim.

Once bitten the newly infected would wander around with a dazed look for a matter of minutes before also going on the hunt. The defining piece of this phase was the insane energy surge the newly infected exhibited. A newly infected individual didn't sleep for about three days. They just rocked along on an impossible surge of adrenaline. That meant they could jump higher, run faster, and lift heavier objects than pretty much any normal individual. There was a good percentage of people who didn't survive this phase.

The ones who fell over dead during the surge phase were the ones whose hearts just couldn't take all the adrenaline. This group was made up mostly of the obese and elderly. They were much more likely to keel over within the first day of surging than any other demographic. The streets of the cities were littered with the carcasses of those who hadn't made the transition to the next phase.

The final phase of the metamorphosis was the night crawler phase. At some point during the surge the light of day became too much for the infected to handle and they started seeking shelter during the day. They'd dig in under houses or if stuck out in the open they'd resort to digging holes to bury themselves in to spend the day. No one knew why they feared the light or why it took a few days for the fear to develop. Numerous videos of the individuals in the night crawler phase showed them losing their minds when exposed to sunlight though. They tended to avoid any sort of bright light, but it was only actual sunlight that sent them into a panic.

If the spore was an extreme hallucinogenic that could explain the fear of the light. Although how it'd cause the same reaction in thousands of different subjects was a big question mark. The knowledge had been put into practice in the last bastions of defenses over in Europe. Massive spotlights protected the walled fortresses of those who'd survived the initial onslaughts. These islands of humanity were kept supplied by airdrops from the USA. Those resupply missions helped to assuage the guilt of the nation for not allowing the survivors to be evacuated to the safe harbor of the US shores.

"When they come out of the dirt like that it's pretty much Night of the Living Dead." Drew said watching the clips on the TV in the loft. LeBron had his smart phone connected to the TV and was sharing the videos he'd downloaded.

"Exactly. Or pretty much like every vampire movie. They fear the light and all that. The drinking blood part works. All of those myths could've originated with people inhaling these mold spores. The legend of the mummy. All of that stuff. It makes so much sense." LeBron said excitedly.

"That's great. All of our nightmares are coming for us. What I'd be more excited about would be a plan to survive. One that helps us get more toilet paper and some fresh fruit." Drew said. It turned out when the rest of the world went dark the good old USA really suffered. Globalization was great until you lost a large section of the globe. Like the one that made car parts or supplied gas or any of the thousands of things that everyone took for granted. Toilet paper for instance. Drew had witnessed three no holds barred, drag out, bloody knuckle all out brawls over the last rolls of Charmin at different stores in the past week.

They were still going to the stores every morning to try and purchase more supplies, but the stores were running very low on everything. It was beginning to look more and more like a communist country as far as shopping went. Drew and LeBron would wake up early every day and go with their dad to stand outside the loading dock at Publix. If a truck showed up, they'd each be given their allotment of whatever was in it for whatever the government mandated price for it was.

Getting up at five in the morning every day to stand in line hoping to slide your credit card for a sack of potatoes or a can of yams wasn't super exciting. It was much better than the alternative of starving to death though. They left their mom and Yue with weapons and instructions to call them if anyone approached the house aggressively. They'd boarded up all the windows in the back and prepped the front to be able to cover those up quickly as well. They hadn't done it yet as they didn't want their home to stand out. After having seen countless videos of the infected in the surge stage diving headfirst through windows to get at victims the boards seemed like a great idea.

"How long until it makes it over here do you think?" Drew asked.

LeBron looked thoughtful. None of them were naïve enough to think that the government would miraculously become efficient enough to actually do what they said they were going to do. There was a good deal of hope that the short gestation time for the disease would keep it from being transmitted across the ocean. There were no recorded cases of someone catching the disease and not going crazy. That made it very unlikely someone would try to sneak an infected person along with them across the ocean or across the border.

"The governments actually doing a pretty good job so far. They shut down the travel and the borders fast enough to shield us. It's only going to take a handful of cases over here to spread it to the whole continent." LeBron said.

"You know that the rich connected people from other countries are still getting in. Our soldiers are still going out and coming back. Someone's going to make a mistake. I trust the plot line of every zombie movie ever made way more than I trust the morons in the government." Drew said.

That was pretty much the consensus among everyone that eventually the disease would make its way over the pond to them. Until then they did their best to try and heed the lessons learned by the Africans, Europeans, and Asians. Large walls went up or were reinforced around military bases. Stadium lighting was being installed as fast as it could be manufactured. Unfortunately, a good deal of the lighting needed was manufactured in China. It turned out pretty much everything was either produced in China or had a piece or part that was made in China. Stuff wasn't made in the USA now so much as it was assembled in the USA.

China had gone down fast. Any country with a tightly packed population had gone down fast so it was to be expected. However, China went down extra fast since they hadn't warned their citizens. No one had time to prepare in any meaningful way. There were pockets who'd managed to escape the first wave of death. Those people faced very long odds in surviving for very long with the millions of crawlers coming at them nightly. The infected had an uncanny ability to sniff out where people were hiding.

"Did you find any more videos on the crawlers?" Drew asked.

LeBron shook his head and sat down on the couch to keep searching. He finally found a clip he hadn't seen before. He cast it up on the TV so him and Drew could watch it together. All they'd seen in the past had been the videos of shapes running past in the dark. Occasionally you'd see them leaping over garbage cans or up onto porches. They'd gotten the 'crawlers' nickname since they moved on all fours. Even walking in those awkward poses, they were able to move way faster than most people.

The clip he found was from a military style infrared camera. The person videoing was standing on a balcony a good ten stories above the street he was recording. Down on the dark street the crawlers were streaming by in the hundreds. Their bodies appearing on the infrared camera like a river of molten lava flowing swiftly by. The camera being used to make the recording didn't have any microphones to capture sound. Judging from all the other reports they'd heard it was safe to assume that the group passing down below was doing so way more quietly than could be considered natural.

"It'll probably be some country like China or Russia that drops off a couple of the infected in Alaska or South America somewhere. They'll want to share the love. Otherwise, when this ends the United States could easily take over the planet." LeBron said thinking back to what one of the anchors on one of the cable news shows had brought up as a talking point. This infection was destroying countries more thoroughly than a cold war nuclear exchange would have. In a nuclear war the concept of mutually assured destruction was very well known. It's how the communist regimes of the world would be thinking now.

It was a week before the first confirmed cases in South America were reported on the nightly news. By this time everyone not classified as essential had stopped going to work. Restaurants were closed since they couldn't get any supplies. The national guard in every state had been fully mobilized. Law enforcement officers were spending their days transporting looters and law breakers to jail. There were so many people who couldn't afford basic supplies due to the exorbitant rates on the black market that robbery was the only option they had.

The economy was now a joke. Cash was no longer even close to being king. The ability to still use currency was only due to the government enforcing it. As soon as the transaction was completed at the grocery store people were trading for stuff on the black market like crazy. Hard to get pharmaceuticals, recreational drugs, booze, guns, and ammunition were the real currency. Barter the new way things were getting done. Multiple houses had their windows boarded up at this point. Bart was working with Drew and LeBron to get theirs done when Yue walked outside to tell them it'd happened.

"I'm more scared of the people around here than I am of those things on the news." LeBron said as they stood around watching the latest reports.

"I never really understood why the government would try to keep things under wraps. I'm getting it now. Totally explains why they're still hiding the alien bodies." Yue added trying to make a joke to lighten the mood. It didn't work.

"Ok. Let's get the windows boarded up and make sure we all know the rally points and the best ways to get out of here if we need to." Bart said.

"Wait a second. This is the part I was telling you about. I think we need to figure out how to reserve a spot." Nancy said before they could all roll out of the house to get back to work. LeBron and Drew were in no hurry to hold up the heavy pieces of wood while their dad yelled at them to not move. They immediately hopped on the sectional to watch the next news clip.

Emergency shelters were being built to emulate the forts the people over in Europe were still surviving in. The supplies normally shipped to stores would be rerouted to the shelters where everyone would receive free meals once they presented themselves at the sites. A ration card system was being worked out and would soon be in place. Emergency shelter designations would be sent out soon as well.

"That explains why they're blocking off the first-floor windows of the high school." Bart said.

"That's good though, right? We need to make sure we're able to get in. Those types of shelters are the only reason those people over in Europe are still alive." Nancy said.

"They're also getting regular supply drops from the United States." LeBron said. He didn't bother following through to the logical conclusion of that statement. If they went into that high school, then no one was going to be making supply drops for them. It'd end up being a death trap.

"We don't know that the whole country will be a loss. Remember they're trying to set it up so the farmers are spaced out and can still put together crates of supplies that helicopters can airlift and deliver." Yue said. There'd been a special on it the other day. An entire hour of television dedicated to the different plans the government was working on to ensure everyone's survival. The show had kept emphasizing that the US would learn from their allies and use that knowledge to avoid suffering a similar fate.

Supply caches, mobilizing the national guard, and declaring martial law had all been done in the name of protecting the country. Travel between states was now severely restricted. It was getting bad, but everyone took some bit of relief from the fact that at least they were prepared. There was a real chance they'd keep the disease isolated even if the infection did hit some parts of the country. No one had really expected the South American countries to be able to keep out the diseased for forever. The news that it'd been detected there though meant that it was only a matter of time before it made it up to the US.

Chapter 5: Crisis at the Border

The border between Mexico and the United States had been completely militarized in a vain attempt to secure it. The refugees scrambling to escape the horrors of the surge didn't care about being arrested. Most of them saw the finish line as being arrested and taken to a secure holding facility where they'd be fed and guarded. The infection was spreading throughout all of South America at this point. The people living there were forced to flee north or die.

The infected in the surge phase tore through the large refugee groups seeking to reach the safety of North America. Horrific videos recorded on smart phones showed the attacks and subsequent rapid spread of the infection. The attacks were happening in broad daylight as the people in the United States and Canada sat terrified in front of their TVs. The news showed massive mobs of South Americans knocking over walls and driving through the desert to escape the terror hounding them.

The United States border patrol disregarded the orders to open fire on the mobs of people streaming across the border. There was no way to stop them all anyway. People running out of a burning building weren't going to stop just because the person in front of them got shot. This is where reality foiled the plans conceived and approved in the capitol buildings. The military couldn't open fire on masses of innocent civilians with no provocation. Especially not in the presence of news cameras. Whether they would've if the cameras hadn't been there was something to be debated another day.

The bulk of the people in the United States were slowly starving as they cowered in their homes. They watched angrily as the news showed refugees being fed three hot meals per day. Meanwhile their own children survived on handfuls of stale Fruit Loops. Sensing the turn in public sentiment the politicians ordered the military to take a harsher stance. By this point the military leaders had already made up their minds what needed to be done and were only paying lip service to the civilian leadership anyway. When it came to making the hard choices, politicians were useless.

Europe had fallen as the refugees overran it. The surge followed right behind them. The exact same scenario was playing out in the United States. The same lack of action was going to doom them all if no one took definitive action quickly. The General of the Air Force took a call from the President to discuss the options available to them. The general hung up the phone after an intense conversation and immediately got in contact with his tactical team. Within the hour ten stealth bombers were dropping thousands of pounds worth of ordinance on the massive groups of refugees headed north through Central America.

The brigades that'd been stationed near the border were deployed to mop up the refugees that made it through the air raids. The soldiers were told that it'd been confirmed that all of the refugees were asymptomatic carriers. That lie wouldn't have held up under close scrutiny but when told to scared young men and women being sent into combat it held up well enough. The soldiers already understood the need to stop the flood of refugees to try to halt the spread of the infections. Even the ones who knew better pretended to believe. It made it easier when you were sniping groups of women and children if you pictured them as monsters. Of course, it was even easier to accidentally miss most of the time.

The border was a bloody disaster. Miscommunication led to most of a battalion dying from friendly fire when a bomber unleashed on them due to the wrong coordinates being called in. The flow of refugees didn't stop. It may have paused for a minute but then it resumed with twice the intensity of before. The surge had caught up with those in the rear of the refugee packs. With the infected stalking them the refugees were more than willing to take their chances running the gauntlet of the US defenses.

Another key difference at the border was that the refugees started fighting back. These weren't groups of the poor trying to sneak up north to work the fields and send money back home. These were desperate groups of people from countries that for all practical purposes no longer existed. Intermingled with the civilians were plenty of men lugging along weapons. When the men guarding the border opened fire the hard-core gang members from places like Columbia had no problem shooting back. They had a lot more experience under live fire than the US soldiers shooting at them.

The pitched battles at the border made for fantastic TV. If only anyone cared about buying ad space anymore. The battles not captured by the media were the unseen ones happening all around them in the air and on the water. The Navy of Brazil has over a hundred ships with almost a hundred thousand marines and sailors. The leaders of Brazil didn't just sit in their houses and let the surge carry them away. They took their families and as many people as they could fit and boarded those ships. They pointed the bows northwards and set sail for the United States. The United States Navy immediately moved to blockade them.

Small planes took people over the border to all the places they'd been dropping off drugs and other contraband for decades. The border had always been more of a filter than a dam. A filter with really big holes in it if you knew where to look.

"We're so screwed." Drew said. They were watching the news as a family like they did every night now. School had been canceled and may never come back. Yue had switched to on-line courses that her professors no longer bothered to show up for. Drew and LeBron had the option to do something similar but hadn't pursued it. Drew because he could care less and LeBron because he was so far beyond the standard virtual school curriculum that it would've been a waste of his time. Bart and Nancy had left it up to them what they wanted to do as far as virtual school went for the time being.

"It's going to be a rough ride all right." Bart agreed. He was standing behind the sectional drinking water out of a tall glass.

The house looked pretty empty. They'd spent a lot of time hiding all the supplies they'd been able to gather. The box springs of every bed in the house had been transformed into secret pantries. The only obvious signs of preparation were the thick pieces of plywood secured in front of every window. Each of them carried a weapon at all times. They could all feel the tension building outside the house. The lack of supplies, the coming invasion from the south, the constant barrage of doom and gloom on the TV, and the complete collapse of anything considered normal were all adding up.

Trucks stopped showing up at Publix. On the news it said the government was working on creating new distribution points for food. Bart snorted loudly causing everyone to look over at him.

"They're not creating new distribution points. They're routing all the supplies to the shelters and military bases. I wouldn't be surprised to be ordered to evacuate here shortly. They figure they can get people to leave their homes easier if they're hungry." Bart said.

"Well, why shouldn't we go to one of the shelters?" Nancy asked. She was pretty big on law and order and following rules. She also had a lot of faith in the human spirit and firmly believed that most people wanted to be good. That faith had been tested many times as a foster care provider but had never failed to see her through.

"We may end up at one of them." Bart said politically. "We'll just have to see how everything works out. It may be good to let the shelters fill up first then see how they pan out on the news before we leave the house unprotected to go jump in one. I see them as a last resort."

"I bet I know what'll drive people to the shelters faster than being hungry." Yue said pointing at the screen. The bottom had a message scrolling across it saying that the infected had been spotted in Texas and California. A frazzled looking reporter appeared in a small room after the break. Commercials had been replaced by an endless loop of which shelter you should go to depending on your zip code and a list of what you were allowed to bring with you.

The reporter was showing footage of the infected from earlier in the day. They'd come running full speed across the desert from Mexico. The soldiers in the military style Hummer that the reporter had been riding in had gunned them down as they sprinted towards them. Once they'd killed them, they'd driven close enough to cover the bodies with gasoline and set them on fire. The reporter then stated he'd been told similar incidents had occurred at the border in California as well.

"We're going to the shelter." Nancy stated adamantly. She wanted to go somewhere they could be protected. Somewhere the government was standing by to help them weather this storm.

"I don't think we make that call quite yet." Bart said.

"Mom. Dad has a lot more experience with this kind of stuff than the rest of us. We should listen to him." Yue said.

"Nobody has experience in this. Your dad included. What sounds good to me is solid walls and men with guns standing on them with big sets of stadium lights turned on all night!" Nancy said starting to get worked up.

"The only people left alive over in Europe are the ones who did it that way." Drew said.

"The only ones the media's showing anyway. It's not like they embedded reporters in every neighborhood to go door to door and see how people are doing." LeBron pointed out. Bart gave him an admiring look. The boy was always thinking. They were going to need him to keep that up.

"Here's what I think." Bart said. "I'm not saying we shouldn't head for a shelter. I'm saying we wait and try to figure out the best shelter to head for. I know we can't stay in the house forever. We have enough supplies for a couple of weeks though. The open road is going to be a very dangerous place to be very soon."

"All the more reason to move now. Before it gets too dangerous." Nancy responded.

Bart didn't have an answer for that. Mostly because he knew she was right. He also knew that he was right. The problem was this wasn't a situation anyone was trained for. They needed to do something though.

"Let's load up the cars. I want each of you to get a go bag ready. Pack it with what you'd need to survive for three days. Water, food, ammunition, and a change of underwear. You can only turn them inside out once or twice before it gets gross." Bart joked.

"We leaving?" Drew asked.

"Not quite yet but you're right honey. We need to be ready to leave at the drop of a hat. There's no telling what may happen." Bart answered.

They spent the next couple of hours loading up the cars and making sure they had everything they'd need. The bungalow home they'd purchased was on a walking trail with a large retention pond on one side of it. The garage was detached from the rest of the structure. They decided to load up Drews pickup and their parents Traverse. Those seemed to be the two best vehicles to take with them. They moved Yue's little Corolla across the street and parked it there. Tired but feeling like they'd accomplished something they all went to sleep.

Chapter 6: A Rude Awakening

The burglar alarm went off with a high-pitched squeal around three in the morning. Bart was out of bed and in the hallway outside his bedroom within ten seconds of it going off. Nancy and Bart slept on the first floor in the master suite. The kids each had a room of their own upstairs. Yue had her own bathroom while Drew and LeBron had to share. Bart glanced out the back door towards the large retention pond and didn't see anything suspicious. Pistol pointed at the floor he headed for the front of the house.

The stairs from the second floor ended by the front door. That's where Drew, LeBron and Yue were all waiting for Bart to show up. Bart quietly ordered Yue and LeBron to stay on the stairs and cover him. He motioned for Drew to go over to the windows on the first floor to see if he could see anything. They had one of the video doorbells on the front door but nothing monitoring the space between the garage and the back door. Bart had meant to put one up, but they lived in a nice neighborhood, so it'd never been a high priority. For that same reason he was pretty much clueless as to how the alarm system worked. He could turn it on and off and that was about it.

He pointed at the flashing alarm panel and LeBron sidled in behind him to key in the code to deactivate it. Bart kept on trying to see if he could tell what was going on by looking through the peephole in the back door. With the main alarm turned off now they could hear another alarm going off. It took them a second to figure out it was the sound of a car alarm. Bart opened the door a crack to look out. He jumped backwards when someone rammed into the door from the outside slamming it back against the chain lock that he'd left engaged. Bart kicked the door shut and engaged the deadbolt all in one motion.

"You see anything?" Bart asked Drew. Bart was rubbing his forehead where the door had hit him earlier. Drew jogged over to where they were all gathered now at the foot of the stairs.

"There's some people going in and out of the garage." Drew said.

"Probably saw us putting supplies in the cars earlier today. That was a dumb mistake." Bart muttered.

"What do we do?" Yue asked. Her eyes were wide open. She was white knuckle gripping her pistol with both hands.

"I'm not sure I'm ready to shoot a bunch of people for stealing our excess canned goods." Bart said.

"We can just shoot near them like you did the guy in the truck." Yue said.

"What guy in the truck?" Drew asked. Since they hadn't told Nancy about the incident in the parking lot, they hadn't mentioned it to Drew either. The less people who knew the better. They ignored his questioning look for the time being which just made him all the more curious.

"That was a choice I made. If you kids are in a situation where you need to use your weapons, I want you to always shoot to kill. You got it?" They all nodded as Bart made eye contact with each of them in turn.

"What if they mess up the cars?" LeBron said. It was a valid point. Without those vehicles they'd need to walk to any shelter if they decided they wanted to get to one. Based on current events Nancy already had a pretty strong argument for them to head out. Now that looters were breaking into their house, she'd be extra motivated to load up the cars and make a run for the closest shelter. Bart sighed and turned around to go towards the front of the house. He told them all to wait there except for Yue.

Bart and Yue padded back to the side of the house by the retention pond leaving Drew and LeBron guarding the back door. Bart ducked into his bedroom and came out with an AR-15. Nancy also came out with him. She was carrying a shot gun. It was her preferred weapon since it didn't require much in the way of aiming to get the job done. She'd been keeping watch out the windows and checking the video from the doorbell camera while they'd been by the garage door. She let Bart know the coast was clear on this side.

"Shut and lock the door behind me. Nobody gets back in except me. Shoot anybody else. You got it?" Bart said. Nancy tried telling him not to go. He shrugged her off with a quick kiss and disappeared out the door. Yue pulled it shut and locked it behind him. A few seconds later the sounds of the AR-15 being fired erupted outside of the house. There were about ten shots in all then Bart reappeared waving at the doorbell camera to be let back in.

Once in the house he jogged to the door leading to the garage and flung it open. He moved smoothly out the door. The barrel of his rifle moving from left to right as he advanced on the garage. Drew and LeBron stood back from the open front door with their pistols pointed at the opening. A flurry of gunshots sounded from inside the garage. Bart came back out the garage door. He nodded at his boys then ducked quickly around the side of the garage where he took a few more shots at whoever had just run out of the other side of the garage.

After a few minutes of silence Bart walked back into the garage to hit the button to lower the garage door. The sound of the garage door lowering was way too loud in the crisp stillness of the night. The acrid smell of gun smoke drifted on the breeze. Bart took a few pictures on his phone. The group text he sent out showed the windows to the Traverse all busted out. The supplies they'd loaded into the SUV were mostly missing. Same with the supplies in the back of Drew's truck. At least they hadn't bothered breaking his windows.

"Well, that sucks." Bart said once he was back in the house. He reactivated the alarm code and they all gathered into the kitchen for an impromptu family meeting. As anticipated Nancy saw this as the catalyst to pack up and drive to a shelter immediately.

"Are you seriously still thinking we're safer here on our own?" Nancy argued. She'd fearfully leapt out of her bed at the sound of the burglar alarm. Before she'd had time to rub the sleep out of her eyes her husband had gone out the door to play Rambo. As far as she was concerned it was time to go. When people start breaking into your garage to steal food in the middle of the night that's a pretty good indicator that the neighborhood's gone to hell.

"We've been stupid. We shouldn't have been so obvious about moving the supplies out into the garage. We should start standing watches. We can drill some holes through the wood so we can see out. We're probably ok for tonight. I say we set the watch and go back to sleep." Bart said.

"Then tomorrow we wake up and drive our happy butts to a shelter." Nancy said with her arms crossed and her eyes flashing.

Bart made a noise that neither confirmed nor denied he was going to go along with the shelter ultimatum. Everyone dispersed back to their respective bedrooms except for Drew who'd been assigned the first watch. When asked why he'd been chosen Bart had informed him they were going to set the watch alphabetically starting with the letter 'D'. Drew had been about to bring up the obvious when he remembered his dad had already run out of the house once tonight firing his weapon. All Drew had to do was stay awake for a few hours.

He almost soiled his pants when the doorbell rang as soon as everyone had gone back to bed. Bart and Nancy came running out of their room as Yue and LeBron thundered down the stairs. Yue was trying to pull up the doorbell app to see who was standing outside.

"It's the police." She said. Considering her dad had just shot an assault rifle at a bunch of neighbors looting their garage she supposed it made sense someone had called 911. Considering it was a very odd hour of the day it even made sense that the 911 call had been answered. Now they just had to hope these cops were the understanding types.

Bart opened the door and greeted the policemen. Both of the cops looked tired. Neither of them looked like they were going to put up with any crap. Bart told them what'd happened while they listened impassively. LeBron stared at the two uniformed men on their doorstep.

"Aren't you going to take notes?" He asked.

"We're good. It's not like anyone's going to be pressing charges. Hell, the jail is filled to the brim as it is. Some dirtbags tried to break in and steal your food. You scared them off without killing any of them. Good for you guys. As long as there aren't a bunch of dead bodies on your front lawn, I'm good. You good Jake?" The other cop on the patio nodded his head.

"I'm good. What are you guys planning to do?" Jake asked curiously.

"Do about what?" Bart asked confused.

"The whole end of the world thing. You've seen the news, right? I assume you don't have a history of running out into your yard to shoot at your neighbors in the middle of the night." The cop responded.

"Oh yeah. We figured we'd stay here for a while and see how things go then maybe head to a shelter." Bart said.

"We're going to go to one tomorrow. Do you have any suggestions on which one?" Nancy asked earning her an annoyed look from Bart which she completely disregarded. The two cops looked at one another. Jake cleared his throat.

"Honestly the ones we've been to kind of suck. The high school right up the street from you guys would probably be the best one if you do end up needing it. It's going to end up packed though and there's not a ton of supplies. You guys have plywood on the windows. If you have any food left this may be the best place to ride it out. Nobody really knows. Our official stance is once the evacuation order's given you should head to the closest shelter." Jake finished with a shrug and took a step back to leave.

"You guys have a good night. Be safe. There's still time to decide. Just keep your TV tuned to the local news." The other cop said as he spun around to join up with Jake. The two of them walked up the sidewalk back to their patrol car. Nancy shut the door so LeBron could reactivate the alarm.

"Well now what?" Nancy asked. They'd all gathered together in the kitchen for another yawn infused family meeting.

"Cops seem to agree with dad on the shelter situation. We should stick with the wait and see plan. Once we leave the house unguarded our stash here won't last long." Drew said. LeBron nodded while Yue and Bart both wisely kept their thoughts to themselves while they waited to see where Nancy's head was at.

"What else can we do to make the house safe?" Nancy asked after a long pause. Everyone relaxed as the tension flowed out of the room.

"First let's get some sleep. The last I heard these things are still trying to get over the border, so we have time. I say we use the time to try and gather what we can and make sure we're good then we watch what the news is saying. Hopefully we can read between the lines to figure out what we should do." Bart said.

"Works for me. Especially the part about trying to get a little more sleep. I'm zonked." Yue and LeBron both headed for the stairs to get more sleep. Drew yawned and headed for the front window to resume his patrol.

Bart and Nancy walked back to their room holding hands.

Chapter 7: Another Day in Paradise

Drew woke up on the couch. He sat up fast enough to give himself a head rush. He'd only meant to lie down for a second. Looking around the room in a panic he saw his dad leaning against the wall looking at him.

"Go upstairs and shower. It's going to be a long day." Bart said. He'd been disappointed about waking up to find Drew asleep on the couch instead of standing watch. He'd need to put the fear of God into all of them at some point.

"Sorry." Drew said as he walked by with his eyes downcast.

Bart didn't answer. He just gave the boy his best disapproving stare. That'd do the job better than yelling anyway. The boy knew he'd screwed up and put them all at risk. The stakes were getting higher every day. They couldn't afford too many more screwups.

Bart made a large pot of coffee while he waited for everyone to wake up and wander downstairs. Nancy liked to sleep in, so he didn't expect to see her any time soon. Yue was his morning girl. She'd always been an early riser. Bart was the same way. It'd led to lots of early morning bonding time between the two of them. Today proved to be the same.

"Morning dad." Yue said walking past him to go over to the coffee pot to pour herself a cup.

"I was wondering if you'd still get up early after all the excitement last night." Bart said smiling over at this daughter.

"I don't understand how everyone else can stay in bed. I could smell the coffee all the way upstairs. No way I can stay away from that." Yue said. She took her coffee over to the sectional and sat down by the end table that had the remote control on it.

"Best enjoy the coffee now. Same with the TV and taking showers. No telling how much longer we're going to be able to do all that stuff." Bart said. He walked over and sat down on the other end of the sectional with his steaming hot cup.

"Wow. What kind of depressing stuff did you put in your coffee? I might as well turn on the news since you're trying to fill the house up with doom and gloom anyway." Yue said smiling at her dad. She knew for a fact that underneath his gruff exterior he was an incurable optimist with a huge heart.

Yue turned the TV on and pulled up the local news first. Normally the local news would have some stories around topics other than whatever the current disaster was. You could count on them in the midst of a hurricane to break away and bring in a story about someone being sued by their HOA for keeping pigs in their backyard. The days of people caring about HOA complaints must be over. The local and national news channels all seemed to be showing pretty much the same content. The only difference being the local news was listing the locations and requirements for the open shelters in their viewing areas. There was also some new information about a curfew that was going to start being enforced. It turned out there'd been some looting.

"I guess we missed our chance to get in on the looting." Yue joked.

"I hope not. We need supplies." Her dad responded straight faced. Yue looked over at him to see if he was serious or not. He nodded his head affirmatively at her inquisitive look. He definitely wasn't kidding.

"We can't just go steal stuff." Yue said. She was picturing jumping out of the car and breaking the glass out of a gas station window to grab all the chips in the front of the store.

"It's either that or starve to death. This whole thing is moving way too slow. Those people who broke in our garage the other night were the first of many. As this thing spreads there won't be any more food being delivered. Everybody's going to hide behind closed doors with whatever they've managed to hoard until they're forced to leave or starve. The only other option will be if those things get in and turn them." Bart declared. Yue turned away from her dad to watch the news. He was probably right, but it was still pretty early to contemplate diving into a life of crime. She needed to at least enjoy her coffee first.

On the TV the talking head behind the anchor desk was talking about how the military was taking the lessons from other countries and applying them in the USA. The news was showing videos of soldiers with bright lights affixed to their rifles sweeping forward to push back the unseen enemy. Drone video showed the miles and miles of fencing that'd been installed along the border. Every clip being aired implied the United States was prepared to fend off this threat. It was a far cry from the previous videos showing the multitude of disasters at the border.

"What a load of crap." Bart announced. Yue shushed him as a general came on to explain how they were working to slow the surge of the infected from South America. Video of row after row of tanks heading for the border were shown. The general gave a lengthy explanation on how they were compartmentalizing the defense by leveraging the local law enforcement and National Guard. He talked about how in the different states they were ensuring none of the infected were able to slip through.

"What are you talking about? I think you need more coffee or something." Yue remarked glancing over at her dad with concern. It wasn't like him to be quite this negative this early in the morning. He was normally pretty jovial until Drew or LeBron showed up.

"The way the news is starting to show all the same videos. The way the scripts the reporters are reading are all positive and trying to show that we have this under control. They're trying to get us to think it's not going to be as bad as we all know it is. Be interesting to see what LeBron can pull up on the world wide web to give us the real story. I was a lot less freaked out before they tried to put a positive spin on it. It means we're completely screwed and on our own. They don't want us regular people rioting and screwing up their plans is my guess. Don't tell your mom." Bart lightheartedly added that last bit to try and soften the blow. He hated to be so direct, but she was a big girl now. She could take it. He wasn't going to lie to try to make her feel good when the truth might give her the edge she needed to survive.

Yue sipped her coffee silently. The fake smiles of the anchors now appeared super sinister to her. She immediately realized her dad was right about all of the broadcasts looking the same now. There were no more videos of reporters from the field showing the advance of the infected. No more talk about how many infected had already crossed into the United States. A cold chill went up her spine. If the government was controlling the media, then that meant her dad was right. They were screwed.

She pulled out her phone and bounced her index finger off the icon for her web browser. Instead of pulling up her normal homepage she was redirected to a webpage on the department of homeland security website. There were a bunch of links for things like local news by zip code, lists of shelters, and all kinds of useful looking links. Unfortunately, the page was frozen. When Yue hit refresh, an error code popped up saying that she couldn't get to the server anymore due to bandwidth restrictions. She tried her different apps for all of her social media sites.

"Locked out of everything?" Bart asked her. He was watching her panic-stricken face as she tried accessing different sites.

"Nothing's working." She muttered.

"May have to use your phone to make phone calls now. Can it actually do that?" Bart wondered if he should just stop trying to make jokes. The look Yue had just shot him had been pretty deadly. He knew he wouldn't be able to help himself. He just needed to be ready to duck in case she threw something at him.

They sat in silence drinking their coffee and flipping through the channels. The reporters kept revisiting the same old stories. The fact that the fences had been setup and the military was in place to hold back the invasion. Video was shown of power plants that'd been retrofitted with massive stadium light systems to keep the infected away. It wouldn't stop the freshly infected but once they hit the stage where they weren't able to tolerate bright light it should serve as an effective deterrent.

Yue hopped up excitedly when she remembered there were other ways of getting on-line besides her phone. She ran up to her room to try her laptop on the WIFI they had from their cable TV provider. The only difference turned out to be that this time the links on the government site worked. She was able to get to the helpful links that were listed on the page. None of them provided any information beyond what was already being shown on the news. She sighed and walked back downstairs leaving her useless computer sitting in the middle of her bed.

By the time she got downstairs Drew and LeBron were sitting on the couch sipping on coffee as well. Bart was telling them why Yue had gone rampaging upstairs to try out her computer. LeBron was already playing around on his phone to see if he could get his to connect.

"Well?" Drew asked looking questioningly at Yue.

"Same deal on my laptop." Yue replied dejectedly. She plopped down on the couch and looked over at LeBron hopefully. He'd be the one able to hack his way around whatever the government had done to the internet. LeBron was intently trying different things on his phone when he looked up and saw everyone staring at him hopefully. He shook his head and leaned back on the couch. He tried a few more things before flinging his phone across the couch in disgust.

Nancy showed up and they had to explain to her what was going on. She wasn't as upset as the rest of them. The internet had never really been her thing. Since she wasn't quite so internet focused, she was the one who came up with the idea that made Bart want to smack himself in the forehead.

"Hey honey. Can you try calling your old office and see if you can get a straight story out of them?" She suggested.

Bart pulled out his phone and ignored the knowing look from Yue. She was reminding him that he'd been the one who'd just told her she may have to use her phone to actually make phone calls. He shrugged and then ignored her as he pulled up his contacts. He couldn't get the main number to work but he was able to get through via the direct number to dispatch. He had them transfer him to the new Sherriff. He stayed on the phone for about five minutes before saying that he understood and wishing the man on the other end of the line good luck.

"The cops are getting the same level of news we are. They're patrolling for looters and the infected. Crime in general is ticking way up since everybody is freaking out. He suggested we check out the shelter but make sure we carry a gun. He said if we had our own supplies to consider just hunkering down at home. The only place he thought was going to be safe any time soon was going to be in the middle of the ocean on a boat." Bart told his family. He hated he hadn't been able to get any more news than that for them. He didn't tell them that based on the overall tone of the brief conversation it wasn't looking good.

"I know some people with boats." Drew brought up.

"Boats won't do us a ton of good without supplies." LeBron said.

"We can fish. We can raid vacation houses. Just a thought. Better than sitting here waiting to die." Drew shot back testily. He was tired and pissed at himself for falling asleep on guard duty.

"It's a thought. We need to keep coming up with ideas like that." Bart trailed off as they all heard sirens in the distance. Knowing that probably wasn't a good thing they followed Nancy out the front door to take a look.

Standing on the sidewalk that ran in front of their bungalow style home they could clearly see an enormous cloud of black smoke drifting up into the air. A few neighbors had emerged from their homes and were looking in the direction of the smoke as well. Everyone looked scared and was sticking to themselves. Drew looked around suspiciously wondering which of the people standing out on the sidewalk may have been the ones who broke into their garage and stole their food.

"It's the shelter." Bart said gauging the distance and direction of the smoke billowing into the air. Once he'd said it out loud it was obvious to everyone. The huge high school that'd been turned into a shelter was the only thing in that general area that'd be big enough to burn like that.

"It could be the stores." LeBron pointed out. The plaza with the Publix he'd worked in was right next to the high school. Even as he said it though he could see that the angle wasn't right. It was most likely the high school.

"It's the school for now. If they don't get it put out, then the stores will be burning too pretty soon." Bart paused as the sound of gun shots drifted to them from the same general direction as the smoke and the sirens. Without another word they all walked back into the house locking the door behind them.

Chapter 8: The Greater Good

They took turns standing watch the night the high school burned. They kept all the house lights turned off to make it look like no one was home. When Nancy asked where all the people who'd gone to the shelter were going to end up no one had an answer for her. Bart was worried about the former shelter residents showing up at their house. His fear was realized the next morning.

Yue had started a pot of coffee then gone upstairs to do the rounds. The rounds consisted of going to every window in the house and staring out the holes they'd drilled in the plywood to see if they could see anything. Yawning as she looked out at the road by their home, she noted the sun was finally coming up. She was pretty happy about that since it meant her shift was almost over. What she wasn't happy about was seeing the small mob walking down the street in their direction. She watched as the group went to the house a few houses down from them. The group stood back while the leader walked up to the door and rang the doorbell.

The group waited patiently in the street for a few minutes. When no one answered the door, they began beating their way into the home. There was about twenty of them in all. They were carrying a wide variety of bats, crowbars, and rocks. It didn't take them very long to get in the house. Yue was shocked by the sheer brazenness of the group. Their plan of ignoring anyone who rang the doorbell wasn't going to work very well in this situation. Fighting to control her fear she rapped quickly on LeBron and Drews doors to get them to wake up. When she didn't immediately hear a response to her knocking, she called out as loud as she dared for them to get up. To their credit neither of them asked why they just hopped out of bed and fell in behind her as she took the stairs two at a time down to the foyer.

"Mom. There's a group of men breaking into houses outside. I'm going to wake dad up." Yue tossed the frightening words over her shoulder as she made her way past the kitchen to the hallway leading to the master suite. The door was open, and her dad was sleeping on top of the covers. He was fully dressed except for his shoes and gun belt. He had those on before he even had his eyes fully opened when Yue poked him to try to explain what was going on.

"Calm down. Take a deep breath, count to three in your head then start from the beginning." Bart told his freaked-out daughter. Yue did as her dad instructed and was able to get out the whole story. The rest of the family had gathered outside the door to listen in as well. Before they could come up with a plan the sound of the doorbell ringing caused Nancy to gasp and point her shotgun towards the front door. Bart walked past Nancy and gently nudged the barrel of the shotgun, so it was pointing at the floor before he walked over to the door. He opened the door as soon as he got there.

"Hello. How can I help you?" Bart asked the disheveled looking man standing on his doorstep. The man had been in the process of getting ready to smash the window beside the door and let himself in. Thrown off by the door swinging open the man took in the calm demeanor of Bart. His eye scanned down to the pistol hanging off Bart's hip. He looked into the room behind Bart and saw Drew and Nancy holding their weapons in nervous grips.

"We're not trying to start anything. The shelter we were staying in burnt down yesterday. We brought pretty much everything we had to the shelter with us so now we're in serious need of supplies. We figured we could just check abandoned houses for food. We're not trying to rob anybody. If you happen to have any extra though we've got women and children with us." The man wheedled.

"How'd the fire start?" Bart ignored the request for food and asked the question that'd been bugging him since he saw the smoke the day before. The investigator in him felt there was more to it than just an accidental fire.

"The guys in charge kept telling us there were more supplies on the way. We were on pretty strict rations. They took whatever you brought and put it into the community pool. People brought a lot of stuff so there was weapons and food and medicine and all of that. I didn't see this next part but a couple guys in the group here talked to some guys who did see it. I guess a truck pulled up and they started loading up all the supplies that were left. Some of the guys here saw what was going on and got into a pissing match with the soldiers. Push came to shove, and the soldiers wasted them."

"So, how'd the fire get started?" Bart asked. The man he'd been talking to just shrugged and shook his head. Another man spoke up.

"The soldiers did it. They must've been trying to cover up what they did. Poured gas all over everything and lit it up before they took off."

"We're seriously not here to steal your stuff. Just hitting the empty houses. We'll let you guys get back to it." The original man who'd rang the doorbell said backing up with his hands held nonthreateningly in the air. The whole group had already started walking towards the next house. Bart watched them walk to the next house where they repeated the doorbell trick. They left that house alone as well when the neighbors answered the door. Bart knew it was only a matter of time before they'd stop caring if people still lived in the homes or not. Especially when he saw the group of about thirty women and children who were trailing along behind the men.

"We could spare some food for them." Nancy was already in his ear. Bart shook his head firmly before walking over to the living room to have a seat on the couch. Nancy stood by the hole in the wood covering the window watching the dirt covered children trudging miserably by. A couple of them were eating random things they'd found in the abandoned homes they'd looted so far.

Bart turned on the TV. It took him a second to press the right buttons since his hands were shaking pretty hard from the adrenaline of the recent confrontation. He'd been in tougher situations over the years but never with his wife and kids lives riding on his actions. The scrolling text on the bottom of the screen indicated the President was making another address at noon. The President had started out strong but then disappeared for the last week. The nonstop news was constantly spewing the government propaganda anyway, so they probably didn't see a need for the President to make any addresses. Bart was curious how the President was planning to spin the 'abandoning everyone' approach.

"You really think the soldiers were stealing the supplies from the shelter?" Drew asked.

"Wouldn't surprise me one bit. Everyone needs supplies and in this kind of environment the guys with the guns end up with the goods. Those soldiers have wives and children to take care of to. Plus, they were probably ordered to do it." Bart answered.

"Your boat idea is starting to sound a lot better." LeBron joked. Drew flipped him off from behind their dad so he wouldn't get yelled at.

"I saw that. There's no excuse for making that ugly gesture at your brother. All we have now is each other." Nancy said walking into the room. A red-faced Drew hurriedly dropped his hand to his side.

They did what was starting to become the normal routine for them. They sat in the living room waiting for the next newscast while mindlessly watching the same drivel they'd seen a thousand times before. The anchors and reporters were dissecting the same old information in slightly different ways. Footage of bombers dropping huge payloads onto the desert to stop the incoming infected. The talking heads no longer bothering to point out that the whole massive bombing run thing had been tried in multiple places in Europe as well and failed.

There was very little footage or news from any of the other countries. At one point it'd been mentioned that Australia was completely clear of any infected. The country had shut down its borders and sent out warnings that any ship or plane crossing those borders would be immediately fired upon with no warning given. It sounded like a pretty solid plan to LeBron.

The noon hour finally arrived. Nancy and Yue had cooked up a batch of basmati rice to eat for lunch. They'd scored several huge bags of the stuff before the store they'd been buying them from had gone into rationing mode. Curious what kind of fantasy the President was going to try to weave into this address they sat around eating their plates of rice waiting for him to get around to addressing the nation. Finally, the screen cleared to show the President sitting in the Oval Office once again.

"They must have a fake Oval Office built out in the bottom of the secret mountain base the government's hiding out in." LeBron observed before being shushed by everyone.

"My fellow Americans. I come to you tonight with a message of hope. It's too early to say for certain but the evidence suggests we're beating back the tide of the infected that's been rising against us. While this news should bring everyone a great deal of relief, we're not out of the woods yet. We need your cooperation to get through this." The President did one of his meaningful pause things. He looked much better rested this time around. It must be a lot less stressful when you were living in a giant mountain base protected by a battalion of marines with a few thousand tons of supplies stocked away.

"We need every American to comply fully with local officials. There have been widespread reports of looting and riots. This must stop now. You've no doubt noted that the majority of internet connections now point to the homeland security website. This is to ensure that timely information can be disseminated to everyone. It also allows for citizens to report looters and anarchists so that the proper authorities can deal with them. Once the crisis has been averted, we will restore regular connectivity. I want to stress that we're all in this together. God bless the ..." Bart had hit the power button.

"I couldn't take it anymore." He said to the irritated looks everyone was giving him.

"What do you mean?" Nancy took the bait.

"Powerful people are scared out of their minds. People so powerful they can control the President. People who have no problem ordering the President to send armed men into the news studios to make sure the anchors read the scripts they're given. That's the reason we're not getting the truth." Bart replied somberly.

"Why would they lie about it?" Yue asked challengingly. She still wasn't sold on the big government conspiracy cover-up that the rest of the family seemed to have latched onto.

"If they can't stop the spread of this infection then the government or the puppet masters or the illuminati or whoever already know we're going to lose. Their best course of action now is to gather their supplies together and retreat into their fortresses. They can wait there in comfort for the whole thing to die out. They're lying so that we'll docilely sit in our houses until the crawler things are at our doorsteps. Otherwise, we may screw up their ability to escape to their private islands or to gather together all the supplies they need." LeBron explained his thoughts on the whole deal. Even to his own ears he sounded like some kind of a conspiracy nut. Yue did not in any way look like she was convinced.

"The other piece the government is focused on is infrastructure. You notice they've got the power plants all lit up. I'm sure they have all kinds of critical things setup to survive. They'll want to be able to rebuild fast once it's over." Bart added.

"Rebuild for who if everybody's dead?" Yue asked.

"Who said everybody's dead?" LeBron said thinking fast. "They could be trying to get us to all sit in our houses while they load up all the military and their families onto cruise ships or something to wait it out. They'll know how many people they can save. They're going to want to keep the ones who haven't been chosen from interfering."

"It doesn't matter." Nancy chimed in forcefully. Her completely unexpected interruption of the conversation instantly captured everyone's curiosity.

"It doesn't matter one bit." She echoed her previous statement. "What matters is that those things are coming. We can't depend on anyone but ourselves to get us through this. We need to figure out how we're going to survive. I don't think the answer is sitting in here until we run out of rice."

They kept talking. The conversation turned to a discussion of every disaster movie they'd ever seen. Bart was the one with the real training, but it didn't really lend itself to end of the world type scenarios. Drew and LeBron started talking zombie movies. The obvious similarity was there with the infected coming for them and the way the infection spread. The biggest difference was the waiting. None of them could remember a movie plot where the heroes knew the end of the world was coming and just sat around waiting for it. Other than the movies where a meteorite was going to hit the earth if Bruce Willis didn't figure out how to stop it in time. It was this random series of conversations that led to Bart's epiphany.

"We can't stay here. I just don't think we can leave quite yet either." Bart stated emphatically out of the blue. LeBron looked up from where he was digging through their DVD collection searching for any relevant movies they could watch for ideas. The internet situation meant they couldn't pull anything up on Prime or Netflix or Hulu or any of their other go to streaming services.

"What are you talking about dad?" Drew asked.

"Like your mom said earlier staying here's a losing battle. If we leave too soon the military guarding the roads are going to sling us in a jail cell or a shelter. Same thing different name. Our best hope is to leave once everything goes completely to hell." He said. He sat there smiling like he'd just come up with a great idea for a new game for them all to play.

Opinions differed on his plan. Everyone seemed to have an opinion on whether they should even trust their dad to come up with the plan. Bart had to remind them a few times that he was sitting right there. Still looking through the zombie flicks spread out on the floor LeBron added that another thing to consider was that the all the people waiting around right now were eating their way through pretty much all of the available food supplies. They'd all just witnessed the group of people going door to door in their own neighborhood eating every morsel of unclaimed food they could find.

Ironically enough the government was abandoning them because the infection hadn't moved quickly enough. There was just no way to logistically support evacuating the population of the United States. Without the use of Google Maps there was a lot of fuzzy math used to come up with the mileage to the border. They were far from confident in their final estimate but were going with the infection most likely making its way to Orlando in another week. Assuming the infected ran like Forrest Gump on crank to reach them. The math got fuzzier when they tried to factor in the infected progressing from the surge phase to the crawler phase.

Chapter 9: Lessons Learned

LeBron sat quietly in the loft listening to the sound of the rain coming down. With the windows boarded up and the overcast sky it might was well be midnight. It was actually early afternoon on the day they'd estimated the first of the infected may start showing up. LeBron was sitting on the loveseat upstairs thinking about the ludicrousness of it all. Their lives had been turned into a bad zombie movie in the span of the last few months.

LeBron had watched every video of the infected he could find back before the internet had been shut off. He'd watched the ones where people in the streets were bitten and minutes later were running around like maniacs trying to find more victims. He'd found a whole channel on YouTube dedicated to the crawler metamorphosis. Three to five days after getting infected people seemed to start calming down. They stopped running around like blood thirsty lunatics and began avoiding bright lights. Once that happened the next time those people were seen they were loping around on all fours like hairless gorillas who'd had one too many banana daiquiris.

Unlike the infected in the surge phase the crawlers had a method to their madness. They'd move along slowly looking for signs of uninfected humans before springing into action. Once they attacked though they did so with the same manic strength as the recently infected. It's like their brains opened up in a way that allowed them to tap the adrenal gland on demand. For whatever reason this new ability impacted their tolerance for light. There were a lot of theories out there, but LeBron was pretty sure Drew had nailed t.

Drew was the only one of them to have ever experimented with hallucinogenic drugs. He'd been in some unsavory situations before winding up with them at the Russel's home. There was a common theory based on the dilation of the infected peoples' pupils that once an exchange of fluids had occurred the infected started tripping like crazy. Drew pointed out that with all that hallucination going on the infected may just reach a stage where they became deathly afraid of the light. When LeBron had looked at him like he was crazy he'd been treated to a story of how Drew had avoided reflective surfaces for a week. That had happened after he'd watched his body melt apart in a mirror after dropping acid. That was from stuff you could buy in the parking lot of a high school. Obviously, the stuff causing the crawlers was at a whole other level.

"Dude why are you sitting in the dark like that. It's creepy. Come downstairs. The President's going to lie to us some more." Drew said. He was using the flashlight on his smart phone to look around the loft. They were very careful about where they shined their lights at night since it could be seen through the holes in the boards. During the day it wasn't as big of a deal. Although during a thunderstorm like the one currently raging outside it probably should be.

LeBron took the stairs slowly. He was still mulling over the data he'd accumulated so far around the people who'd been infected. A lot of the data seemed to contradict itself. It was beyond frustrating that all his sources of information had been abruptly cutoff. The internet had become just as useful and expected a utility as water, sewage, and cable TV. It was completely unjustifiable to him how they could still have power but no data. Nothing but the utterly useless horribly slow homeland defense server anyway. At the foot of the stairs, he grabbed his bowl of rice and two adult Gummy multivitamins. Nancy hoped the multivitamins would make up for the lack of variation in their diets.

"He's coming on." Yue announced to get everyone to shut up and sit down. For a bunch of people who were supposed to be hiding out they sure talked a lot. Thinking about hiding out she got up and tugged the curtains tight to make sure they were completely closed since they had the TV turned on.

Bart walked over with a bowl of rice and tapped Drew on the back. Drew being the first one to finish his food pretty much every time they ate.

"Hey. Go stand over by the window and keep a look out while we're watching this." He asked Drew. Drew grumbled at having to get up off the couch but dutifully began walking the rounds for the bottom windows. The group Yue had spotted the day before had cemented in their minds how important it was to maintain a constant vigilance. If she hadn't seen what was going on outside that interaction with the shelter survivors could've ended a whole lot less peacefully. The screen of the TV was showing the seal of the President as Drew walked over to look out the first window.

"My fellow Americans. I'm heartbroken that I have to start this address out with an apology. The government has failed you. I have failed you. We weren't able to contain the infected at the border. It's anticipated they'll have spread across the majority of North America within the next few weeks." The President paused to let that point sink in. This time there was no need for him to have to try to appear serious. The weight of what he'd just admitted was heavy enough to need no clearer explanation. After an acceptable pause for everyone to reflect the President continued speaking.

"Our experts predicted we wouldn't be able to stop the spread of this contagion. I prayed that they were wrong. We launched strike after strike along the border to try to stop it. We were unable to do so. Parallel to those efforts we also began the evacuation of key government, civilian, and military personnel to secure locations. We executed contingency plans that have long been in place for such extinction level events. We shut down access to the internet to ensure that no one reported the evacuation before we were able to effectively execute on the plan. I know it will be of small concern to many of you struggling to keep your family alive in the coming months but hopefully it'll bring some comfort to know that the United States will continue. We will continue to fight this virulent pandemic. Someday we hope to return and rebuild the USA together with those of you who manage to survive this catastrophe."

"Many of you may be wondering why I'm bothering with this address. This is basically a speech to let you know you're on your own. There was a great deal of debate within my cabinet as to whether this final address was a good idea or not. I felt that we had an immense moral obligation to tell you all the truth. I also believe we can give you some guidance on how to survive the plague soon to sweep across the entirety of the continent. I want to make it clear that I'm rooting for all of you. Americans have proven time after time to be the most resourceful people on the planet."

"I leave you now with some of what we've learned. I pray it helps some of you to survive. First of all, don't expect the threat to simply die out. We've confirmed the shadowy figures seen in the original video from Egypt weren't just people from the crew who got infected earlier and fell into the vault. We sent a team that captured one of the figures. Various techniques were used to confirm the specimen we pulled out was thousands of years old. Thousands of years old but still alive. The team of operators we sent in to capture the specimen all became infected. They were infected without being bitten. This confirmed for us that the contagion can become airborne. Keep in mind they were in a confined space with a very old specimen."

"After this address we fully suspect riots and unrest to rip the country apart. More people may die at the hands of fellow Americans than from the infected. Please be aware this may happen and plan accordingly. If you have two weeks' worth of food in your home and decide to shelter in place you can plan on starving to death in two weeks. What our specialists suggest you do is band together for protection and seek out remote locations to live where you can raise your own food. It's understood that to give you all a chance to survive you need information. To that end I've ordered internet access to be restored. Please take advantage of it to contact your loved ones as well as to gather the information you'll need to survive. That access will disappear as the power plants across the country are shut down."

"One final note. There are locations that've been deemed critical to maintain. These sites will be needed to rebuild the United States. Critical sites have been marked as vital and booby trapped to discourage trespassing. These sites include dams, power plants, and any other sites deemed critical. Other than those sites the full resources of the United States are at your disposal. Those of you still alive in another month have a legitimate chance of living a long and full life. May God protect you all." The very somber looking face of the President faded off the screen.

"At least now we know not to mess up the stuff the rich people will need once the rest of us die off." LeBron commented sarcastically.

"I was like five seconds from running out to sabotage the local power plant. Good thing we didn't stop the speech early." Drew tagged on.

Everyone else was quiet and contemplative. Nancy was crying softly into Bart's shoulder while Yue rubbed her back. They sat around in various states of disbelief. It wasn't easy absorbing the fact that the President had just announced most of the people in North America would be infected or dead within the next month. It wasn't easy hearing that there'd be no help coming.

"We're going to need more supplies. Drew and I will go get them tonight. We'll leave you guys here to guard the house." Bart suddenly announced.

"Where are you going to get more supplies from exactly?" Yue asked.

"Stores, gas stations, restaurants, fast food places or wherever else we see. Basically, anywhere that we can break into where there may be food. We need to collect enough to survive the first wave of the infected." Bart answered.

"What about the first wave of the rioters and whoever else shows up with guns to take what we have?" Drew asked.

"We kill them. That's the world now. Those that adapt the fastest will be the ones left standing. I fully intend for us to adapt faster than anybody else. Nothing matters moving forward more than each other." Bart said.

LeBron was busy making a list in a spiral notebook he'd pulled out of a drawer in the kitchen. He'd titled the list 'Lessons Learned' and was busy jotting down everything he'd learned so far on the internet as well as the intel the President had just provided. He finished a page and tore it out to pass it around to everyone. The more they knew the better. LeBron was literally trying to make sure they were all on the same page as far as what was happening in the world around them.

They installed an extra layer of plywood on the downstairs windows. Their neighbors walked over to talk to them while they were screwing in the big pieces of wood. The neighbors were a friendly couple from England. They'd all gotten along well enough. Bart had even had a few beers over the years with the husband Shaun. The couple didn't have any children and were considerably younger than Bart and Nancy so that'd been about the extent of the friendship.

"How are you doing in all of this?" Shaun asked once Bart had finished drilling.

"About as well as can be expected. How about you two?" Bart asked. He looked over at the neighbor's bungalow. They'd spent the extra money to install the hurricane shutters. Bart had made fun of them for that since they lived so far inland. Now he was kicking himself for not having selected to have that done to their own home. It wasn't like the slightly higher mortgage payment would matter at this point.

"No worries. We had a few facetime calls with our family back in England. What's coming isn't pretty." Shaun said. His wife was nodding sadly behind him. She looked pretty well plastered. Given the circumstances you couldn't really blame her.

"Alright then." Bart said and continued screwing in their last sheet of plywood while Drew and LeBron held it straight. Shaun waited for them to finish then asked Bart if he could possibly buy a gun off of him. Bart looked like he was coming up with a nice way to say no when Shaun interrupted him.

"I know how valuable weapons are at this point. I'm not stupid enough to offer you cash. What I do have is a lot of instant noodles, rice, potatoes and what not. I can trade you for a pistol and some ammunition. It's not a bad thing to have someone the house over shooting at the same bad guys that you're shooting at."

Chapter 10: A Looting We Will Go

Drew glanced over at Shaun's house as him and his dad crept out of the house later that night. Bart had come to an agreement with Shaun which had netted them a few large boxes packed with food. It turned out Shaun was a bit of a prepper. He'd stocked up on tons of instant food in case of a hurricane or alligator attacks or whatever it was that freaked out people from England who moved to Florida. Whatever the reason they'd made a deal where Bart parted with a nine-millimeter handgun along with three magazines worth of bullets in exchange for a ridiculously large amount of food. He'd have felt bad about how much food they took except that it didn't even really put a dent in the massive supply Shaun had stored in his garage.

They were walking tonight. There was a trail that ran past their home all the way to the local downtown area. It ran past a couple of restaurants and grocery stores as it twisted along through the woods. They'd biked, skated, and walked the trail together as a family about a million times. It was something their mom had liked to do every night. Drew had never felt unsafe stepping out onto the narrow-paved trail before. Now the trail lurked ominously in front of them. The biggest fear they'd ever had in the past was that there might be a gator hidden in the weeds since it ran along the side of several large retention ponds. Now Drew imagined everything from crawlers to desperate refugees lurking in the weeds on either side of the narrow trail.

"Hurry up!" His dad hissed at him. Bart had already warned him that once they went out the door they needed to move fast. They needed to put as much distance between themselves and the house as they could. LeBron, Yue, and Nancy were all loaded up and ready to defend the house, but it'd be much better if they didn't have to. Drew jogged along behind his dad down the trail for about five minutes before Bart slowed to a stop. His dad had either decided to stop because he judged they'd gone far enough or because he was on the verge of a heart attack.

"Maybe it's time to stop using the treadmill to hang wet clothes on." Drew suggested with a smirk. He was standing beside his dad who was now hunched over trying to catch his breath. Bart started to say something back to Drew but was trying too hard not to puke up the ramen noodles he'd wolfed down before they left. Drew wasn't even breathing hard.

"Let's go." Bart said once he was finally able to straighten up. Drew was right. He'd definitely let himself go in retirement. He couldn't remember the last time he'd actually jogged further than the refrigerator. He only did that when he was in a hurry to get a snack before the commercials ended. It was a long cry from the excellent shape he'd kept himself in earlier in life. Like the end of the world didn't already suck enough now he was going to have to work on his cardio. Otherwise, he'd end up crawling through the night trying to eat people for the rest of his life.

They'd gotten enough dried goods from Shaun earlier to bolster their stores to the levels he thought they needed. The reason Bart had decided to still go on the supply run with Drew was to get in some recon of the local area. It was one thing to stare out the drill holes in your plywood covered windows at random freaks running through the neighborhood. It's another thing entirely to venture out a few miles and really see what's going on. He was hoping to get a feel for how hard it was going to be to escape later. He was reconsidering staying in the house and wondering if they should make their run now instead. If they happened to find a bunch of canned food that he could make Drew carry back home that'd just be icing on the cake.

Bart had decided for them to head out in the opposite direction from the school that'd been burnt down. He assumed that entire area was a big burnt-out mess. The Publix over there had probably already been picked through completely. He was hoping going in the other direction would be safer. He realized as they walked along that there might no longer be a safe direction. The sound of gun fire in the distance was followed by the sounds of screaming. The screaming tapered off and an uneasy silence fell across the world once again.

Bart fought against his cop reflex to run towards the sounds of people in trouble. That wasn't something he'd be able to do anymore. At least not for a while. The world was going to fall apart around them. His job was to keep his family alive at all costs. There were going to be some very hard decisions that had to be made. Decisions he knew he was going to have a hard time living with.

"Did you hear that?" Drew asked him. He was referring to the distant screams and gunshots. He'd stopped walking beside the concrete covered trail that'd take them in the direction of the people who needed help. Bart kept right on marching the other way. He'd instilled a strong sense of community in Drew. The boy knew right from wrong. He had honor. He'd have to squash all that to survive the next few months.

Drew stared up the sidewalk another second or two then turned and followed his father into the darkness. The trail they were on skirted the suburb they lived in before disappearing deeper into the wooded preserve areas. Carrying his rifle in the crook of his arm with the now familiar weight of the pistol hanging on his belt Drew felt like an impostor. Like a kid who's just a little too old for make believe dressing up to go out in the yard and play regardless. He couldn't imagine actually killing someone. He thought of the weapons they were carrying more as a deterrent. A sign that people should leave him and his dad alone.

"What's that?" Drew hissed looking up the trail at some lights coming towards them. Bart immediately looked to the left and right to see if there was somewhere that they could hide. They were surrounded by swampy woods though and the lights would be on them in less than a minute. Cussing himself out for getting them into this situation Bart told Drew to let him do the talking as the lights got closer.

The lights coalesced into a small group of men on mountain bikes. The men were armed with rifles strapped to their bikes and pistols hanging off their belts. A couple of the men had baklavas pulled up to hide their faces. There were six men total. They stopped pedaling and coasted to a stop as they got close enough to clearly make out the two of them.

"You out here alone?" One of the men on the bikes asked. The bikers were shining their lights into Bart's and Drew's faces effectively blinding them. Drew was backing up slowly wondering when he was going to feel a bullet rip through him.

"Drop the lights or I'll drop a couple of you." Bart answered the man. Bart hadn't pointed a weapon at the group or made any other sort of threatening move, but the tone of his voice clearly conveyed he wasn't bluffing.

"No problem. All friends here just trying to survive the end of the world." The mountain bike guy said. The men angled their handlebars so that the lights mounted to them were no longer pointed straight at Drew and Bart. The bikers all sat on their bikes with weapons in easy reach waiting to see what was going to happen next. Everybody was taking this end of the world stuff one step at a time. It wasn't like the apocalypse came with a handbook.

"Yeah. Friends. Where are you guys headed?" Bart asked.

"Just out for a little ride. How about you two?" The man asked casually. The group of bikers were slowly moving to encircle them. Drew nervously flexed his arms and subtly checked to see if the safety on his rifle was engaged or not.

"You guys really need those rifles and everything?" One of the other men had put the kickstand on his bike down and was getting in Drews face. Drew was big and athletic but the man in his face was bigger. Drew looked desperately over at Bart.

The man swung an arm to grab Drew in a headlock. He may be bigger than Drew, but he wasn't anywhere near as well trained. He was definitely not in the same kind of shape as the star athlete he'd just attacked.

Drew had grown up fighting. Someone twice his size swinging a fist at him was nothing new. The man's fist sailed harmlessly over his head as Drew ducked then swung his fist hard into the man's crotch. Without needing to think too much about it he then stood up and grabbed the hunched over man by the hair. Drew slammed his knee into the guys face then flung him into the swampy woods. He watched a little too long as the guy tumbled into the murky water.

A fist slammed into the side of his head. Drew hit the ground rolling to avoid the kick his instincts expected. Bright flashes of light and the loud roar of gunshots. Drew rolled and scrambled off to the side of the road. His brain was screaming at him that he was going to die. He finally latched onto the fact that his dad was in the middle of that firefight. That thought goaded him into action.

He'd rolled himself out of close proximity to the fight. He sat up Indian style and flipped off the safety on his AR-15. He focused on the madness in front of him while doing his best to control his breathing. He saw his dad calmly standing off to the side in a firing stance putting rounds into the bikers as they struggled to figure out what was going on. Everything was moving in slow motion for Drew. He began firing into the crowd of bikers. His only concession to aiming being to make sure that he didn't shoot his dad. He pulled the trigger until he heard the firing pin hit an empty chamber. The mountain bikers were lying on the ground moaning in a tumble of limbs and blood and bikes.

Bart jogged over to Drew and held out his arm. Drew reached for the hand that Bart was offering him. The sharp crack of point-blank gunshots. His dad jerked around and fell to the ground screaming in pain. Drew spun around looking for the shooter. He was expecting the next bullets to rip into him. Bright flashes of light and more gunshots sounded. Drew saw the man he'd thrown into the swamp stumbling out of the weeds firing a pistol at him. The man was screaming at the top of his lungs while he yanked the trigger.

Seeing the pistol in the attacker's hand reminded Drew he had one as well. Tossing his empty AR-15 out of the way he fumbled the pistol out of its holster. He swung it up just like his dad had shown him and rested the sights on the chest of the attacker. The man was frantically reloading his pistol. Hearing his dad screaming in pain and knowing this man would kill them both as soon as he got his pistol reloaded Drew fired his weapon. The tall man spun in a circle on the first hit with a surprised look on his face. He fell to one knee still trying to load his pistol. Drew took a dazed step forward and pointed his pistol at the man.

"Don't shoot. I'll leave. All good kid." The attacker stuttered from his kneeling position. He'd lost the bullets he was trying to shove in the chamber of his revolver. Drew waved the pistol to the side signaling the man to get up and leave.

"Drop your pistol." Drew ordered. He watched until the man dropped his pistol into the dirt and started backing away. Drew knelt down next to his dad to see how bad he was hurt. Some of the bikers that'd been shot had survived. They were crying out in pain as they lay on the cold concrete bleeding out.

Bart was sitting up bandaging his own leg. He had blood covering a good portion of his clothes. In a weak shaky voice, he told Drew he was doing ok but would need help getting back home. Wondering if he could rig up something with one of the bikes Drew glanced over to the pile of bodies and bikes scattered around the path. The pile was partially illuminated by flashlights that were throwing light at random angles creating some really freaky shadows.

In the light Drew saw the man he'd shot rooting around in the bodies. The man saw that he'd been seen.

"Just trying to see if I can save my friend." The man said pointing down at the pile and leaning over to adjust the man he'd pointed at. Drew lowered his weapon and began to turn back to take care of his dad. Luckily, he realized he was being a moron by turning his back on the guy. Drew turned back around to tell the guy to get lost. The guy who was now holding a pistol in his hand and trying to stand up with it.

Drew shot him adding one more corpse to the pile of bodies. Drew sent random shots into the pile of moaning bodies until he ran out of bullets. That seemed to shut up the whiners. At least he thought it did since his own hearing was pretty much crap after all the gunplay. He understood now why Bart always insisted they wear the bulky earmuffs when he took them to the range. Drew focused back on his dad. He was ashamed to realize he'd almost forgotten about him with all the violence going on. He shoved his pistol back in the holster and knelt down next to his dad again.

"I just killed somebody." Drew said loudly. The temporary deafness causing him to yell when he thought he was using a normal voice.

"I just killed like five guys. Screw 'em. They were going to kill us. Let's get the hell out of here and back home before anything else happens." Bart said before lapsing into a coughing fit. Drew had been thinking about grabbing some of the weapons the bikers had dropped. Hearing the coughing and the weakness in his dad's voice all thoughts of corpse robbing immediately left his mind. He was suddenly overcome with the dark certainty that his father was going to die on the trail.

Drew bent down and scooped his dad up into a fireman's carry. He shifted him around on his shoulders then started jogging down the trail back towards their house. He'd expected to hear a ton of complaints on this undignified and probably very painful mode of transport. The silence was a lot more concerning. He doubled his pace while straining to see ahead of him in the darkness.

The weight across his shoulders was just another day for Drew. One of the sports he excelled at was wrestling. He'd won his way to the varsity slot as a freshman and then proceeded to rack up a ton of medals for victories at the state, regional and district levels. Bart had assumed correctly that it'd be a great way to constructively channel his rage at the world. A good portion of that anger control had been learned running bleachers after he got in fights at practice or in school. Once you spend enough time running bleachers you really start to weigh whether fighting someone is worth having to run yet more bleachers. Running bleachers really sucks.

A standard warmup exercise that the wrestling team did almost every practice was putting each other in fireman's carries and running laps around the inside of the school. They'd run the hall then go up a flight of stairs then run that hall and go down the stairs and then switch off for the next lap. Even with the weapons they were both carrying Drew had no problem carrying Bart while he ran down the trail. His dad actually felt a lot lighter and frailer than Drew would've ever thought. He'd always looked at the man like he was some sort of indestructible superhero. Worried that his dad might be dying on his back Drew put his head down and sprinted back home.

He pounded up the stairs breathing raggedly in the chill night air. The door was flung open before he'd even made it all the way to the porch. Yue, LeBron, and Nancy all getting comically stuck together in the doorway that they all tried to run out of at the same time.

"What happened?" Yue asked loudly stepping back to let their mom go out before her.

"Let him get inside!" LeBron said hustling behind Drew to try and see where Bart had been hurt.

"Is he alive?" A frantic Nancy asked. She was blocking the way inside while trying hard to look at Bart whose eyes were closed. He'd passed out from the shock and pain at some point on the run back to the house.

"Get him inside." LeBron repeated guiding Drew past Nancy and into the house. Nancy followed along holding one of her husband's limp hands. She was searching for a pulse but unable to locate one as he was bounced around on Drew's shoulders.

"Put him on the couch." Yue ordered Drew. They all helped Drew get Bart off his shoulders and laid out on the sectional. Bright red blood getting smeared all over the back of the off-white leather. Nancy let out another moan at the sight of all the blood.

They worked together to strip him down to his boxers. They got him cleaned up and bandaged as well as they could with band aids, tape, and clean shirts. He grumbled and rolled around in pain. Once they'd cleaned him up as much as they could with what they had Nancy shook him until he woke up.

"Is that going to come out of the leather?" Bart asked squinting at the blood everywhere.

"You should've splurged on that guard policy." Yue said with tears in her eyes. It was an old family joke. Bart and Nancy fought over things like appliance warranties and leather protection plans reliably every time they made a purchase. It was so predictable that the kids refused to go with them when they were making those sorts of purchases. They refused because of how awkward it got afterwards when the sales rep inevitably smiled and started talking about the valuable, easily affordable protection plans that could be added on.

"What do we do?" Nancy asked Bart. She was kneeling down by his head.

"Check the holes. Make sure the bullet has an entry and an exit. You may have to get some tweezers and get the bullet out of me before you sterilize and bandage me up. Also, pain killers. The ones we have from when Drew got his wisdom teeth removed. I need those very soon." Bart said through gritted teeth.

Yue held up her phone to show them all she'd found the directions online for treating bullet wounds. The lights flickered then went out. They'd just lost power. Nancy had her hands pressed down on Bart's hands. She put her head against the couch and started taking deep breaths. She put her head back up a few seconds later and sent LeBron off to find the pain pills. She got Yue to go look for flashlights and candles. She had Drew shift Bart around so she could check for entry and exit wounds. Bart loudly moaned every time he was moved.

It was going to be a long night.

Chapter 11: Lights Out

By the time the sun came up the next morning they were all completely frazzled. They'd found an entry and an exit wound for two out of the three places Bart had been shot. The third bullet had gotten lodged in his shin bone. The bullet was right where they could see it, so they'd been able to pry it out using a pair of tweezers and a spoon. It'd been holding Bart down while they did it that'd been the challenge. Bart may not spend a lot of time at the gym, but he was able to summon some serious Hulk rage when they started prying around in his shin bone with a soup spoon.

The general consensus was that Bart would probably live if they could find some antibiotics to give him. That meant driving to the local drug store and looting what they needed. Unless the drive through happened to be open and still accepting credit cards. The most likely scenario was having to fight other looters to get what they needed.

The morning had snuck up on them. The removal of the bullet and working to clean Bart's wounds had taken longer than any of them realized. It was LeBron who noticed the light peeking in from the holes in the plywood covering the kitchen window. It was also LeBron who brought up the fact that if they didn't leave soon there wouldn't be anything left for them to loot. Drew was keeping quiet on the looting side of things. Nancy however wasn't happy.

"Who exactly is going to run over to the pharmacy to grab these supplies? How do you propose to break in? Do you not see what happened to your father? We've been pulling bullets out of him all night and now you think it's a good idea to go back out there? I don't want to spend all my time pulling bullets out of everybody. I know Bart wouldn't want you to go back out there without him. He's going to get better. No one's going anywhere." Nancy finished resolutely.

"If we don't go out there then everything that I Googled says he'll get an infection. He could die." Yue said into the silence following Nancy putting her foot down. She could still access the data network on her phone. The WIFI in their house had died when they lost power the night before. If she wasn't so exhausted, she'd be working right now on trying to download every piece of useful information she could find. She'd snagged a few first aid documents and a couple of survival guides. She kept trying to find maps she could download to her phone in between scrubbing blood stains off the floor and couch.

"No one's going anywhere. If Bart were awake, he'd say the same thing. We're your parents. We're not going to have you risking your lives like that. We're definitely not sending you out into all that violence right now on what'd probably be a wild goose chase." Nancy reiterated her opposition to the whole idea. She was as exhausted as the rest of them. She was determined to stay awake though. She needed to maintain her grip on her husband's hand and make sure the kids didn't do anything stupid.

Yue pulled up some more information on her phone. She stared at the skin around the gunshot wounds on Bart comparing them with the images from WebMD. She was looking to see if there was redness around the wound which would indicate infection. The wounds already looked infected to her. Nancy tried to downplay it when Yue showed her the images and told her about how bad the infection could be. She tried to downplay it, but her exhaustion kept her from being a good actress. She was terrified. Not for herself but for her family.

"I'm going to get some medicine for dad." LeBron told Yue quietly while they were both standing in the kitchen. The sinks and tubs in the house were all filled with water. They were being very careful about keeping it as clean as possible. They'd been draining and refilling the tubs and sinks for the past week now in preparation for this eventuality.

"I'm coming with you. Wait until mom passes out. She can't possibly stay awake much longer." Yue said quietly. LeBron nodded suddenly understanding why Yue had kept bringing their mom pillows. She'd been working hard to make their mom comfortable ever since the outburst where Nancy had told them they weren't leaving the house. He wondered idly how many times Yue had manipulated him into doing what she wanted. He stopped thinking about it deciding he was better off not knowing.

"What about Drew?" LeBron whispered the question.

"I don't know. He's taking this pretty hard. We leave him here to guard the house once mom falls asleep." Yue responded. They both glanced over at Drew who'd leaned his head back and fallen asleep on the couch next to their dad. His mouth wide open as he shifted around uncomfortably on the couch.

Yue got their mom up off the floor and stretched her out on the couch as well. Less than five minutes later Nancy was asleep, and they were working on waking up Drew. Immediately after waking him up, they found themselves in a hushed but very heated argument with him about who should go.

"I've been out there. You guys don't know how dangerous it is. If anybody is going it should be me." Drew said.

"You already carried him for miles. You saved his life once already. Let LeBron and me do our part." Yue said. LeBron looked up at her admiringly. He'd been about to just fall into the regular pattern of arguing. Yue had approached it from a much better angle.

"Nice try. I'm going." Drew said standing up.

"Then who stays here to guard the house and make sure nothing happens to mom and dad?" Yue asked pointedly.

"You're the one who read all the first aid books and LeBron's the smart one. I'm just the muscle. It makes much more sense for me to go. Besides with mobs rioting in the streets sending you out is like asking for you to get attacked." Drew said making a very valid point.

"Chivalry is probably dead at this point." LeBron echoed. "I think we need to be real about this. Drew and I should be the ones to go." Yue got a stubborn look on her face. She may not be an armband wearing feminist, but she definitely wasn't going to stand by and be told she couldn't do something just because she was a girl.

"Chivalry goes both ways. The woman allows it as much as the man does it. LeBron's better at the internet than both of us. He can stay here and download the info we're going to need. Drew and I'll run to the drug store and pick up whatever we can find to help dad. No more arguing." Yue turned around and walked to the front door where she picked up a rifle and brought it back over to LeBron.

"Ok then let's roll." Drew said following Yue over to the front door where they grabbed their rifles and the car keys.

"Watch the house LeBron. It's just as dangerous here as it is anywhere else." Yue said to LeBron before they exited the house. They paused outside to make sure LeBron got the door closed and locked then they headed into the garage. Without hesitating to choose between the vehicles they hopped up into Drew's truck. Drew got into the driver's seat while Yue rode shotgun. Riding shotgun now having come full circle back to its original meaning.

Yue got back out of the truck and into the truck bed a minute later to find the emergency release for the garage door. It was ridiculous how much electricity had become a part of everyday life. Even though they'd been using flashlights to get into the truck it hadn't occurred to either of them that that hitting the magic button on the opener wouldn't make the door go up. Drew had been pointing his flashlight at his opener trying to figure out why it wasn't working when Yue had hopped out to manually open the door.

Drew backed the truck into the street then jumped out to help Yue get the garage door down and locked back into position. Once they figured that out, they slowly drove towards the exit to their neighborhood.

In the early morning light, they saw first-hand the destruction brought on by the door-to-door looters. Every other house had its front door hanging wide open. Most of them had the front windows broken out to provide easy access. Seeing an odd-looking shape in the pile of garbage in front of one of the houses Yue recoiled when she realized it was a dead body. She wondered how many more bodies were slowly decaying inside the houses. How many elderly and unarmed had died for whatever supplies they had sitting in their pantry.

They'd heard the sound of gunfire sporadically throughout the night. It was becoming as common a background noise as crickets chirping. What they hadn't heard was any sirens. No one was coming to save them. The President had made it clear everyone was on their own. Concern welled up in her breast for LeBron and their parents. They were sitting at home now with just LeBron to defend the house until their mom woke up. When they'd left, she'd hoped to make it back before Nancy woke up. Now she was second guessing not waking her up to begin with.

They felt the eyes of their neighbors boring into them as they drove down the eerily quiet street. Yue urged Drew to speed up. Neither of them had mentioned the body they'd seen rotting away in a pile of trash on someone's front lawn. Drew had hoped Yue had missed seeing it and vice versa. Drew rounded a corner then braked quickly. A woman walked across the street in front of them without once glancing in their direction. Her face was swollen on one side, and she was sporting a massive black eye.

"We have to hurry." Yue reminded Drew. She'd seen him reach for the door handle. She knew his instinct would be to try and help the woman. She felt the same way. They were going to have to bury that human part of them. Compassion would just lead to an early death. They had to reign it in. Drew nodded and sped past the woman. He didn't look back.

They exited the neighborhood turning left onto the road that'd take them to the closest drug store. They drove past the plaza with the Publix supermarket in it. Yue checked it out hopefully as Drew slowed down to go through the intersection. The store was a burnt-out husk. People were creeping around furtively in the parking lot. A few of them stopped to stare as they drove by.

"You think there's still stuff worth getting in the Publix? They have a pharmacy. Can you tell if that part is burnt down?" Drew asked slowing down even more. Up ahead he'd noticed a line of people crossing the street into the apartment complex. He imagined from above they looked like a line of ants connecting an ant pile to a discarded candy bar wrapper.

Yue had seen the same line of people. She'd also noticed men with guns watching the line closely. She remembered their dad's admonition that the guys with the guns got the supplies. Knowing she could count herself and Drew in that group gave her some level of comfort. However, it didn't give her enough comfort to want to go confront whoever was running the rip-off of the Publix.

"Let's call that plan 'B' for now. If the Walgreens is empty, we'll come back and give it a shot. We don't have time to drive around all day, but we don't have the time to get shot or forced into a chain gang either."

"I'm good with the not getting shot plan." Drew said tiredly. He smiled over at his sister to show he was good with the plan.

They continued driving through the war zone that used to be a sleepy little city. Drew thought the scenery outside his window looked a lot like the movies he'd watched about a future where people were allowed to hit the streets and purge once every year. The blatant looting, the furtive movements of scared people trying to survive all intertwined with the occasional crazed reveler set against a backdrop of looted and burnt buildings.

Anarchy surrounded them as they navigated the road past the Publix and headed towards the Walgreens. Drew drove slowly through an intersection passing a car crash where the body of the driver was still stuck in the driver's seat. Glass and metal littered the entire intersection. A random thought once again struck Yue. If they got a flat tire, they'd have to change it themselves. The AAA cards they both had courtesy of their mom were useless now. Like most of the lifelines they'd had all of their lives. There was no one to call to come save them. It was a frightening feeling.

"That doesn't look good." Drew said pointing up ahead at the line of cars by the gas station next to the Walgreens. They'd stocked up the garage with jugs of gas so should be good on gas for a while. The people who'd broken in hadn't taken any of the jugs as far as they could tell. The idea had been for them to have enough gas to be able to make the coast or get out of the state if needed.

They drove past the long line of scared people sitting in their cars waiting to get gas. Quite a few of the cars were stalled out where the owners had run out of gas waiting in line. The people who'd run out of gas had evidently just abandoned their cars there. Drew and Yue were careful not to make eye contact with anyone as they drove past. People were staring openly at Drew's truck. More than a few of them looked like they wouldn't mind getting a little violent. Yue figured all the timid people were safely locked away in their homes where they'd eventually die while hoping the badness went away on its own.

The Walgreens parking lot was packed with cars and people. Drew drove around to the side and went in the exit to see if they could get close enough to get in the store. Towards the front of the parking lot a crowd had gathered. They were standing around watching as two men walked supplies out of the Walgreens and tossed them into the back of a U-Haul. It was one of the large rental trucks that you could use to move a two to three-bedroom home.

The front doors of the store had been smashed to pieces. A few men and women were busy going in and out of the store transferring as much as they could from the store to the U-Haul. Three men were standing in front of the entrance with hunting rifles guarding the people going in and out. They were nervously moving their weapons this way and that urging the crowd to stay back. The crowd kept encroaching on the space as more people arrived to try to get medicine and food.

"We should get out of here." Yue said nervously.

"Probably." Drew agreed nodding. "How bad does dad need that medicine?"

"His skin was red all around the bullet holes. Especially where we had to pry the bullet out of his bone. It's not like we were using surgically sterilized equipment for it like you're supposed to. We literally held a lighter underneath a soup spoon to clean it. We operated on our dad with the same level of hygiene crackheads use to prep their drugs." Yue said. She was trying to joke but it was coming out more sad than funny.

"So, we need the antibiotics." Drew summarized.

"Pain pills, ointment, real gauze and pretty much anything else we can get our hands on." Yue said staring at the men guarding the U-Haul. They were skinny white guys dressed in hunting coveralls. Not super intimidating. The rifles they held up were nice but made for shooting out of a deer stand. They weren't designed for combat.

"The Publix is played out and this place is going to be empty in another thirty minutes. I don't think we have a chance if we try to find somewhere else. They're all going to be like this." Drew said. His heartbeat was starting to accelerate. He felt a cold chill in his blood. He felt like he had to pee really bad. All that just from thinking about what he knew they had to do.

"We can't get in there. They're guarding the hell out of it." Yue said.

"We have guns. That crowd will either scatter or attack them depending on how desperate they are. I'm leaning towards they attack them. I don't see us sitting here nicely waiting our turn and hoping something's left when we have better weapons." Drew said nervously pulling his pistol into his lap and making sure the magazine was fully inserted.

"Ok. I agree. I think we should hijack them though. We try and fight them right here that crowd is going to end up cleaning out the store and the U-Haul anyway. Let's wait until they get everything loaded then follow them and take the truck." Yue was thinking on the spot. Her plan became the de facto plan anyway as the little redneck gang robbing the Walgreens all hopped up in the U-Haul to drive away. Three of them in the front of it and three of them jumping in the back with the supplies they'd just gathered.

"You drive." Drew said jumping out of the cab and into the truck bed. He'd killed one man already today. Hopefully these guys would give up but if not, he'd do what he had to do to get the medicine his dad needed.

Chapter 12: Pancakes to Piracy

Yue sped up to catch the U-Haul that was barreling down a side street in front of them. The road they were on was the same one Yue used as a shortcut to get to her waitress gig. That life seemed like a million years ago now as she worked on circling around the moving truck to get her brother a clear shot at the driver. She was having a hard time wrapping her mind around the circumstances leading to her needing to Mad Max this U-Haul to get the medical supplies needed to save their dad.

The U-Haul slowed down to make a turn. The driver conveniently putting on his turn signal to let them know which way they were going. Yue pictured the guy slapping himself in the head and swiping the turn signal to turn it off once he realized the pickup behind them wasn't just casual traffic. She accelerated rapidly to get them even with the driver of the U-Haul. He looked down at them looking like he might wave at Yue before he noticed Drew sitting in the back pointing the AR-15 at him.

Before Drew could pull the trigger, the U-Haul slowed to a stop. The man driving desperately holding his hand up in the air and yelling not to shoot. Yue pulled up in front of the U-Haul and leapt out of the seat onto the street. She immediately raised her own rifle and aimed it at the big window on the front of the U-Haul. She made sure to let her peripheral vision expand to take in the back of the truck. She'd need to be able to see if the people in the back jumped out.

"Throw your rifles out the window and get out keeping your hands where I can see them! I'll shoot anyone who looks weird! Do what we say, and we'll let you go! We're just looking for some medical supplies." Drew yelled. He was standing up in the truck bed aiming at the occupants of the cab of the U-Haul. The occupants of the cab were looking back at him from point blank range. They knew they were screwed based on the petrified looks on their faces. They rolled their windows down and began carefully pushing their rifles out.

A loud shot rang out. The side view mirror beside where Yue was standing shattered throwing glass everywhere. A woman was standing by the end of the U-Haul with a pistol aimed at Yue. The woman was yelling something. Yue and Drew couldn't hear the woman over the sound of their own return fire. That single poorly aimed pistol shot earned the U-Haul riders a combined forty shot volley in return. The return shots were much better aimed.

Drew had shot holes all along the windshield of the U-Haul. He was pretty sure he'd gotten at least the driver and one of the passengers. The middle seat guy had dropped almost instantly out of sight as soon as the first shot rang out. Yue stopped firing long enough to look at her own handiwork. The woman who'd fired the pistol at her was lying motionless in the street in a pool of her own blood.

Drew jumped down from the bed of the truck. Together they moved up to the driver side window. Drew yelled at the general area of the window that if anyone inside wanted to live they should just go out the other side. Yue stood behind him covering his back while they gave anyone left alive in the cab a few seconds to comply. A man shouted not to shoot and opened the door on the other side of the truck. Drew ran around to the other side and caught the man lying prone on the ground aiming a rifle at Yue's legs.

Drew shot the man in the head then picked up the dead man's rifle off the ground. Without putting his head too close to the open door he fired a few rounds into the cab. Not hearing anything he climbed quickly into the cab and verified he'd gotten the other two men already. The keys were still in the ignition. Having checked all of that Drew climbed back out of the cab and ran around to meet Yue.

"Now what?" She asked after she got over the relief of seeing him come around the cab. She'd been worried the shots she'd heard may have meant Drew was the one on the ground.

"We need to get the other two out of the back if they haven't already taken off. Then we drive this bad boy back home like bosses." Drew said. This was going way too well. He couldn't believe they were actually going to be able to claim an entire U-Haul full of supplies. He kept waiting for the other shoe to drop. The fact that they'd just killed four people hadn't sunk in yet.

"Ok." Yue said.

Drew looked over at her noticing a tremor in her voice. He could see that she was shaking all over. He kept his eyes on the back of the truck.

"It's going to be just like paintball. Except I'm going to put some holes in the side of the truck to flush them out. You cover me. It'll all be good in a few minutes. We'll be on our way home with everything we need." Drew said. He didn't bother looking behind him. Freaking out or not he didn't have the slightest doubt in the world that his sister would have his back.

Drew walked at a steady pace towards the rear of the truck. He stopped a couple of times to shoot holes through the side of it. The third time he started to do it he heard voices yelling from the back of the truck.

"Hey! We're unarmed! You can have the truck! We're going to run! Don't shoot us!"

"You have ten seconds to get out of range!" Drew yelled back. He counted off five seconds in his head and swung around the end of the truck leading with his rifle barrel. Yue came right behind him. Two people in camouflage coveralls were running like their pants were on fire through the parking lot on the other side of the street.

The people who'd been in the back had positioned a few boards to keep the door from locking on them. Drew threw those boards out and pulled the sliding door down on the back of the U-Haul to secure it. Yue ran back over to his pickup truck and climbed in ready to go. Drew liked how she'd picked the vehicle without a bunch of broken glass and corpses in it to drive. He jumped up into the cab of the U-Haul and fumbled around with the seat belt in the front to let him pitch the driver out onto the street. If the idiot hadn't been wearing a seatbelt, then he might have ducked faster and avoided getting his brains blown out the back of his skull. Drew reached over and undid the other guy's belt and tossed him out as well. No point in driving around with a cab full of dead bodies if he didn't have to.

His phone rang. He dropped it under the seat by accident and had to dig for it. It's hard answering on a touch screen device when your hands are drenched in blood. He was hoping it wasn't their mom when he answered it. It was Yue. She had him put the phone on the dash with the speaker on so they could talk while they drove home.

"How much longer you think cell service is going to last?" Drew asked.

"That's more of a LeBron question but I'm thinking at some point whatever makes cell towers work will run out of power like everything else." Yue said back.

That reminded Drew that LeBron had been texting them like crazy. He opened up the texts and was relieved there was nothing bad. Their dad was still breathing, and no mobs had attacked the house yet. Their mom was still sound asleep. Drew texted LeBron they were going to be rolling in with a U-Haul full of goodies. A set of bubbles appeared and sat there for a few seconds. Drew was impatient to get going. He wasn't going to try driving this U-Haul through an apocalyptic event like this while reading text messages though. If LeBron had thought of something that they hadn't it could save their lives.

"How the hell are we hiding this thing?" Drew asked Yue over the speaker phone. LeBron had come up with that question right off the bat. Drew had just been excited to have been able to snag so much stuff at once. Stuff that people were willing to kill for. Now they were going to dangle it like candy in front of a horde of opportunistic well-armed trick or treaters on the way back to their house.

"I have no idea. We just drive and hope nobody cares enough to try and stop us." Yue said. She was planning on taking a different route back to their house. She didn't trust the people she'd seen in the Publix parking lot. She definitely didn't want to drive back by the Walgreens. If that riled up little mob was still in the area, they'd know what kind of treasures the U-Haul held.

Yue drove down the road and Drew followed. The whole drive home was a real butt clencher as Bart liked to say. Drew felt like a diamond might fall out of his boxers if this got any more tense. People stared hard at the U-Haul as they drove past. The shattered windshield and random bullet holes weren't even the interesting part to most of the people standing along the streets. The only part those people were curious about was what was in the back of the truck.

They made it almost all the way to the main entrance to their subdivision without anything happening. As they were getting ready to turn in a cop car pulled out behind them and turned its flashers on. Not knowing what else to do Drew pulled over. He didn't want to lead the cops to their house, and it wasn't like he could outrun them. Yue kept right on going skipping by the entrance to their neighborhood.

"Make sure to talk really loud so I know what the cops are doing." Yue said over the speaker phone.

"He's probably pulling me over to see what's in the back and take what he wants. That's if he's a bad cop who's already given up. If he's a good cop who still thinks he's protecting people, then he may have some questions about the bullet holes and the blood covering the seats up here. It could just be some freak who found an abandoned cop car and is just going to shoot me and take the truck once he walks up here." Drew responded nervously.

"So, it's a lose-lose scenario pretty much then. Ok. Let me know if it's one cop or two and what side of the truck he's walking towards you on." Yue said.

Suspicious of why that information was relevant Drew watched as the cop opened his car door and got out. He appeared to be alone although it was hard to tell using the U-Haul side mirrors. He let Yue know. The cop didn't even pretend this was a normal stop. He disappeared from view in the back of the truck. Drew felt the vibration of the back door being slid open. A minute later the cop reappeared in the side view mirror with his pistol dangling from his hand. He looked excited as he walked towards Drew. Drew kept up the play by play over speaker phone with Yue.

"Put your hands on the steering wheel where I can see them." The cop said once he reached the front of the truck.

"Why?" Drew asked. The simple question seemed to throw the cop off.

"Shut your mouth and open the door nice and slow or I'm going to open it for you. You're not going to like how I open it." The cop said holding up his pistol. Drew had his own pistol in his lap ready to go. He reached for the door handle right as he saw Yue driving towards them. He hesitated on the door handle wondering what she was up to.

"Did I do something wrong officer?" Drew asked. It was completely out of place to ask. The cop took his eyes off the approaching truck and looked back up at Drew with a grin.

"It looks like you either robbed a drug store or killed the guys who robbed a drug store. Either way you're a criminal with a truck full of stuff my family can use to survive. I'm taking it. Whether you live or die depends – " The cop stopped talking when Yue pulled up and called out to him.

"Excuse me officer do you know CPR?" Yue asked him in a high-pitched tone. The cop looked over at her as Drew opened his door. The cop looked back at Drew and held up his hand to stop the door from opening. Yue used that time to pull her pistol up and stick it out the window at the cop. The cop glanced back at Yue and did a double take. He started to lift his own pistol up.

"Don't do it." Drew said aiming his pistol at the back of the cop's head through the open window. Glancing back and forth the cop saw it was a lost cause and set his gun down on the ground.

"Now what?" Yue asked after they'd handcuffed the cop and put him in the back of his own squad car. They'd already taken the opportunity to snag every bit of gear they could get out of the car. The trunk of the police car had been like a survivalist's treasure chest. Drew reached in the car and yanked all the cables out of the radio. They'd already taken the cops phone when they locked him in the back of his car with just a pair of boxers and socks on.

"Let's leave the cruiser on the side of the road and send the cop packing. It won't hurt to have a spare car sitting out here in case we need it." Drew said. They didn't want to kill the cop. He hadn't tried to kill them. He'd been about to rip them off but that was different. Neither of them wanted to execute the cop in cold blood. Other than a few odd looks from a minivan that drove by there was no immediate consequence to sending the mostly naked officer jogging up the road with his arms cuffed in front of him. Neither of them noticed the cuffed man stopping briefly to memorize the license plate on Drew's truck.

Leaving the police cruiser locked up on the grassy median they drove the U-Haul into their subdivision. This time Drew was confident they had everyone's attention. Mothers and fathers of children who were going to starve to death in the very near future would be super curious what was in the back of their truck. If they deduced the U-Haul was full of food, medical supplies and assorted other goodies then there was no doubt the neighbors would turn into a pitchfork and torches mob. The sooner they got this truck unloaded and out of sight the better.

They drove over to their house and parked in the front. Drew saw more than one set of curtains shifting around. A couple of people went so far as to walk out on their patios to try and see what kind of goods they had in the back. Seeing the blood stains and the weapons no one quite had the guts to ask them what was in the truck.

"This is a really bad idea." Yue said looking around.

"You guys were supposed to run out and get some Amoxicillin or something. Not steal an entire drug store and lead a parade of desperation back to our house. WTF?" LeBron said as he walked out of the garage staring at the big ass U-Haul parked in the alley. His neck whipping back and forth as he took in all the observers. The alley had looked pretty much deserted until his brother and sister had shown up with what amounted to a giant picnic basket.

"Let's get it unloaded." Drew said.

"The sooner the supplies are inside and secure the sooner we can all get ready for people to start beating on our door trying to take them." LeBron said.

"Yeah, probably big guys with big guns." Drew commented as he walked towards the truck to open it up.

"It's not guys with guns I'm worried about." Yue said seriously enough that both LeBron and Drew focused on her words. "It's the guys with little starving kids who are going to be the death of us."

Completely bummed out by the truth of what Yue had just said they began unloading the back of the U-Haul as fast as they could. Not trusting the garage to secure their goods they carried everything into the house and stacked it in the living room. Anything that looked like it might help their dad they sat in a separate pile on the kitchen counter. That pile was pretty big by the time they were halfway done unloading.

Nancy woke up while they were carrying stuff in and had to be told what'd happened. She hugged each of them tight and got to work sorting out the supplies they were carrying in. She cried softly to herself when she saw the gigantic stack of different kinds of pain pills and antibiotics. She didn't know what she'd done to deserve such wonderful kids but somehow the universe had come through for her. Despite not being able to have more of their own they'd still ended up with the large loving family she'd always wanted.

It seemed to take forever but eventually they finished unloading the truck. They wanted to pass out on the couch more than anything but there was still work that needed to be done. If nothing else, they had to ditch the U-Haul as soon as possible. Just in case everyone in the city hadn't already seen it parked in front of their house. Drew dragged his aching body out to the truck and drove it out of the neighborhood with LeBron following him.

They ditched it in the large overflow parking lot of a church that was right up the road from them. They left it parked right where a carnival normally setup every year. Drew jumped in the truck with LeBron, and they drove back home. They parked the truck in the garage and made sure it was all locked up then went back in the house. Nancy was humming and smiling. She gave them both another hug when they walked in. They'd gotten a few more lights going to help them sort out all the gear. Nancy noticed the state of Drews clothes and ordered him to go give himself a sponge bath and ditch the blood-stained clothes he was wearing.

Drew fairly bounced up the stairs after his dad sat up on the couch and thanked him for getting all the supplies. The giddiness from getting the rare praise from his old man lasted until he realized the grey mushy stuff that he was picking out of his hair must be brain matter from the guy he'd shot in the U-Haul. Nothing like finding pieces of some dude's brain in your hair to kill the mood.

Chapter 13: Fort Russel

"That cops going to get his friends and come find us." Bart said from the couch. His words were slightly slurred from the pain killers. He was insisting on taking just enough to take the edge off the pain without making him loopy. He was convinced they'd be attacked before the day was out.

"Not if he tries calling them, we won't." Yue said holding up her phone sadly. A desperate looking LeBron started shaking his phone like it was an etch a sketch.

"I don't think shaking it will get the tower back." Drew said irritably. He was covered in sweat from going up and down the stairs with the supplies. The crew that'd loaded up the U-Haul had done an excellent job clearing out the drug store. They now had a veritable ton of supplies that should see them through a month or two of sitting in the house without having to even ration them.

They had so much stuff that storing it was an actual problem. They'd mostly solved the problem by emptying out their closets and designating those as storage pantries. There was still going to be a ton of stuff just sitting around. Their living room looked like an episode of "Hoarders" with a medical spin. Yue and Nancy were covered for pretty much any feminine hygiene issue they could dream up.

"I guess we were lucky it lasted this long." Yue said dejectedly. She slid her phone into her pocket and grabbed a plastic bag filled with candy to shove into the pantry.

There was a loud knock at the front door. They all froze staring at one another. Yue pulled her phone out before realizing without WIFI and the internet she wasn't going to be able to see the video of who was outside. Drew sat down the bags of assorted stuff he was about to carry up the stairs and picked up his rifle instead. Nancy stood up by the couch with her shotgun in her hands. Yue went to the window by the front door and peeked out the hole in the plywood to see who was on the porch.

It was an old woman shifting nervously from foot to foot waiting to see if they'd answer the door. She had a paper sack in her hands. Yue looked but didn't see anyone else. LeBron had circled the house looking out all the peepholes and not seen anyone either. Bart asked them to turn out all the lights before opening the door to talk to the woman. With all the lights turned off Yue answered the door.

"Hi. I'm from down the street. We saw you unloaded a bunch of supplies earlier. It looked like some might be medicinal. My husband has a condition and needs Apixaban or Heparin to survive. He has some but it's only going to last another week. I was hoping you had some you didn't need. I have money." The old woman opened the paper sack so Yue could see the crumpled bills that'd been shoved into it.

"Moneys useless. What else do you have?" Yue asked. She knew they probably had the medicine and none of them needed it. It was going to be a very valuable commodity here in the near future though as people started running out. A light went on behind her and she heard someone sorting through the piles of medication they had lined up all along the kitchen counters.

"We have a little bit of food and water." The woman said hesitantly.

"How about weapons?" Yue asked. The woman shook her head sadly.

"Here. This is all I could find. Don't come back. Don't tell anyone where you got it from." Nancy said squeezing past Yue and handing the old woman a Ziploc bag with ten pills in it.

"Thank you! Bless You!" The woman said happily eyeing the ten tiny little pills. She was mentally adding them to the ones still in the bottle at home to see how long until her partner of fifty years was going to die.

"She's going to either tell people or come back." Yue said admonishing her mom.

"If she's coming back, she better hurry." LeBron said from the other side of the house.

"Why?" Drew asked looking over at his younger brother. Everyone had turned to face that direction to hear the response.

"I've been looking up videos and pictures of the infected people have been uploading. There's a video of the infected tearing through Jacksonville. If they're that close, then they'll start showing up here anytime now." LeBron said. All of the main websites had started going offline soon after the President's speech. The ones that remained hadn't been updated very often. All of the main social media sites had gone offline except for some video sharing sites like YouTube.

"The crawlers are going to have to hurry if they want to kill us. There's two police cars and a big SUV coming down the road now." Drew said walking down from the loft where he'd just gone to drop off another batch of supplies.

"They don't know which house we're in." Yue said.

"They're talking to that old woman you just gave the pills to mom!" Drew yelled down from upstairs. His irritability at doing all the physical labor in a house that felt like a sauna completely forgotten. He felt like a trapped rat. They couldn't even really shoot at the cops from inside the house since they had plywood covering all of the windows. All they had going for them was that the cops weren't going to have any choice but to come in and get the supplies.

"What do we do?" Nancy asked Bart. Bart was struggling to sit up straight.

"They're parked in front of the house!" Drew yelled down the stairs.

"How many of them are there?" Bart yelled up to him. Drew counted a total of five men getting out of the cars. He recognized one of the men as the cop they'd sent running away in his boxers earlier. No good deed goes unpunished. The officers were armed to the teeth and wearing bullet proof vests. They were approaching the house like they knew what they were doing. Or at least they looked like professionals to Drew, and he'd watched a lot of cop movies so he should know.

"If we hurt them bad enough then they'll leave." Bart said. He rolled himself onto the floor and had Nancy hand him a rifle before ordering her to get down low behind the kitchen counter.

"They're almost at the door. Two of them just split off to go around the back!" Drew yelled down. Bart continued to cover the front door but yelled for Yue and LeBron to cover the back.

"Are they at the doors?" Bart yelled up to Drew.

"I think so!" Drew yelled back down straining to see straight down through the tiny holes they'd drilled.

"Ten shots each through the doors!" Bart yelled and started shooting. Yue and LeBron followed his lead and started punching neat holes through the doors. Upstairs Drew watched as the cops in the front fell back. One of them holding the side of his head with a hand covered in blood.

The back door to their house took a couple of shot gun blasts and two large men in SWAT gear tried to force their way in. They were driven back after a brief exchange of fire with LeBron and Yue. They sat in the stupid hot house sweating and scared. The cops tossed a couple of smoke grenades into the house. Visibility on the first floor quickly dropped to zero.

"You're all under arrest for theft and murder! Lower your weapons and come out and you'll not be harmed! Continue to resist and you'll be killed!" Someone yelled into the house. LeBron put some metal downrange in the general direction of the voice as their answer. He was rewarded with a yelp of pain. Yue grinned over at him and gave him a thumbs up.

A blinding flash of light accompanied by a huge burst of sound rocked them all back. The remainder of the door was beaten off its hinges as all five cops came storming into the house. Drew ran downstairs in the smoke and confusion to help in the fight. Nancy stepped in between the approaching cops and her babies and started blasting away with her shotgun. She was screaming in a mad rage while she pulled the trigger. The buckshot she was slinging was ripping the flesh off of every bit of the exposed skin of the invading men. They returned fire viciously even as their charge faltered.

Yue, LeBron, and Bart carefully placed shots into the front of the house all around the last place they'd seen Nancy. The smoke cleared enough that Yue could see her mom's body lying on the floor. She stood up and rushed to help her. Bullets flying all around as the cops retreated dragging their wounded with them. They left out the door continuing to pour bullets into the house as they retreated. Bart walked right through that hail of bullets. He continued firing at the retreating men until they'd disappeared. Looking down with disbelieving eyes he saw Yue on the ground beside the body of his wife.

Nancy was dead. She'd died placing herself between the attackers and her children. She'd fallen defending those she loved. Yue sat on the ground sobbing with her mom's bloody head in her lap. Drew and LeBron stood next to Bart staring down in disbelief. Bart collapsed to the floor and added his plaintive sobs to those of Yue.

"What about the cops?" LeBron asked. Drew looked up with tears running down his face and nodded. He ran up the stairs to spy on the men who'd attacked them.

"They're leaving!" He yelled a minute later as he came bounding back down the stairs. He ran back over to where they were all gathered around the body of their mom. Bart looked up from where he'd collapsed on the floor and told them they needed to get to work on fixing the doors and windows. He told Yue to bring him a washrag and his mom's favorite comforter.

Bart could barely move after the battle. He directed Yue to clean up Nancy and get her dressed and rolled up in the comforter. He debated on what to do as far as a burial and finally decided on a fire. They didn't have a casket or the strength or the time to bury her properly. He wasn't about to dishonor her memory her by letting her body sit around until it started to smell. He carefully directed Yue on preparing Nancy until the body needed to be moved. At that point he had Drew and LeBron come downstairs.

They all prayed over the body of the woman they'd all cherished. A woman who was larger than life. A woman who'd had such a huge positive impact on so many lives. They said their goodbyes to her in the entryway to the bungalow she'd loved. The hallway in the house she'd wanted for the family she loved. When they were done, they sewed up the comforter and carried it out beside the pond. They carried out a bunch of the spare wood from the garage and one of the jugs of gasoline.

They stepped back and Drew lit the gas-soaked comforter on fire. With tears in his eyes Bart watched from a chair on the porch. He wasn't able to stand on his wounded leg any longer. He was seeping blood through all of his bandages after doing his part to repel the assault. The neighbors waved to them sadly. LeBron noted the man was wearing the pistol on his hip that they'd traded for with him. When the fire had burned down, they all returned to the house. Bart set them to repairs and building the house back stronger than before.

Drew went to each of the upstairs windows to cut out firing holes. He wasn't going to be stuck staring out of tiny holes again with no way to fight back. Downstairs LeBron and Yue were adding two by fours across the windows to strengthen the plywood. They'd completely sealed off the front door so that the only downstairs entry point now was the backdoor. When Drew finished upstairs, he was going to put in some firing slots downstairs as well.

Before Bart passed out, he'd ordered them to turn the place into a fortress. He didn't want to see any more of his family die. They'd taken that order to heart and started working on building a fortress to protect that which their mom had gladly given her life for. As worn out as they all were the manual labor was welcomed to keep their minds occupied. Idle hands were the devil's playthings after all.

Chapter 14: The Surge

They worked late into the night fortifying the house. They did everything that they could think of to give them an advantage against another assault. To sit down and relax was to think of their mom's pale face looking up at them from inside the pink flower covered comforter. There were still caches of supplies from the drug store that were sitting around the house in unorganized piles. There were still plenty of items that needed to be carried up the stairs. The more tedious the work the better. Whatever it took to get their minds off the fact that they'd just wrapped their mom's body up in a blanket and set it on fire in the backyard.

Drew accidentally fell asleep as the sun came up. The large holes they'd cut into the plywood allowed enough light in that they could finally see inside the house. Drew had sat down on the couch in the loft to rest his eyes for a second. His exhausted body had taken control leaving him passed out in a sitting position. Yue and LeBron found him that way a few minutes later. LeBron was rocking back and forth he was so tired. Yue was seeing double as she strained to keep her eyelids open. It felt like each eyelid had tiny weights strapped to the lashes.

"One of us has to sleep and one of us has to keep watch." Yue slurred through her fatigue. She couldn't remember ever being this tired. She was emotionally and physically spent.

"Go to sleep. I think we have some Ritalin in the drug pile downstairs. I definitely saw some caffeine pills. I'll *Breaking Bad* my way through the next few hours then wake up one of you to take my spot." LeBron said. It struck Yue that she really must be next door to a fugue state. She couldn't find any flaw in the obviously flawed plan her little brother had just outlined. She sat on the couch next to Drew then lay down lifting her feet up into his lap.

"Wake me up if you start falling asleep. Somebody has to be awake all the time." She said with her eyes already closed as she drifted off.

LeBron picked up one of the blankets they kept in the loft and threw it over his snoozing siblings. His eyes filled up with tears remembering how he'd thrown a blanket over his mom's body the day before. He couldn't even contemplate what he'd do if he had to throw one over his sister or brother next. Thinking about family members in mortal danger reminded him he needed to go downstairs to check on his dad.

Bart was spread out on the big sectional below. They'd pumped him full of painkillers and antibiotics after their mom's impromptu funeral. The mixture they'd concocted must've done the trick. He hadn't moved from the spot they'd left him passed out in. It was a bit alarming how little he'd moved. LeBron reached over and held his hand over his dad's mouth to make sure he was still breathing. Having confirmed his dad was still alive LeBron went over to the kitchen and began digging through the diet pills and vitamins looking for something to help him stay awake.

He found a big bottle of Ritalin next to a pile of packets of Walgreen branded caffeine pills. The kind long-haul truckers always grabbed a few of whenever they were checking out. Hoping the pills worked he gulped down a few of them with sips of warm Mountain Dew. He then proceeded to drag his drained body around to each window and peer out into the early dawn. The medicine must've worked because he was still making the same rounds four hours later when his dad asked him if he'd gotten any sleep yet.

"Not yet. Letting Yue and Drew nap it up until I can't keep going anymore." LeBron rattled off before walking quickly to the next window. He was covered in sweat. Living in Florida without power sucked. If this whole apocalypse thing was going to last much longer, they were going to have to seriously consider moving north.

"What'd you take?" Bart asked sitting up to look at LeBron with concern.

"Caffeine pills and Ritalin." LeBron answered suddenly worried he was going to get into trouble for doing drugs. He wondered where the paranoia was coming from. This was obviously an acceptable time to do a little experimentation.

"Ok. Well, try not to get hooked. They're not going to be making any more of those anytime soon. How's your brother and sister?" Bart asked disregarding the drug cocktail LeBron had whipped up to stay awake. It'd obviously served its purpose. LeBron thought of pointing out that they had a super-sized bucket of Ritalin on the counter but decided to keep that to himself.

"They're both asleep on the couch upstairs. We worked all night on the house. We were all trying to get our minds off what happened to mom." LeBron said the last part quietly. Bart nodded along.

"I'm not going to lie. It's going to be hard for me to get past what happened yesterday. When I think of all the times she asked if we could just leave and go to a shelter. She never felt safe here. I don't think this new reality we're headed for is a world she'd have wanted to be a part of anyway. It's going to get a lot uglier, and your mom had a beautiful soul." Bart said. His eyes were misty and far away. LeBron headed up the stairs to continue his rounds and give his dad time to pull himself together. He didn't think he'd be able to take watching his dad cry without ending up bawling himself.

LeBron made sure to spend a little extra time upstairs. He found himself standing in the hallway looking over the bannister at the family photos lined up on the wall. LeBron, Drew, and Bart all unanimously despised the two times a year picture day came around. Nancy had always gotten the coupons for the JC Penny's photo studio for Christmas and Easter photos. She always used them. They'd all have to wear the same color shirt and ensure they'd had their hair cut recently.

They all loathed having to dress up and pose for the endless pictures then stand around waiting forever for Nancy and Yue to pick out the best ones. They all kept their mouths shut and just wandered around the furniture section of the store like lost puppies though. They smiled and bore it because their mom really didn't ask for very much. She sacrificed and did everything for them with a smile. She held them all individually to a very high standard and made sure they were each doing the best for themselves. She always put herself second. It didn't surprise LeBron at all that she hadn't hesitated to step up and put her own life on the line to defend them.

Smiling at the memories of the behind the scenes of the portraits he walked back downstairs. He peeked around the wall to make sure his dad had been able to get control of himself. He'd rather walk crotch first into a cactus naked than walk in on his dad crying. Seeing that everything looked ok he walked on down to continue his rounds.

"Everything ok upstairs?" Bart asked.

"All good in the hood." LeBron joked. He'd actually thought of going by his middle name a few times. He just didn't know how to get people to flip from calling him LeBron to calling him Charles. He resented being a black kid named LeBron when he had almost zero interest in sports. It was especially awkward that he sucked at basketball. Drew was always teasing him about it. He struggled a lot with his identity. Passed around in the foster system he'd never really felt like he fit in anywhere until the Russel's had adopted him.

Bart quizzed him on what all improvements they'd made to the house. He nodded at the fact they'd cut in the wider holes to see and shoot out of while also reinforcing the plywood with the two by fours. The investment in buying all the wood Drew could get in his truck on his original Home Depot run seemed to be paying off. LeBron asked his dad if he thought the cops or anybody else would bother them again.

"I doubt it. We rocked those guys back on their heels pretty hard. I wouldn't be surprised if a couple of the bastards didn't make it. The neighbors saw what happened when five fully armed and trained men tried to bust in here. They'd be stupid to think they could do any better. What I'm worried about is what you said yesterday. About the infected already showing up in Jacksonville?" Bart finished with a questioning look at his youngest son. He was ridiculously proud of how smart LeBron was. They were going to need to leverage that high IQ to have any hope at survival.

"The ones on the videos aren't even the main ones to worry about. They're just the ones in the surge phase. The ones who really spread this are the crawlers. The ones in the surge phase, they call them surgers on the internet, are pretty easy to take out if you're ready for them. The ones that make it to the next phase are the ones to really worry about. They call them crawlerz with a 'z'. They're as strong as the surgers, but they only move around at night. They're the ones really spreading this. They're creepy. Most of the videos of them are from like surveillance cams and video doorbells and stuff like that. They come at night, and they come hard." LeBron finished answering his dad. He was shuddering at the thought of having to test their makeshift carpentry against the monsters he'd watched on the internet.

"All we can do is prep and pray at this point." Bart said. He'd watched some of the videos LeBron was referring to. The warped looking crawlerz creeping around at night on all fours. Scampering up trees like monkeys. Ripping the knobs off the doors to houses then slamming into the doors until they broke in. They were the stuff of nightmares. A horror movie coming soon to a porch near them.

That sounded about right to LeBron. Every time he looked out the windows upstairs, he expected to see one of the surgers running down the street screaming for blood. Every bump and creak he heard at night made his heart race. His mind instantly going to those night vision videos like he'd showed his dad. The human shaped monsters with the glassy dead eyes coming out of the darkness.

Preparing for a deadly storm was pretty familiar to all of them. Living in Florida they'd dealt with a ton of hurricanes over the years. They'd done their fair share of boarding up windows and stocking up on water and toilet paper. They'd listened to the reporters talking about how if you didn't evacuate when ordered the government wouldn't send anyone to save you. They were well aware that the biggest killer in the hurricanes was the storm surge that arrived before the actual storm and just kept coming. It snuck up on people and trapped them in their homes. The water rushing in and rising until they drowned in their attics. LeBron imagined the first wave of the infected would hit like that.

LeBron decided to wake up Drew when he went back upstairs. Drew stumbled sleepily to the sink where he carefully dipped out some water to splash on his face. If they were really trying to fortify this house, they'd need to figure out how to handle getting extra water sooner rather than later. Drinking the runoff out of the retention pond outside was the easy option. As long as they were able to get out of the house. LeBron sat down watching Drew head off to start the rounds.

"How are you doing?" LeBron asked Drew as he crisscrossed the loft to the opposite windows to check the alley. Drew stopped to look seriously at LeBron.

"Not great. If I'd killed that cop, then mom would still be alive. If I'd killed the moron that I tossed into the woods, then dad wouldn't be hurt. We have to start making the hard choices. It's not a nice world anymore." Drew said sadly. Yawning he turned around and walked over to the window.

"Don't blame yourself. Nobody else blames you. There's no way to know what to do anymore. We just have to – " LeBron stopped talking immediately when Drew raised his hand in the air and made a shushing noise. Hand still in the air he motioned for LeBron to join him at the window.

Drew moved out of the way so LeBron would be able to see out the window into the alley below. A morbidly obese man was sprinting down the middle of the alley. The man's T-shirt had ridden up around his stomach which was bouncing around like a Jell-O mold in an earthquake. Watching him LeBron realized he'd have a really hard time outrunning somebody moving that fast. The man's eyes were fixed on the house down the street. He looked like he might be screaming as he ran but LeBron didn't hear anything from where they were watching.

"What are you looking at?" Yue asked from behind them. A startled LeBron leapt forward banging his head into the two by four. Drew spun around with his fists up ready to fight. Yue stood there with her eyes wide open trying to figure out what she'd just walked into. LeBron rubbed his head where he'd slammed it into the wood and moved out of the way so Yue could take a look.

"Fat surger." He whispered to her as she watched the overweight monster in the alley break all kinds of track and field records.

"I think he just died." Yue said standing back so Drew and LeBron could see. The large man who'd been riding the surge of adrenaline the newly infected get was now lying in the middle of the alley. He looked like the pictures of the bodies in the streets all over the world that showcased the dead the morning after the surge. It wasn't a shocker that someone with that much extra meat on their bones hadn't made it. It was actually pretty crazy his heart had held out for that long.

"It'd be pretty ironic if we survived in the United States just because we have way more fatties than the rest of the world." Drew said sarcastically. It was funny but LeBron thought he may actually have a point.

Startling all of them again Bart made an appearance. He'd managed to drag himself up the stairs using the bannister as a crutch. His face was pained but he wanted to see what was going on. Looking at him Yue made the call in her head that their dad should just stay upstairs in the loft moving forward. She helped him hobble over to the window to look out.

"I guess LeBron was right then. I was kind of hoping just this once your brain might've misfired." Bart said staring down at the dead guy in the alley.

LeBron couldn't physically keep his eyes open anymore. He went in his room and collapsed on the bed. Everyone else was awake at this point. Between the vulture buffet in the alley and all the other recent events they were all waiting to see what was going to happen next. Yue was the next to see one of the surgers sprinting by. She barely caught a glimpse of a woman running impossibly fast down the sidewalk in front of their home before the woman disappeared from sight down the street.

An hour later Drew saw one that was shuffling slowly down the street. It was turning its head rapidly back and forth as it walked. It appeared to be looking for prey. Drew felt naked and exposed peering through the slit in the second-floor window. The dead eyes of the surger below taking on the supernatural ability to see through walls in Drews mind. He slowly slid down the wall and focused on his breathing. Yue found him still sitting there ten minutes later too scared to move.

They kept spotting the surgers periodically throughout the day. They were all being overly cautious now about moving the curtains to look out the windows. They kept their voices at a whisper when talking to one another. The last thing any of them wanted to do was attract the notice of the surgers stalking by. As terrified as they were of the surgers they knew the coming night would be even worse.

Based on everything they'd heard the crawlerz were at a whole other level as far as massacre and mayhem went. Some sort of metamorphosis took place when a surger evolved into one of the crawlerz. They lost the ability to function around light, but they gained an otherworldly control of their adrenaline bursts. Stories of galloping crawlerz jumping from the street through second story windows to get at victims were so common they had to be believed.

Worse than their physical abilities the metamorphosis seemed to unlock some primal cognitive and telepathic capabilities. LeBron had read plenty of descriptions of coordinated attacks by the crawlerz where the most plausible explanation was that they were communicating with one another using telepathy. It was one way to tell the crawlerz from the surgers. The crawlerz moved silently through the world while the surgers ran around screaming anytime they saw something they associated with prey.

For these reasons and more they all feared the coming darkness. They were all holding out hope that maybe the crawlerz were still a night or two away from showing up. Since they only moved at night that was a possibility. The strength of their will wasn't enough to stop the earth from rotating though. The sun fled from the sky like it was also afraid of what was coming. The two by four enforced plywood window coverings that'd seemed so solid in the daylight now looked way too flimsy to keep out the monsters roaming the darkness outside.

Chapter 15: The First Night

The house was pitch dark. They didn't dare turn on a light or make any more noise than they had to. Going off the intel that the crawlerz were way more perceptive than the surgers Bart decided they'd all just congregate upstairs in the loft to sleep through the night. They setup a watch schedule of two-hour shifts and everyone else tried to go to sleep.

The only one who actually fell asleep was Bart. He was helped along by the generous dosage of pain killers Yue crushed up and included in his before bed round of medication. She was keeping him constantly filled up with antibiotics and painkillers at this point. The paranoia had set in with her that his wounds would get infected, and he'd die. She didn't know if she could take burying both her parents in the same week. She wasn't even sure they'd be able to leave the house again anyway. With the surgers roaming around during the day and the crawlerz coming out at night there was no safe time to conduct a funeral service.

The distant gunshots and screams started up a little after midnight. Even with the surgers roaming the streets today it'd been relatively quiet outside. The nice thing about being the last people on the planet to have to deal with the infected was that they knew what was coming. It was also the worst part of it. Kind of like being told how horrifying a roller coaster ride is. You don't really understand the fear until you've been stupid enough to strap yourself in. Once you're sitting at the top staring straight down at a ground that's way too far away with your belly threatening to rebel that's when you get it.

The three of them huddled together on the floor by their snoring dad listening to the sounds of violence all around them. At the sound of gunfire right down the street Drew got up and walked unsteadily over to the window closest to where the noise was coming from. Looking down the street he saw the flashes of light that lined up with the roar of the shotgun someone was shooting into the street. That poor soul had managed to end up outside on their porch fighting against a steadily increasing number of the ghoulish monsters.

Drew watched as whoever it was fired straight into the figures lunging for him. The infected mostly shrugged off the shotgun blasts and kept coming up on the patio. Before they could get to him though a blur came out of nowhere and ripped the man down to the ground. The blur now distinguishable as a humanoid figure buried its face into the struggling prey it'd just tossed to the ground. Whatever madness drove the infected told its host when to stop feasting on the prone man and continue hunting. The surgers and the crawlerz quickly leaving the porch to seek their next victim.

LeBron and Yue joined Drew in looking out the window. All of them watched as the body of the man left on the porch slowly rose to its feet. Hesitantly at first then with more confidence the freshly turned surger moved out into the street. It left the shotgun lying on the porch along with its humanity. It ran off in the direction of distant gunfire. On the way it passed a few infected who were still sprinting towards the sound of the shots it'd fired from the porch before being turned. That's how fast it'd all happened.

Drew was glad his brother and sister had walked over and seen what he'd just seen. He was terrified of even whispering at this point. Worried that anything they did may bring the wrath of the infected down on them. The few crawlerz he'd seen had all moved through the shadows with inhuman speed. The surgers were fast but at least they ran standing upright. The crawlerz ran like they'd been possessed. There was no trace of humanity left in them. The contorted way they moved made their speed seem even more unnatural.

The sounds of breaking glass and gunfire continued throughout the night. They walked around peering out the holes in the windows without touching the curtains in any way. They had no way of knowing if they were being overly cautions or not. There wasn't a way to know if they were going to end up ripped apart by some fiend regardless of whether they wore socks or shoes to move around the loft. The number of crawlerz swelled as the night went on. When it got to the point that they couldn't look below without seeing a dozen of the demonic figures Yue decided they should just huddle together in the middle of the floor.

LeBron followed her docilely enough, but Drew seemed to think if he couldn't see the crawlerz then they might come crashing into the house. He resisted Yue at first until she got close enough to him to whisper that curiosity killed the cat. She filled her voice with such animosity that he had no choice but to listen. The old timey saying shattered through the black ice of his current terror and managed to sink deep enough for him to see reason.

As luck would have it though as soon as they'd abandoned making the circuit to look out the windows something slammed into the door downstairs. Drew shot an accusatory glare at Yue. She couldn't see him in the darkness though, so the glare was pretty much wasted. Seeing it wouldn't have mattered as she was too busy being completely petrified the same as LeBron. Drew was scared too but his first instinct was to fight. He started searching his pockets to make sure he had his flashlight in case whatever was slamming into the door managed to get in.

The loud bangs from downstairs continued for a few more minutes. As randomly as the assault on the downstairs door had begun it ended. The sudden silence casting doubt into their minds if the door had held or not. The loud sounds had included what could've been boards cracking. For all they knew the assault had ended because the door had opened up enough to let a crowd of crawlerz inside to hang out in their living room. Knowing they had to check and knowing she was the least likely to make any noise Yue stood up. Her brothers intuited what she was doing and stood up to follow her. She pushed them both gently back, so they'd know she was going by herself.

Hoping they got the message and wouldn't come thundering down the stairs after her she tip-toed over to the top of the stairs. One step at a time she descended into the darkness below. Heart working like a jackhammer as her imagination filled the darkness with the faces of the damned. In her mind's eye a group of the hunched over crawlerz gathered by the foot of the stairs. Drool leaking out of their mouths as they stared at the sacrifice willingly descending to the slaughter.

Heart threatening to thump out of her chest she made it to the bottom of the stairs without anything taking a bite out of her. She struggled to control her breathing. She'd held her breath the entire time down the stairs without even realizing it. Starved for air she gasped like a marathon runner who'd just made it across the finish line. She walked over to the door and could tell that it'd taken a beating. Based on how it was wiggling around when she pushed gently against it, they were very lucky whatever had been trying to get in had given up when it had.

A cool breeze was the only benefit of the loose-fitting door. The house was hot. Even at night it felt like they were living in a sauna. Her clothes were sticking to her. She was going to start getting a rash pretty soon unless they all decided to start walking around in their underwear. The Florida heat was no joke. She remembered their dad had tried to hold out one time for a second bid on their AC system when the one they had in one of their old houses had conked out. He was positive the first company they'd called had been trying to rip them off. He'd made it about two hours before calling them back and paying the exorbitant price to get the new system installed. It was Yue's firm belief that if it weren't for air conditioning Florida would've been the only state in the country with a population of less than fifty people.

Judging by all the screams and gunfire they'd heard earlier they may very well be on track to hit that fifty-person population. Assuming you didn't count the crawlerz as people. Allowing herself to enjoy the cool air seeping in around the abused doorframe she listened to the screams coming from outside. These weren't the muted screams they were able to barely hear in the loft. It hadn't even occurred to her that ignoring those distant cries for help was a moral dilemma. What she was hearing now was coming from somewhere close by.

She was working on angling her head to see out the side window when her suspicions were confirmed. The loud blasts of a pistol being fired multiple times mingled with a woman's screams from the house next door. She didn't even need to move the sheer part of the curtain out of the way to see the bright flashes of light as the pistol was fired. She assumed it was the pistol her dad had traded Shaun for the boxes of food they'd emptied into their pantry. They'd given him three magazines worth of ammunition, but he didn't even get all the way through one of them by her count. She felt bad for them, but the analytical part of her coldly noted that there was now a houseful of food and at least a couple magazines worth of ammunition available next door.

She went upstairs and quietly gathered Drew and LeBron to come down with her. They painstakingly spent the next hour quietly moving furniture to shore up the door. Hopefully they'd be able to do some carpentry work once the sun came up to further strengthen the door. They'd just have to manually screw the boards and take their time so as to not make much noise. The three of them working together should be able to figure it out. Now that she thought about it, they should've been doing that now instead of trying to lean couches against the door.

A loud whack from the back of the house froze them all in place again. That noise was followed by others as it seemed like all of the plywood on all of the windows in the back of the house were tested. Each time one of the boards was struck the sound echoed throughout the house. Thinking of some of the videos they'd watched online they knew the worst was still to come. Some of the footage that'd been uploaded of towns that'd been hit by the crawlerz looked like they'd been hit by a hurricane. Windows were smashed, cars were dented in, houses were burnt to the ground and there were always corpses scattered haphazardly around the area.

Yue tugged on each of her brothers to get them to head back upstairs with her. Drew followed along easily enough, but LeBron hesitated. In the extremely dim light seeping in from the moon she saw that LeBron seemed transfixed by the pile of crap they'd just spent all that time putting in front of the broken door. She grabbed his shoulder and tugged it harder to break him out of his trance. He shook his head to clear it as he turned to follow her up the stairs.

They sat silently in the loft until morning. They jumped each time they heard the random smacks on the outside of the house. The strikes intensified in ferocity and frequency the closer it got to daybreak. By the time the sun came up there hadn't been any attempts to break in through the windows downstairs for at least an hour. The coming of daylight lifted a gigantic weight off their shoulders. Dog tired their spirits were buoyed by the fact that they'd survived the night. At different points over the evening each of them had been sure they weren't going to make it. Seeing the sun come up was a big deal.

Feeling someone's eyes on them the siblings looked up to see Bart had finally woken up. He smiled down at the three of them.

"I feel great. Thanks for letting me sleep. I miss anything?"

Chapter 16: Hump Day

The situation didn't get a whole lot better once the sun came up. The crawlerz all disappeared but the surgers were running around everywhere now. The extent of the damage to their house was staggering. The crawlerz hadn't even made a serious attempt to get inside. The random attempts had been powerful though. Plywood was bent and cracked. Windowpanes had shattered from the battering they'd received leaving shards of glass all over the floor.

It was a complete disaster outside. Bodies were scattered all over the alley. The bloated corpse of the first surger they'd seen was now part of a set. Vultures were feasting on the corpses of the dead. Here and there dogs and cats could be seen slinking around. The dogs occasionally either barking their heads off or whining in fear. The surgers ignored the animals for the most part. They were focused on finding people. Whatever chemical cocktail was eating away at their sanity gave them a single-minded focus on finding and attacking anyone who wasn't one of them.

Bart was sitting in a puddle of his own sweat up in the loft. Every time he moved around, he started seeping blood again. On the plus side they had more gauze wraps than the costume trailer for a mummy movie. Yue was able to change the dressings on her dad's wounds multiple times a day. She was hoping the cleaner they kept it the faster it would heal. It wasn't like she normally had much else to do lately. Today was an exception. They easily had a full day's worth of hot, sweaty repair work to do on the house.

"I should've grabbed bricks and bags of mortar instead of wood." Drew whispered looking around the room. It was much easier to look around thanks to the light leaking through all the cracked and loosened wood. If only he'd been thinking of the three little pigs when he'd been ransacking the Home Depot building supply aisles.

"Those things weren't even trying to get in here last night. Maybe we just take for granted that they're going to get in tonight. We could work on sealing off the upstairs instead." LeBron said thoughtfully.

"We don't have enough wood left to block off the second floor." Drew said. He was looking at LeBron like he was crazy for suggesting it might be a good idea to let the crawlerz get into the first floor.

"What if we took all the doors and cabinets off their hinges and used those?" LeBron suggested quietly. He was staring at the gap in the ceiling above the stairs where they worked their way up into the second floor.

"How are you going to do all of that quietly in one day and make it good enough that the crawlerz can't beat their way through it to get upstairs?" Yue asked. She hated the stair idea but was liking the inner doors as a source of building material idea.

"Yeah, they get in here we're screwed." Drew said. The three of them stood there indecisively staring around the living room. Outside the din of the surgers continuing to tear apart the neighborhood was loud enough that Yue thought they could almost risk building a deck on the second floor. Mostly she felt claustrophobic. The walls were starting to close in on her. It sucked to be claustrophobic and agoraphobic at the same time. The thought of being caught out in the open with all those things was even worse than the feeling that the walls were closing in on her.

Drew won the door placement argument by default since he was the only one of them who was good with his hands. Bart was a hobbyist at wood working and loved building projects. He'd tried to transfer that skill and passion to all three of them, but Drew was the only one who'd caught the bug. While the surgers howled away outside they carefully repaired all of the windows and doorways as best they could from the inside of the house. When that was done, they followed Drew around the house cautiously pulling doors out of doorways and off of the cabinets.

The fun part of doing that was trying to quietly knock the doors out of the hinges. They had a mallet, but it was sitting out in the garage. No way any of them were risking their lives for a mallet. That meant they had to use a hammer. A bit of trial and error with the hammer and a blanket and they were able to make it all work without too much noise. In the end the doors were duct taped to the wall while leaning on the floor in front of the windows. They manually put a few screws through each door to hold it to the wall. They'd searched high and low to locate a whopping three drywall anchors. Drew knew they had some in the wall he might be able to reuse but by the time they finished it was getting pretty late.

They stumbled their way up the stairs. If nothing else, they'd succeeded in making the downstairs section of the house completely dark again. The darkness didn't fool any of them into believing they'd actually done a great job hardening the defenses down there. They were literally using duct tape to protect themselves from killer freaks with superhuman strength. None of them were feeling super confident about their chances of surviving the night. They reported in upstairs to Bart and let him know what they'd accomplished.

"What's the plan if those things get in here?" Bart asked. His three sweat soaked miserable looking kids didn't answer as they plopped themselves down in the areas that they'd each claimed as their own. Once all three of them were comfortable he asked the question again.

"Blaze of glory time?" Drew asked sarcastically. It was the wrong answer. His dad ignored him.

"You need to always have a backup plan. Those things might get in here tonight. Hell, based on what you told me happened last night I'm willing to bet that no amount of duct tape is going to keep them out if they decide they want to come in. Now what's the plan if they get in?" Bart asked again.

"We hide?" Yue said tentatively.

"That could work. Where are we hiding at?" Bart asked.

"We could knock the wood off the windows and hide in the master bathroom." LeBron said. He was talking in that hyper way he had that meant he had an idea spinning around in his head.

"Why are we knocking the wood off the window?" Drew asked trying to keep up.

"So, when the sun comes up none of the crawlerz decide to hang out in the bedroom for the day. Once the light starts coming in, they'll leave." Yue said excitedly. She started getting into the plan. She loved the idea of having a backup plan. It was helping her deal with the feelings of helplessness she'd been coping with.

"The roof to the patio is right outside the bathroom window. That'll make it easy for us to climb down if we need to abandon the house." LeBron added.

"You think it'd be nice to have any of your stuff with you if you need to ditch the house?" Bart asked trying to lead them into a plan that would give them a decent chance at survival.

They continued discussing the aspects of this plan they'd come up with. Working together they came up with ideas on what they could do now to enable them to pull it off later if they had to. With only an hour to two of decent daylight left they got to work. It turned out they weren't going to be able to get the plywood off the bedroom window unless they went outside and used a ladder and a drill. The window had the big firing port sawed out of it though, so they settled for just getting rid of the curtains. That should let in enough light to discourage the light averse crawlerz from taking a siesta in Yue's room.

They stocked the bathroom with medicine, food, and weapons. They put together 'go bags' using their backpacks. Bart advised them on what should go in the bags. The general idea was they should be able to survive for a couple of days off of the supplies in the bag. They should have some medical supplies and other essentials like food and water in the bag. Every other cubic inch of space in the bags should be shoved full of ammunition. Bart made sure to reiterate multiple times that you could never have enough ammunition with you.

Yue dropped a couple of rolls of duct tape off in the bathroom as the final element in their panic room. She'd have really liked not to be seriously planning on duct taping the door shut if they ended up locked up in the small space. On top of the lameness of the redneck panic room irking her she was also seriously worried about her dad. He'd been enthusiastic in getting the room built out. Some of the things he'd said had seemed off to her though. She assumed LeBron had noticed as well but Drew was likely oblivious.

Satisfied they'd done all the prep they could without making too much noise they gathered together up in the loft. They all felt a little better about the coming night now that they'd built out their fallback position. The lingering question mark was if they were forced out of the house then where would they go? The plan was to fight their way to the garage and take the Traverse if they had to make a run for it. They were still working on what their destination would be after they got on the road.

"What do you want in your pack?" Drew asked their dad. Yue and LeBron both perked up. Maybe Drew was more perceptive than they'd thought. Or he was just trying to be helpful. Either way this response should be interesting.

"If those things get in the house. You'll have to jump off the porch and fight your way to the garage. I won't need a pack because I won't be going. There's no way I'll make that jump with multiple holes still oozing blood out of my body. I'm not going to slow you guys down and risk us all dying." Bart said with passion. He'd been planning on keeping that particular thought nugget a secret until they actually had to jump. He suspected he could blame his loose lips on whatever drugs Yue was slipping him.

Yue had in fact been slipping a little Valium into her dad's medicine. Considering the situation that they were in she was worried about him losing himself in depression. She was worried about him doing something stupid. Something exactly like he'd just admitted he was planning on doing.

"So, if I break my leg when we go out the window should Yue and LeBron just leave me laying there while they run for the garage?" Drew asked. The subdued anger in his voice rivaling the passion of Bart's earlier declaration. Bart said nothing. He didn't trust himself to open his mouth.

"We're not leaving you behind dad." LeBron said.

"That's right. We're not leaving anybody behind." Yue echoed her brothers' sentiments. Bart grumbled something and shifted around on the couch so that he was no longer facing them.

The sun went down. Darkness filling the house like a heavy fog settling in thick around them. LeBron pulled the first watch. The rest of them settled down to try and rest in the humid loft. It was getting musty up there. All of them could use a shower. They'd been slathering on deodorant to avoid smelling like a dead hobo, but they could really use some air conditioning.

LeBron gazed longingly at the ceiling fans in the living room as he made his rounds. It was amazing how much they'd taken for granted before this all happened. Walking past the refrigerator he shivered at the thought of an actual glass of ice-cold soda. He could almost hear the ice cubes clinking together inside one of their tall glasses. The master bedroom had an even funkier smell than the rest of the house. It was the master bath that they were using when they had to go to the bathroom. Going to the bathroom in this case meaning the boys got to pee in the toilet tank while Yue was welcome to the actual bowl. Once they filled up the tank, they were able to flush it. If you needed to do more than tinkle there was a small box of garbage bags in the corner. It was all pretty disgusting.

Hurriedly leaving the gag room LeBron continued up the stairs on his rounds. The sounds of their neighborhood dying outside was just background noise now. The random scream as some poor bastard got caught out by the infected. The occasional sharp retort of gunfire punctuating the night. On at least one memorable occasion someone had shot off a ton of those expensive mortar fireworks like you can buy in South Carolina. The ones that come in the colorful wrapping paper and are only to be used to scare off crows from your cornfield. None of them could think of a good reason for anybody to have set off a bunch of fireworks like that. There wasn't a cornfield for miles.

Drew had come up with what was probably the right answer. He thought the people who'd set them off must've been making a run for it. They were using the fireworks as a distraction while they took off the other way. Since no other reason made any sense and because it didn't really matter anyway, they all went with that explanation. It occurred to LeBron as he paced the house that the only reason that he was still even thinking about it was because Drew had come up with the best explanation sooner than he had. He was used to Drew beating him at pretty much any sort of physical contest. He prided himself on solving puzzles and coming up with answers to riddles faster though.

LeBron walked to the window in the corner of the loft to look down. He was careful to be quiet so as not to wake up anyone. That care went out the window when the sound of banging and splintering wood came from the first floor.

It was too dark to see but LeBron heard his family scrambling up off the floor. Down below the smashing sounds ceased. It'd been loud. Whatever had wanted to get in the house this time hadn't stopped until they were in. They stood together in the darkness listening to the sounds of something moving around in the house below. Yue gasped loudly when she heard the sound of something heavy below smashing into the floor. For a couple of seconds afterwards the sounds from below completely stopped. The silence somehow way more chilling than the crashing noises had been.

They stood there in the darkness holding their breaths. All of them doing their best not to make a sound. Tears of terror rolled down Yue's cheeks. The smacking of footsteps moving quickly to the base of the stairs. Then the sound changed to the hollower sound of someone coming up the stairs. Halfway up the sounds stopped as if whoever it was had stopped again to listen. Drew was closest to the stairs. He had his hand on his pistol but hadn't pulled it out of the holster. He was fighting back his fear. Praying that whatever was on the stairs would just turn around and go back down them.

Instead, the footsteps sped up as the thing on the stairs moved quickly up to the loft. Light flooded the space as Bart flipped on his flashlight. He'd done it just so he could line up a clean shot at the monster threatening them. The sudden light revealed a middle-aged woman with curly auburn hair. Her clothes and body were filthy. Like she'd slept in a muddy ditch all day. Her neck had been savaged by someone in the very recent past. It was coated in dried blood. A strip of ragged flesh hanging off with the muscle showing from underneath.

The sudden light and proximity to uninfected humans sent the woman into a flurry of limbs and teeth. She was on top of Drew before Drew could even clear his pistol from the holster. LeBron and Yue were there a second later grabbing the woman by the hair and neck to keep her teeth off of their brother. Bart was ignoring the pain from his own wounds while shining the light and maneuvering around to try to get a clear shot.

The flailing woman reached back and grabbed LeBron by the shirt. She flung him across the room completely shredding his shirt in her claw like grip. He smashed into the dry wall hard enough to dent it in where his head hit. Yue was thrown off next. The crawler forgetting about Drew to jump at her. Bart blasted away as soon as she moved off Drew to attack Yue. The bullets ripping into the woman's side didn't seem to even slow her down. Yue scrambled backwards trying to get away. More bullets from both Drew and Bart smashing through the crazed crawler's torso.

The woman fell on top of Yue when one of the bullets pierced her skull. Others had already hit her in the heart and lungs. The bits and pieces thrown off the woman by the attack coated Yue's clothes. She stood up as Bart ran to make sure she was ok. Ignoring her dad, she went over to where they'd stacked their medicine and frantically moved everything around until she found a bottle of peroxide. She ripped her shirt off and threw it to the ground. She then dumped half the bottle on herself and the other half on Drew and told him to scrub it in.

Bart was shining the light for them as they gargled with the peroxide when another of the crawlerz came thundering up the stairs. LeBron had positioned himself at the top of the straight flight of stairs with his mom's shotgun. Not even able to see the monster coming at him he just started shooting down the narrow stairwell. They heard the monster gasp and grunt before it fell and rolled back down the stairs.

Less than a minute later there was banging on the door on the other side of the house. Bart shined his light down the stairwell right as a pale faced skinny high school aged looking kid came streaking up the stairs. LeBron pumping buckshot down the stairs as fast as he could rack the shell and pull the trigger. The kid took one of the hits right in the face but kept coming at an impossible speed. Half the skin missing from his face and the monster didn't even slow down. Even with the last shot hitting him right in the stomach from a distance of less than a foot the monstrosity still leapt up the stairs to grab LeBron.

Bart sidled right up to the boy and shot him through the head twice dropping him to the ground. Without hesitating Bart then turned his aim and his flashlight to the stairwell where yet another of the beasts was streaking towards them. He emptied his magazine at this one's face to stop it from making it up the stairs. With himself and LeBron running low on ammunition he yelled for them all to fall back to the panic room. They grabbed whatever was near them and ran with it towards the bathroom in the back that they'd worked on securing and stocking with supplies earlier.

Noticing the flashlight waving around erratically Drew ran back to the loft by the stairs and bodily picked up Bart to carry him along. The man's leg had given out on him after all the commotion. The sound of movement from the first floor egged Drew to sprint full speed down the hallway into Yue's room. Yue slammed her bedroom door and dropped down the makeshift wooden lock they'd rigged up to try and keep the monsters out. Based on what they'd seen so far of the crawlerz strength none of them were foolish enough to think it'd hold.

Drew tripped over the bed slamming Bart into the wall by accident. He got up and dragged him into the panic room right as the first strike sounded against the bedroom door. Inside the bathroom they shut that door and used the duct tape to seal it off. They had devised more wooden locks for this door. They dropped the sections of two by four into the locks and then all huddled on the ground trembling as they heard the bedroom door getting smashed in. LeBron had grabbed his dad's flashlight and clicked it off before carrying it into the bathroom with them.

They held each other in the darkness listening as the crawlerz slunk around their home seeking the victims they sensed must be there somewhere.

Chapter 17: A Time to Panic

The crawlerz were in a frenzy. While they huddled in their makeshift panic room with their guns aimed at the bathroom door the house was being ripped apart. Just because the crawlerz only came out at night didn't mean they were super graceful about it. Whatever evolutionary impacts it had on controlling adrenaline bursts must not help any with seeing in the dark. Either that or the psycho killers just went all rock star mode when they got frustrated trying to find people in the house.

A hand smashed through the drywall separating Yue's room from the bathroom. They watched as the crawler's hand bounced up and down in the hole it'd created. It got entangled in electrical wire which it then ripped out of the wall. The whole bathroom wall shook immediately after the wire disappeared when the crawler threw itself against it. Dust drifted down from the ceiling as they watched from the floor in disbelief. The crawler was hitting the wall like it was being shot out of a cannon. The drywall was cracking and popping off of the broken wall studs.

The wall stopped shaking abruptly. The sounds of a wall on the other side of the room getting ripped apart hinted at a brief respite from them being found and killed. They lowered their weapons relieved they weren't going to have to start shooting immediately. The bathroom door flew into the bathroom slamming into the wall. A large shape filled the doorframe. It caught the bullets from all four of their weapons. It still managed to take one step forward before crumpling to the ground.

"Time to go!" Bart yelled.

Drew was already prying the plywood off the bathroom window. They'd loosened it up when they came up with the plan for the panic room so it shouldn't take him too long to get it off. They'd also lined up their go bags on the bathroom counter right by the window. Meanwhile their next set of problems were thundering up the stairs at a million miles per hour. LeBron and Yue ran into the master bedroom and started laying down fire in the narrow hallway. They were blasting away every time they saw something move. The plaster dust and darkness conspiring to ruin any chance of visibility. Bart was pulling himself along by the wall to go help them.

Drew had given up on gently levering the plywood off the window like the original plan had called for. Considering the ridiculous amount of noise his family was making behind him silence was pretty much out the window anyway. They needed to get themselves the hell out of the window before the upstairs became crawler central.

Drew slammed his hammer into the board multiple times until it finally loosened up. He pushed it hard. The plywood ripped out of the wall leaving the window open for them to climb out of. He quickly tossed all four of their bags out the window onto the porch roof.

"Let's go!" Drew yelled over the deafening roar of guns in the room beside him. Picking his rifle up off the bathroom counter he ran back into the master bedroom to usher everyone along.

Yue was standing alone in the hallway firing her pistol. Bart was attempting to help LeBron to his feet. A small shape lying face down on the ground beside LeBron turned out to be a dead kid. Drew gulped realizing they were going to have to shoot kids. Either his brother or sister had already had to kill one.

"I'm out!" Yue yelled falling back and digging in her pocket to find another magazine. Drew stepped into the space she'd just vacated. Everything made more complicated by how dark the room was. Looking down the hallway he realized that Yue and LeBron must not have even been able to really see their targets. All you could see were blurs in the darkness. If it moved, you just had to shoot at it.

"Go! Get out! I'm right behind you!" Drew yelled shooting down the hall at a man shape that'd popped into view. As he fired the flash from his round going off briefly illuminated the hallway. The short section of carpeted bungalow was lined with the dead. LeBron and Yue had been busy. Drew shot until he didn't see anything moving then took a step backwards to run back in the bathroom.

He tripped over the body of the dead kid and landed face first in the corpse of the crawler they'd killed earlier. Thinking he was going to need a few gallons of hydrogen peroxide and some steel wool he hopped back to his feet. Completely disgusted he was suddenly twisted in a vicious circle when something grabbed him by the back. That something pulled him backwards until they both fell down. Drew spun in the air and got his hands around the things neck. He started slamming its head into the floor.

The crawler who'd grabbed him was a teen about the same size as Drew. It ignored being choked and having its head slammed into the floor. With an insanely powerful heave it jumped back to its feet hurling Drew up onto Yue's bed. Drew let his momentum carry him off the other side of the bed. As soon as he felt himself falling towards the floor, he pulled out his pistol. He had no clue where his rifle had ended up.

When the crawler came flying over the bed to get at him Drew shot it in the head and chest until it stopped moving. He pushed the fresh corpse to the side and scrambled out from beside the bed. Moving fast he hurdled the sprawled-out bodies of the dead as he rushed to rejoin his family. Yue was already standing out on the porch roof looking down. She'd shrugged on her go bag already. The weight of all the ammunition they'd shoved in it tilting her backwards on her feet. LeBron was arguing with their dad.

"We have to go now!" Drew yelled in full on panic mode. He wasn't understanding how his brother and dad weren't realizing how important it was to immediately get the hell out of Dodge. He also wanted to make sure he was heard. He was feeling pretty deaf after all the shooting in the enclosed spaces and assumed everyone else was as well.

"Dad says he's not going!" LeBron shouted. Drew moved forward to get directly in Bart's face. LeBron's eyes grew huge as Bart pulled his pistol out and aimed it in the general direction of Drew's head.

"Duck!" Bart screamed at Drew. Drew pulled both his legs up in the air so that he fell straight to the ground on his knees. His dad stepped forward shooting through the space Drew had occupied half a second prior. The crawlerz who'd slunk into the bathroom behind Drew absorbing the rounds from the pistol. Neither of the demonic looking crawlerz bothered to duck out of the way of the roaring gun. They didn't do much more than grunt as the bullets slammed into them. Bart emptied his pistol for the fourth time in the last five minutes to put them on the deck.

Drew stood up breathing raggedly. He thought he'd been deaf before. Having the pistol being shot directly above his head had really set his eardrums to ringing. Without being able to hear himself he yelled for LeBron to get out the damned window. Bart was leaning against the counter working on getting a fresh magazine jammed into his pistol. He looked like death warmed over. He was waving at Drew and pointing him towards the window. Drew couldn't hear a word the man was saying but it was pretty obvious his dad wanted him to go out the window after LeBron.

Knowing their dad was planning to stay in the house to cover their retreat Drew went a different direction. He slammed his fist into his dad's face then grabbed him in a fireman's carry. Turning sideways he ran and stuffed Bart part way through the window. LeBron and Yue pulled him the rest of the way out. Seeing Bart had dropped his pistol Drew grabbed it and looked towards the bathroom door. A crawler ran into the bathroom and tripped over one of its dead brethren. It tried to leap at Drew at the same time but just ended up jumping at a weird angle face first into the bathroom mirror.

It fell across the counter with a bloodied face and a snapped neck. Even as it fell to the ground its eyes were focused on Drew. It's mouth snapping open and shut. An ancient hatred directed at him from those mad eyes. Even in the dusty, dark, mostly destroyed bathroom Drew found himself mesmerized by the intensity of the insane rage glowing in the deadened eyes. He'd have died in the bathroom staring into the eyes of a paralyzed monster if his dad hadn't managed to kick him painfully in the ear by accident.

Hoping he hadn't lost a chunk of his lobe Drew turned and squeezed through the window as soon as Yue and LeBron got their dad through it. Once through the window he immediately turned around and pointed the pistol back into their bathroom. Yue noted Drew was out and got ready to jump. Motion and a metallic sound beneath her feet got her attention. Looking down she saw a crawler pulling itself up the gutter to get at her. She put her rifle on the things forehead and pulled the trigger once to get rid of the threat.

She could see more crawlerz running their way. The distinctive way they ran using their hands as well as their feet was horrifying. It dehumanized the forms coming for them. She didn't see how they were going to make it. She heard Drew open fire behind her. More of the demons must be in the bathroom already. Knowing their dad had come out on the crowded porch roof gave her some comfort. At least they'd all die together. With that cheerful thought she aimed for the hedges beside the privacy fence and jumped.

She completely missed the hedge. The rucksack full of ammunition and supplies weighed way too much. They'd seriously overestimated how much they could realistically carry while jumping off roofs. Instead of landing on her feet with the hedge taking the edge off the pain from her fall she landed flat on her back on the lawn. Her breath was completely knocked out of her. She literally could see stars circling around in the darkness above her. Those stars were blocked off a second or two later by the body of her brother who'd also aimed for the hedges.

Drew looked below and saw LeBron land on top of Yue. Hoping they both weren't dead he flung the last two go bags off the roof onto the ground below. His dad was screaming something at him, but Drew was still mostly deaf. Assuming his dad was trying to tell him to leave him behind Drew picked him up and jumped for the hedges. He actually landed on the hedges. The stiff branches ripping at every bit of his skin as he plummeted through them with his dad's weight added to his own. He rolled out of them immediately after hitting the ground to check on Yue and LeBron.

LeBron was pulling Yue up onto her feet. She looked dazed and confused. Trying to catch her breath she gamely started stumbling around the house towards their detached garage. LeBron had his rifle up and was surveilling for crawlerz. They appeared to have lost them for the moment at least. Drew bent down and scooped up both the packs he'd thrown down from the roof. He waited for a pissed off looking Bart to crawl out of the broken hedges. Then they both started hobbling towards the garage behind LeBron and Yue. All of them shifting their packs around to make sure they had loaded weapons in their hands.

LeBron and Yue ran around the corner straight into a crawler who was in the process of climbing out of one of their broken windows. They both opened fire on the things back. It collapsed dead inside the window frame. The gunfire attracted others though. Including a couple who came around the corner screaming their heads off. Yue assumed those two must still be in surge mode since they were making so much noise. She shot the one on the right seeing his nose replaced by a big bloody hole. LeBron was out of ammunition so fell back to let Drew shoot the other one.

Drew shot it three times in the body and the large surger kept coming at them. Yue swung her rifle to aim and put two shots in the side of the monster's head. It collapsed to the ground with its body flopping around like a fish out of water. More movement from the front door as LeBron struggled to get the garage door unlocked. Yue and Bart just started shooting everything they had into the house while Drew frantically tried looking in every other direction at once to cover them.

"It's open! It's open!" LeBron was screaming behind them.

Drew yanked Yue and Bart backwards into the garage with him. LeBron slammed the door shut. They'd barely gotten over to the Traverse when they heard the door being slammed into. Yue had the keys in her bag. They all tossed their bags in the backseat while Drew scrambled to find the rope to pop up the garage door. Yue got in the driver's seat. Bart was laid out across the back seat trying not to black out from all the pain. Pain that had to be seriously significant to cut through the fog of the pain killers Yue had been feeding him.

Drew found the rope and pulled it. The garage door popped up a foot. Drew ran over and pushed it up high enough for Yue to get out of. LeBron walked beside the Traverse on the same side as Drew shooting at anything in the darkness that moved and wasn't Drew shaped. His night vision thrown completely off by the lights from the car. The garage door slammed into the top of the Traverse as Drew let go of it thinking it'd stay up. Sparks flew as Yue just powered through it. LeBron and Drew jumped in the car to join her. A fist smashed into the back window shattering it into approximately a zillion pieces.

Yue screamed and put the car in drive. Drew and LeBron both started shooting out the back window. Nothing clawed its way through the window to try to rip their heads off so at least one of their bullets must've found a home. They were both thrown across Bart when Yue accelerated way too fast down the narrow alley. She'd flicked the high beams on hoping to screw up any of the crawlerz coming at them. She could clearly see they were going to be running over corpses. Much more concerning to her was that there were at least a few of the psychos running straight for them.

Yue had no idea how they made it out of the alley. She'd never admit it, but her eyes had been closed tight about half of the time. She'd stomped her foot down hard on the accelerator and tried to keep the wheel straight as they bounced over bloated bodies and got slammed into by crawlerz. The windshield was a cracking mess of safety glass with a head shaped indent on the passenger side. Shocked to have survived running that gauntlet Yue eased up on the accelerator and turned sharply for the main road. Over her own ragged breathing she clearly heard Drew teasing LeBron.

"That would've been so much easier if we just had some fireworks to shoot off to distract them, right?"

Chapter 18: Are We There Yet?

"Hurry up!" LeBron hissed. He was staring at the subdivision across the street where a house was engulfed in flames. He thought he'd heard someone screaming off in the distance as well. Both excellent reasons for Drew to hurry up and get the tire changed. Yue had driven them straight through an intersection full of broken glass and twisted metal. Judging by the multiple burnt out husks of vehicles there'd been at least a couple of accidents there. Everything had been fine until she'd mentioned she hoped they didn't get a flat tire. Five seconds later the Traverse had tilted forward slightly followed by the *'whomp whomp'* noise of a flat tire.

"So, you're saying I shouldn't take my time?" Drew snapped back through clenched teeth. He'd ripped half the skin off two of his knuckles trying to rush the tire change. If LeBron would just squat down and help him instead of standing there telling him to hurry, they'd be on their way a lot sooner.

Drew tightened the final nut and stood up pleased with himself. His time may not qualify him for a place on a NASCAR pit crew, but he'd just changed a tire in the middle of an apocalypse without anything eating him. It was important to celebrate the little victories. Not that the feeling of satisfaction from changing a tire did a lot to balance the crushing losses they'd recently suffered.

His momentary pleasure at successfully surviving the tire change was short lived. LeBron yelled to him to hurry up and get in. Glancing over in the direction LeBron was staring he saw a group of crawlerz vaulting over the privacy fence surrounding the neighborhood where the one house was blazing away. The crawlerz were hitting the ground and sprinting in their weird all fours way straight for them. That was all the encouragement Drew needed to jump headfirst into the backseat of the Traverse.

LeBron reached over Drew and slammed the back door shut. He was yelling at Yue to drive. She'd already been accelerating the second Drews feet had left the ground for his desperate leap into the backseat. Bart was rolling around in the small third row where they'd seat belted him in. He'd been moaning in pain, so Yue had pumped him full of more painkillers. His bandages were hanging off him like he was some kind of dollar store mummy. Spots of blood standing out in bright scarlet on the cloth bands flapping around in the breeze.

Yue flicked the light on and then pulled back on the lever to turn on the high beams. Light from anything but the sun didn't force the crawlerz into hiding. It did make them act even more erratic than normal, however. Not that they didn't act erratically enough already. In the sudden surge of light Yue saw the group of crawlerz spilt off in multiple directions. One slowed down completely and began calmly walking towards them. The others seemed to be working on encircling the Traverse.

They couldn't encircle what wasn't there. Yue didn't slow for the crawler walking towards them. She was kind of freaked out by the calm way it continued pacing towards them right up until she slammed into it at full speed. The other crawlerz were a much bigger problem. They sprang onto the roof and hood of the car. She was driving blind with an overweight older woman spread out across what was left of the smashed windshield. LeBron was pumping lead into the mass of pale white flesh squeezing into the car through the rapidly failing rest of the windshield.

The woman seemed pretty dead, but she wasn't rolling off the car. She was stuck to the windshield like a massive bloody bug. Yue was hunched over standing on the floorboards to see out of the narrow gap of window left at the top. She was navigating like that while the rest of them were shooting out their own windows trying to get rid of the crawlerz who were crawling all over the speeding car. Drew was super impressed that Yue hadn't crashed yet considering the conditions she was driving under.

Drew cussed himself out for jinxing them with his errant thoughts a second later when the car went into a spin on the side of the road. Luckily the spin was brought to a quick end by the impact with the telephone pole on the side of the road. They bounced off the pole and somehow ended up back out on the road. Best part of the almost dying in a fiery car crash was that it'd cleared off the uninvited hitchhikers. It'd also served to knock loose most of the rest of the glass that'd been trying to hang on in the windows.

The only one in the car with a seatbelt on was Bart. A quick check showed that he was still snoozing peacefully in the backseat. A testament to the healing power of modern pharmaceuticals. LeBron had tears in his eyes and was holding his wrist. Drew was bleeding all over the place from a cut on his forehead. Yue had managed to perform some cirque de soleil worthy acrobatics to maintain her grip on the steering wheel throughout the hydro sliding extravaganza.

Drew pulled his t-shirt most of the way off so that the shirt was hanging down his back. He moved it around gingerly so that the neck part was covering the gash in his forehead. It served the purpose for now of stemming the flow of blood into his eyes. He shifted the shirt around some as he slid over to check on LeBron. He poked LeBron in the shoulder to get his attention. LeBron looked up still holding one of his hands.

"What's wrong with your hand?" Drew asked. LeBron held up his left hand. The top half of the pinkie finger on that hand was basically just dangling off the rest of the finger by the skin.

"It hurts so bad." LeBron stuttered out.

"I bet it does." Drew said with all the empathy he could muster. What he wanted to say was that it looked pretty damned disgusting. He kept that thought to himself and started poking around for something to set his brothers finger with. It wasn't the same as checking WebMD, but he did ask Yue what she thought they should do. All that either of them could come up with was feeding LeBron some drugs and taping up the finger. They'd leave the tape on for a few weeks and hope it magically healed.

He found the tape in the box of medical supplies they'd left in the car and turned back around to LeBron. He was a few shades paler than usual. Probably because he'd been listening to the medical consult between his siblings. The shrugs and confused sounding whispers of 'I don't know' probably hadn't filled him with a whole bunch of confidence. Not to mention that what Drew was about do to his finger was probably going to hurt a lot. Drew gave LeBron an Oxy from their dad's stash to prep him. He didn't say it out loud, but he was thinking the kid should probably have snorted it instead of dry swallowing the tiny pill. He was going to want pain relief way before that pill finally kicked in.

There'd been so many boxes of medical supplies in the U-Haul that they'd left a few bags of stuff out in the Traverse in case they needed it. They'd figured it was worth the risk of it being stolen to have some in the car in case they executed a quick getaway. That bet was paying off now. Out of the massive haul of supplies they'd dragged into the house all they'd run out to the garage with was what they were carrying or had shoved into their backpacks. The other gear in the car was extra stuff they'd thought it'd be nice to have like a box of canned food and some gallon jugs of purified water. The crazy way Yue was driving Drew was thinking they were going to be losing the car pretty soon too. Then they'd really be down to what they could carry.

In one of the bags there was a finger splint kit. It wasn't meant for pinkies, but it was way better than taping a pencil to his brother's finger and hoping for the best. Yue had suggested a popsicle stick, but it wasn't like they had a box of popsicles sitting in the trunk. Drew casually knocked the pencil away from the roll of white tape he'd found and opened the package for the splint. He spent some time trying to decipher the directions then just went with what the little pictures were showing. It wasn't like the directions were super helpful anyway. Lawyers tend to have more input into the directions on medical packaging than doctors. It's more about protection from liability than actually healing people.

"What do the directions say?" LeBron said pulling his hand back behind him and away from Drew.

"That we should call 911 or take you to an emergency room." Drew said scooting across the bench seat closer to LeBron who continued to scoot away from him until he was pressed up against the side of the car.

"Should we wake up dad?" LeBron gasped in obvious physical pain. The finger was starting to swell up already. Waking up Bart was the smart play. As a retired Sherriff who'd spent most of his life as a law enforcement professional in one capacity or another their dad was a trained first responder. If anybody in the car was going to know what to do about LeBron's dangling pinkie it was him. However, their dad had just slept through them slamming into trees and firing shotguns at monsters hanging off their roof. Drew wasn't really sure they could wake him up.

"I'll give it a try but if he doesn't wake up, we need to try out this splint. We can always fix it once dad wakes up if we do something wrong." Drew said climbing into the backseat and nudging their dad on the shoulder.

"Yesh." Bart slurred struggling to open his eyes. Yue had pretty much roofied the poor guy.

"LeBron broke his pinkie. We have a splint. What do we need to do?" Drew asked. He was enunciating each word clearly and loudly like he was trying to explain to someone who didn't speak English very well and also happened to be slightly deaf. Bart sat up.

"Show me." He said. His eyes focusing for a minute or two while he poked at LeBron's finger completely ignoring LeBron's howls of pain. He nodded and started to lie back down and go back to sleep.

"Well?" Drew asked nudging him some more.

"Put ice on it. Tape it to another finger or splint it the way it should go. Get him to the ER." Bart said with his eyes already closed. He was back asleep before Drew could come up with any follow-up questions. Seeing how his dad had pretty much echoed the directions under the drawings on the informative paper that came with the splint Drew decided it was go time. Disregarding the rest of the size one font instructions he grabbed LeBron's wrist and pulled it over so he could take a look at it.

Cringing on the inside he moved the top of the pinkie back to where it should be. The pinkie was flopping around while he tried to put the splint on. It was messed up enough that Drew could feel his stomach getting upset. He'd sprained his fingers and hurt himself plenty of times in wrestling and football but what LeBron had managed to do surpassed anything Drew had ever seen.

"Be careful! It hurts!" LeBron yelled at him. Yue chose that moment to run over some kind of big hump in the road causing Drew to bang LeBron's broken finger around. That resulted in a lot of cursing and LeBron getting some impressively large tears rolling down his cheeks.

"Sorry!" Yue called from up front. She was busy driving them through the Armageddon that was the small downtown area of the town next to them. Drew looked around and saw that he needed to hurry up with LeBron's finger because there could very well be more pressing matters popping up any second.

"No time to screw around bro! This is going to hurt." Drew said grabbing LeBron's hand again. LeBron took a deep breath and steeled himself for the pain. Once he looked ready enough Drew readjusted the pinkie to where he thought it should go. Hurrying before LeBron could snatch his hand away again, he splinted the pinkie and the finger next to it together. He wrapped it all up with a generous amount of tape and declared it a done deal.

"Thanks." LeBron said around his deep breathing. He sounded more like he was prepping to teach a Lamaze class than like he'd just gotten his finger splinted. Drew twirled around the blood-soaked T-Shirt on his head to try and get a non-blood-soaked spot over the bleeding gash on his forehead. He was getting a little concerned by the amount of blood pumping out up there. He hadn't brought a lot of extra shirts with him. Then he realized he had bags of bandages sitting all around him that he'd been rooting through for the splint he'd used on LeBron.

"How are we doing?" Drew asked Yue after he pulled out some gauze and thick bandages pads from one of the bags. Yue was driving, LeBron had a badly splinted broken pinkie, and his dad was in La La Land in the backseat, so Drew worked on putting the bandage on his head himself while talking to Yue. He was having a hard time looking out the window while trying to get the bandage situated. He needed one more hand and he'd be good.

"It looks like downtown got bombed. I haven't seen any crawlerz at all which has been a nice surprise." Yue reported.

"You do know you shouldn't say things like that out loud, right?" Drew said. He was half joking but when you're in a situation as bad as they were in why tempt fate?

"Whatever. How's dad? Where are we going? I think we need to look for another car. This ones accelerating funny and it's out of windows." Yue responded. She was unimpressed by Drew's superstitious nature. He always wore the same boxers on game day. He had a rabbit's foot on his key chain. She was surprised he could leave the house in the morning without eating a bowl of Lucky Charms.

The question about where they were going was a good one. They had almost a hundred gallons worth of gas in jugs in the back. That gave them a pretty good reach. They had a good space of time where they wouldn't have to worry about siphoning gas or attempting to figure out how to make a gas pump work with no electricity. Assuming every gas pump in America hadn't been drained dry in the space of time between finding out the crawlerz were coming and the crawlerz actually coming. Where could they go? Where would be better than where they'd started from?

"I say we head north. Florida sucks without air conditioning." LeBron said. His words sounded sleepy. The Oxy must finally be kicking in. About time.

"If we take the turnpike to the interstate there's pretty much no major towns for a long time. Besides maybe Gainesville?" Yue was thinking out loud while she drove. The streets were pretty empty other than the occasional wrecked or abandoned car. They passed one little hybrid looking deal that had a dead body sticking out of the windshield and both doors standing wide open. A crawler must've jumped in and broken its neck on impact. The occupants had ditched the car and taken off running. Drew guessed they probably hadn't made it too far. This wasn't a world where people squeamish about picking a cadaver out of their windshield had much of a future.

"North works for me. I'm tired of walking around with permanent jock itch." Drew chimed in.

"TMI." LeBron said

"Gross". His sister echoed the sentiment at the same time.

"Really." Drew said pointing at the dashboard. "There are bloody chunks from the inside of a dead stranger smeared all over the dashboard. Me mentioning my crotch rash is what gets at you both though?"

That cracked LeBron up. It may have been the Oxy fueling his inappropriate laughter, but it still got Yue and Drew chuckling along as well. It felt good to laugh about something again.

"North it is." Yue said turning onto the on-ramp that'd take them up on the toll road leading eventually to the turnpike. Drew decided that Yue had probably reached her threshold for dealing with stuff for the day. He generously forbade himself from asking why she was still using her blinkers every time she made a turn. At least for the rest of the night. He promised himself that if they were still alive in a day or two, he'd give her crap about it then.

Chapter 19: North

The turnpike was a great idea until it wasn't. Yue had been worried when they first got on the toll road that there was going to be massive car pileups. She'd pictured them having to get out and walk down the side of the road past mile after mile of stalled vehicles. It was the standard scene from a zillion end of the world type movies she'd watched with her brothers. It'd actually turned out to be pretty clear sailing until they hit the overturned tractor trailers on the turnpike. Thinking about it she realized there'd never really been a mass exodus type day. People had plenty of time to get where they wanted to be before the crawlerz started actually spreading across the country.

The overturned eighteen wheelers were stretched from guardrail to guardrail. It was still about an hour before the sun would be all the way up. There was already enough light to see the guardrails had been smashed flat on one side. Of course, it was the side with a steep slope going down into a drainage ditch that ran along the road.

"We might be able to make it around." Drew said doubtfully. He got out of the car and walked over to the edge of the road with his flashlight and rifle to check it out. LeBron followed along a second later.

They'd need to transform the Traverse into a gravity defying hovercar to make it around that side. LeBron and Drew had a rough time getting around it on foot. Once they finally made it around, they immediately walked over to check out the other side to see if it was a valid option instead. The other side was nice and flat. If it wasn't for the guardrail blocking them on that side, it would've been perfect. They hopped over the guard rail to walk back to the car. LeBron shined his light into the cab of the tractor trailer as they walked past. The dead body of the driver was seat belted in place. His face covered in dried blood as he dangled off the seat staring sightlessly forward.

"That guys going to be hanging out in his truck for forever." Drew attempted a joke. His delivery was flat thanks to having gotten way too good of a look at the driver. This was all a lot to process. The fact that civilization was done. Wiped out by some weird fungus infested Discovery channel mummy freak show. It was a bad zombie movie. It still didn't feel real. They were walking past a dead guy like it wasn't even a big deal.

"Eventually it'll be over. Someone will clean it all up. It may not be for a long time, but it'll happen. We just have to make sure we're still around." LeBron said in response. He was feeling a lot better now that the Oxy had kicked in. His broken finger had gone from debilitating pain to a dull throb.

"You sound like the overly serious narrator guy at the end of a movie. Have you been sneaking extra Oxy?" Drew asked smiling at his semi-stoned brother.

They walked back to the car and gave Yue the bad news. Since they couldn't go around the wreck, they were going to have to backtrack. Yue got them turned around while Drew worked on figuring out where they were. He was really missing the convenience of just being able to ask Siri to get him wherever he was going. Not that they really had a clue where they were going.

"If we get off at the next exit, we should be able to go around and get back on further north. Or, honestly, we could just stay on HWY-27. It pretty much goes straight north too." Drew said staring at the atlas.

"Does it go through a bunch of towns though? We want to stay away from towns. That's why I like turnpikes and interstates." Yue said before breaking into a big yawn. The yawn reminded all of them they'd been going hard with minimal sleep.

"Maybe we should stop and rest once we get off the turnpike. Look for a side road or something?" Drew asked.

"Sounds good to me. I'm in no real hurry to get to wherever it is we're going to end up going. If we could find a car with windows and less intestines that'd make me pretty happy." Yue said as she drove them the wrong way down the onramp to get off the turnpike. There was forest on both sides of the road. Yue looked for an opening then drove off the road and into the woods until they were hidden from view by the dense trees.

Drew started to say he'd take first watch, but Yue cut him off and told him to rest. She wanted to spend some time checking on their dad. She needed to change out his bandages and give him another dose of medicine. She was planning on checking Drews work on LeBron's finger as well. Drew put his head back on the seat and almost instantly fell asleep. LeBron had already passed out on the drive to the exit. Yue climbed over them to get into the third row with her dad.

Bart didn't look good. The stubble on his face didn't do anything to cover up how pale he looked. He'd always been such a vibrant passionate force in Yue's life that to see him as frail wasn't really something she'd been prepared for. Fighting back her emotions she shoved her hand over his mouth to make sure she could feel him breathing. She could but it seemed like really shallow breaths to her. She jostled him around as she swapped out his bandages hoping to wake him up. She smiled to herself thinking it was the same strategy she used to use on the infants she'd babysat for her mom's friends. If you didn't make them a little angry then they'd just keep falling asleep halfway through their bottles and the moms would freak out that you were starving their babies to death.

Poking Bart around didn't work. He was out for the count. Yue sat down and levered Bart's head into her lap. She stared down at his grizzled white stubble covered face while wondering how she was supposed to feed antibiotic pills to a sleeping man. Everything they were trying to do made her feel ineffectual and useless. She didn't have any delusions that she was up to the task of keeping her family alive. She needed Bart to wake up and take control. She needed her dad.

Sitting in the back with her dad's head resting in her lap she let herself cry silently for a few minutes. Once she felt like she'd taken the edge off of her frustration she got her thermos straw and the pills in position and smacked Bart on the cheek. When that didn't work, she smacked him harder and told him to wake up. Drew stirred around on the seat in front of her, but her dad remained sleeping. She poured some of the water from her thermos onto her dad's face while telling him to wake up again.

The water did the trick. She was able to get him to swallow a couple of pills before he closed his eyes and went back to sleep. Shifting his head off of her she moved up a seat to take care of LeBron. Drew had actually done a decent job splinting up his brother's finger, so she left that in place. Once she'd finished swapping out Drews blood-soaked head rag the Traverse was starting to look like a MASH rerun. She sat back down in the front seat of the running car and enjoyed the AC on her face.

What she didn't enjoy was the rain shower that passed over. It spent just enough time above them to make the inside of the car just the right level of miserably damp. She started checking the radio stations while she was sitting there. The FM bands all gave her nothing but static. The AM band had one station that she could just make out. She listened intently for about thirty minutes to the ramblings of the announcer. According to the man on the radio this was all some sort of UFO driven pod people government conspiracy to turn them all into impossible burgers to feed the people from Atlantis. In the thirty minutes she painstakingly spent picking out what the man was saying around the bursts of static the only two things she didn't hear blamed for the current situation were the loch ness monster and bigfoot.

She sighed and turned the radio off after a quick scan to validate none of the other channels were broadcasting anything. She turned the air conditioning up to get a few more blasts of cold air before she killed the engine. They were going to have to suffer some to conserve gas. She put her own seat back and reclined backwards looking out the broken windows around the car. Feeling comfortable with the cold air from the vent hitting her in the chest she closed her eyes to relax for a second.

She woke up confused. She'd been in the middle of a dream about being in the shower. It was dark outside. She was lying in a wet car seat that wasn't even reclined. Seeing the broken shards of glass around the edges of the window finally woke her up. She was supposed to be on guard duty! She sat up so fast she gave herself a head rush. She swiveled around to look behind her and saw that the boys were still both asleep. A loud roll of thunder echoed through the open car. Drew stirred then looked up at her.

"Is it night already? How long did I sleep?" He mumbled. He started fumbling around for the door handle. He needed to get out urgently and relieve the pressure in his bladder.

"It's not nighttime yet I don't think. Just the standard Florid afternoon liquid sunshine." Yue said nervously. Seeing Drew getting out of the car and standing in the rain made her realize she needed to urgently do the same thing. Except for her it was all a bit more complicated than just standing beside the car and letting it fly.

"Well what time is it?" Drew asked from the other side of the car as Yue positioned herself in the rain trying to hold the small umbrella over her head and squat down all at the same time. She decided to ignore him since she had no idea what the answer was. For all she knew it really was getting dark outside.

"It's about five." LeBron called out from inside the car. Evidently everyone had decided it was time to wake up. Yue realized the car was dead because it'd ran out of gas when she fell asleep with the engine still running. That meant she was going to have to fill up the tank. That also meant she was going to have to explain why the tank was empty.

"Hey Drew, can you help me top off the tank?" Yue asked. She was hoping he wouldn't notice that topping it off really meant filling it up. She was standing up holding the umbrella over her head as the wind picked up and started driving the rain sideways. Around the back LeBron had popped up the rear cargo door using it as a nice wide shelter to stand under while he took care of his business. He was the only one of them who wasn't soaking wet. He zipped up and went to sit back down in the car waggling his wounded hand around in the air.

"Sorry I can't be much help!" LeBron told Yue as he passed by her on his way to get back into the car. Not that it was going to be a whole lot more pleasant inside the windowless auto considering the rain was now pouring in from every direction. Yue muttered something unpleasant to LeBron as she met Drew in the trunk of the car. Drew grabbed a gas jug and Yue went with him to help pour it in the tank. It didn't really take two of them, but she was feeling guilty about having wasted the gas in the first place. She also wanted to make sure he didn't spill any of it.

"Did you fall asleep with the engine running?" Drew asked her quietly. Faced with the direct question Yue didn't see a way to avoid telling Drew the truth. She decided to just not answer.

"I'm going to check on dad." She replied to Drew who was grinning and shaking his head mockingly at her. Yue was pretty much always the perfect one in the family, so she was mortified to have been caught out in having made such a dumb mistake. A mistake that could've resulted in something a lot worse than just running out of gas.

She forgot all about her screwup when she looked into the third row and saw how miserable her dad looked. Bart was sweating like crazy. He smiled up at Yue as she lowered her hand to his forehead. He was burning up.

"I've got to hit the head." He told her. She stared at him strangely for a second before doing the mental math and translating his request. She'd heard the term before, but her dad had never used it with her, so it seemed weird. She chalked it up to the high fever and probable infection. She called out to Drew to come help her get dad out so he could use the head. Drew grinned at her use of the odd phrase.

"Aye aye shipmate." Drew spouted out as he put the jug of gas back into the Traverse and pressed the button for the lift gate to lower itself. He half-jogged around to the side and helped Yue get their dad out in the rain so he could take care of that trip to the head. By the time he was done they were all soaked to the bone. Yue was actually thankful for the heat and humidity. Hot and miserable was better than cold and miserable. She just wished they could be dry and miserable instead of wet and miserable.

"Now what?" LeBron asked loudly.

"Beats me but at least we shouldn't have to pull over for anyone to pee for a while." Drew said. Not that they should even bother considering they were all drenched anyway. The floorboards were covered in a decent amount of water. That couldn't be good. Especially considering all the electronic doodads this car was loaded down with. The sales rep had been sneaky enough to make sure their mom got in the most expensive car with the zillion cool features as the first step in the car search.

"I say we try and find a car with windows. This sucks." Yue said. She turned the key and the car started up on the first try. She let out a relieved sigh. She'd been afraid she'd also killed the battery by leaving the car on for so long.

"We need to find a vehicle with windows then a safe place to spend the night." Bart said from the third row. He was sitting up now which everyone took as a good sign. He was also making a lot of sense. Once the sun went down, they didn't want to be caught driving around in a car with no windows.

"Ok. Let's go." Yue said putting the car in drive and hoping they didn't get stuck in the mud driving out of the woods back to the road.

Chapter 20: That New Car Smell

Luckily the pricey soccer mom mobile came with all-wheel drive. Otherwise, Yue doubted they'd have made it through the rain-soaked ground back to the road. She'd offered to switch with Drew and let him drive so she could watch their dad, but Drew wanted his hands free so he could shoot. LeBron was going to have a hard time aiming with a rifle until his finger healed so he was sitting in his seat with a pistol in his good hand.

The misery meter was pegging out at this point. Everyone was suffering from something. Yue felt pretty lucky to only be dealing with some bruised ribs from jumping off the porch. Considering how much lead had been flying around when the policemen had come at them it'd been a miracle none of them were hurt. A miracle enabled by their mom's heroic sacrifice.

She couldn't make herself blame the cops. The cop they'd let go had seen all of the blood in the cab. The cop knew they'd murdered people for those supplies. They'd been absolutely in the wrong there. She was still having a hard time believing that they'd done that. It'd started the events that had eventually led to their mom dying. At the end of the day, they hadn't even taken a hundredth of those supplies with them when they were forced out of their house.

It was getting late so Yue was driving as fast as she thought was safe. They needed to be safely hidden before darkness came around. It was tough driving with no windshield. The faster she drove the more annoying the rain was. She was getting more and more frustrated as time wore on. She really wanted to hurry so they could look for a new vehicle. The country they were driving through right now was nothing but trees and empty fields. It was a good-sized road though so she knew it'd end up somewhere they should be able find a new ride.

"The first big town we're going to hit is Leesburg." Drew said from the middle seat. He was doing his best to keep the atlas from being destroyed by the wind and rain. He'd opened the umbrella and was using it to shield the atlas from the rain. He felt kind of bad about it knowing Yue was having to take the storm right in her face in the driver's seat. He didn't feel bad enough to switch spots with her though.

Off to the sides of the road they started seeing traces of civilization through the thick sheets of rain pouring down. Yue slammed on the brakes suddenly causing everyone to rock forward in their seats. The tires lost traction and they went sideways for a few sphincter tightening seconds. They only slid a few feet before the tires caught again. The tires squealed loudly. The smell of burnt rubber drifted up through the busted-out windows. Drew was fumbling with the umbrella trying to see what was going on. He'd dropped the freakin atlas down into the kiddie pool of a floor. LeBron was screaming in pain where he'd jammed his pinkie into the back of the seat.

"What is it?" Bart asked loudly from the backseat. He was looking out each window one at a time with his pistol pointed up at the ceiling.

"Roadblock." Yue said.

Up ahead of them were a couple of cop cars parked hood to hood across the road to keep people from going any further. No cops challenged them though. The lights on the cars weren't on. There were a couple of bodies lying on the road around the parked police vehicles. There was room to go around the cars in the median and keep going. Yue was thinking they may have just found their new ride though.

"Those Expeditions are pretty nice. I bet the keys are still in them." Bart said from the back. He'd been thinking along the same lines as his daughter.

Drew noticed everyone had kind of turned to stare at him. Sighing he got out of the Traverse and walked slowly towards the police vehicles. They were the nice extra-large Ford Expeditions. They'd be loaded down with weapons and supplies hopefully. Not to mention the Expeditions wouldn't be the normal ones you could buy off the Ford lot. These would be the supped-up law enforcement models.

The rain began to taper off after he got out of the car. Florida afternoon storms were often like that. They blew in strong then were gone almost as fast as they appeared. The decaying bodies on the road by the police cars were gross. None of the bodies were dressed like cops. Drew quickly surmised that the cops manning the roadblock must have been charged by a large pack of the infected. They'd taken out some of them but been bitten in the process. The cops who'd been bitten were now wandering the countryside looking for brains. He felt vaguely sorry for the police officers. Based on where the bodies had been dropped, they'd held their fire until it was obvious the people running at them were really going to attack them.

He didn't think any less of them for holding their fire. No one had been prepared for this. Thinking back to the President's speech there were probably some people living it up in semi-normal circumstances on secret bases right now, but the bulk of humanity was circling the toilet bowl. He got in and looked for the keys. They were nowhere to be found in the first car but in the second they were still in the ignition. A few quick checks later and Drew was bouncing out of the car to run back over to Yue.

"The battery's dead but otherwise we should be good. I say we dump some gas in the tank and jump it. It's way nicer than this cesspool we've been riding around in." Drew said indicating the general nastiness of their current ride.

A few minutes later they had Bart transferred to their new ride and were hooking up jumper cables. The powerful engine on the Ford rumbled back to life once they'd let the cables sit on it for a minute. They transferred the rest of their gear and collected an abandoned shotgun and service pistol off the road. They were wet and nasty after lying on the ground in the rain and heat for days. They'd be fine once they wiped them down and got rid of the dead body funk.

"The front of this thing is pretty much built for ramming into crawlerz." LeBron announced from where he was standing admiring the cow catcher looking steel contraption covering the grill of the big beast of a truck.

"I know you must be tired from carrying the bags of gauze and everything, but can you help get the gas jugs in the back. You can use your non-handicapped hand." Yue said. She sounded a little pissed off. Between LeBron babying his hand and Drew playing with all the buttons and knobs in the front of the truck she'd been the one carrying the bulk of the stuff from their old car to the new one.

"There's somebody coming down the road." LeBron said squinting his eyes to try and see better. He couldn't tell if it was just some guy running towards them or a blood thirsty adrenaline-fueled monster who wanted to rip their heads off and dine on their eyeballs. When the guy started screaming like a lunatic that pretty much answered the question.

"Help me get the gas in the back!" Yue said nervously. She was struggling with the heavy jugs. All she could think was if they drove off and left them, they were then at the mercy of the random gas gods. They'd already been forced to leave behind way too many of their supplies.

LeBron ran around to the back and picked the jugs up as high as he could with one arm while Yue swung them into the back. Bart was yelling at them to forget the damned gas and get in the truck. Drew was in the truck waiting to floor the accelerator once his brother and sister got back in. He was focused on trying to get past the surger before it bashed in their windows. He assumed it was a surger anyway since it was screaming and running around in the daylight.

Bart carefully aimed and put some holes in the surger when it got close enough for him to feel like he wasn't wasting bullets. As soon as the surger hit the ground Bart leaned back in his seat to wipe the sweat off his forehead. The act of shooting had sapped a lot of his energy. He was burning up even though the air conditioning vent was blasting cold air directly down on him.

Attracted by the sound of the weapon firing more surgers were emerging from the woods. The roadblock had been in front of a fairly large suburb of Leesburg. The population of that town was in the middle of the nightmarish process of being converted from normal humans to crawlerz. In that transition period there were still plenty of them in the surger phase where they didn't freak out when they saw the sun. They basically only freaked out when they saw or heard something that told them prey was nearby. They'd begun their permanent acid trip into oblivion.

The surgers ran through the strip of woods separating the highway from the large golf course community. They broke through and sprinted full speed in the direction of the young man and woman struggling to get jugs of gas into the back of a police utility vehicle. They screamed in a mixture of lustfulness and rage as they ran. In their chemically crazed consciousnesses they were mighty animals filled with hunger and the humans ahead were their prey. Driven by multiple versions of that insane vision they accessed parts of themselves normal humans couldn't consciously summon. The surgers launched into extreme tachycardia as their hearts pumped blood at an insane rate through their bodies. Their adrenal glands opened up giving them superhuman strength.

Yue punched the button to automatically lower the back door and shoved LeBron around the truck. He looked back at her to see what the hurry was. He'd seen Bart shoot the surger charging at them. That quick glance backwards showed him a line of surgers bouncing towards them faster than should be possible. The sound wave of their ferocious cries reached him as he looked curdling his blood. He whirled around to go where Yue was shoving him. When he whirled around, he hit the side of the truck with his splinted hand.

Yelping in pain he scrambled to the door and jumped in. Yue climbed in directly behind him. She'd barely shut the door before Drew was rocketing them down the road. The surgers barreling into the side of the police car like rams. How they'd made it across the road impossibly fast like that was unfathomable to everyone in the truck. Drew jerked the wheel to the right and an old paper coffee cup from Dunkin Donuts basically exploded throwing coffee all over his lap. A middle-aged man with a face blistering from a horrible sunburn slammed his head into the driver's side window. The window rocked inward but didn't shatter. The surger tripped and flipped back into the road.

Another thump where one of the surgers tried to jump headfirst into the big SUV and wound up split apart on the cow catcher mechanism. A splatter of blood flew up onto the windshield. Drew fumbled around to find the windshield wipers and get the window cleaning spray shooting out. The wipers smeared the scarlet fluid all over the windows before finally getting sprayed off. It left a fine red line where the wipers didn't reach. Behind them the surgers turned and sprinted after their taillights. One of them keeled over with an exploded heart. It's feet still twitching trying to catch up with the truck. Not a single thought of self-preservation firing off in its rewired brain.

"It's getting dark out." LeBron announced spinning back around to face the front.

"We're only about ten miles from where we Grand Theft Autoed this ride. We've still got some time before it gets too dark." Drew said. The headlights had already come on since they were set to auto. Yue of course hadn't missed that little detail.

"The truck thinks it's dark. Why don't we pull in over in that park?" She asked. "I need a place to get everybody bandaged and medicated. I don't feel like doing it with those things ripping the truck apart around me."

Drew almost argued some more before realizing he really had no reason to be arguing. It wasn't like they had an appointment to get to. The only thing on their current itinerary was basically 'try not to die'. That high priority task pretty much busied out every day on their calendars. It was the kind of mission he could really get behind. Yue was probably right with the slow and easy approach being the best. With those thoughts in mind, he cut across the grassy median and down the dirt road leading to a park featuring multiple baseball diamonds.

There was a gate across the road leading into the park that was locked with a chain and padlock. The gate had an aluminum closed sign dangling off it. Drew felt like the people in charge of the security for the field should be fired. There was no fence or anything to keep him from simply driving around the gate. There were some short hedges, but it wasn't like Drew was super worried about the paint job on their new cop mobile. He drove through the hedges then followed the road to the furthest parking lot and put the Expedition in park.

Yue shuffled around checking on everyone's injuries. She proclaimed Drew to be pretty much healed as long as he didn't pick at the big scab forming on his forehead. Assuming he'd pick at the big scab she went ahead and put a new bandage around his head to cover the big gash and keep it clean. She told LeBron to stop whacking his broken finger against stuff every five seconds or he was never going to heal. She saved their dad for last since he was the one that she was most worried about. She realized she was treating everyone in sort of a reverse triage. She wondered if that was to try and build up her courage to check on her dad's wounds.

Her fears were realized when she took off the bandage on his shin and saw the angry red lines leading out from the wound. Bart was burning up. They'd scored about thirty thermometers in the U-Haul load from the drug store but none of them had made it into the supplies they'd ended up with in the Traverse. Not that they really needed one to tell that Bart was seriously sick. He accepted the news with good grace. He knew he was burning up with a fever already and knew exactly what those red lines meant.

"Listen up kids. I know you're going to want to try and save me but if the antibiotics Yue is pumping me full of aren't doing the trick my time may be fast approaching." Bart said looking around to make sure everyone was listening.

"We just need to find a different kind of antibiotic. It's not like I'm a pharmacist or something." Yue interrupted. She was in a state of extreme frustration. She'd done everything she could think of to do for their dad. He still wasn't doing better. Based on how his wounds looked today he was starting to do a lot worse.

"I'm not saying to start picking out my coffin just yet. I'm saying that you will not risk your lives to try and save mine. I want the three of you focused on each other. You're going to have to do things to survive. I want you to do them with a clear conscience. At the end of the day all that really matters is the three of you surviving. Just keep going north until you find somewhere you can live your lives." Bart said. A little dramatically to Yue's ear. LeBron and Drew seemed to be eating it up though.

"You're not dying. You're going to rest in the back seat and suck down medicine until you're good to go. Now shut up and go to sleep. No more talk. You're depressing me." Yue finished talking giving Bart a kiss on his forehead to show she loved him. Bart was already fast asleep. She hoped he'd at least heard her little speech before he closed his eyes to rest. His forehead felt like it was on fire to Yue's lips when she kissed it.

In the last lingering rays of light, they all got out to stretch and relieve themselves. Drew walked over to the truck when he was done and rubbed his hands over the side of it. Yue saw him and asked what he was doing.

"Come check this crap out." Drew said in an awed sounding voice.

LeBron and Yue had been on the opposite side of the truck. They walked over and stared in awe at what Drew had noticed. There were some pretty massive dents in the side of the Expedition that hadn't been there before.

"Are those from the surgers?" LeBron asked.

"I don't remember pissing off any water buffalo at the drive thru safari today." Drew responded.

"You've been waiting to say that ever since you saw these dents, haven't you?" Yue asked. She meant it as a joke, but it came out flat. The size of those dents meant the surgers were even stronger than they'd thought.

"I guess that explains the crawlerz being able to beat their way through the wall and right into our bathroom hideout." LeBron said seriously.

Touching the dents and feeling how deep they were was sobering for all of them. If they'd gotten cornered, they'd already be dead. It brought home to them in a big way that they needed to avoid populated areas. Yue climbed in the truck after LeBron thinking to herself that the selection of the baseball field had been an excellent choice. She couldn't even imagine driving through a city like Leesburg at night with those things running around hunting them.

Drew took first watch. They left the engine running but had the air on very low to try and conserve gas. None of them were sure if that actually helped or not but they figured they should at least try. It wasn't like they could go to the local gas station and get a fill-up. If they wanted gas or groceries or anything else, they'd be digging through people's houses rather than through the mostly ripped apart husks of grocery stores and gas stations.

In the woods across the field from where they were camped for the night several piles of leaves began shifting around as the sun descended further from the sky. The crawlerz who'd tunneled into the leaves had been running through the woods earlier chasing vague sounds they'd heard on the wind. When they'd sensed the sun coming up the pack of five had quickly buried themselves in the mud and muck to keep the light from piercing their brains with its painful images.

They stood in the woods now attracted to another sound. The sound of an engine running somewhere nearby. They meandered around for a minute getting a fix on the sound. Once one of them figured it out they all sprinted out of the woods towards the Expedition on the other side of the baseball diamond. They ran unnaturally fast without making a sound. Their blood lust lending them the energy needed to virtually fly across the field to attack.

Chapter 21: Death by the Dashboard Lights

Drew was staring out the front window of the truck mechanically loading bullets into extra rifle magazines when he thought he saw something in the side mirror on the passenger side. He leaned over to get a better look right as LeBron managed to roll onto his finger and wake up moaning in pain.

"You ok?" Drew asked shifting back into the driver's seat. He glanced back to see LeBron waving his hand around in the air like that was going to somehow help with the pain. Yue had been pretty stingy with the pain pills for LeBron. She'd kept him on high strength Tylenol. Drew was thinking they should let him pop a Demerol if it'd shut him up. He was going to give away their location if he kept hurting himself and yelling like that.

"Yeah, I'm great man. I'm going to take a quick whiz since I'm up. Probably get attacked by a raccoon and it'll bite my stupid finger." LeBron said.

"If a raccoon bites something while you're outside taking a whiz you better hope it's your finger." Drew joked as LeBron pulled up on his door handle. The overhead dome light popped on when the door opened. Drew was wondering how to turn that off when the back window shattered.

LeBron immediately tried pulling his door shut but instead found himself in a tug of war with a hand that'd snaked into the small opening that'd been there. A loud slam on the other side of the truck told Drew they were under attack. He put the truck in reverse and floored it. He could see the crawlerz in the rear-view camera. Except for the one trying to get in LeBron's door. LeBron's door had flown open when Drew put the truck in reverse.

For a second LeBron had been staring at an older woman with psycho eyes who couldn't figure out why the door was flying open and pulling her arm with it. The grey-haired woman was wearing a turtleneck and a pencil skirt. The teal covered turtleneck was covered in blood on the front of it. She looked like the cover model for a library themed zombie movie. Her lips peeled back from her teeth as she lunged forward to attack LeBron. LeBron was frozen in fear. He felt like his insides had all been soaked in ice water. He was positive he was about to die right until the open door slammed into the librarian from hell knocking her spinning to the ground.

"What the hell!" Bart yelled from the back trying to sit up and see through the haze of narcotics Yue had given him. Now the extremely buzzed old warrior was waving his pistol around trying to figure out if he should be shooting something. None of that boded well for the people in the truck. The crawlerz were probably perfectly safe.

Yue was turned around in her seat with her pistol pointed into the back where they'd all heard the window shatter. That loud completely unexpected noise had been what startled Yue and Bart awake. Waking up to the big truck going backwards at full speed through a dark parking lot with enraged nightmare beasts trying to break in from every angle was a lot. Yue started yelling at Bart to get down so she could see if there actually was something in the back of the Expedition. She couldn't tell with her dad sitting up flailing his pistol everywhere.

The librarian had gotten up and was chasing them across the parking lot. A pair of arms appeared on the side of the busted out back window followed by a face a second later. A face that Yue and Bart put multiple bullets through and all around. They kept shooting until the body tumbled off to the side. Yue wasn't sure how accurate her dad he been in all the excitement. She wouldn't be super surprised if they found holes in the roof the following day. Assuming they were still alive the following day.

A big assumption at the moment. Drew saw the trees and bushes at the end of the parking lot in the rear-view camera view. A pale hand slapped the glass right next to his face. Not really knowing what was going to happen he slammed on the brakes and turned the wheel hard to the left. The rear of the car swung to the left which was fortunate since that was the way he wanted to go. Hoping he wasn't going to blow up the transmission he shifted into drive. Nothing exploded, so he switched his foot back from the brake to the accelerator and stomped down hard.

The Expedition spun out for a couple of seconds then the tires grabbed hold and they shot off towards the main road. The crawlerz chasing them shifted their trajectories to aim right at them again. Drew couldn't tell how many of them there were. He'd heard Yue yelling at him that she'd killed one. They were everywhere banging on the sides of the truck trying to get in. He saw LeBron prepping to shoot the next time he saw anything through his window. So much for having a vehicle that kept the rain outside of it.

Yue screamed when a bloody hand smashed through the window right beside her head. They'd heard the crawler out there beating on the side of the Expedition. It must've been squatting on the runner and beating on the door. The hand it shoved at Yue now was a broken mess. It hadn't been able to handle the abuse of pounding on the side of the heavy-duty Expedition. The broken fingers refused to work right for the monster which is why Yue wasn't snatched right out of the window.

She raised her pistol shooting at the crawler while sliding backwards away from the shattered glass. The eerily quiet crawler was pushing its way in through the shattered window when one of Yue's bullets found its mark. She was basically on top of LeBron by that point. Yue continued screaming her head off and pulling the trigger without even looking. She didn't look up until she was out of bullets. The body of her attacker was firmly stuck in the window with multiple blood drenched bullet holes.

Drew turned the wheel hard to miss one that was trying to jump right through the windshield. They skidded off the dirt road onto the baseball diamond. Drew kept the pedal floored to round the bases as fast as possible. He wanted nothing more than to be driving them out over the same hedges they'd arrived through earlier.

"Do you see them!" He yelled back behind him.

"There's two of them still coming!" LeBron yelled back. Yue was busy trying to push the corpse of her kill back out the window before it dripped brain gunk all over her. She'd be hitting the hand sanitizer hard if they made it out of there alive.

Drew didn't slow down when he saw the small drainage ditch in front of them. He had no idea how many of those things were out there converging on them right now. Slowing down was death. Driving at a high-speed right into a ditch might also be death. He yelled into the backseat for seat belts. He knew they probably didn't have time but at least he could say that he'd tried.

The truck hit the ditch and shuddered before popping out of it and going airborne. It was a big truck to go off the ground like that. The chrome grill caught a crawler on the scalp as it jumped at them. Drew never even saw the one that left its hair and part of its skull stuck between the chrome fender pieces. The truck landed in the outfield of the final field hard and bounced again before digging deep into the mud. The wheels spun and their momentum carried them forward at a breakneck pace.

Drew flipped on the high beams and saw a man shape running at them from the left. He was more interested in the hedges up ahead. He ignored the shape darting towards them and focused on hitting the hedges in the same spot he'd hit them on the way in. He didn't want to find out now that there were concrete barriers, or anything else hidden by the innocent looking shrubbery. Ignoring all the other distractions he kept the truck pointed at the hole in the hedges he wanted to hit. Directly behind him he heard shots fired. He hoped that meant the shape he'd seen had gotten close enough to be taken out.

They ripped through the hedge and bounced again as Drew drove like a maniac to get them back on the main road. He didn't want to have to slow down to turn left onto the road, so he angled them to go up through the median again instead. The shocks were sorely tested but his gamble paid off as they transitioned semi-smoothly onto the main road with no need to slow down. With the tires gripping the concrete Drew continued to drive it like he stole it.

"I think we lost them!" LeBron yelled. His statement followed by the grotesque sound of a human body sliding out of a broken window. It fell to the road below to be left behind like an oversized bag of fast-food wrappers tossed out the window.

A human shaped shadow slammed into the front grill of the Expedition where it splattered like a water balloon filled with chunky red sauce. Drew got the wipers going after swerving all over the road and almost crashing. It had taken him a second to realize the person yelling in fear was himself.

"There's more coming! Drive!" LeBron screamed at him.

Drew took off again. His hands were shaking so bad it was hard for him to hold the wheel. Yue was asking if they should turn off the lights. He put on the high beams instead.

"This isn't the time to be an obstinate ass!" Yue yelled at him. It was one of her favorite things to call him. The familiarity of being called an obstinate ass actually relieved some of his shaking.

"Trying to find county road 48. It'll take us back to the toll road. If we miss it then we end up in Leesburg where we'll probably end up not good." Drew replied. It was annoying being underestimated all the time. Just because he was a jock didn't mean he was dumb.

They tore along a long stretch of road surrounded by the woods again. They were all really starting to love the middle of nowhere. Yue was thinking she'd love to transport them all to BFE right now. Wherever that formerly derogatory phrase ended up dropping them off at. Drew was driving at least seventy even when there were cars and crap in the road he had to dodge. Crawlerz were still popping out of the woods and giving chase fairly frequently.

"How are they so fast?" LeBron asked as one almost caught up to them after sprinting across the median to try to get at them. The things limbs were a blur as it galloped behind striving to catch up. It's hands seeming to hit the ground as often as its feet. It's eyes glowing red in the brake lights behind them. LeBron stared in fascinated horror.

"You're the one who showed us all of those videos." Yue said. The videos had shown the phenomenal physical capabilities of the crawlerz. It'd been like one of those got talent shows but featuring demon possessed people instead of janitors who could sing really good. They'd watched disbelievingly as crawlerz scurried straight up telephone poles and easily leapt onto the tops of one-story homes.

Somehow those videos had served to make the threat seem less real. Watching something like that on TV filmed somewhere like Sweden didn't inspire Americans to pack their bags and load their guns. The bulk of the citizens of the good old USA had done what they typically did when a threat was reported on the news. They'd watched and waited assuming the news people were overreacting. Even if something like that was happening in Sweden it'd never make it across the whole world to impact them.

It was the same reason the media shouldn't report the little storms off the coast of Africa that were going to turn into hurricanes. After hearing so often of storms coming to destroy them most people in the standard hurricane zones learned to only half-listen to the news reporters. The men in the yellow slickers standing beside the beach trying to look like the sprinkles they were getting hit by justified the full-on foul weather gear from head to toe. It becomes obvious they're hamming it up for the ratings when you see a kid on a tricycle ride by behind them on the street.

Unfortunately, this time no one had been crying wolf. The threat was a million times worse than anyone had imagined. The price of complacency in this case was a very steep one. One that Drew was determined his family wouldn't pay. Losing their mom had been bad enough. As if that train of thought was an answered prayer the lights revealed the street sign that he'd been feverishly scanning the intersections they drove through for. He'd been getting paranoid they'd drive right past it.

Yue had to blast another crawler out of her window when Drew slowed down to make the left turn in the intersection. Bart had woken up and was slumped against his back window staring out at the landscape as they drove. Drew gunned it hearing the big engine roar with power. They drove through a big pile of debris in the middle of the road with Drew saying the millionth prayer of the night in hopes that they didn't rip open any tires. He couldn't see them, but he could feel that there was a contingent of crawlerz closing in on them. It was that fear that was driving him to drive too fast.

One more crawler got close enough to pound on the driver side door. It tried to reach through his window but stumbled on something in the road and quickly fell behind the speeding truck. Drew continued to accelerate as he went around turns at a speed that had everyone convinced that they were on the verge of rolling into a ditch.

"Slow down! We'll be just as dead if we crash!" Yue berated Drew. He slowly let his foot off the accelerator after multiple assurances that they'd outrun the threats. In the middle of nowhere again Drew took a hard right onto a small road leading to a dairy farm. He drove them through a field and into a small thicket of trees where he turned the engine off. They sat there just listening for a few minutes to see if they heard anything. When they didn't hear or see anything they relaxed.

"Let's keep it down this time. I'm leaving the engine turned off. Two of us on watch all night long. One looking forward one looking back." Drew ordered.

"Got it. No Metallica and keep the lights off. How do we get these stupid dome lights to stay off?" Yue asked. She was playing with the light in the ceiling. She finally got the cover off and solved the problem by removing the little light bulbs.

Drew looked at his phone really quickly and noted it'd only been dark for about two hours. It was going to be a long night.

Chapter 22: Ghetto Tank

They made it through the night without any more excitement. It turned out you just couldn't sleep without air conditioning. With the truck turned off it was uncomfortably hot and humid in the little copse of trees Drew had parked them in. Every time they heard a squirrel drop a nut outside, they grabbed their guns positive they were all about to die. They switched off who was on watch periodically, but no one really got anything in the neighborhood of good rest. They did the two awake and one sleeping arrangement the entire night since they wanted Bart to get as much sleep as possible.

"Life without air conditioning isn't worth living." Yue grumbled grumpily as the sun came up. Dawn was the signal for ending the moratorium on conversations. They still needed to be quiet, but it wasn't quite as life or death. There weren't as many surgers running around during the day as there were crawlerz at night.

"I feel you." LeBron said. He looked up at this brother in the front seat. Drew was out cold. There was a long string of drool dangling out of his mouth.

"That would make a great profile pic." Yue joked. She sobered up quickly when she crawled into the backseat to check on their dad. Bart grinned up at her from the backseat. There was a fine sheen of sweat on his forehead.

"Good morning sugar bear. How are you feeling today?" He asked.

"Fine dad. The question is how are you feeling today?" She sat down on the end of the bench seat by his feet and stared at him waiting for a response. He kept quiet for a moment working up an inventory of all his aches and pains to report to her. She waited patiently knowing she'd have to multiply his daily pain report by five to get close to the real number. She was a little worried he might get hooked on the pain pills. She'd decided she'd rather deal with him becoming an addict than make him deal with being in a ton of pain though. It was one of those damned if you do and damned if you don't kind of scenarios.

"Other than the raging fire in my body from the infection, missing your mom and the general discomfort of sleeping outside in Florida not too bad. Oh yeah. There's the pain also. I'm not a big fan of the pain." Bart said smiling to soften the impact of his report. The misty-eyed look he got when he talked about their mom just about broke Yue's heart.

"Great dad. Here's a bunch of drugs to shut you up." Yue handed Bart two antibiotics, a Tylenol, and a Tylenol with codeine. She'd decided if one antibiotic didn't do the trick, she'd double it up and try different ones. She had no idea if they might counteract one another or anything. She was glad her dad's spirits seemed slightly better. She'd given him a whole valium the day before because he'd seemed overly depressed. He'd talked to himself while giggling for about an hour. She really wanted to avoid giving him another valium. She never wanted to relive that ultra-awkward experience ever again.

"I really wish those freaks would stop busting our windows out." Drew muttered through a big yawn as he woke up. LeBron had poked him a few times to get him moving. It'd belatedly occurred to LeBron that they should have had one of the people who were awake sitting in the driver's seat the night before. They'd left Drew in that seat the entire night. If something had happened, they'd have had to wake Drew up to drive away. As someone who'd had to wake Drew up many times LeBron knew it wasn't always a quick or pretty process.

"Yeah. The most annoying things about the killer clowns chasing us is having to replace the broken windows. We're going to have a really hard time getting decent rates on car insurance again when this is all over." LeBron replied sarcastically. He was scratching himself vigorously. His exposed skin had provided sustenance to a swarm of ravenous mosquitoes thanks to the missing windows. He really hoped the virus that created the aforementioned killer clowns wasn't transmittable by bug bites. He also wished he hadn't thought about the possibility of catching it by bug bite. Now he was going to be paranoid.

"I know. The death is way worse. The window thing does suck though. Is there anything in the back we could use to seal off the windows?" Drew asked. He was picturing duct tape and ponchos.

There was indeed duct tape and ponchos available in the back of the big utility vehicle. There was also a bunch of other gear including a nice sized toolbox filled with random tools. Drew was looking at a giant pack of zip ties he'd found. He had an idea. He didn't want to say it out loud because he was afraid it'd sound stupid if actually verbalized. Then he realized it was just his sister and brother standing there.

"What if we armor up the windows with stop signs? We could poke holes in the metal and then just tie wrap the signs over the windows. We could run the tie wrap around the window frame." Drew was standing up showing them what he was thinking of. The more he showed them the more animated he got. He was thinking it might be a pretty good idea after all.

"How do we see?" Yue asked him.

"We could poke holes in the signs so we could see out of them. There's metal shears and loppers in the back of the truck. There's hammers and screwdrivers to make holes in the signs to thread the tie wraps through." Drew said.

"Won't the sharp metal inside the holes cut the tie wraps apart?" LeBron asked.

"I really don't know dude. I haven't ever tried to tie wrap a bunch of signs to a big truck to save myself from superhuman psychos before." Drew said testily.

"We have plenty of duct tape. We could use that to dull the edges." LeBron said thinking through the problems he was seeing in his head. He completely ignored Drew getting frustrated with him.

"What about the front windshield?" Yue asked.

"What about it?" Drew shot back. He really just wanted to get started on strapping signs over the currently broken windows. Leave it to Yue and LeBron to make everything extra complicated.

The conversation went around in circles for a few more minutes. It got heated a couple of times thanks to everyone being on edge and having basically zero sleep. They finally decided as a group that it was an idea worth pursuing. Which was a good thing since otherwise Drew would've just tried it himself. They told Bart the idea when Yue woke him up to change his bandages and he said it sounded good to him. He recommended they try to scrape up some chicken wire for the front windshield if they could find some. As far as the back window went, they had the fancy rear view cameras so covering it up was no big deal.

They agreed to stop when they saw signs along the way that they could use. Or if anything else looked like it might work, they'd stop for it. If they weren't avoiding populated areas the ideal situation would've been to find a Home Depot or someplace similar. That'd obviously be a lot easier than trying to duct tape traffic signs to cover the missing windows. Ideal or not that was what they were planning to do. You have to do what you can with what you've got where you're at.

They started the morning just a few miles from the toll road, but it was late afternoon by the time they rolled up to the on-ramp. The police SUV had received an apocalypse makeover. A pretty rough one. A bent stop sign was strapped to the back-passenger door. It was covered by a poncho duct taped over it. A deer crossing sign and another stop sign sealed off the back window. Those two had taken the rest of the duct tape and a lot of zip ties to get to stop flapping around when they started driving over twenty miles per hour.

They'd put a ton of work plus at least one fingernail into something they all knew wouldn't last more than a few seconds if they were attacked. Duct tape and tie wraps wasn't going to stop creatures that could pound huge dents into the solid metal sides of the truck they were in. It'd slow them down a lot more than glass would though. Hopefully giving them the edge that they may need to escape. Then they could spend the next day replacing ripped tie wraps and sign hunting.

The first test for their metalworking skills was running down the on-ramp straight at them. It was a guy dressed up in full on fireman regalia including the helmet with the shield covering his eyes. If he hadn't been running faster than an Olympic track star they may have wondered if he was actually infected or not. As it was, they were feeling pretty good about shooting the guy.

Drew stopped the truck about thirty yards from the man. LeBron lined up a shot using the bottom of the window to help him steady his rifle since his pinkie was all messed up. The first shot rocked the fireman's head backwards. The strap around his chin kept the helmet from flying off. Yue poked her brother in the back.

"Stop showing off and just drop the guy. Dad told us not to try for headshots unless they were close. Also, he's wearing a helmet genius." She said.

LeBron muttered something under his breath in reply then dropped the barrel down slightly to sight in on the area around the guy's heart instead. The fireman was already running full speed at them again. LeBron focused on his breathing like his dad had showed him and let the sound of the gun firing surprise him. A small red geyser erupted out of the front of the man's coveralls, but he kept coming. LeBron put a few more bullets into the fireman's chest.

The man finally collapsed onto the ground. He was still struggling to move his body to get at them until he eventually just lay there without moving in a slowly widening pool of blood. Drew kept the vehicle sitting where he'd stopped for LeBron to shoot. None of them said anything for a minute while LeBron slowly pulled his rifle back into the truck. It was like they'd hit a new level of wanton killing. LeBron was shaking.

"I thought you were going to let him try to punch through the stop sign." Drew joked from the front seat as he started driving up the ramp past the body of the fireman.

"We went with the not letting it into the car to eat us alive plan instead." Yue responded rubbing LeBron's back.

"Alright. Let's stick with that plan. Where to today kids?" Drew called out jauntily trying to raise everyone's spirits. He didn't like the weird place they'd all gone after dropping that guy.

"North." LeBron said quietly trying to join in on the banter.

Drew nodded. That was definitely still the plan. They'd talked it over during the day with Bart joining in the discussion during those periods of time he was actually awake. They'd continue heading north and hopefully come up with a more detailed plan along the way. Worst case they'd get far enough north that the humidity and heat wouldn't suck so much before they ran out of gas. They were planning on travelling exclusively during daylight hours. The infected people in the surger phase would get less and less as time went on making daytime the safe time.

The turnpike was deserted other than that one infected fireman they'd killed on the onramp. They drove past a toll plaza and kept on going. Once they passed the toll plaza there was pretty much nothing else to see until they reached the merger with I-75. They'd only been driving on the interstate for a few minutes when they saw a car on the side of the road. Two men were working on changing a tire. There was another car sitting behind that one with a woman and a few kids in it.

Drew slowed down to see if they could help. The men changing the tires stood up and turned around with long guns in their hands. The expressions on their faces made it obvious what'd happen if Drew pulled over. LeBron gave the men a jaunty wave as Drew accelerated past them. That was the kind of world it was now. You looked out for yourself and your family. Everyone else could go to hell. He could get used to that.

Chapter 23: Don't be a Hero

For whatever reason the interstate was packed in comparison to the turnpike. After passing the people working on changing their tire the traffic picked up to the point where it was almost like a normal day. Albeit a normal day where every car speeding up to pass you had to be considered a threat. Not to mention the random surgers who'd jump out on the road and try to beat their way into the truck. They did get to test out the stop sign idea and it worked. It was a good thing it worked because they needed to do it for another window after driving the interstate gauntlet for less than an hour. The surger who'd smashed that window had almost made it into the front passenger seat. A very freaked out Drew had come close to losing control of the truck. He'd screamed out in surprise while pulling the trigger on his pistol as fast as he could to get rid of the unwanted hitchhiker.

"Do you guys think it'll be the crawlerz who get us or just some regular people who need gas?" LeBron asked. It was a dark question around a dark topic but very relevant to their situation.

"We avoid everybody. Drew if you see a pretty girl on the side of the road showing some leg, I want you to drive like the devil himself is chasing us. The same if you see a little kid or an old woman. It's a different world today than it was a couple of months ago. People will cut our throats now for the jugs of gas we have in the trunk." Bart advised seriously from the third row.

"What if we see a kitten who really looks like it could use some milk?" Drew asked with a straight face.

"Runover that little thieving furball. Milk don't grow on trees." LeBron said smirking.

"Good lord. We could've picked from like a million different kids to adopt. It's like we used up all of our luck when we got Yue." Bart said shaking his head and trying to hold back an errant grin.

"You absolutely should've stopped while you were ahead." Yue said.

The good-natured back and forth in the car kept going as Yue leaned back and listened. Her brothers busy competing to see who could come up with the hardest type of hitchhiker for them to bypass. Yue was happy to hear their dad occasionally chime in. He'd been quiet most of the morning. When she changed his bandages, she'd noted the infection appeared to be getting worse. If she saw someone on the side of the road in a doctor or nurses' outfit, she'd gladly toss them a jug of gas for a second opinion.

She looked out the window as Drew drove past an RV. What a great idea! They were driving around in a big comfortable house on wheels. They didn't have anything welded over the windows though, so they were most likely sacrificing security for comfort. The big, bearded guy sitting in the front passenger seat was glaring at them pretty hard as they drove by. He had good reason to be glaring since Yue was already thinking of ways to steal the guy's RV.

"What's that guy's deal?" Drew asked loudly. It'd been a while since anyone had said anything. Bart had fallen back asleep at some point and LeBron had lapsed into a semi-depressed slump. Yue was the only other person in the truck who'd even noticed the angry bearded RV guy.

"Who cares. I'm more interested in trying to find ourselves an RV. The sleeping arrangements in here suck. I'm going to need my own private chiropractor and a bucket of muscle relaxers after another night or two of sleeping in here." Yue rubbed the back of her neck for emphasis.

"Getting diesel may be an issue. Probably the same deal as regular gas would be is my guess." Drew said thinking it over. They were driving through a populated section of the interstate so the number of surgers had increased. There were also a lot more wrecked vehicles scattered around that he had to dodge. The increased number of surgers probably correlated directly to the increased number of wrecks on this section of the interstate.

"We could get a travel trailer or something to pull along behind us. Seal up the windows somehow and we'd have a nice safe place to spend every night." Yue said. They were both thinking of the dents in the side of the Expedition they were driving. Not to mention how fast the crawlerz had ripped apart the defenses they'd put up around their house. A cheap light weight pop up camper wasn't going to be the long-term solution in a world like this.

Drew was guesstimating how much extra gas it'd take to tug along a travel trailer when his musings were cut short by the sound of gunfire up ahead. They were driving fast to avoid the random surgers who kept coming at them. If they slowed down to turn around the surgers would be all over them on this confined section of the road. If they kept going, they were heading straight into whatever kind of trouble was associated with the noisy gunfire coming from up ahead. They'd been trying to get through Ocala, the city they were currently driving through before it got dark.

Yue didn't bother saying anything when Drew started accelerating. She reached over and shook LeBron awake before turning around to check on their dad. He was asleep again, so she decided to leave him alone for the moment. She turned back around to face the front right as Drew took his foot off the gas. Up ahead the reason he'd slowed down was turned over on its side with a few dozen surgers rushing towards it.

One of those short school buses like you'd see for an afterschool dance or karate place was on its side in the middle of the grassy median. A woman was standing on one side of it firing a hunting rifle with an expensive looking scope at the surgers rushing towards her. A man was lifting a young girl onto the top of the overturned bus to try and save her. He had his rifle in a sling on his back. The desperate last stand played out quickly over the next few seconds. So quickly that Drew never even had a chance to get them all killed by trying to rescue the doomed little group.

The girl was barely stable on top of the bus when a surger leapt into the air and grabbed her. The surger let its momentum carry it and the girl off to the other side of the bus where it rode her like a sled through the grass. A few surgers on that side of the bus lunged towards the pair. The man was pulled down from behind by an oversized man beast who'd managed to wade right through the hail of bullets being laid down by the woman. The woman's magazine dried up on her and she was carried to the ground screaming in a pile of teeth and clawed fingers.

Two surgers smacked into the side of the Expedition hard enough to snap them out of watching the drama unfold. Drew floored it to beat through the mob converging on the overturned bus. Momentum was their friend. They passed the bus and kept moving. A depressed silence reigning supreme until the surger covered bus was out of sight.

"Why'd you slow down?" Yue asked Drew out of the blue.

"They were in trouble. I don't know." Drew said staring straight ahead.

"You do know if you'd tried to help them, we'd all be dead right now. Including your little brother, right? There was nothing we could do for those people." Yue said. She wanted to be compassionate. She knew her brother had a huge heart. That huge heart could end up getting them all killed.

"That little girl though…" Drew started to say something, but the rest was lost in sobs. Yue leaned forward and put her hand on his shoulder. Partially to comfort him but mostly because they were driving almost eighty miles an hour down a road littered with wrecks and bloodthirsty cannibals who were trying their best to run out in front of them. Having their driver half blind from tears wasn't a great thing at the moment. At least they'd made it through Ocala proper now it looked like. Nothing but woods on both sides of the road as far as the eye could see.

A dinging noise saved Yue from having to justify why they shouldn't try to save little girls lives. Which was good because she didn't have any justification. Secretly she knew that she'd have slowed down the truck as well. Blowing past a couple of adults with weapons was one thing. Driving past a little girl being attacked by monsters. A desperate little terrified girl. Trying to justify doing that would turn you into a monster yourself. No matter what their dad tried to tell them. There were things you had to risk dying for to be able to look at yourself in the mirror afterwards. Knowing their dad and having heard his cop stories a million times she knew he'd have been the first one out the door to help save the girl.

"We need gas already?" Yue questioned trying to see over the steering wheel and Drew.

"Yeah, we do. I guess constantly slowing down and then flooring it is using up more gas than just keeping it on cruise control would." Drew said obviously happy to have such a mundane problem to deal with. He immediately started scanning the side of the road for a semi safe place to pull over. They were in the middle of nowhere at the moment, so this was as good a place as any. Even though the dashboard display had flashed that they had fifty miles to go until empty.

"For our next car we need to check the window sticker for AM." LeBron said leaning forward and joining in the conversation. Yue hadn't even known that he'd d been listening. She went ahead and took the bait.

"AM? I think you mean Sirius." She replied looking over at him and waiting for it.

"Apocalypse mileage. I mean you can't really go off highway and town mileage when you're going to be – " LeBron stopped talking when Yue chuckled and punched him in the arm. He grinned and leaned back in the seat while Drew shook his head with a grimace. He was not amused.

Drew pulled over leaving the Expedition running. He punched the button to raise the back door and was rewarded with the high-pitched whine of metal on metal. The back door stopped after only moving up a few inches. Bart was setting up in the back awakened by the fact that they'd stopped.

"It's stuck on the signs." He said. He reached into the back and dragged a jug of gas out handing it up to Yue who opened her door and handed it to Drew. Drew grabbed the big red container and hurried around to the side of the SUV where he busied himself filling up the tank. He stopped pouring it in when the container went dry. It'd been a good amount of gas, so he decided not to use another jug yet. Instead, he circled the truck to manually close the back door. He wanted to check and see if they'd caused any damage trying to open it.

The outside of the big white police vehicle had taken a serious beating. There were dings all over it from the crawlerz trying to get in. There was one long scratch Drew knew was from when he'd driven too close to a wrecked car and caught a corner of it on the side of the Expedition. Sparks had flown everywhere. He'd been scared they were going to spin out when he hit it. Spinning out in this big beast could easily end up with them upside down.

He pushed hard on the back door until he was rewarded by the click of the door closing. He made a mental note to remind everyone not to use the back door anymore. Just because it'd closed this time didn't mean it would next time. Once she'd verified Drew was done topping off the tank Yue declared it bathroom break time. She went first then came back to help Bart go. LeBron and Drew stood on either end of the Expedition looking up and down the road as well as glancing into the woods to make sure no surgers were coming at them.

Drew helped Yue get Bart back in the car then him and LeBron took their turns recycling the crystal light flavored water they'd been drinking. They were rapidly running out of the boxes of packets they'd brought with them. There'd been a big cardboard box full of boxes of the packets in the Traverse they'd originally taken from their garage. They'd talked about rationing the flavor packets but that would've meant having to drink the hot water they had with them plain. There'd come a point when they had to drink unflavored water but until then they agreed it was way better to just use the packets. It was amazing how much little stuff like that they'd taken for granted in their old lives.

Yue stood guard with her AR-15 on the driver's side of the truck while the boys took care of nature's call. She scanned back and forth for the infected but what ended up catching her eye was a jacked up pickup truck that came cruising up the road. It was the first vehicle she'd seen since the overturned bus tragedy had played out in front of them. She'd expected it to be the angry bearded man RV when she first saw the glint of the sunshine striking the window of an oncoming vehicle. The big truck pulled up at a safe distance beside them. She could see the dents on the side of it where it'd been mauled by the infected as well. A man leaned out the busted passenger window and waved to Yue.

"You guys ok?" The man asked. He wore his hair short and was growing out a scraggly looking beard. He didn't have an accent which surprised Yue since she'd been expecting to hear a thick southern drawl based on the monster truck the guy was riding in.

"We're fine. Thank you." She replied simply.

"Yes, you are. Love me a woman who can handle a big gun like that." The man said continuing to smile down at her. He went from a basically normal guy in a big truck to a super creepy guy in a big truck with that lecherous grin and statement. Drew and LeBron emerged from around the truck with their weapons in hand. Based on the look on their faces they'd both heard the creeps attempt at a pickup line.

"You guys need something?" Drew asked. He gestured for Yue to get back in her seat. He was hoping getting her out of the way would get these losers moving along.

"What you got?" The creepy dude asked.

"Nothing. I guess we're good here. Good luck." Drew said and started getting back in his own seat. LeBron began to walk around to his side to get in. Creepy dude smiled and waved as the big, wheeled truck took off down the road. Looking in the direction the truck had come from LeBron saw a few vaguely humanoid figures in the distance coming their way fast. He mentioned that to Drew, and they got moving out of there fast.

"I wanted to ask him if those big tires actually helped with keeping the infected off them." Yue said.

"I'm sure he'd have been happy to give you a ride." LeBron teased.

"You guys need to work on avoiding people. The sick people we can dodge all right. It's the healthy ones you have to worry about. There are going to be a lot of evil people trying to take advantage of the situation. With the infected you know where you stand. They want to throw you on the ground to rip your throat out. Boys like creep boy back there will smile at you the whole time their friend is sneaking around to stab you in the back." Bart said. It was the most he'd said all day.

"Thanks for the lecture dad." Drew said. The same way he'd said it so many times back in the old days when Bart had told him to focus on his schoolwork instead of just the athletic field. The tone immediately made them all nostalgic for the good old days.

"Lectures are how you learn without having to have your heart ripped out. Would you rather have somebody who'd been there and done that help you avoid issues, or do you want to risk your lives figuring it out yourselves for the first time?" Bart asked before succumbing to a coughing fit. Yue didn't like how pale her dad was. He was also burning up with a fever. She poured some non-flavored water on a t-shirt and handed it to him to put over his head. LeBron and Drew were both looking on with concern. Bart stopped coughing long enough to tell Drew to get them moving.

Based on how the day had gone they absolutely needed to make sure they got past Gainesville and found a secure place to spend the night before darkness fell.

Chapter 24: Go Gators!

It started to rain. No big surprise there since it was the afternoon in Florida. It reduced how far the sounds of their engine would travel which was good. It was going to make the road super slippery which was bad. Especially when you were trying to make an oversized SUV swerve around accidents and attackers at a high rate of speed. Stuck in between two cities they couldn't really just stay where they were. The place would be literally crawling with crawlerz once the sun went down.

LeBron had a theory that Gainesville might not be so bad anyway. The entire city existed basically because the University of Florida was there. In the month leading up to the final breakdown of civilization the college experience had gone through multiple iterations. A lot of campuses had remained open either to try to maintain a sense of normalcy or because closing down meant sending their international students back home to countries devastated by the disease. As the disease approached more and more colleges buckled down since pretty soon sending their students anywhere was a death sentence.

The results had pretty much been the same everywhere. Students who were sent home at least got to see their families again before being killed or turned. In Florida the colleges were used to treating every emergency like a hurricane. That meant bust out the emergency shelter rules and try to make everyone comfortable. Thanks to dealing with a couple of other pandemics in the recent past they also had plans in place for those. None of those plans covered the aggressive nature of the spread of this ancient disease though.

"I'm thinking zombie cheerleaders." Drew announced from the front seat.

"When aren't you thinking about cheerleaders?" Yue asked with a smirk.

"We wish they were zombies. Zombies are slow." LeBron said.

"Depends on which movie you're talking about. There's fast ones, slow ones and every other kind you can imagine." Drew responded.

"My point is that if these things were slower, they'd be so much easier to survive. I don't even understand how people lose to slow zombies. I mean just walk away briskly." LeBron argued.

"I'm not sitting here for this right now. We need to focus on getting through Gainesville." Yue interrupted. She'd once watched bemused as Drew and LeBron almost got into a fist fight over which Marvel character was the strongest. The two of them could argue hypotheticals with the single mindedness and passion of a two-year-old who sees a toy they want at Target.

"Please listen to your sister!" Bart said loudly from the third row. Yue immediately turned around to begin fussing over his bandages and make sure he was ok. She'd thought he'd fallen asleep again. Anytime she heard him awake she used as a time for a checkup on him since she didn't want to bother him while he was resting. Little did she know this had led to her dad lying quietly in the back seat to avoid having his bandages checked fifty times a day. He too remembered the superhero argument though. He had zero desire to be stuck in the same vehicle as his two sons in the middle of a similar argument.

The miles ticked down quickly. There was way too much water leaking through the duct tape and broken windows on the Expedition. They stopped to rig up a covering to try to make it better. The front window treatment they came up with definitely wasn't going to stop a crawler. Not unless they were allergic to cheap grocery bags and duct tape. Their ride was starting to look like a mobile dumpster. LeBron commented it looked like the truck Oscar the grouch would drive if he were in the apocalypse. A joke that for some reason reignited the argument between the two of them.

"Shut up!" Their dad roared out from the third row. Turning around to look at him LeBron and Yue saw that he'd actually sat all the way up in the third row. He must be super pissed. Or he was just sitting up to monitor the situation as they drove through Gainesville since Ocala had been such a cluster. Completely understandable for the pucker factor to go up exponentially as they approached anything resembling a city. Yue found herself really hoping LeBron's theories on lower populations in college towns turned out to be accurate. Of course, it'd only take a few surgers or one armed nutjob willing to kill for gas to ruin their day.

The city of Gainesville snuck up on you. The interstate rolled past the outskirts of it which was another reason they were hoping it wouldn't be as bad as the last city they'd driven through. It was also a great reason to be taking the interstates. The smaller highways that cut north through Florida all ran directly through the middle of large cities on the way to the Georgia border. Centers of population weren't a place they wanted to be.

Covering half the road underneath the sign telling them which exit to take for the university was a fire scorched firetruck. LeBron felt like that was the perfect symbol for how well the world had reacted to the appearance of this disease. Drew drove them slowly around it checking for any sign of an ambush. In the rows of seats behind him everyone was on guard. Sitting up with weapons ready struggling to see what was going on through the blocked-up windows and the rain that was coming down even harder now.

Drew was the first to figure out the white thing on the other side of the firetruck was the jacked-up truck the creep had been driving. It looked like the creep had creeped out the wrong people. A small group of men were unloading supplies from the back of the big truck. The truck was leaning forward on one flat tire with all the windows shot out. The bodies of the creep and some other guy were lying on the ground. A man about Drews age noticed them watching and jogged over in their direction. The other men around him formed up and followed him.

The group quickly surrounded the Expedition. It looked to be a group of college kids wearing the contents of a looted camping store. They were all carrying hunting rifles. None of them looked shy about using the rifles. Drew rolled down his window wishing that he could roll down the passenger side instead.

"Hi!" He called out to the one who appeared to be leading the others. In the back of the Expedition everyone got ready to fight. Even though they'd just be picked off like fish in a barrel considering the position they were in. The only chance they'd have is if they all ducked and Drew floored it.

"Hi." The leader said in a thick European accent. LeBron smiled and mentally gave himself a high five. He'd totally been right on the international students getting stuck here. The ambushers continued to maneuver into position to take them out if needed. All it'd take would be one mistake and they'd be dead. Yue got ready to go out shooting knowing that their lives depended on Drew not saying anything stupid.

"I see you guys wasted the creep that was driving the big truck." Drew said. The leader nodded.

"Did you know him?" The leader asked.

"Nope. Guy tried to pick up my sister. It was super awkward. You going to let us through here or what? You guys rob everybody who comes through here or just the jerks?" Drew motioned towards the motionless bodies lying in the rain.

"Those men. They try and kidnap my girlfriend. Then they say they give us supplies for her. They try and trade a box of beans and some gas for the love of my life. They didn't know how many of us there were. Normally we have everyone hidden for ambush. They went for their weapons, and they did not win." Drew and the others got the gist of the heavily accented story tossed at them across ten feet of heavy rain.

"So, are we good to go then?" Drew asked in as friendly a tone as he could muster. He was leaning neighborly on one arm while his other was being used to get his pistol in position in case he needed it quickly.

"No. Get out of the police car so we can search it for things we may need." The man said in a decidedly unfriendly tone.

"Go!" Bart yelled from the backseat as he started blasting away through one of the unbroken back windows. Drew put his foot down hard while simultaneously pulling up his pistol and snapping off some unaimed shots. The shots had the desired effect of sending the people standing around that side of the car leaping for cover. Yue was curled up on the floor since the woman on her side of the car had started shooting as soon as Bart had. The bullets hammered into the side of the Expedition and easily pierced the stop sign strapped over the window. LeBron had ducked down low. He was holding his pistol up in his good hand sending random shots out through his window. If they survived this encounter, they were going to be needing a lot more duct tape. LeBron really hoped no one shot him in his good hand.

A few shots pinged off the signs covering the back window. A couple of the shots made new holes in the signs and bounced around inside the Expedition. Drew was driving like a mad man trying to evade the bullets he imagined were aimed at their tires and the back of his head. Bart was yelling for everyone to sound off if they were ok or not. He relaxed once everyone checked in and the bullets stopped hitting the back of the truck.

"Why'd you yell to go!" Drew yelled over his shoulder. He was freaked out. There was enough adrenaline pumping through him that he felt like he could've masqueraded as a surger.

"I didn't really want to be executed on the side of the road while they took our ride. You want your dead body lying next to those two dead monster truck guys for eternity? It wouldn't surprise me if that ditch on the other side of the road wasn't full of dead bodies and stripped-down cars." Bart said in a calm voice before lying back down and promptly passing out.

"Can't really argue with that." LeBron said to Drew who was still fuming. Drew's heart was beating like crazy. He was in shock they were even alive. He was also soaking wet from the rain pouring in through his window. He wondered if they should even bother looking for a new vehicle. At this point it was pretty obvious they'd just shoot the windows out the first chance they got anyway.

Drew kept checking the side mirrors to make sure they weren't being chased. He was so busy looking at the side mirrors he almost missed the gang of surgers rushing at them from the median. Yue yelling in his ear to look to his left Drew yanked the steering wheel to the right avoiding the first surger jumping for them. That turn wasn't enough to keep them from smacking head on into another two. One of whom smashed right through the duct taped grocery bag windshield onto Drew. Screaming Drew slammed on the brakes sending the truck into a vicious skid.

"He's dead! Keep going!" Yue screamed into Drews face. Drew looked down and saw that Yue had picked up the adolescent surger by the shoulders. The things spine was literally sticking out of a big hole ripped in the top of its back. Blood was everywhere. The kid's eyes were still wide open.

A much larger surger stuck its head through the open driver's side window and began scrambling in on top of Drew. Drew whipped off his seatbelt and fell over backwards into the passenger seat trying to get away. He started kicking his attacker in the face. The truck was slowly accelerating with no one at the steering wheel except the upside-down dead kid. Yue shot the big surger in the head as another one started pounding on the stop sign next to her. She ignored that one to spin around and shoot the one trying to get in the truck through her dad's window.

"Drive!" Yue screamed again. LeBron had curled into a ball against his seat pointing his rifle out his open window and shaking like a leaf. Drew was screaming and kicking the dead guy in the face while the Expedition rolled down the interstate with no one steering it. Yue opened her door to hop out and try to pull the dead guy out the window so Drew could get back in the seat. Her door was slammed back in her face by another surger who'd been running at the truck. It caught the corner of her suddenly opening door right in the head and went down. Yue put a couple of rounds into its body to make sure it stayed down then tried hopping out again. She kept yelling for Drew to get his ass back in the driver's seat.

Jogging to get to the front door she grabbed the oversized surger by the legs and pulled hard. The mostly headless dead guy came out of the window on top of Yue like a giant load of bloody afterbirth. The safety glass still clinging to the window frame raining down all over her. Pulling that guy out shifted around the kid who tumbled down to the floorboards landing on the accelerator. Yue watched in frustration as the truck took off without her. She sighed and started running along behind it hoping Drew would pull his head out of his butt and get the truck stopped for her. More than likely Bart had slept through the whole ordeal.

In the Expedition Drew struggled to pull the dead kid off the ground and regain control of the truck. The kids spinal cord got stuck on the steering wheel and Drew had to basically rip him out of there. He opened the door and shoved the kid back down after he maneuvered around so that his foot was the one controlling the accelerator. He stopped the truck once he was back in control and worked the gore covered dead kid out of the truck onto the road. He gagged his way through the whole disgusting process.

"We left Yue." LeBron said quietly pointing at the open door and empty seat beside him. Drew immediately forgot about the gore he had smeared all over him in his haste to get outside and see where Yue was. Seeing her running up to the truck he breathed a little easier. Looking behind her he saw another surger tearing across the concrete trying to catch up to her. Checking his holster, he realized he'd lost his gun somewhere.

"Get down!" Bart yelled with his head stuck out his window and his rifle pointed in the direction of Yue's head. Yue threw herself to the ground. She knew her dad pointing the weapon in her direction and yelling to get down meant there was more than likely a monster about to jump on her from behind. She'd barely had time to rip her jeans open on the rough concrete when her dad started blasting away. A blood covered Drew then helped Yue up off the road before flinging her back in her seat. He slammed her door shut and got back in.

"I hate to say this, but I think we need a new car." Drew said once he had them moving down the road again. Shopping bags were fluttering around like crazy at the unsafe speed he was driving at. He shifted around uncomfortably in the puddle of blood he was sitting in.

"I think we need to find a nice safe hole to crawl into. This open road stuff sucks." LeBron said to the general agreement of everyone in the truck.

"Let's get the hell out of Florida and figure it out." Bart said before once more lying down to rest. Yue hurried to dig up some pills for him to take before he went to sleep.

Chapter 25: The Hell Out of Florida

Despite Yue's complete lack of enthusiasm, they opted to spend the night in the Expedition again. The late afternoon rain had brought the mosquitos out so that was wonderful. It really helped to enhance the overall ambience along with the humidity and blood-soaked seats. They'd kept driving north for another hour after leaving Gainesville in the rearview before deciding to look for a place to pull over. They'd driven past an exit that looked pretty deserted. Drew had turned around, gotten off the interstate there then driven them deep into the woods to spend another fabulous night being eaten alive by the bugs.

They hadn't seen anyone else on the road recently. That observation corroborated their dad's insistence not to get out of the truck back where they'd been ambushed. The number of people they'd seen on the road prior to the ambush site had been a pleasant surprise. Even if most of them had been super creepy. At least none of them had tried to massacre them to steal eighty gallons of unleaded and a bunch of ace bandages. It was still nice to know there were other survivors out there. Hopefully a lot of people just weren't up to road tripping quite yet.

"We need to loot a Ross or something. I'm on my last pair of boxers." Drew complained. They'd all taken the time to give themselves sponge baths and change into whatever fresh clothes they had left. The problem with dirty clothes in the apocalypse was that dirty had evolved to mean completely unwearable. That's what happened when about once a day you ended up covered in the insides of another human being. On top of being gross their clothing became a biohazard as well. If any of the juicy grossness they kept getting covered in managed to get in their bloodstream they could end up with an insatiable hunger for brains.

Not that they had any clue why they hadn't all turned already anyway. All of them were covered in scrapes and cuts. They'd all been drenched in blood and other squishy sticky substances pouring out of dead humans who were infected. They actually tried not to think too much about what all they'd been covered in. Their working theory was that whatever made you turn must be in the mouths of the infected. Maybe that's where the bulk of the bacteria/virus/bio mold or whatever the hell was the cause of all this stuff accumulated in the quantity needed to make someone turn.

"I honestly don't know why you bother getting out of the truck to take a piss bro." LeBron said indicating the blood caked boxers Drew had thrown into the grass in disgust.

It was a valid statement. When you're marinating your nether regions in some kind of nasty zombie goo for a couple of hours in the hot Florida sun a nice cleansing urine rinse may be exactly what the doctor ordered. At a certain point you just couldn't ratchet up the gross factor any higher.

"Ok. We need a new ride, more ammunition, fresh clothes, and supplies. I know dad just wants us to get out of Florida but honestly where exactly are we supposed to go? Everywhere is going to suck. The weather just happens to be better for camping up north." Drew was venting. It wasn't the first time he'd brought this up. They were rushing north with no real plan in mind. They were burning through valuable resources to get them there. At the rate they were going they'd wind up broken down and hungry on the side of the road in the middle of nowhere. They'd be stuck trying to defend themselves with hammers and screwdrivers. To top it off they'd be wearing ace bandages wrapped around their crotches since they'd be out of wearable clothes by the time they got there. Wherever 'there' was.

"What do you think we should do?" Bart asked. He was sitting up and listening in. Yue had helped him out earlier to pee. He was so shaky on his feet now that they'd had to hold him up while he went. The heat from his fever radiated off him in waves. If that fever didn't break soon Yue had no idea what they were going to do. They couldn't exactly hit up an urgent care or pull up WebMD on their smart phones. Smart phones had gotten pretty dumb when the cloud died. Yue mostly used hers for setting alarms to make sure they didn't get caught out in the dark by accident.

"There's a couple of truck stops on this exit. I say we go check them out and see what we can find." Drew suggested.

"They'll have already been looted. We're better off searching houses." LeBron said.

"A lot more likely to get shot trying to break into houses. Anybody who's still alive will have learned to stay quiet. They'll have weapons to defend their places. They won't like us trying to bash our way in to steal their stuff. We beep the horn to see if anybody's home and we'll have curious surgers coming around to see what's going on." Bart said.

Bart didn't think he'd be around much longer between the infection and the way the world was going. He was lost without Nancy by his side. Before he went though, he wanted to do his best to set the kids up for success. He hoped he could hang on long enough to make a difference. In the interim he'd decided one thing he could focus on was explaining all of his answers to them. He wanted them to learn from his experience. He needed them to see why he was pushing them in a certain direction. He really hoped his high fever wasn't making all his answers come out sounding like a bunch of gibberish.

"That makes sense. Let's go hit the truck stops. Maybe the showers are still working." Drew said.

"That'd be so awesome." Yue responded shuddering in pleasure at the thought of getting truly clean.

They piled back into the Expedition after a brief discussion on whether it was better to sneak up on foot or drive over and park. They opted for driving in since that gave them the option of easily driving out. None of them were delusional enough to think they could outrun a surger if they happened to bump into one. Drew drove them out of the woods and over to the truck stop by the interstate.

They parked between the gas pumps and the station. As they'd anticipated the front windows of the store were busted out. From where they were sitting the inside of the place looked like a tornado had torn through it. The shelves were toppled over, the freezer doors were flung open and there was junk all over the place. It was hard to tell from the parking lot if any of the stuff they were seeing was actually worth getting out of the truck for.

LeBron and Drew went in through the broken window while Yue shifted over to the driver's seat. Bart sat up worriedly in the back struggling to keep an eye on his boys through the haze of his ever-increasing temperature. Inside the store LeBron and Drew sifted through key chains, bandanas, and rotten fruit. Beside a toppled case of DVDs, they found a nice cache of personal hygiene products. Deodorant was a rare commodity in the apocalypse. At some point people were just going to have to get used to everybody smelling bad. The little personal packs of moist towelette wipes they found were going to make them Yue's favorite brothers ever.

They ended up dragging a decent amount of stuff out of the building. Most of it being the toiletries they'd stumbled over. LeBron and Drew were both sporting T-Shirts proclaiming how much they loved Florida. They'd taken every stitch of clothing they could locate including the pile of bandanas. There'd also been a couple of knives left in a big knife display up by the counter. Someone had shattered the glass on the top and taken the ones they wanted leaving just the folding knives in it. They hadn't been able to find any food or water. The showers weren't working either.

"Alright. There's still another truck stop a couple gas stations and that horror movie looking motel." Drew said climbing in the truck after LeBron.

Yue nodded and took them across the street to the gas station and did a quick drive by. It looked like there might actually be some supplies in there worth getting. The window to this one had been broken out too. Drew and LeBron hesitated to jump right in since there was a dead body in the parking lot and a few more cadavers littered the floor inside the station. Drew checked his weapons and took a deep breath before walking the short distance to the broken window to climb inside. LeBron stood outside covering him and waiting for the all clear.

Yue watched nervously as Drew entered the gas station. She couldn't shake the feeling something wasn't quite right. It wasn't like they hadn't seen dead bodies lying all over the place before so that wasn't it. As sad and horrible as it was the sight of dead people was becoming pretty commonplace. There was something else that was pulling at her. It suddenly struck her. Why did this store still have supplies in it when the others they'd seen were pretty much empty?

Drew stood tall in the dimly lit building. The overhang to the walkway leading to the pumps cast a long shadow across the front of the building. The front row of shelves looked picked clean as expected. The rows towards the back looked like some of them might not have even been touched yet. Drew cautiously walked down the aisle towards the shelves with merchandise still neatly stacked on them. He carefully placed his heel then his toe down with each step moving as silently as possible. He noted the big piles of garbage strewn around the back. The interior of the store smelled strongly of rotting meat.

The pile of garbage by the freezers shifted and a fat rat came running straight at Drew. He danced backwards almost pulling the trigger on the charging rodent. The rat turned to the left at the last second and disappeared down a different aisle. When Drew jumped backwards to avoid the rat, he unknowingly leapt out of the way of the crawler who'd been stalking him since he entered the building. The lithe young, infected man hissed quietly in anger as it missed the prey that'd wandered into his lair. He spun around on all fours to try again and was mesmerized by a beam of light coming in from the window.

A startled and confused Drew lined up a shot at the suddenly stationary crawler and blew a hole through its head. Hearing something behind him Drew whirled around to find a wide-eyed LeBron standing behind him with his rifle aimed in the general direction of where the crawler had been standing. Drew started to put his rifle down then remembered how the crawler had snuck up on him. He whirled back around and motioned for LeBron to help him clear the store. They didn't see any more crawlerz. They did find a few more dead bodies and lots of supplies to lug out to the truck.

"We may run out of bullets and gas, but we have enough Vienna sausages to get us to Canada and back." Yue announced with a slightly disgusted look on her face.

"I never knew there were this many flavors available." LeBron added with a slightly sickened emphasis on the word flavors. Drew completely missed the sarcasm. He loved the little miniature sausages made of God knew what parts of what animal. Bart was a Vienna connoisseur as well.

"At least we have Yoo-Hoo to wash them down with." Yue said smirking.

"I guess high blood pressure and a gradual descent into morbid obesity are the least of our worries right now." LeBron said pulling out the cutters from the toolbox in the trunk. The store had tarps in it which they were going to use to make themselves some windows for the Expedition. They'd actually considered trying to tie a freezer door to the front of the truck to serve as a windshield. They gave up on that idea when they couldn't figure out how to keep it there at high speeds. Duct taping a freezer door to the front of the thing they were riding in at eighty miles per hour just didn't seem like a great idea. Instead, they were all wearing cheap sunglasses now to shield their eyes from the wind and debris that'd be whipping in.

"Should we check out the other places?" Yue asked.

"I don't really see why. We're pretty much stocked up now. Unless there's a gun store or we can figure out how to turn the pumps on and get some gas." Drew said.

"We could siphon the gas if we had a hose. Then we'd just have to find cars that still have gas in them." LeBron chimed in. Drew and Yue questioned him a little more about that idea since they'd both heard of people doing that too. It turned out LeBron also had no real idea of how it worked. He'd just seen it in a movie. It was decided if they could find a hose then they'd experiment to try to figure out how to do it. Bart had gone back to sleep at some point during the excitement or they would've just asked him. It seemed like something an old cop would know how to do. The rest of them had about the same idea of how to do it as of how to hotwire a car. It looked easy enough on TV.

Yue traded spots with Drew so she could continue to check on Bart as they headed for the interstate. Drew had only driven about a mile when Yue yelled for him to stop. Drew slammed on the brakes as Yue yelled for someone to get her a t-shirt or a towel or something. LeBron pulled a t-shirt out of the stack they'd taken from the tourist junk in the truck stop. Looking in the rearview mirror Drew saw Yue wiping their dad off with the shirt and cleaning up around him.

"What happened?" Drew asked craning his neck to see what was going on. He'd brought them to a hard stop on the side of the road. The smell of brunt rubber emphasizing his reaction to Yue's panicked cries to stop.

"Dad just yacked all over himself." LeBron said trying to help Yue get their dad cleaned off.

"I'm fine. Hand me the towel." Bart mumbled trying to grab the t-shirt Yue was using to wipe the puke off him. She gently pushed his hand down then worked on getting him out of the shirt he was wearing. She needed to change it since it was covered in vomit. They had the big pile of spare shirts now so the only thing that'd suffer would be his sense of fashion.

She had his shirt half off when he spewed again. This time he full on exorcist spewed. It was like he opened up a fire hydrant of chunky watered-down spam. Yue had no idea where it'd all come from. She couldn't remember him eating anything that looked like the hot steamy stuff now dripping out of her vomit-soaked hair. She shrugged aside her natural disgust and focused on trying to help her dad feel better. LeBron had the back-passenger door to the Expedition wide open in an attempt to air out the interior.

Working together they got their dad cleaned up with a new shirt on. They spent a few minutes cleaning the supplies off that'd gotten puke all over them. Yue let herself care about her hair enough to waste a whole bottled water rinsing the bulk of the chunky stomach chowder out of it. Mostly she was just concerned about their dad. He hadn't been able to pee when they got him out of the truck to clean him off. His temperature had backed off to be replaced by cold clammy skin and sweat. That didn't seem like a good thing either. They made him as comfortable as possible in the back seat once they had it cleaned up.

Having done all that they could for Bart they kept driving north. Drew sticking to a nice steady fifty miles per hour to try and avoid having the wind blow the taped-up tarps off the windows. The inside of the truck was a complete junkyard at this point. On the plus side driving around in a wind tunnel kept the puke smell from building up too much inside the packed SUV. Having their dad hose down the inside of the Expedition with his stomach juices had been the icing on top of the stink cake they all had to eat a slice of.

Drew pointed out the welcome center they drove past to LeBron and Yue. He didn't point it out to show that they were almost out of the state. The whole welcome center parking lot was packed with camouflage paint covered green war machines. The national guard must have made the welcome center into a base. More than likely it'd been a check point to keep people from getting into the state who were infected. That'd been the plan to stop the spread of the infection according to the news anyway.

It turned out the crawlerz didn't have much use for interstates though. They came through the woods in packs at night ripping into the national guardsmen. It was guns and bullets in the dark against a supernaturally strong enemy with no capacity for mercy. An enemy who gave no quarter and had seemingly limitless reinforcements. Drew stared over at the camo covered graveyard before suddenly slowing down to cut across the median.

The welcome center had been turned into a vulture picked nightmare. There weren't as many bodies as Drew had expected to see though. LeBron answered that unspoken question by mentioning that since soldiers tended to be in better physical shape than most people, they'd be more likely to survive the surge. As to why the soldiers hadn't been able to kill more of the crawlerz when they attacked. That was anyone's guess. Most likely they'd still been operating as if they were facing a conventional enemy. You can't employ standard military tactics when faced with a nightmare and hope to survive.

The dead soldiers they did find helped replenish their ammunition and weapons supply greatly. They'd become way less squeamish about picking through the dead to gather supplies. The pickings were slim between the lack of dead soldiers and the fact that they evidently weren't the first to have had this idea. The dead men had been lying in the hot Florida sun and rain for a long time. That didn't help when trying to flip over a carcass to see what treasures the body may be hiding.

Finally convinced they'd found enough to have made the stop useful Drew acquiesced to Yue's suggestion that they get the hell out of there. She wanted to hurry up and find a place to camp for the night. The next morning, she wanted to spend some time searching for somewhere to spend a few days. She wanted to make sure Bart had a nice place to rest while he recovered. She was beyond distressed by how pale and weak he'd gotten after the puking fiasco.

They crammed in the weapons and other supplies they'd looted off the dead warriors and set back off. Less than thirty minutes later they were cruising past the welcome to Georgia sign. They'd made it out of Florida. Now they just needed to figure out what came next.

Chapter 26: Orphaned Again

"That thing came out of nowhere. It had to be waiting. If that rat hadn't popped out..." LeBron trailed off. If the rat hadn't popped out and made Drew stumble back a few steps, they both knew what would've happened. The crawler would've ripped Drew's face off.

"How was it moving around during the day though?" Drew wondered out loud. It wasn't like an exhaustive study had been performed on crawlerz in their natural habitat then published in scientific journals. Everything they knew about the crawlerz came from YouTube videos and the highly censored nightly news. The closest thing they had to a *crawlerologist* was LeBron. He'd been the one who'd really put in the hours watching all of the videos on all the obscure websites. On top of all the videos he'd taken the next step and actually read all the blogs and such that'd popped up before and after the government took control of the internet.

"It stopped moving when the light got in its face. It looked at the sun like it was hypnotized or something. There were plenty of theories that the infection caused massive hallucinations that disconnect the crawlerz from reality." LeBron lectured.

"Ok professor. You're saying that the crawlerz are just a bunch of people walking around tripping balls? They can't come out in the light because it makes them go off the deep end. This whole apocalypse is just some kind of Grateful Dead afterparty gone wrong?" Drew asked sarcastically.

"Shut up both of you. We need to find somewhere to get dad in a real bed and we need to do it now. He's scaring me." Yue announced from the back. That shut both her brothers up. They immediately began checking the exit signs. The next exit had a big shopping plaza and a ton of signs for places to eat. If it had all that then there must be some nice houses somewhere too.

Drew turned off at the exit then drove quickly past all the typical interstate exit carnage. There were burnt buildings along the sides of the road. The vehicles scattered around were a mix of military and civilian ones parked at odd angles. Here and there human sized lumps lie in the road covered in the rags that used to be their clothes. Nature slowly working away at the leathery flesh and faded yellow bones that were all that remained of what used to be living, breathing, laughing people. Each lump had their own story. None of them ever dreaming their story would end up like it had. Going out as a pile of rotting meat on the street of some exit in the middle of nowhere.

Drew dodged the fleshy speed bumps and headed down a road named Lakes Blvd. The name of the road made him think this exit might have been a good option after all. He took the first left turn once they got out of the main part of the town and followed it as it looped through a ritzy looking neighborhood. Continuing on down the road he veered sharply to the right to get on a loop that ran around a lake. They could see the sky-blue water peeking at them through gaps in the trees they were passing.

"This is where the rich people live." LeBron said in awe as Drew drove them down a random driveway towards the lake. The driveway he'd selected didn't lead to the biggest house. He'd chosen one instead that was set back off the road further than the others. The large house had a dock with a boathouse on the end of it down by the lake. Drew parked in the driveway in front of the four-car garage.

"I wonder if they have stables?" Drew asked no one in particular. He was also impressed by the expensive looking lake house. For some reason it'd gotten him thinking about the possibility of riding horses around. It might be the future of transportation as gas supplies continued to dwindle. Yue ripped him right out of the saddle of his horse-riding fantasy back to the harsh reality of their lives.

"Hurry up and clear the house. We need to get dad somewhere safe and comfortable. He's not waking up at all now." She said poking at Bart and fussing over him. She looked scared.

Drew and LeBron got out of the truck quickly. They walked towards the large house with weapons at the ready. Even with the extra ammunition they'd found on the dead soldiers back at the rest stop in Florida they were running dangerously low. Dangerously low defined as anything less than a couple of barrels full of bullets each. They had multiple green ammo boxes full of loose bullets plus the twenty or so magazines they kept loaded. They'd seen how fast those rounds disappeared when they got into a serious confrontation though.

The house was locked up tight. Assuming the owners weren't sitting inside getting ready to shoot them in the face through the tinted bay windows that was actually a great sign. No windows were broken, and the doors were all locked. That meant that there probably weren't any crawlerz curled up inside on the couch waiting for a couple of nimrods to come busting in the front door. Drew was thinking this was some rich dudes vacation house. He was less concerned now with clearing the house than with how they could get in without breaking a window.

"Let's go around back." He whispered to LeBron who nodded in understanding. They moved around the house checking each window as they went. A full revolution of the house later they were standing back where they'd started. They were still trying to figure out a way in that didn't involve breaking a window. Yue kept looking over at them and making hand motions for them to hurry up.

Drew told LeBron to wait then ran back over to the truck. He hopped in the driver's seat and backed the truck up until he actually hit one of the ornately carved wooden supports for the front porch. With Yue fuming at him to just bust out a window on the bottom floor he jumped out and crawled across the hood of the Expedition to get on the roof. He walked quickly across the roof of the big SUV and used that extra height to boost himself up on the roof of the wraparound porch. He waved down at LeBron and Yue then went to check the windows up on the second floor.

The three windows he could get to from up there were all locked. One of them was a fancy window that opened vertically instead of horizontally. It flexed when Drew pushed on it. He kept applying more and more pressure until the top part of the frame snapped. He kept pushing until one side of the window came loose. Once he had that side open, he unlocked it to open the other side then quickly slithered in.

Yue could be frustrated all she wanted but Drew had gone through all the extra hassle for their dad. They needed a place that was comfortable that they wouldn't have to run from any time soon. That's why he didn't want to go around breaking windows to show that someone was in the house. If nothing had broken in previously it stood to reason that they should be safe to spend a few days here. Not that reason was something you could necessarily depend on in this new normal. Drew put the window back in the frame as well as he could making a mental note to bring up a roll of duct tape to seal it back off.

Drew walked quickly through the dark house pausing to poke his head into each room. He didn't see anything after doing a full circuit of the second-floor room so headed downstairs. The downstairs took less time to check. He opened the front door so LeBron could join him in checking the garage to finish off the sweep. The garage doors had light filtering in from the outside. The dusty light illuminated a couple of motorcycles and what turned out to be a tarp covered bright yellow Hummer with gigantic tires.

"Well, that'll take every last bit of gas we've got." LeBron said checking out the banana-colored behemoth.

"Yeah. To get to the end of the driveway. But at least we'd be inconspicuous driving it around. These may work better." Drew said walking over to get a better look at the beefed-up looking dirt bikes.

"Let's look later man. Yue's going to have a heart attack if we don't get dad tucked into a real bed real soon." LeBron said spinning on his heel to head out of the garage. At the mention of Yue and their dad Drew followed quickly behind.

Walking out the front door Drew shot Yue a thumbs up gesture to let her know the house looked empty and that they should be good to go. He hurried down the stairs to help Yue and LeBron carry in their dad. They carefully pulled Bart out of the backseat. Bart moaned a few times when he was being pulled out but didn't wake up. LeBron moved forward to help Drew carry their dad, but Drew waved him off. The man had gotten so light that he could easily carry him cradled like a child in his arms. Shocked by how frail and light their dad had become Drew was suddenly struck by that same intense fear he saw on Yue's face.

LeBron held the door open as Drew carried Bart up the stairs into the house. Yue grabbed some of their gear out of the battered Expedition and followed them inside. She pushed the downstairs door closed and followed Drew through the house to the master bedroom. Despite her fear for their dad, she was still impressed by the beauty of the décor in the huge master bedroom. That only distracted her for a split second before she rushed forward to help Drew and LeBron get Bart comfortable on the massive white comforted bed pushed against the wall.

"Now what can we do?" LeBron asked Yue once they had Bart cleaned up and tucked in. LeBron's voice quivered with the same powerful mix of emotions they were all feeling.

"We let him rest. What was that?" Yue asked looking around. They'd all heard the distant noises coming from outside. Sound carried pretty well in a world devoid of mankind's noise making contraptions. Leaving Yue to watch over Bart, LeBron, and Drew left to see where the noise was coming from.

"It's coming from the front of the house." Drew said slipping his rifle strap down so he could easily get to it. He waited for LeBron to adjust his as well. Once LeBron was ready, they crept through the house to the front door as silently as they could. Not that it should make a difference with all the racket they were hearing from outside. It sounded like somebody was beating the holy hell out of the Expedition they'd left parked out front. Either that or a sledgehammer was mating with a bunch of oversized cymbals.

Drew motioned for LeBron to stay still while he snuck over to the window to see what was going on outside. A lone surger was systematically ripping their ride apart. Drew stared out the window watching while the tall freak ripped the signs off the truck. Once it had the signs ripped off it dove inside through a window. It beat the tie wrap secured signs off the back window and then just lay in the back kicking the roof repetitively for whatever reason. Finally, it smashed its way out through the back and wandered in a complete circle around the Expedition.

Drew was on the verge of backing off when the surger spun in a tight circle for no apparent reason and stared right at him. Drew held that eye contact for a split second too long before backing rapidly away from the window trying to piece together what'd just happened. He'd only taken maybe three steps when the front door reverberated loudly from being struck hard from the outside. Drew and LeBron quickly aimed their weapons at the door waiting to see what would happen.

The door shook hard one more time then suddenly flew off its hinges as the berserk surger rampaged into the room. LeBron and Drew both opened fire blowing holes in the wall, floor, and door. They pretty much hit everything except for the freak charging straight at them with its mouth wide open. The surger sprang through the air for Drew who kept pulling the trigger on his AR-15 as quickly as he could. LeBron was struggling to bring his weapon to bear thanks to his finger splint getting in the way.

A few of Drews bullets found their mark right as the surger slammed into him. Drew and the rapidly dying surger rolled on the ground in a growing pool of the surger's life blood. He gripped the surger around the neck as it continued to try and bite him. Eventually it grew too weak to keep trying to bite him. Looking up Drew saw his brother standing next to him with the barrel of his rifle pointing at the surger's head.

"You ok? He didn't bite you right? I didn't want to shoot him and hit you in the hand if he was dying anyway." LeBron rapid fired the questions at Drew while looking extremely upset.

"All good. Just need some wet wipes and a gallon of bleach." Drew said pushing the body of the surger to the side.

"You're going to need like fifty rolls of duct tape to fix that entryway." Yue called out from down the hallway where she had them covered with her rifle. She stayed long enough to make sure they weren't hurt then turned to go back to take care of Bart. Drew and LeBron turned to continue unloading the truck and see what they needed to do to fix the front door.

"Be ready. We're probably going to have company on the way after all that noise." Drew told his brother as they hurried outside.

It turns out you can fit a lot of supplies into an Expedition Max. Even after leaving a lot of items in the vehicle because they were covered in some sort of disgusting goo, the pile they had covered most of the living room. Once they'd jogged back and forth what felt like a hundred times transferring everything from the truck to the bullet riddled foyer, they set themselves to trying to figure out how to seal off the front door.

They had the door hanging in the frame with duct tape all around it within a few minutes. They could no longer go in and out that way using the door but from the outside the house should look fairly normal. They talked it over and decided they should move the truck inside the garage and see if it made sense to put their supplies in the Hummer instead of leaving them in a big pile in the foyer. If they were in the Hummer and they had to leave fast at least they wouldn't have to leave all their gear behind. It wasn't like multiflavored tins of Vienna Sausages grew on trees.

They went out in the garage and started poking around looking for the keys to the Hummer. They were nowhere to be found in the garage, so they decided to move the truck inside then keep looking in the house for the keys. Before they just threw open the garage door Drew pulled a step ladder over and climbed up it to look out the dusty windows to make sure the coast was clear. The coast was not clear.

There were quite a few surgers milling around the driveway. He couldn't even see the other side of the Expedition where for all he knew there were hundreds of the adrenalized cannibal psychos doing jumping jacks. He carefully climbed down off the ladder trying his best not to make any noise. Seeing LeBron looking over and obviously getting ready to ask him a question Drew put his finger to his lips to silence him. Motioning for LeBron to follow him Drew left the garage and walked back to the master bedroom.

Yue was sitting on the bed with her back to them holding their dad's hand. Drew slid up next to her to let her know that they needed to leave. The house was getting surrounded by surgers which meant the crawlerz would swarm the place after the sun went down. They only had an hour to find the keys to the Hummer and bust out. Yue looked up at Drew then over at LeBron. Tears ran unashamedly down her face.

"I'm sorry. I didn't know what to do." She sobbed out.

Drew was completely lost. He did know she needed to be quiet though. There were way too many of the surgers around to be making noise. What was she sorry about?

LeBron put the pieces together faster than Drew. He'd been expecting this to happen even as he prayed with all his heart that it wouldn't. He sat down on the bed beside Yue and put his hand over hers. They both sat there sadly with Drew slowly comprehending what was going on. Drew's whole body fought against the evidence laid out in front of him. He looked at Yue then LeBron both of his siblings tearfully shaking their heads. Yue had tucked their dads face under the blanket so all he could see was a comforter with the vague shape of a body underneath it.

    He moved the comforter back to expose his dads cold, pale face. Yue had closed his eyes, so he looked like he was sleeping. His skin was cold though. Drew pulled his hand back like he'd been shocked. It felt like he was dreaming. Like his body was being controlled by someone else. His grief overwhelmed him. First his mom then his dad. The people who'd taken him in and made him part of a family. He couldn't take it. He fell down on his knees and sobbed along with his brother and sister.

    The sound of the duct taped front door being torn out of the frame signaled the need to pause their grief unless they wanted this house to become the family crypt.

Chapter 27: A Dark Cloud

Drew stood up and calmly walked out of the room. Yue and LeBron followed behind him. They were all walking like robots. Drew came alive when the surgers came tearing through the house shrieking at him. Screaming in rage Drew shot down the first mentally deranged freak coming at him. Behind him LeBron and Yue fanned out to either side. Together they blew away the surgers who'd made it into the house. More were coming though. They were having to keep up a steady barrage just to keep the ones out who were busy trying to force their way into the home.

"We need to break through them and get to the truck!" Yue yelled. They all started pushing forward. Swapping out magazines as they drained them.

"What about dad!" LeBron suddenly stopped in place as he remembered they were leaving their dad lying in the bed. It didn't seem right to just leave his body there.

"We'll come back!" Drew yelled stepping around the piles of gear they'd so painstakingly removed from the Expedition earlier. Yue ran past him and looked out a window into the front yard. She turned right back around and screamed for them to go out the back door instead. Judging by the panicked look on her face there wasn't time to pack. She flew past them to fling open the sliding glass door leading out to the backyard.

Drew and LeBron ran out right behind Yue who turned around and immediately slammed the slider shut. She'd barely shut it when a tween looking freak slammed into the glass. The tween hit it hard enough to make them all wonder if the thick glass slider was going to break or come out of the wall. Seeing another six or seven surgers coming right after that one Yue yelled for them to run.

"We can't outrun them!" Drew yelled.

"There's a ton of them in the front yard!" Yue answered breathing hard. She was staring down the little overgrown brick lined path at the dock below. She started running that way with LeBron and Drew coming right behind her. Drew spun around when he heard the sound of glass breaking behind them. He brought up his rifle as the surgers poured out through the broken slider. Yue and LeBron lined up beside him and they found themselves once again trying to hold the line.

"We have to break away and get to the dock! There's too many of them!" Yue yelled over the sound of their rifles. These surgers were mostly silent. A few of them did scream out a challenge when they saw them, but the bulk of them were as silent as the dead. The silence was way creepier than screaming would've been. It made them seem more intense. Like the infection was in full control of them. Riding their bodies like a rage filled jockey urging its mount on until it finished the race or fell over dead from the extreme exertion.

LeBron tripped and fell into the tall grass shooting a round straight into the sky. He peeked behind them and saw they were getting close to the edge of the dock. He looked at the house and saw they were never going to be able to stop the onslaught completely. It was a miracle they hadn't been overrun already. There were a lot of infected crawling towards them. They hadn't been trying for head shots. Just aiming for center of mass and hoping that slowed their attackers down enough for them to make it to the dock.

"We have to run!" LeBron yelled. If they didn't run, they'd just sit there shooting until they ran out of ammunition. Once they ran out of ammunition they'd be overrun. LeBron punched Drew in the shoulder and yelled out the need to run again. Drew was in full on Rambo mode standing tall screaming and hurling lead at the enemy. LeBron gave up on verbal communications and grabbed Drew with his good hand to drag him backwards. Drew finally got the point. They broke contact with the enemy and turned to make a desperate run for the dock.

They managed to make it onto the dock before the first pursuer caught up with them. Drew had been trying to stay in the back to cover his brother and sister. He felt a pair of hands tugging at his shirt from behind trying to fling him on the ground. Instead of going down he launched into a spin move like the starting varsity running back he'd been in his former life. The surger slammed into the wooden dock face first and instantly started scrambling back up. Drew pointed his rifle and pulled the trigger twice. The first round blew the back of the surgers head off. The second time he pulled the trigger he just heard an impotent click.

There was no time to change out mags. More attackers were sprinting across the lawn for them. Drew pulled out his pistol and began jogging backwards down the dock shooting the surgers when they got too close. He didn't want to waste any more bullets than he had to. The boathouse had an expensive looking covered ski boat hanging off a complicated looking pulley system. There was a pegboard beside it with a bunch of lifejackets hanging off it under a small roof. In the dusky light more surgers were pounding down the dock towards them. They were coming on unbelievably fast as the three of them used up the rest of the bullets in their magazines.

One got past the bullets filling the air and took LeBron with it off the dock into the lake. Drew unhesitatingly pulled out his knife and jumped into the water where LeBron had disappeared. Yue yanked a bunch of the lifejackets off the holder and tossed them into the water. She was about to jump in when a completely insane older woman wearing a stain covered bra and equally dirty bloomers rammed into her from behind causing them both to tumble off the dock.

Drew hit the water letting himself sink down with his eyes wide open searching for LeBron. He couldn't really see anything in the murky water. He flailed his arms around hoping to get lucky enough to grab LeBron. A set of hands grabbed him by the head pulling him backwards. He fought off the hands by ripping at the face of the person trying to pull him down. He needed to find LeBron. A kick landed in his crotch. The sudden pain caused him to let out his breath. He desperately struggled to paddle his way up for a breath of air. His face broke the surface of the water and LeBron punched him hard right in the nose.

"Sorry!" LeBron gasped as soon as he realized who he'd hit.

"Are you ok?" Drew asked in a worried voice. The coppery taste of blood filled his mouth, but he could care less about being kicked and hit. He was terrified the surger who'd ridden his brother off the dock might've bitten him. He couldn't fail another member of his family. A couple of lifejackets hit the water next to them and they both reached for them to rest their arms. Drew looked up to see if Yue was diving in yet. He was anxious to see her safe as well.

The old lady and Yue fell right on top of them. The falling bodies propelling all four of them into a painful submersion. The three uninfected popped back to the surface thankful not to have been bitten or had anything broken from being hit that hard. The woman didn't pop up.

"I guess they can't swim." Yue choked out. She'd swallowed a good portion of the lake water. Her head had gone underwater right as her stomach collided with Drew's shoulder.

"They can jump like crazy though. Swim!" LeBron said grabbing one of the lifejackets and kicking for the middle of the large lake. On the dock more of the infected appeared. They all stopped to take a minute to figure out where the humans were then leapt like they were being shot out of a cannon. Each time one jumped the three of them dove under the water to evade the deadly missiles. Once the surgers went underwater they lost all grip on reality and just sank. It seemed to be a stimulation similar to when the sunlight overwhelmed them.

As happy as they were to find out the infected sucked at swimming it was an even better feeling once they got far enough away that they stopped having to dodge the cannibalistic cannon balls. They swam into the setting sun. Too depressed and miserable to enjoy the sight of the golden fire dancing along the surface of the glimmering water. They swam in silence kicking through the smooth water with their shoes, clothes, backpacks, and weapons weighing them down. If Yue hadn't had the presence of mind to fling in those life preservers, they wouldn't have had a chance.

They swam until they couldn't see the dock anymore. Huddling in a small circle in the water they got as close together as they could to stave off the cold. The water wasn't cold enough that any of them were worried about instant hypothermia, but it wasn't super comfortable either. Just in case they weren't miserable enough clouds moved in and a light misty rain started falling.

"At least now we can talk." Drew said in a low voice. They were in the middle of a lake with the rain coming down in the middle of the night. If they couldn't safely have a conversation here, then they were going to all need to learn sign language.

"We can't just tread water all night." Yue said. They weren't technically treading water since the lifejackets were doing most of the work. They were all exhausted from kicking and hanging on to the jackets though.

"Do we go back to the house dad's in now?" LeBron asked. He was actually glad for all the physical exhaustion and bone chilling terror. It was distracting them all from the real tragedy. They were orphans again. Thinking that thought, swimming in the dark with his brother and sister, LeBron began to cry in earnest. He felt the arms of Yue and Drew wrap around him tightly. These were the last two people he had on this planet. He couldn't control the great wracking sobs that shuddered through him. He couldn't tell if it was from his dad passing or his fear that he'd lose his older siblings next. It was a mix of both and everything.

They all cried. It was cathartic and essential that they do so. Their parents had been beautiful people who loved them deeply. Losing them both in such a short amount of time hurt badly. There were holes inside of them that would likely never be filled back up. They'd still all been struggling with the loss of their mom when they'd lost their dad. A man who'd dedicated his life to protecting others as a cop and then as a father. A man who'd put his family before everything else. A man who'd want them to survive now. Bart would've pushed them to fight on no matter what.

All of them eventually came to that same thought. Yue, Drew, and LeBron may not be related by blood, but they weren't stepbrother or adopted foster friends or any of that crap. They were brothers and sisters. They were family. They'd live and die to support one another through this dumpster fire of a new normal. Their mom could've told them that already. She'd known they belonged together when she started the adoption process for each of them.

"We can't go back to the house. It's going to be crawling with crawlerz. They'll probably cram in there to hide when the sun starts coming up. There's a ton of surgers already there. Assuming they don't finish turning today." Drew said. He was wondering as he said it how come there'd been so many surgers. Why was it taking so long for some to turn fully into crawlerz? He'd have to ask LeBron once the kid was feeling better.

"Well, we can't just tread water all night. Eventually we'll get hypothermia or cramps or something. Either way my pants are rubbing me raw in some seriously tender places." Yue announced once everyone had calmed down. She was actively trying to keep her mind from drifting back to the second she'd felt the life leave her dad. He'd never regained consciousness. She hadn't even had the chance to say goodbye.

"It's completely dark, raining and we have no idea which way shore is. Let's get this done. Hopefully we wash up on a beach not covered in crawlerz." Drew said. He picked a direction and started swimming expecting the others to follow. Yue did almost immediately. LeBron looked to the sky first to see if he could see the stars. He wasn't excited about swimming around in circles all night and wanted to see if there might be a natural way to navigate. It turned out the rain was falling out of clouds though. That poster he'd made in the third grade about the water cycle was right after all. Feeling stupid for even looking he sighed and started kicking along behind his brother and sister.

Either the lake was huge, or they were indeed swimming in circles. It felt like they'd been paddling for hours and not getting anywhere. They'd all seen the opposite shoreline earlier, so they were aware it was a big lake. It wasn't like it was the ocean though. They'd been able to clearly see the opposite shoreline. Drew figured he'd probably picked the wrong direction and they were busy swimming towards the furthest possible point of the shoreline. He'd have expected nothing less from their luck.

The rain stopped and the clouds eventually dispersed. They kept mechanically kicking and stroking their way forward. Completely exhausted it never even occurred to LeBron to look up at the stars when the rain finally stopped. He was too busy keeping his head from slipping underwater and demanding his legs keep pumping up and down. It was Drew that first noticed they were approaching a shoreline. With the moon no longer hidden behind the clouds their visibility had gone from zero to not so great. Not so great was good enough to see an amorphous black blob that was hopefully an uninhabited shoreline.

They swam their way up to a muddy tree lined beach and pulled their weary bodies ashore. They had no idea where they were but for the moment all that mattered was that they were no longer in the water. None of them said a word. For all they knew a group of crawlerz could be hanging out nearby. They were at a loss as to what do next. They were low on everything now. They'd used up most of their available ammunition getting themselves into the lake in the first place.

Soaking wet and miserable they snuggled together as close as they could trying to get some sleep in the leaf covered mud. It was suicide to wander around at night with their reduced capabilities. Once the sun came up, they could better figure out what to do. Drew indicated silently that he'd take the first watch. He sat Indian style while LeBron and Yue shivered themselves into a restless slumber. He'd almost rather have been back in the water than sitting on the shore alone with his thoughts.

It physically hurt to remember the way his dad looked lying cold and still in that bed. Abandoning his body there still felt like a betrayal. Drew spent the watch silently counting the ammunition he had left. He shivered in the chill night air. He periodically checked on Yue and LeBron to make sure they were still alive. He also needed to occasionally poke them awake to get them to try and stop letting their teeth chatter quite so much. Nothing quite as frustrating as trying to get a couple of freezing people to stop letting their teeth chatter while asleep in a pile of cold mud.

Those chattering teeth could lead to their deaths if the sound drifted into the wrong set of ears. Drew gave up after half a dozen attempts at winning the teeth chattering battle. There was only so much they could do to try and survive. He sat there with his rifle in his lap waiting for death to come for them until the sun surprised him by making an appearance.

He let LeBron and Yue sleep in while he stood up to take a look around the lake in the early dawn hours. It appeared they'd swum to an unpopulated section of the shore which may explain why the chattering teeth hadn't brought on an army of the damned. The far shore wasn't particularly far away. They must've swum at the exact wrong angle to have spent so much time in the water the previous night. Seeing a gap in the trees it looked like they were next to a road.

Tired of his damp clothes he nudged the two sleeping beauties with the toe of his soggy Nikes to wake them up. He was proud of how both LeBron and Yue instantly came awake and moved to their feet with their weapons strapped on within easy reach. Both of his siblings were carefully looking around and noting the same details Drew had already taken into account. They may have lost pretty much everything, but they still had one another. They were alive and the sun was up.

It was a brand-new day.

Chapter 28: A New Day

Drew walked up the bank to the road and saw there was water on the other side of it as well. They were on some kind of land bridge that cut the lake in half. Considering one direction to be as good as the other Drew started walking up the road with Yue and LeBron in tow. He was walking point keeping a lookout for any threats. He was fantasizing about finding dry underwear when he noticed a huge house through the trees up ahead.

He pointed it out to LeBron and Yue. They all started walking with a bit more pep in their step. A house that size was sure to be full of useful items like dry underwear and shoes. If they got really lucky, they may even be able to procure some new weapons. They might not be able to find anything to replace their AR-15s, but the possibility of a couple of shotguns and a bunch of shells was very real. This was Georgia so finding a bunch of hunting rifles wasn't too crazy to consider either. They'd probably have to figure out a way to break into a gun safe to get at them.

They were all busy counting their chickens before they hatched as they walked down the driveway towards the big house. Standing around in the parking lot outside the home they were forced to reconsider. The house was still gorgeous. The sun reflecting off the water made this a truly spectacular day. That missing door meant the home could be infected with crawlerz. After his run in at the gas station Drew was pretty paranoid about going into an enclosed space that could have one of those deadly stalkers hanging out in it.

"Should we try a different house?" LeBron whispered. He said it almost too quietly for them to hear him. When the sun was out, they were a little less cautious about making noise, but they still had to watch the volume. Whether that would work out for them in the long run or not remained to be seen. They were pretty much making this up as they went along. It wasn't like there was a guidebook. They couldn't even pull up the house on Yelp and see how many stars previous looters had left for it.

None of them wanted to walk another step in their damp clothes. They knew it wasn't super smart to risk their lives to avoid additional chafing but that's what it was coming down to. Carefully avoiding thinking of what Bart would've told them if they did this they lined up at the front door and took the plunge.

Drew went first. He had a flashlight he was using to scan the inside of the house. He was holding it with his pistol the same way he'd seen people on TV doing it. That way wherever he looked the pistol was also pointed. That seemed like a pretty good way to explore the house to him. Plus, as an added bonus, the flashlight by itself was an effective stunning weapon against the light fearing crawlerz. Anything that might throw off a crawler lunging at him full speed out of the dark was a good thing.

LeBron was in the middle of the train. Being the least athletic of the three of them it made sense to put him there. He was also the youngest which made the older two feel protective of him. If they had a few more people, they probably would've had LeBron sit outside while they cleared the house. As it was each of them played an integral part. In addition to guarding their backs Yue was also doing her best to let some light into the house. She took every opportunity to quietly open curtains and twist Venetian blinds open to let in those gorgeous crawler crushing rays.

The entryway was one big well-lit foyer. A set of windows high up on the walls making the inside of the home as bright as the outside once they got past the mudroom area. The furniture in the large open sitting room had been tossed around at some point. The couch was tipped over and the lamps and side tables were knocked all over the place. A knife was sitting on the ground in the middle of a large stain on the expensive looking tile. With nothing to loot in this room they continued on through the large brick lined arch that led into the house proper. Each of them marveling at the cool architectural feature. It must be nice to be rich.

The next room was similarly torn apart. This one had a few bodies lying around as well. The fight that'd started in the foyer must've carried over into this room. Drew let the light play over the unmoving bodies on the floor then shined it around the walls. The drywall had been completely ripped off in a few places revealing the studs. They all vividly remembered seeing the crawler rip apart their bathroom wall, so it was easy for them to picture what had happened here. The desperate fight in the foyer followed by a retreat into the living room. A few members of the family dying defending the home. They'd probably locked the kids in that back bedroom. The final act of that drama being the infected parents joining the other crawlerz in ripping apart the walls to murder their own children.

"Looks like they fought pretty hard." LeBron said under his breath. The others nodded. This family hadn't gone down without a fight.

The far wall was one gigantic series of sliding glass doors. They were covered currently by hanging blinds that stretched the entire length of the wall. Yue imagined the view was going to be pretty spectacular once they opened up those blinds. Based on the way the house was sitting on the property it should give them a panoramic view of the lake. Even better than the Zillow highlighted view it should definitely let in a ton of sunlight. That would be a good thing since the corpse littered living room was creeping her out.

"Shine the light around again. Then let's go open up those shades." Yue told Drew. The three of them watched as Drew shined the powerful flashlight over every piece of the living room visible from where they were standing. There were a few places still in the shadows, but they felt like they'd taken most of the risk out of it.

"Smooth is fast and fast is smooth." LeBron reminded them. It was a favorite saying of their dads. It seemed like a pretty apt description of the proper mindset to try to get to for traipsing across a living room turned morgue in the middle of an apocalypse.

Without another word Drew quickly began walking across the living room. He'd already sketched out the best route in his head and was now hurrying to get through it. He was worried they were being stalked like he'd been back in the gas station. His imagination pumping up the fear a thousand percent by highlighting all the places in the room he hadn't been able to see from the door. Not to mention what may be lurking in the shadows in the other rooms in the big house. There was a lot of it left to explore. First, they had to survive the living room though.

Heart hammering in his chest Drew spun to the left when he heard the sound of something skittering across the cold tile. His light caught the silhouette of a young boy racing towards them. He was pulling on the trigger of his pistol when the boy disappeared behind the couch. Yue took off running towards the blinds. One of the 'corpses' they'd seen by the blinds suddenly sat up and jumped for her. Taken completely by surprise Yue tumbled to the ground with the crawler snapping at her face with its teeth.

Drew gave up on the homicidal tween behind the couch and ran for Yue. He hit his knees and slid across the floor with his pistol extended in front of him. As soon as he got close enough, he rested the barrel on the little monster's head and pulled the trigger blowing the contents of its skull all over an ottoman. A nice leather ottoman that Drew was willing to bet cost more than their entire living room set back at their old house. Somehow, he doubted the owners of a mansion on a lake shopped for their furniture at Rooms to Go. Yue shoved the crawler off her as Drew spun to check on the crawler that he'd left behind. Yue ignored the gore and stood up to help Drew.

The crawler he'd left behind had multiplied into five crawlerz snaking through the living room towards them. Drew pulled his pistol up and dropped into a firing stance. Before he could start blasting away, he heard the sound of ripping fabric. The living room was suddenly a lot less dark. The light exposed the crawlerz in mid leap. Two of them froze to just stare at the light while the other three whirled around like they were being burnt alive. Those three scampered around knocking over furniture before eventually hauling ass up the stairs and out of view.

Behind them LeBron continued to rip the fabric off the motorized device that would've normally been activated to open and close the blinds. From what he'd seen as he ripped the coarse material down the view out the back window really was spectacular. Not that he'd had time to really stand back and take it in. Two of the fingers on his good hand were bleeding. He'd torn off the fingernails while ripping the wide room darkening strips of fabric out of the trolley mechanism that took them back and forth across the windows. Ignoring the pain, he continued shredding the window coverings as fast as he could. Opening up more and more of the home's interior to the bright light of day.

"What do we do about those two?" Yue asked in a shaky voice. She was pointing at the two crawlerz who were standing there staring at the light beams. They looked pretty peaceful standing there like that. A complete one eighty from the vicious vibes spewing off them moments before. There was no doubt that as soon as the sun set these two would be back to hunting them though. Drew stepped forward to finish them.

"Wait." LeBron said.

"Yes?" Drew questioned him. It was obvious LeBron had something to say but was hesitant to spit it out.

"Maybe you shouldn't shoot them." LeBron said. He rushed to clarify himself when he saw the look that crossed Drew's face. Drew had totally misinterpreted what LeBron had said. He thought his younger brother was asking for mercy for the two killing machines currently mesmerized by the beams of light. "I mean you shouldn't waste the bullets or make that much noise. You already shot the pistol once, so we already have to leave. Maybe kill them a different way?" LeBron trailed off uncomfortably. Shooting the beasts in cold blood was bad enough.

Drew nodded his head as he got what LeBron was saying. He agreed completely now that LeBron had pointed out the obvious. It was the thought of doing it that was making him a little queasy. LeBron stepped forward fumbling with his folding knife like they were going to let him do the honors. Killing them as they stood there defenseless. Killing them in cold blood. That was going to lead to a lot of sleepless nights. Drew put his hand on LeBron's chest and shook his head.

"Ok. Let's do it fast and get out of here. We have a few minutes max before some surgers start sniffing around." Yue said. She gulped and turned her head the other way when Drew stepped towards the defenseless crawlerz. Standing there like that they looked more like filthy people than super powered homicidal maniacs. It was like they were letting their brother kill a couple of stoned homeless people. Yue grabbed LeBron and spun him around to face the lake muttering something about heading to the dock to look for a boat.

Drew caught up with them a minute later. He was scrubbing at the blood on his hands with a piece of the ripped fabric from the blinds. Looking at his face neither LeBron nor Yue thought it'd be a good time to ask how it'd went. It was enough that he'd shouldered the burden and done it for them. Yue put her hand on his shoulder for a second to try and convey her appreciation. Hoping the simple gesture had made him feel better they all walked quickly towards the detached garage on the other side of the driveway.

"There's a boat coming this way." LeBron whispered. That halted their progress as they stopped to look out at the water. Headed straight for the dock was a pontoon boat. It had a bright yellow cover on the top of it. From the angle they were at they couldn't see who was driving it. The dock was downhill from them, so they were looking down on the top of the covered boat making its way in.

"I hope they're friendly cause otherwise we're treading water again." Yue said pointing to the top of the driveway where a couple of figures had just stepped into view. The three of them moved quickly out of sight into the weeds hoping they hadn't been spotted. Without another word they began jogging for the dock forcing their weary legs to function after a night that'd sapped them of pretty much all of their energy.

The pontoon boat was drifting towards the dock when they got there. The people on the boat didn't seem super surprised to see them. They did stop the boat so that it didn't come all the way in yet.

"Act friendly." Drew whispered. They didn't want to spook whoever was in the boat. He made sure to keep his hands off his rifle as they jogged down the dock.

The people in the boat became visible as they got further down the dock. A skinny bald guy in glasses was standing next to an Amazonian looking woman in a tank top. The woman looked tall and muscular enough to easily walk on to any WNBA team. Two kids looking to be in their mid-teens were standing towards the back of the boat. All of them were sunburnt but otherwise looked ok. The woman was holding a shotgun while the husband drove the boat.

"You guys ok?" The woman called out loudly. Drew, LeBron, and Yue all just stared back at the woman. If they weren't in trouble they were now. How did this woman not know to keep her mouth shut?

"We've got company coming. Surgers were just coming down the driveway when we ran down here. They'll be here soon. We could use a lift." Drew said loudly but not quite as loudly as the woman had done. The woman and the man held a whispered discussion before the man piloted the pontoon boat close enough for them to climb aboard. The second they were all on board the man whipped the pontoon boat into full reverse to get them moving back out towards the middle of the lake.

Drew turned to monitor the dock and saw a sprinting surger tearing towards them. He brought his rifle up and used three of his bullets to slow the demon down enough that they could make their getaway. He turned around to a sea of shocked faces. On the dock more of the surgers had gathered and were staring out at the pontoon boat as it pulled away. The infected were evidently able to control themselves well enough not to dive into the water and drown if they didn't have any chance of reaching their prey.

This time when Drew turned around, he was confronted by the woman with the shot gun pointing it at his face.

"I'm going to need all of you to drop your weapons on the deck." The woman said.

"Do it guys. Don't make any moves. I think we're good here." Yue said. Drew relaxed slightly knowing that Yue was the politician in the family. She typically had a good sense about people. If she thought that they were ok dropping their weapons, then it probably wasn't a horrible idea. Drew carefully put his rifle on the ground then shrugged out of his pack and put that down as well. Lastly, he dropped his belt with his gun and a straight bladed hunting knife hanging on it.

Beside Drew his siblings were going through the same weapon removal process. All of them keeping a careful eye on the tall woman with the shot gun. The bald man with the glasses looked on nervously while the two teens stared at them with their mouths hanging open. Once they were all unarmed the woman had them move to the back of the pontoon boat away from their weapons. The nerdy looking guy driving the boat apologetically walked over to them to check for hidden weapons. He claimed a couple of knives but otherwise didn't find anything that made them look bad. The man went back to the other side of the boat to confer with the woman once again.

"What made you think we could trust them?" Drew asked under his breath. He was expecting to hear some cryptic answer about some body language or something Yue had noted. He assumed she had a good reason for telling them to comply.

"I mean they didn't shoot us when our backs were turned. They rescued us off the dock. If they'd just cruised away, we'd be treading water right about now. What else are you looking for? I'd rather be sitting here unarmed than back in that damned lake swimming again." Yue answered. She seemed a little upset to be called out on telling them to go along with the woman's orders.

"I think we're going to be fine." LeBron said indicating with a head nod that the man and woman were walking back to talk to them.

"I'm Candace and this is my husband, Jim. These are our kids Lisa and Daniel. We're more than happy to take you to the undeveloped shore side and drop you guys off if that works for you?" The woman said. She waited expectantly for them to introduce themselves and agree to the offer she'd just made them.

It didn't sound like fresh, dry underwear were anywhere in their future. Instead, they were going to get ditched on another weed covered beach. That would force them to beat their way through the woods back to the road where they kept almost being killed. Returning this time with even less ammunition.

Chapter 29: Cut Bait

They cruised silently under the cover of the pontoon boat. The sun was really beating down on them, so they were thankful to have that cover at least. Jim was busy ignoring them while he headed for the drop off point. Candace had already mentioned that gas was a scarce commodity so they should be thankful for the water Uber to the safe side of the lake. Candace had kept her family on board the pontoon boat ever since people had started getting infected. She didn't say anything, but it was obvious they'd hidden caches of supplies around the lake to keep them going. They'd noticed early on the infected couldn't swim so they'd spent as much time as they could in the boat.

Once Candace heard that they were all still soaked from their night in the lake she rummaged around in the bow of the boat and returned with a garbage bag full of clothes. One thing they'd scavenged a ton of was clothing, so she had no problem parting with some dry underwear. Even though she said she knew she might regret it in another few months. It wasn't like you could just run down to Costco and buy a ten pack of your favorite color panties.

The setup seemed pretty ideal to Yue. Especially when Candace let drop that there were multiple lakes around the area. They'd pretty much lay claim to this one. They'd actually gone to check out one of the neighboring lakes early on when the infection had first started spreading. They'd turned around and come straight back when they'd seen a couple boats moored in the middle of the next lake over full of drunk guys waving guns around. Since then, they'd heard plenty of shooting from every direction. They stayed on the less developed side of the lake as much as they could. They only ventured onto the developed side when they needed to gather more supplies.

They'd been on their way over to gather supplies when they'd heard the single gunshot and seen the three people running down to the dock. Candace told them normally they'd have just turned around and cruised the other way, but something had moved her to come help them. She noticed Drew looking over at the packs and weapons she'd made them leave on the deck.

"We have our kids on board so we can't be too careful. Don't worry we'll give you your stuff back when we drop you off. Throwing you out into the world today with no weapons would be the same as killing you. Between the day walkers and the ones that come out at night I don't see how anybody can stand to have their feet on dry land anymore." Candace said. She seemed slightly oblivious to the fact that she was going to be casting them off onto the shore in the very near future.

They arrived at the far shore way too soon. None of them were really ready to leave the comfortable boat seats to force their way through the briars and bushes quite yet. Fortunately, it didn't seem like Candace was in any sort of hurry to see them off either. She offered to fix them some lunch first and they eagerly agreed. It wasn't like anyone had offered to fix them lunch in a while.

Over a warm meal of baked beans with fresh scallions on top they told the family what they'd seen in their travels so far. Candace and her family listened wide eyed as Yue and LeBron told their story about the trip from Florida to here. Their whole life had become the two lakes they were stuck on. Being stuck out on the lake had given them plenty of time to observe the behavior of the infected on the shores though. They referred to the infected who walked around in the light of day as day walkers. They were extremely interested in why LeBron had settled on the term surgers instead.

"They can walk in the day light for a lot longer than three days though." Jim said breaking his silence after LeBron explained what he'd pieced together about the surgers. Everyone looked over at him to see what he had to say. When he didn't keep on talking right away LeBron prodded him along.

"It's not an exact science but what they were saying on the news was that once you get bitten you start avoiding the sun after a few days. I even saw sites where people were discussing how that could've been how the vampire legends started. Back when the virus was loose in the world and people noticed that the people who got bitten couldn't stand the sunlight." LeBron said. He was really hoping Jim would tell them some more about what he'd observed. You could never know too much about your enemy. He was also hoping the conversation would continue long enough for him to reasonably request another helping of the beans. The fresh scallions were stupid good. The family must have to risk their lives to pick them, but some things were just worth the risk.

"I guess we should stock up on garlic and crosses then." Candace joked.

"I don't think they care too much about herbs. They definitely suck at crossing bodies of water though. There's another point to your vampire mythology. I've watched them pretty much every day. Two or three of them have been what you call surgers for about a month now. Maybe the infection hits different ones different ways or it just takes longer for the toxins to build up in some of their systems, but I definitely wouldn't put too much 'stake' in the three-day thing." Jim said smiling. The only person who got it was LeBron.

"Come on guys. Stake? Vampires?" He looked around as the light dawned in Yue's eyes, Candace looked slightly bemused, and Drew was completely lost. LeBron was busily assimilating this new intel into his understanding of the infection. He liked what Jim had said about it taking longer for the toxin to accumulate in certain people. It also made sense that as the infection spread across the world it may slowly weaken or mutate. If a cobra bit ten people, the first two or three may die but the impact would be progressively less for the rest of the people as the snake ran low on venom. If he could somehow trick Drew into taking them to a library, he was going to snag every book on epidemiology he could find. He knew there were bound to be flaws in his logic. If he could just get his hands on the right textbooks, he may discover the concepts that saved their lives.

A few awkward goodbyes later they were standing on a sandy little beach next to an overgrown service road that looped around the lake. They watched as the pontoon boat motored away from them. The two teens in the boat staring dejectedly back after them. Candace and Jim resolutely refusing to look back. Drew got why they'd been ditched so quickly. Candace and Jim were good people. If they hadn't dropped them off right away, they'd have probably tried to figure out how to let them stay. If LeBron, Yue, and Drew all stayed that would've been three more mouths to feed. There was a finite supply of food available to pilfer from the lake houses. The parents were just doing survivor math and looking out for their two kids. Drew respected that.

Yue and LeBron respected the boat dwelling family's decision as well. They definitely all appreciated that rather than taking their weapons and supplies from them Candace kept her promise and sent them away with everything they'd brought on board. She actually hooked them up with some extra clothes and food. The three of them had been careful to ask multiple questions as to how to get to the interstate once dropped off. Even though they had no intention of heading towards the interstate once dropped off.

They trooped into the woods as a group stopping once they were out of sight of the lake. Now they could either keep walking through the woods until they wound up on the interstate or they could go back to the house where all of their supplies were. The house where the body of their father was in need of burying. The house with the bad ass looking Hummer. It was true that the house was more than likely still covered in the infected but where wasn't?

"Back to the house dad's body's at?" Drew asked quietly. LeBron and Yue both nodded with zero hesitation. They really didn't have a choice. Hitting the road low on supplies with no vehicle once it got dark was basically suicide. None of them liked the idea of walking away without getting the chance to say goodbye to their dad either. This exit had done a number on them, but they weren't ready to cut bait and make a run for it quite yet.

Chapter 30: Saying Goodbye

They tromped along through chest high weeds hidden from the lake by a thin line of trees covered in Spanish moss. They hadn't spoken since agreeing to go back to the house they'd left their dad in. Jim had mentioned he sometimes saw the infected pop up at random spots around the lake. Even on the uninhabited side where there was no real reason for them to be at, he'd seen them appear in their endless search for prey. LeBron thought the main reason there were infected all around the lake hinged on the fact that there was a family in the middle of the lake who didn't have a firm grasp on whispering.

Regardless of why the infected had surrounded the lake they needed to be extra careful to avoid them now that they found themselves backtracking around it. In the tall weeds a surger could be coming for them and they'd never even see it until it was right on top of them. Especially if it were one of the younger infected. None of them wanted to duke it out with a psychotic ten-year-old tweaker who's adrenaline was pumping so hard it could lift a car. Just the thought of infected kids and the tall weeds had each of them flashing back to the *Children of the Corn* movies their mom had made them watch. That classic had easily out creeped the other movie they'd rented where a clown kept killing kids through a sewage drain.

Sweating and surrounded by small clouds of mosquitoes they stoically marched along the sorry excuse for a road. They couldn't even slap at the mosquitoes for fear of the noise carrying too far. LeBron kept his theory on the spread of the infection by bug bite to himself. It wasn't like any of them could do anything to stop the bugs at this point. Without the constant chemicals sprayed by the mosquito control officers the bug problems were just going to keep getting worse anyway. LeBron made a mental note to stock up on insect repellant the next chance he got. Until then he'd just cuss quietly to himself while trying to Mr. Miyagi the flying pests out of the air with his fingers.

Drew suddenly stopped walking and pointed up in the air. Expecting the worse Yue and LeBron craned their necks backwards to see what new threat was coming for them. It wouldn't have surprised them at this point to see the infected had managed to learn how to levitate and were now hunting them from the sky. What they saw flying by instead was a plane. Not a big deal in the good old days but a novelty post apocalypse. They watched for a few seconds before Drew began moving forward again. Turning their eyes away from the heavens they kept up the pilgrimage to see their father one last time.

The trees on the side opposite of the lake cleared out revealing the source of the mosquitos. A sludgy looking scum covered pond was spread out on the right side of them. It was the overflow and treatment center for the crystal blue rich people water in the lake. Not that money mattered anymore. Anyone who'd gone into the apocalypse with a bunch of money sitting in their bank accounts had wasted the opportunity to spend a bunch of money. The inflationary power of an oncoming cataclysmic event had been pretty amazing. Stocks may have fallen but the value of a case of spam had gone through the roof.

It was getting late by the time they'd made it back to about where they'd started that morning. There was no way they were making it all the way back to the house they'd left their dad's body in before dusk. At least not on foot. Once they got there, they still had to secure the Hummer and bury their father. They didn't even know if they'd be able to find the keys to the Hummer or not.

"Find a boat?" LeBron had stopped walking and was pointing at the row of docks visible along the lake. They might not be able to figure out the pulley system holding the nice boats up out of the water but there was bound to be a simpler boat somewhere. A canoe or two would actually be perfect. Drew and Yue paused to consider what LeBron had just suggested. They both concluded it was brilliant. Worse case if it got too late, they'd just sleep in whatever boats they found. That way they could have the funeral for their dad and reclaim their supplies in the morning.

Not another word was spoken as they got into the residential area on the developed side of the lake again. They were all very much aware that the area around them was infested with surgers. At least they didn't have to worry too much about the crawlerz until the sun went down. Except for when they actually went into the houses. From now on they planned on opening every outside door and window before entering any houses so they could let in as much light as possible. They all agreed that was a better tactic than getting surrounded by vicious man-eating monsters in small, dark enclosed spaces.

Shoes sinking into the squelchy leaf littered ground they followed a path that wound its way through the trees by the edge of the lake. They'd already made it past two docks when they saw something that looked promising. Yue spotted a john boat sticking out from behind one of the detached garages. Trying to make as little noise as possible they slid the boat down to the lake and pushed it in. There was a small motor on the back, but they used the paddles they'd found by the boat until they got a decent distance from shore. The last thing they wanted was to be trying to get a motor to work in waist deep water within easy jumping range of the shoreline.

Once they got out on the water, they put a little more effort into figuring out the motor. Drew had assumed it was a gas motor. He'd thought that since every movie he'd ever seen with a guy with a john boat showed the guy pulling the rip cord to get the motor started. Once they'd determined it was an electric motor, they still almost gave up on figuring it out. Luckily, Drew happened to randomly decide to hold down the correct two buttons while pulling up on the stick attached to it. The little motor hummed along smoothly and quietly propelling them effortlessly over the clear blue water.

"Is that it?" Drew asked pointing to a dock up ahead. All of the docks looked pretty much the same. The one he was pointing at had a body lying on it.

"We only killed one of them?" LeBron asked. He remembered a lot more shooting than that. Letting his eyes wander up the dock to the yard he realized there were probably quite a few more bullet riddle corpses up in that direction. Then again, the infected were insanely hard to kill between the adrenaline-fueled crazy speed and the fact that that they kept going way past the point a normal human would've just keeled over.

There were still a couple of hours left before it'd get dark outside. Rather than trying to sleep in the boat Drew decided to go scout out the house and see if it was empty. If it was empty, they could go ahead and do what they needed to do without bothering to spend an uncomfortable sleepless night out on the water. Instead, he wanted them to spend an uncomfortable sleepless night out on the road somewhere in the Hummer. It didn't take a ton of convincing for Yue and LeBron to decide a little recon mission was the best way to go. All Drew really had to do was casually mention the AC the Hummer would have.

The main dock was too high out of the water for them to tie the john boat up to it. They tied it to one of the pilings beside a ladder and used the ladder to climb up on the dock instead. They'd talked about leaving one person behind to get the boat moving if needed but since none of them wanted to be the one to stay behind they nixed that idea. They agreed that they'd bug out and run back to the boat at the first sign of any sort of complication. None of them really believed they would though. Everything they did now was complicated.

Jogging quietly in single file they made it off the dock quickly and settled in behind the detachable garage. There were a few scattered bodies left over from the previous days firefight but nothing else to worry about so far. The big fear now that the house had been left open was that the crawlerz could've moved in and made themselves at home. The thought of the crawlerz oozing around their dad's body completely grossed them out. It was an indignity they refused to let him suffer. The coast looked clear all the way up to the house. From this angle they could see the bodies scattered around the front yard. The beat to hell Expedition sitting in the middle of it all. The police lights on the top somehow having made it through everything unscathed.

The back door was standing wide open. A good sign since the sunlight would be penetrating into at least one room thanks to the open door and slight breeze. Drew took a deep breath and checked his weapons one final time.

"On me." He said quietly and ran across the open space to stand with his back to the wall next to the open door. His brother and sister joined him seconds later. Taking another deep breath Drew stepped in front of the open door. Heart hammering in his chest he reached through the door and grabbed the manual slider to move the blinds completely out of the way. He slid the blinds as far over as he could get them then yanked his arm out like it was about to get crushed in an elevator door. He'd been waiting to feel the crush of teeth on his wrist the entire time.

The home was just like they'd left it. The three of them walked inside with guns at the ready. They were met by the musty smell of death. The supplies they'd unloaded from the Expedition had been scattered all over by the infected. Yue chuckled to herself looking at a dented can of barbeque flavored Vienna sausages. She was thinking back to the look on Drew's face as he'd carried the canned wieners out to the Expedition. He'd been so excited to show them to Bart. It'd always been one of their favorite snacks to eat together. The fact that it grossed everyone else out just made it all the better.

None of them made a move towards the room their dad was in yet. They couldn't bring themselves to see him lying there. They'd seen plenty of bodies the animals had gotten to already. What if that'd happened to their dad? What if the rats were feasting on his intestines or the vultures were slurping his brains out through his eye sockets? Horrid images flashing through her mind Yue fairly flew into the back bedroom to make sure their dad's body wasn't being defiled. She wanted to get there first to protect Drew and LeBron from the multiple horrors that may have happened according to her hyperactive imagination.

Drew rushed in right after Yue. He was worried she was going to get jumped by a hidden crawler in her haste. LeBron came right after him scanning the room anxiously for any sign of danger. Yue was sitting on the side of the bed silently bawling her eyes out. LeBron ran over and gave her a hug studiously ignoring the large lump in the comforter. Drew stood off to the side trying to be as vigilant as possible. Their dad wouldn't have liked it if they all got killed coming back to bury him. He could almost hear the chewing out they'd have gotten.

Drew went over to the windows. The curtains were already half open. He ripped them completely off the wall letting the sunlight saturate the large master bedroom. He didn't want any crawlerz sneaking by them on a technicality thanks to a shadowy corner. They had a lot to do in a short time. First and foremost, they needed to make sure their dad's remains were taken care of respectfully. He wasn't a hundred percent sure how they'd be able to handle that. Thinking on the fly he came up with a plan that'd let them put it off until later.

They said their final goodbyes in that sun lit clinically white oversized bedroom. Yue had pulled the comforter off of Bart's face to say their farewells. Each of them took a turn holding his cold hand and whispering their heartfelt appreciation for everything that he'd done for them. That they all loved him went without saying but each of them still said it plenty. Once they'd spent a respectful amount of time, they rolled him up in the white comforter and duct taped it around his body. Knowing exactly what their dad would've had to say about them duct taping his corpse into an old blanket brought a smile to each of their lips. A welcome bit of humor penetrating the heavy cloud of sadness pervading the room.

They carried their oversized bundle out into the yard looking for a good spot to send him off. Settling on a slight rise that overlooked the lake Drew set his dad down. He went back inside and grabbed one of their gasoline containers pouring a liberal amount on the comforter. It'd only take a spark now to send Bart to his reward to be with his Nancy.

They proceeded to tear the house apart looking for the keys to the Hummer. They finally found them pushed back on the top of the fridge in a Ziploc bag. Not bothering to waste time wondering why someone would put car keys in a Ziploc bag Yue rushed out to the Hummer to see if it'd start. The big yellow emblem of capitalistic excess rumbled to life on the first try. Yue hopped out and began helping her brothers carry as much of their scattered supplies as they could from the living room out to the Hummer. Considering how many dead bodies were lying around in that area of the house she thought they may need to change the name from living room to something else.

By the time they finished loading the Hummer it was getting dark. Yue was worried they'd pushed the envelope too hard trying to get everything done in such a short amount of time. LeBron kept nervously peeking out the windows to see if a parade of crawlerz were heading their way. They gathered together in the yard with their dad and said a few last words. They held hands and said the Lord's Prayer as they'd done a zillion times on Sundays as a family back before the death of civilization. Then Drew bent down with a lighter and set the comforter on fire.

They didn't have time to stay and watch it burn. Trusting in the gasoline-soaked blanket to handle the task they'd set for it they jogged back to the Hummer and put the garage door up. Yue drove while Drew rode literal shotgun. He was happy to be driving down the road in a vehicle that actually had all of its windows. He knew that wouldn't last long. Other than trying to say a few comforting words Yue and Drew both ignored the continued sobbing coming from LeBron in the back seat.

Chapter 31: All for One

"Do you think we should paint a three on the door?" Drew broke the long silence. He'd been trying to remember the number from the movie for the last twenty miles.

"I've been thinking that since we first saw this thing sitting in the garage." LeBron said. Yue looked over at him happy to see that Drew had managed to wring a smile out of their perma-depressed brother.

"I'll be happy if we can keep the windows in this one. We're going to have to figure out that syphoning trick too. Using the turn signal on this thing eats up a gallon of gas." Drew said looking uneasily at the gas gauge on the overly masculine dashboard. Whoever had bought this thing was definitely trying to compensate for something.

LeBron's smile slipped slowly away as silence reclaimed the interior of the Hummer. None of them were ok. The toll of losing both their parents so horrifically in such a short amount of time was a terrible burden on all of them. Drew kept remembering that he'd only been legally adopted since right before this all started. He'd only been able to really call them mom and dad for a short amount of time. Until they'd actually taken him to the courthouse and signed the papers, he hadn't really believed it was going to happen. Deep down he'd felt like he was going to be rejected again.

LeBron was a wreck while Yue seemed to be doing ok. Part of that was her trying to be strong for her little brothers. Bart and Nancy had been the only parents she'd ever known. She didn't remember foster care or the adoption process or any of that. She just remembered being brought up in a house filled with love. The values and strength her parents had instilled in her were what was helping her cope with their deaths now. She wished she could transfer some of that inner strength to her brothers.

"We need a plan." Yue announced.

"You're saying that driving north isn't going to fix everything?" Drew joked.

"I'm saying I want to live a long healthy life. I'd like the same for both of you. That's not going to happen if we get killed. Driving north for the sake of driving north isn't going to cut it. Where do we stop? How do we know when we've got where we going? We need a destination. We need a plan." Yue said dramatically.

The conversation about a plan brought LeBron back out of his shell. He'd been thinking a lot about what they should do. His overly analytical brain ripped apart everything he came up with though. The idea of finding an isolated farm like the President had brought up in his speech sounded great on the surface. Until you realized that there'd be a ton of survivors trying out that option since the President had mentioned it. Survivors tended to be very territorial. They also tended to be well armed. Considering none of them had ever so much as grown vegetables in the backyard they could put that option towards the bottom of the list.

After seeing how the family had been surviving on the pontoon boat, he liked the idea of living in a large lake with places along the banks to loot, hunt or pick food. Just because they couldn't farm didn't mean they couldn't pick fruit and vegetables. LeBron had no idea how corn worked. He assumed that if you had a big cornfield one year then the corn would grow there again the following year. Even if that's not how corn worked, he did know that apples and grapes and fruits would keep on growing on the same trees and vines every year.

They had weapons. They could always hunt for what they needed. With most of the human population wiped out there was going to be wildlife galore. By next summer they'd probably be tripping over deer and other wild game. The same could be said for the fish populations as well. With a little bit of effort, they could survive out in the middle of nowhere.

Scavenging wasn't going to be an easy long-term solution. Pretty much all of the brick-and-mortar retail stores had been cleaned out before the crawlerz even made it over the border. If they wanted to carve out an existence by scavenging, then they'd have to do it by house hopping. Even that might not get them what they needed to survive. Back in their old house they'd watched as at least one group of refugees went door to door collecting all the supplies they could. The only houses not looted by the refugees had been the ones with armed survivors protecting them. It was going to be hit or miss if those people had survived in their houses long enough to eat through all of their supplies or not.

"It's not impossible to survive by looting houses. Our neighbors had a house full of supplies and they died less than a week into it. We abandoned our house. It was full of food and weapons. We find enough houses like that we can survive for a long time." LeBron said. He'd been talking non-stop for at least the last thirty minutes laying out his thoughts on what they could do. Yue felt like she should be taking notes while Drew just wanted LeBron to summarize and tell them what they should do. He thought the living on a boat eating fresh fruit idea sounded pretty good.

"Dad warned us about going house to house though. He made it sound like that'd be the most dangerous way to try to survive." Yue challenged the door to door scavenging idea. It seemed like that may be where LeBron had been driving the conversation to. As soon as she said it, she felt bad about it. LeBron had been so animated in describing his ideas that he'd broken out of his depression. She hoped she hadn't just driven him right back into it by bringing up one of the last conversations they'd had with their dad.

"I've thought about that, and I totally agree. One thing we haven't talked about has been joining up with other survivors. At some point we're going to need some sort of social interaction. Also, there's a certain amount of safety that comes with numbers." LeBron said seemingly unphased by Yue bringing up their dad.

"If by social interaction you're talking about meeting hot chics I'm in." Drew said from the driver's seat. That plan definitely sounded better than eating apples on a boat with his brother and sister for the next few years. He moved it up to plan number one in his mental list.

"How would we meet other people though? The ones we've run into so far haven't been super friendly." Yue said. She was thinking of the creep in the jacked-up truck. The guy who'd been killed by the foreign exchange students turned highway robbers. Even some of the cops they'd interacted with since all of this started had been more intent on ripping them off than helping them out. Of course, they had murdered a bunch of people to steal a U-Haul full of supplies. It wasn't like they were innocent in all of this either.

"I don't know. I guess I'm thinking of towns that managed to wall out the infected and are still keeping them out. Of course, that'd mean they're also keeping outsiders away. Otherwise, they wouldn't stay uninfected for very long. Somewhere out there the government has set themselves up too. The President said they'd enacted some plan to ensure the United States survives. To me that means they've got secret bases somewhere loaded down with supplies. Of course, I'd bet they're also shooting outsiders who get too close. There's also a good chance the bases are so remote we'll never be able to find them." LeBron said.

"Sounds like we're back to driving north." Drew deadpanned from the front seat. He'd really been hoping after all of that talking LeBron had a better plan in mind than keep going and hope no one killed them.

"The family back on the pontoon boat were nice." Yue reminded them.

"Yeah. They very nicely told us to get the hell out of their territory. The scallions were good though." Drew said.

They kept the conversation going a little longer trying to figure out what they were going to do. There were just too many variables though. The country sped by as Drew kept them at a steady sixty miles per hour. There were long stretches of the interstate where you couldn't tell anything was even going on. These stretches were inevitable ruined by a wrecked car or bodies lying on the side of the road. They hadn't seen a surger in a few hours. Probably because they were in the middle of nowhere. Which was exactly where they wanted to stay. LeBron and Yue were already trying to figure out the best way to bypass Atlanta.

Yue reached up and flipped on the overhead dome light so she could see the map better. They'd found a state map in the glove box. Yue's heart stopped beating.

"Why are we driving at night?" She asked loudly.

"Ah hell." Drew said. He immediately started looking to see what the next exit looked like. He was praying it was going to be as desolate as everywhere else they'd been driving past. If he pulled off into a populated area they were screwed. He couldn't believe none of them had noticed it was getting dark. He'd turned on the headlights without even thinking about it.

The exit they pulled off on was about as desolate as you could hope for. It was so deserted it made you wonder why they'd bothered building an exit there. Drew took them down a long off ramp then took a hard right at the bottom of it. The place looked untouched by the apocalypse. Other than the lack of any lights in the few buildings they drove past nothing was out of the ordinary. Despite how empty the landscape looked Drew still gunned the engine to get them far enough down the road to avoid any unwanted visitors.

Hearts beating like baby rabbits dropped into a cage with a hungry python the three of them sat in the Hummer once they settled on a place to park. The worst failed to materialize. They set watches and spent an uneventful night trying to sleep inside the packed Hummer. It was a no harm no foul kind of situation, but they all felt like complete idiots for having let that happen. If they'd been in a more populated area, they'd be dead by now. They'd gotten lucky. Lady luck couldn't be counted on moving forward.

The next morning Yue got serious about making sure they didn't manage to get caught out in the dark again. She had her alarm sound setup to be an audio file she'd recorded during her turn on watch. It simply announced it was getting dark over and over again. She'd had one set before but had gotten used to just ignoring it. At some point she'd turned it off without ever reactivating it. She took each of their phones and setup a similar alarm at staggered times. LeBron couldn't help but bring up that it'd be really ironic if the alarm going off actually alerted the infected that they were in the area. Yue considered that then set them all up to vibrate instead of using the initial audio files she'd painstakingly recorded for each device.

Alarm situation figured out they drove out of the field they'd spent the night in. They drove back to the interstate and took the onramp just in time to stop and watch three big rigs roll by. The trailers were covered in apocalypse inspired graffiti. Grinning skulls and the flames of hell seeming to be the most popular. Warnings to anyone who may try to interfere with the truckers was written all over it too.

"Beware of the dog?" LeBron questioned one of the odder warnings.

"That must be a pretty badass dog." Yue responded trying to take in all the other warnings and images that were cruising by at a high rate of speed.

The fronts of the trucks were Mad Max masterpieces. Wooden lances stuck out all around them making them look like balding porcupines. The windows had been knocked out and replaced with chain link fencing. The quick peeks they got of the people driving made it look like they'd dressed to match their trucks. Goggles and shiny blood red football helmets prevailed. The truckers looked down on the bright yellow Hummer as they drove by. One of them gave them the bird. Drew gave it right back until Yue slapped his hand down.

"You trying to piss off the crazy looking people in the big trucks?" She hissed.

"They flipped us off first." Drew mumbled feeling like an eight-year-old even as the words left his lips. The look on Yue's face corroborated his self-assessment.

"We going to sit here and wait for the surgers to show up or get moving?" LeBron asked looking back and forth between his brother and sister.

Drew was happy to break off the fight with his sister since he knew he'd been the idiot in that scenario. He turned around in his seat and gassed the engine. The big toy truck accelerated easily up the rest of the onramp. They got back on the interstate and drove about a mile before seeing the big trucks had stopped up ahead. They were parked at an angle to block the road. Drew could just make out the people standing behind the trailers. He braked the Hummer and looked over at Yue.

"What are you looking at me for! Get us out of here!" She yelled.

A dozen giant hornets were buzzing their way towards them. The high-pitched whine of the dirt bikes the ambushers were riding started up out of nowhere. The trucks must have stopped and let out the riders then driven another mile down the road to setup the ambush. An army of the bikers were headed right for them from the opposite side of the interstate. Drew spun the wheel while flooring the accelerator and drove right through them. Miraculously the dirt bike riding troop all managed to dodge the oversized Tonka truck Drew was trying to kill them with.

Completing the turn in the grassy median Drew accelerated slinging a rooster tail of mud into the air behind them. The dirt bikers were on top of them almost immediately riding one handed while pointing pistols and sawed-off shotguns at them from every side. Drew ignored them and kept driving. If they could just pick up a little more speed, they should be able to outrun the dirt bikes. The riders must have sensed that Drew wasn't planning to stop for anything. The bikers rode away from the doors. Drew was feeling pretty good about that until the lead rider started shooting at their front tire.

Drew yanked the wheel to the right sending the bikers on that side spinning off into the median. The leader did a wheelie and rode right in front of them. Drew felt the moment the guy finally scored a hit on the tire. The Hummer pulled hard to the left and he found himself driving on a rim. The bikers were circling them now like great whites circling a dying whale. They'd streak in and take their pound of flesh then dart off before they could retaliate. Once they ran out of gas it'd just be a matter of time before they were forced away from the Hummer to be taken prisoner or killed. Most likely these freaks would leave their dead bodies in a ditch while they rode away with their stuff.

Screw that.

Instead of continuing down the interstate Drew turned the wheel to aim for the trees. They smashed over the edge of the road bouncing into the wooded area below. Drew wrenched the wheel to the left as they side swiped a big pine tree. He was yelling for everyone to get out and make a run for it when they ran headfirst into a much bigger tree. He was bouncing off the console when the air bag deployed as he was trying to pull his pistol out. Everything went black.

LeBron was the only one who didn't lose consciousness. He was in the back seat with his seat belt on. Yue and Drew had both banged off the consoles and had the air bags explode in their faces. They were out for the count. LeBron had almost blacked out from the blinding whiplash when they unexpectedly slammed into the tree. The pain of ramming his messed-up finger into the seat in front of him had actually kept him from joining his brother and sister in La La Land. He fumbled for the doorknob and opened it. He stepped out of the door onto the forest floor with his pistol in his hand.

A helmeted figure stepped out of the shadows and smashed him in the face with the butt of a shotgun. LeBron dropped the pistol and fell to his knees. His vision was blurry, he tasted blood and every part of his body hurt. He couldn't even see the person who'd just hit him. He groped around in his pocket until he found the novelty folding knife that he'd taken from the shattered case in a truck stop. He was trying to unfold it when the figure in the helmet sighed and kicked him in the jaw hard enough to knock him out.

Chapter 32: Step Right Up

"Wake up." The words drifted to LeBron from far away. He didn't want to wake up. He'd maneuvered himself into a position where the pain was equalized around his body. He was afraid that if he moved, he'd lose that equilibrium. He was floating now using the unconsciousness to buffer him from the pain.

"Do you think he's ok?" The words pierced the cocoon LeBron was struggling to keep intact around himself. Outside the cocoon was pain and death. Inside of it he'd found balance. A face appeared in his thoughts. The person talking was his sister. If he could hear her talking, she must not be dead. He was sitting on something hard and scratchy. His face hurt like crazy. He opened his eyes to a small room illuminated by a weird red glow. Moving his head to the left and right slowly he smiled painfully at this brother and sister. They were squatting to either side of him staring down.

"Where are we?" LeBron asked. It hurt to move his jaw to ask the question. He was guessing one whole side of his face was a bruise. He hoped he didn't have any facial fractures. The tip of his tongue felt weird. His mouth tasted like snotty blood and dirt.

"We're locked up in a room inside one of their trucks. We both woke up when they were dragging us out of the Hummer. I was worried you might be dead the way you were laid out on the ground. I tried to check on you, but they bashed me in the head a few times. I woke up in here." Drew said.

"I skipped the second round of facial pummeling. They were holding me too tight to get away anyway. They talked to some guy over walkie talkies and told him what'd happened. He told them to throw us in the cat cage and lock us up." Yue said hesitatingly. Drew gave her a hard look.

"Did he say anything else?" Drew asked. He felt like Yue was holding something back.

"They talked about whether they should kill us or not. It didn't sound like there was a really conclusive answer. I think they were pretty pissed we didn't just pull over and give them all of our stuff." Yue said. She felt better for saying it. It actually didn't even seem as bad now that she'd said it out loud.

"You see anything when they were taking us all to this room?" LeBron asked.

"Not really. I think this was part of a circus or something. The truck was already setup for them to hang their dirt bikes off the ceiling and there were lots of storage rooms built in. They did a pretty thorough job of taking all of our stuff." Yue finished. She sighed and leaned back against the wall. There was nothing else to say really.

They sat in the eerie red room for what felt like an eternity. There was just enough moldy straw left in the box to be itchy without providing any real cushioning. Whatever cat had been locked in the huge crate previously had really enjoyed marking its territory. The strong acidic smell was probably the main reason why the decent sized space was available to use as a temporary jail cell for the three of them. Thank God for PETA and the Tiger King pushing all the animal people to make their cages nice and roomy. They were jostled around occasionally as the truck swerved or hit a bump.

The wooden door rattled surprising the three of them. A short black woman with a brightly colored bandana tied around her head opened up the door. She looked around at the three of them then handed Yue a box filled with water and cans of food. There was also a plastic bag with a few pills in it. Yue snorted out a laugh when she saw the cans of food that they'd been handed were basically a variety pack of the Vienna sausages out of the Hummer. The woman had the nerve to serve them out of their own stash. The woman grinned when she saw Yue had recognized the food.

"You guys need anything else? I assumed you really liked the little sausages considering how many of them we found in that car you wrecked. Eat your food and someone will come by to take you to the bathroom in a little bit. If you can't wait, I don't think it's possible for you to make the inside of this box smell any worse." The woman smiled again indicating the stench they were all dealing with. She took a step backwards and prepared to close the door.

"Excuse me. What's the plan for us? Why do you have us caged up in here?" Yue asked looking the woman in the eyes.

"Are you guys from a circus?" Drew asked. The woman gave him a condescending look at the word circus.

"We're a type of circus you could say. A carnival macabre is how we've been introduced. An ancient clan of the Roma travelling the world to entertain royalty. Or at least that's what we used to pretend to be. Now we're three trucks full of freaks in a world full of freaks. We honestly haven't decided what to do with you three yet. We're saving that to puzzle out later." Questions answered as much as she was willing to answer them the woman started to shut the door again.

"Hey! You could just pretend we'd just pulled over. You have our stuff already. Just let us go." LeBron sounded more than a little desperate. Not that there was any reason whatsoever not to sound desperate in a situation like this.

"Silly boy. If you'd just pulled over and let us take you stuff, we'd have slit your throats and left you in the ditch. The only reason you're still alive is that you tried to run us down then shoot us. You were pretty much in a coma and yet you still tried to unfold a knife to attack us. You may not be the brightest or strongest, but you've got heart. Heart is all that matters." The woman finished talking with a flourish. With one hand over her heart, she let her smile disappear as she sealed them back in their crate.

"I didn't realize how weird an apocalypse could get." Yue joked while she split up the food and passed it out.

The sausages turned out to be a god send for LeBron. Something was definitely wrong with his jaw. He couldn't really tell which part of his jaw hurt the most because everything hurt. Yue opened the can for him so he could pick them out. He was able to kind of mush the sausages around in his mouth until he could swallow them. The pills were just regular Tylenol tablets. Yue assumed the people who'd captured them had kept all the good stuff for themselves. She beat the tablets with her shoe until they were in small enough pieces for LeBron to swallow along with his water.

They were taken one at a time to use the bathroom. The bathroom turning out to be a hole cut in the bottom of the trailer with a toilet seat mounted above it. There was a solid steel plate mounted on sliders to allow for sealing off the small hole when not in use. The smell was about what you'd expect. It wasn't nearly as bad as the cat piss smell of the crate they were spending all of their time in. The interior of the trailer was lit with the red lights. There were all kinds of supplies shoved pretty much everywhere.

There was a good dozen people keeping a watchful eye on them as they did their business. Between the pain in his face and dozen people staring at him it took LeBron a good five minutes to get a stream going. His escort thought it was hilarious which didn't help him at all. Looking around he saw piercings and crazy hairstyles. One guy lounging nearby on top of a stack of crates looked like he was three hundred pounds of solid muscle. His massive biceps covered in the amateur tattoos LeBron associated with outlaws. This guy must've spent all of his time behind bars on the weight pile in between shooting up roids.

They got another pee break a few hours later. Other than that, they spent their time sitting in the recently emptied giant litterbox staring at each other. They'd tried to come up with a plan but there really wasn't a great way to get out of the situation they were in. They didn't have much to go on beyond the cryptic answers the gypsy looking black woman had given them. Based on the extremely eclectic mix of people they saw on their trips outside the box to pee the circus macabre title definitely fit.

LeBron had his head in Yue's lap. She was stroking his hair while he tried to sleep when they felt the truck come to a jolting stop. LeBron tried to sit up, but Yue shushed him and got him to lie still. Drew was watching LeBron with fire in his eyes. He wished he could kick the door off this crate and walk through the trailer with guns blazing. He'd love to cause some serious pain to the circus clown who'd done that to LeBron. He could understand chasing them down to steal their supplies. Once they'd hit the tree though the freaks could've taken everything they wanted and just left them there. What the hell was up with putting them in this stupid box?

The crate door opened an hour later. They'd been alerted by the sound of the lock being jangled around on the other side. All of them assumed it was just another bathroom break. It turned out they were partially right. Instead of being hauled out one at a time to piss in the hole all three of them were ushered out at the same time. They were given drinks and offered the chance to use the hole which they each did. Once they were ready, they were marched to the back of the trailer where the doors were. There were three people standing there waiting for them. The black woman with the bandana, the massively muscled felon and a dark-haired man with greasy hair who was wearing a top hat. The rest of the people from the trailer were gathering behind them now.

"You're the three morons who wouldn't pull over. You don't look related. How do you know each other?" The man in the top hat asked.

"These are my brothers." Yue said simply. The one thing they'd all agreed on was to let her do the talking. Drew was too hot headed, and LeBron was a tad too introverted. Plus, LeBron was doing all he could just to stand up with the pain he was in. Doing a lot of conversing was out of the question.

"I see. Interesting. Which one do you love more?" The man asked.

"I'm sorry. I love them both. They're my brothers." Yue repeated wondering what this slimy little top hat wearing used car selling piece of garbage was getting at.

"Let me put it this way. Tell me which one gets to live. You have three seconds." The man had pulled out a pistol and was pointing it at LeBron. He waggled his eyebrows and pointed it at Drew then moved the barrel back and forth.

"Kill me you little bitch!" Drew took a big step forward getting right in the man's face. The pistol came to rest on Drews forehead. Drew slapped the gun away. Before the man could react, he dropped to his knee and went for the top hat wearing guy's leg. He caught the huge guy's knee in his face and was laid out flat on his back. LeBron was tossed on top of him a second later when he took a clumsy swing at top hat. Two men from the crowd grabbed Yue by the arms to keep her from jumping in.

"Well, that went sideways pretty fast." Top hat said pointing the gun down at Drew and LeBron who were working on getting disentangled. A smile was playing across his face as he watched the two of them. He put the pistol back in his holster and addressed Yue once again.

"I'm Blaze. I'm happy to meet you." The man emphasized the word 'you' while grinning mischievously. "Sorry I couldn't help it. I love a good pun." A few people snickered. Yue wasn't sure if they knew her name was Yue or if they were just sucking up to the boss. She was pretty sure at this point that Blaze must be the man in charge. She was also sensing that under all of the schtick lurked a cunning mind.

"Are you planning on letting us go?" Yue asked. Blaze let the awkward silence build up. He acted as if he were pondering her question for the first time. Yue waited with her hands restrained behind her by men she couldn't see. She was doing her best to look calm and collected. On the inside she was vibrating with a mix of cold fear and red-hot rage.

"No. We're not planning on letting you go. We've lost well over half of our clan in the last month. There should be another three trucks in this convoy. We need fresh blood. Your little family seems like it might be a good fit. We like the odd and we love the foolishly brave. It seems to me that three adopted kids from different races may fit the odd mold. Individually you're not much but together you're unique. We find strength through diversity and all that good stuff. I honestly would've had a hard time believing it if Charani hadn't showed me your driver's licenses. Your brothers already showed me they've got the guts to fight for their family. Maybe not a lot going on in the brains department though." Blaze finished glancing down at Drew and LeBron who were both in obvious pain.

"Before all this happened, we were talking about how we needed to find other people to work with. This could be perfect." Yue tried hard to inject enthusiasm into her voice. She was thinking fast. Given the general weirdness of what was going on choosing to walk away wasn't going to be an option. If they couldn't walk away, then the next best thing was going to be to try and go all in. They'd earn trust faster that way which would be useful if they did decide to make a run for it. Maybe this freak show would work out to be a decent place to hang out in the apocalypse.

"That sounded super fake, but I'll give you a 'B' for effort. You really think you can bullshit a bunch of road gypsies?" Blaze didn't bother waiting for an answer. "Here's what we're going to do. You and the brother without the broken face are going to stay in this truck reporting to Charani. We're taking the black kid with the broken face to our trailer. We have a doctor there who can take care of him. If you guys decide to make a run for it, we'll feed him to the lion. Do what you're told, and you'll be fed and have a safe place to sleep at night. I don't think you're going to find a better offer than that anywhere else anyway."

"You still have a lion?" Drew asked from a sitting position down on the floor. He'd have thought they'd have gotten rid of all the big cats.

"You got me. We ate the lions and the tigers and the bears. Oh my. Only fresh meat we've had in a while. Both of our trainers were zombified early on so we couldn't do much with the big fleabags anyway. You good with the deal?" Blaze said redirecting his attention to Yue who was obviously the spokesperson for the sibling trio.

Yue nodded her head in agreement. The three of them were shuffled back to their crate to spend the night. One of the unbreakable rules was that once the sun went down the doors didn't open again until the lead truck ordered it.

"So, we're like Gypsy assistants now?" Drew asked. His face was covered in flecks of the dried blood he was trying to wipe off with his shirt sleeve.

"Better than being the people the Gypsies killed and left on the side of the road." Yue answered. LeBron nodded along to that for a second before the pain of simply nodding his head struck him and he had to stop.

"At least they took our Vienna sausages, so we'll have plenty to eat." Drew said smiling at the face Yue made.

Chapter 33: Story Time

LeBron was taken away first thing in the morning. Drew and Yue watched with dread as their younger brother followed Blaze out the open back doors of the truck and disappeared around the side. A few minutes later the doors were shut and sealed from the inside. They felt the shudder of the engines starting as the truck came to life. Charani had them sit down on a couple of crates in front of a plush leather recliner. Charani sat in the recliner and looked at them both.

"Either of you have any special talents or skills? Hobbies we should know about. Medical problems or anything like that?" She asked them.

"I was a waitress going to college and my brother's an athlete." Yue answered.

"I like working with wood." Drew added. Charani didn't look impressed.

"Have either of you killed anyone?" Charani asked with a bored expression. Her eyes lit up and she leaned forward attentively when Drew and Yue exchanged a guilty glance.

"We've both killed the infected. Our dad was a cop and a soldier before that. He taught all three of us to shoot." Yue finally answered. Charani could tell there was more but chose not to go down that path quite yet.

"Being able to shoot is a good thing. For the next little bit, I want you to use your listening skills. Feel free to ask me questions. I won't bite. We have nothing to do today while we bounce around in the back of the vardo. Unless the ringmaster sees another bright yellow Hummer that he wants."

Charani was a born storyteller. She spent the next hour patiently answering their questions while filling them in on what was going on with the strangely painted trucks. The trucks that the clan called vardo. They weren't a real gypsy clan. Like she'd mentioned before they were more of a sideshow. Blaze was the majority owner and the manager of the group. Depending on who they were negotiating with he was called a ringmaster, CEO, or a Gypsy king. Whatever title got them to the most money the fastest was what he was.

The clan mostly called him Blaze now. He'd answer to pretty much any honorific you wanted to throw out there. As would most of the clan or troupe or whatever you wanted to call them. They were all multifaceted actors ready to pretend to be a wandering group of the Rom or a small circus as needed. They'd mostly played large music festivals as a sideshow. They regularly had people flying back and forth to Vegas doing different acts like juggling, magicians, cat shows, mentalism, and the like. They also got calls to do private shows for the rich. Those could get a little risqué but also brought in some pretty big dollars.

Vardo was the gypsy word for a wagon. Blaze had adopted it to mean their trucks. He enjoyed taking aspects of the Rom and the circus and blending them into a semi-secret language only the clan could follow. Each vardo had a leader. Blaze was the leader for the first vardo and Charani was the leader of the vardo they were currently riding in. Harley was the name of the giant muscular dude riding with them. He actually owned the second vardo. It was stuffed with supplies not people, so he chose to ride with Charani instead.

The clan had been in New Orleans when the news came that the crawlerz were coming up through Central America. At first, they hadn't taken it seriously. Enough of them had relatives scattered across the world that pretty soon they couldn't just ignore it anymore. They'd loaded up the full caravan minus anyone who had some other home worth going back to. They'd set out with seven fully loaded trucks. A flotilla of smaller vehicles kept pace. Blaze had taken them all to a remote campground to setup and see what happened. They'd thought they had plenty of time.

When they tried to leave the state, they were turned back twice by state troopers heavily reinforced by the military. Reading the signs based on the news blackouts and talking to their contacts Blaze knew they had to either get out or find a solid place to hide. The remote campground they were in had seemed good enough. Good enough hadn't cut it. They'd been there a week longer than Blaze had hoped they'd be. They'd been fairly silent the whole time. With that many flamboyant personalities wandering the site it was impossible to keep the noise level too moderated though. Not that it was just noise that attracted the crawlerz.

They'd come an hour after sunset. Just a few of the crazy fast homicidal freaks. That'd been all it took to wipe out a third of the clan. Screams and gunfire had ripped through the night. Everyone panicked and ran around shooting and screaming. Charani remembered seeing a guy who made Harley look small get his head twisted around so far that he was looking backward before falling dead to the ground. The crawler that'd done it was a ten-year-old girl.

"I still remember how her eyes bored into me. I lost all my nerve. My knees turned to water. I slammed the back of the truck closed and locked it. I heard some people screaming outside but I never opened the door until the next morning." Charani said. She paused then to stare off above their heads. Yue and Drew waited respectfully for her to come back to them. They both knew about that horrifying gaze the crawlerz had. Charani took a minute to shake that memory off then continued with her story.

The next morning when the clan had emerged from the trailers, they'd done so to find most of the people attacked the night before had turned to surgers. They'd spent that morning fighting for their lives against their demon possessed friends. They'd lost even more of the clan that morning. They realized then how lucky they were most of their trucks could be opened and closed easily from the inside. They'd rigged them like that since a lot of them ended up sleeping in the trailers during gigs to save money.

The state troopers post that kept turning them back had been attacked as well. The remainder of the troopers tried to turn the clan back around again. Blaze had just blasted the horn and driven right through the bullets. One driver caught a bullet in his shoulder, and one truck pulled over with a flat tire but everyone else made it through the gauntlet.

They'd learned to only drive during the day to avoid the crawlerz. At night they always slept inside the locked trailers not emerging until the sun was up. They had some webcams and small holes they'd drilled in strategic places to let them check if it was safe or not to come out. There were plenty of times they had to beat down a surger or two in order for the driver and his escort to make it up to the front of the truck. A few nights had been like living through a nightmarish hailstorm as the crawlerz pounded on every inch of the trailers trying to find a way in.

They'd come up with the porcupine look to keep surgers off the fronts of the trucks when they were moving. The long poles worked to sweep most of the charging surgers off their feet before they could leap for the drivers. One trailer they'd lost had been filled with crawlerz when they opened it. The people inside had turned into surgers or ripped apart. They'd lost another two people when they sent them to investigate. There was no definitive reason for it having happened. Someone had either hidden a bite, or a crawler had managed to rip its way in somehow. Maybe through the latrine hole they had under the mounted toilet in each truck.

"That's about it. Pretty much the worse road trip ever. That dirt bike thing we did to you was something new. I thought you'd just pull over and let us take your crap. Would've been way smarter than running into a tree. We do this act where we set a globe on fire and ride around the inside of the globe on the dirt bikes, so we have some pretty good riders. Enough about us though. How'd such a diverse trio of siblings wind up out here on the road?" Charani leaned forward and put her chin on her fists to listen. All the others who'd been half-listening to Charani tell their story leaned in to listen as well. This was what passed for entertainment in this brave new world.

Yue told their story occasionally pausing for Drew to pitch in. Their audience was spellbound as the story played out. At both their mothers and father's deaths there were the typical words of condolence. Drew had a hard time accepting the condolences of the people who'd just tried to kill them to steal their ride. Charani seemed particularly interested in the family living on the boat when they got to that part of their story. Anything that resembled a long-term survival strategy was valuable intel. The fact that the infected couldn't swim was news to the clan as well.

Once story time was over Yue asked what was next. Charani leaned back in her chair and closed her eyes. She started talking with her eyes still closed. She used her pointer fingers to massage her temples while she spoke.

"What's next' is the million-dollar question. You said you wanted to join a group of survivors. You'd be hard pressed to find a group more interested in survival than this one. We're on our way right now to a place even more remote than the last one. We can't travel too far since the longer we're on the road the more likely something goes wrong. For now, feel free to socialize. I'll have different people teach you different things as we travel. You'll follow our rules or be punished. That's about it." Charani signaled she was done with them by leaning back and hitting the button for the bottom of the recliner to shoot out. She almost tagged Drew in the chin, but he jumped back out of the way in time.

"Too bad you didn't move that fast when I smacked you with my knee." Harley said to Drew. Drew looked back and saw the big man had a big grin on his face. It wasn't an ill-natured grin at all. Now that Harley wasn't trying to be intimidating it looked like he might not be so bad after all.

"Yeah, that came out of nowhere. I was going for Blaze and didn't even think about looking over at you. My mistake." Drew said standing up to be on eye level with the big man. Harley was sitting on the seat of one of the dirt bikes. He was so big he made the bike look like a kid's toy.

"Ha. I love the way you pikers say Blaze. His real name is Louis Percival. Now that you're part of the team and whatnot I can tell you that. You see a couple of rubes on the midway though you make sure to call him Blaze. For some reason he really thinks it sounds cool. My real name's Richard Rickenbacker. I have a theory that we all ended up here just so we could give ourselves cooler names." Harley said.

"LeBron may take you up on that offer. He's talked to me about changing his name a few times." Yue replied sidling over to join in the conversation. She wanted to personalize their brother to the big guy. Harley took the bait with a glint in his eyes that indicated he knew exactly what she was doing.

"LeBron seems like a fine name for a proud young black man." Despite himself Harley was now a little curious what the deal was.

"He's not good at basketball. Horrible actually. Loves to sit in his room and read all day. He won't even watch sports. It'd be like if I was named Joe Montana. Except I'm actually pretty awesome at football so I guess it's not the same thing at all." Drew said. He didn't know where Yue was going with this but intuited this was the right thing for him to say.

"That's kind of a boy named Sue situation." Harley joked. Yue and Drew stared back at him completely lost.

"Johnny Cash?" Harley tried. When they both still sat there staring at him, he muttered something about millennials and told them they should go grab some food since they'd be working later.

"What are we going to be doing?" Drew asked. With all the circus talk he had visions of pounding in stakes to help setup a tent. He kept wondering if this was all just some weird dream and he was really face down in the air bag in the Hummer. He could easily have gone into a coma or something when they hit that tree. Harley's response to his question made him think being in a coma in a broken-down car surrounded by crawlerz might be better than their new reality. The pain in his face and the burn marks on his skin from the air bag dashed his hopes of it all just being a dream.

"You two get to be our canaries. When we stop there'll be plenty of cameras and the drivers will be able to look around. The place we're heading for should be deserted, but you never know for sure. The best way to find out is to send a couple of pikers like you guys to walk around for a bit. If no scary monsters come running to try and eat you that means the rest of us can come out and have a picnic before the sun goes down. Once the sun starts going down the rule is everyone back in the trucks for quiet time no matter what."

Chapter 34: Canaries

The trucks slowed to turn off the highway. Once off the highway they began twisting and turning down a long winding road. Yue and Drew sat near the back doors next to a man and woman in their late twenties. Both of them had shaved heads and were wearing too much jewelry. One of them caught Drew checking out their heads.

"We're quick-change artists. We use wigs in our act so keeping our heads shaved just works for us. Although I guess we don't really need to worry about it so much now. Just habit I guess." The man said.

"More like it gets itchy when it starts growing back. So far, we haven't had any issues getting our hands-on shaving cream and razors. We must be the only ones in the world still worried about shaving. Although my legs are probably hairier than his at this point." The woman said grinning over at them.

Yue smiled politely back at the couple while Drew just ignored them. He'd made up his mind he didn't like these people and he wasn't as good of an actor as Yue was. She had to keep reminding him to play nice since these people had LeBron locked up in another trailer. Based on the general weirdness of these people there was quite literally no telling what they may do to LeBron if they screwed up. The truck slowed then came to a stop.

"Your time to shine." Charani appeared out of the depths of the trailer. She was holding a handheld radio. Harley was walking behind her with a big black duffle bag. The huge muscles in his arm twitching as he set the bag down on the floor in front of them.

"It's your gear that we took off of you. Go ahead and pull out what you want. You can leave the rest in the bag. It's your bag so we won't be taking anything out of it now that you've agreed to be one of us. We don't steal from one another. Anyone else is fair game." Harley nudged the bag towards them with his foot to get them to open it.

Inside the bag were all of the weapons they'd been wearing when captured plus a good portion of their other gear. They spent a few minutes sliding back into their rigs. It felt good to have the weapons on again. Drew realized now how naked he'd felt without them.

"What about the rest of our stuff?" Drew asked as he was busy shoving knives and magazines into his pockets. Yue gave him an exasperated look. They really should be pretty happy with being armed again.

"Bulk food and ammunition supplies are stockpiled to be shared for the good of the clan. You'll get more storage place and privacy the longer you're here. We're not a bunch of hippies but we're pooling our supplies together to get through this. You have a problem sharing all your cans of tiny, flavored sausages?" Charani fixed Drew with a stare that showed why she was fierce enough to be in charge of one of the vardo.

"What do we do now?" Yue asked looking to change the subject. She wanted to get this job done and see if they could check on LeBron.

"Once we get the word you and your brother will exit the truck and walk the perimeter. Basically, just do a big circle around where we're parked and see if you see anything suspicious. We'll scan everything with webcams first to see if anything pops up. The drivers were checking the whole time we came in as well. We'll give you both radios. If you're still alive in thirty minutes, then the rest of us come out and stretch our legs for a bit." Harley filled them in on what they'd be doing.

"You guys trust us now?" Drew asked indicating the fully loaded AR-15 he was cradling under his arm.

"We trust you not to want to get your brother killed. You're also seriously outgunned if you did want to try and pull something. Although I really had to control myself not to snag one of those sweet assault rifles for myself." Harley was looking at Charani while he talked. When she heard the order come across the radio, she nodded at him.

Harley waved Yue and Drew over then opened the doors. Drew took the lead moving quickly out the back of the truck. Yue came right after him since Harley was making it super obvious that he was in a hurry to get the door shut and locked. They began the loop around the trucks under the watchful eyes of the drivers and their escorts. The trucks hadn't been turned off yet since the drivers were ready to drop the hammer at a moment's notice if they needed to get the hell out of there. They were sitting ducks up in their cabs.

The spot they'd parked in for the night was a parking lot next to a sandy beach on a huge lake. Drew stomped around the perimeter angrily. He was holding his rifle like he'd welcome the chance to put some rounds into something. Yue followed behind hoping to temper Drews temper before it blew up in their faces. They were both so preoccupied with his simmering anger at having LeBron held hostage that they lost precious seconds when a small group of surgers came running at them from the woods on the other side of the road.

Losing a few seconds when dealing with attackers who move as unnaturally fast as the surgers was a big deal. If one of them hadn't been screaming they'd have probably been pulled to the ground and eaten before getting off a single shot. As it was Yue swung around first and immediately yelled for Drew to help.

There was a total of five surgers sprinting towards them. They were dressed for camping and their clothing was still relatively fresh looking indicating they hadn't been turned that long ago. Yue got two shots off before a skinny kid sprung forward and knocked her to the ground. Drew was standing beside her firing at the three still running for them. He had no time to bend down to help Yue who was grunting as she rolled around on the ground with the surger. She was desperately fending off the things teeth as it snaked its arms behind her crushing her into a lovers embrace.

Drew put rounds in two more of the surgers before one got past and knocked him to the ground beside Yue. Somewhere off in the distance Drew heard shots ringing out. He felt his wrist twisted around so hard he knew it must be sprained. It might even be broken. He pulled his pistol and fired four times into the torso of the older man in red flannel who'd taken him down. Using the old man to help him steady his hand he shot the woman trying to pull Yue close enough to bite her. He kept shooting her until she collapsed on top of his hyperventilating sister. Disregarding her respiratory crisis, he rolled on his back to shoot the other surgers he'd seen coming at them.

Nothing was coming at them. Blinking in surprise he slowly sat up looking in every direction. He finally noticed the escort in the truck closest to him had his hunting rifle stuck out the window. He waved jauntily over at Drew when he saw that Drew had finally noticed him. Drew stood all the way up and helped Yue to her feet. She waved a thank you to the truck escort as well before they returned to their perimeter check.

They walked the perimeter a few more times before whoever was in charge of making the call made the call. The backs of two of the trucks opened up and the clan hopped out. This couple of hours bleeding into dusk were the best part of the day for most of them. A life spent trapped in the big metal coffin on wheels was a life most of them didn't think was worth living. On the flip side they understood that the big metal coffins and their extremely unique lifestyles were the only things that'd kept them alive this long.

"The gun shots will probably bring us a lot of visitors tonight but we're staying anyway. Drew, we're going to have you keep walking the perimeter for the next hour. Yue, feel free to go check on your brother in the first vardo but then join back up with Drew on sentry duty." Charani had walked straight over to them when she came out of the truck. She gave her orders and turned to leave.

"Can I go see LeBron too?" Drew asked.

"Nope. Follow orders boy. It's what's going to keep you alive." Charani tossed the reprimand over her shoulder as she headed towards the lake to take in the view. A revolver dangled from her hand for defense. Drew nodded in appreciation on seeing that. The surgers came so fast that you might not have time to figure out where your holster was. Having one of those things coming straight for you could be a bit stressful.

Drew grumbled a reply and took off on his rounds while Yue went to check on LeBron. She met up with Drew again about an hour later. She'd been allowed into the first vardo with her weapons and taken to see LeBron. He was sitting in a nice recliner like the one Charani had claimed as her throne in the vardo they were riding in. He had a book open in front of him and a cool glass of ice water beside him. A couple cans worth of Vienna sausages were on a paper plate beside him. Yue looked closer at the books and saw they had titles like 'Foundations of Epidemiology' and 'Epidemiology and Biostatics'.

"A little light reading?" She'd asked him. LeBron had been startled at being addressed. He'd been completely engulfed in the textbook in front of him. He smiled and nodded at her offering her the plate of Vienna sausages. She declined those morsels but did take a big swig of his ice water. The doctor, a veterinarian, who was treating him saw Yue standing there and had come over to tell her what was going on. They had no X-Ray machines but best guess he had a fractured jaw. Probably just a hairline fracture. The plan was to keep him immobile until it healed. Until then he wasn't supposed to talk or move his mouth very much at all.

"So, LeBron's doing good." Yue said. Even in his ticked off mood Drew recognized something odd about the way Yue was acting.

"What else is going on?" He asked. He'd noticed everyone was starting to wander back towards the trailers. Between the gunshots and the talking outside everyone was pretty surprised no more surgers had already shown up. No one wanted to be caught outside when it got dark enough for the crawlerz to emerge.

"Blaze asked me to eat dinner with him." Yue said so fast that Drew almost missed it.

"You said no right?" Drew stopped walking to stare at her.

"I said yes. He kind of holds our lives in his palm right now. I have to go back to his truck for the night to meet up with him. I'll see you tomorrow though." Yue was backing away from the anger smoldering in her brother's eyes.

"You mean his 'vardo' don't you? The guys like twenty years older than you." Drew hissed. Yue pulled away.

"Don't worry. I'm a big girl. It's just dinner anyway. Honestly with a name like Blaze I would've thought he'd have invited you to dinner instead of me." Yue walked towards the trailer she'd be spending the night in while a super sulky Drew walked towards his. A scream from the other side of the trailers captured both their attention.

Drew ran around the truck in time to see a naked obese man sink his teeth into the flesh on the back of the bald woman they'd talked to earlier that day. The other half of the couple was lying on the ground a few feet away with his throat and half of the skin on his face ripped off. The obese man's face snapped up when Drew yelled to get his attention. The woman squirmed out from under the greasy mound of fat rolls and curly black hair. She disappeared underneath the truck. Drew put three rounds into the fat surger before it could even get close to him.

Drew nodded at Yue who'd come around from the other side of the truck to help. She took in the situation and nodded back then left for her date. They were both moving extra fast and being extra quiet since there were obviously now surgers in the area. Charani was at the door with Harley waiting for everyone to get back in so they could close up for the night. She asked about the hairless couple since they were the only others not accounted for. Drew shook his head to indicate the couple hadn't made it.

The bald woman walked around the opposite side of the truck and stared at Drew. She was in the early stages of the transition. Drew had seen this stage plenty of times in the videos LeBron had shown him. It wouldn't be long now before she went from looking roofied to trying to rip his head off. He raised the barrel of his rifle slightly. The woman's eyes narrowed, and she leapt at him with a low growl. He fired his rifle at the same time Harley gave her both of his barrels. One of the slugs from Harley caught her in the middle of her head.

Drew scrambled up into the back of the trailer. Charani took one last sad look down at the body of the bald woman before helping Harley shut and lock the back doors. She didn't ask Drew where Yue was. Drew took that to mean that the whole truck knew his sister was on a date with the boss. That wasn't gross at all.

Drew stormed to the back of the truck and found a place to sleep as far from the cat piss smelling crate as possible. As worked up as he was, he doubted he'd even be able to fall asleep. The stress warred with his exhaustion and the exhaustion eventually won.

Chapter 35: The Man in the Suit

"Wake up."

Drew shifted away from the prodding boot and overly loud voice. He kept his eyes tightly shut and willed whoever it was to go away so he could sleep another five minutes. Whoever it was didn't respond to Drews subconscious snooze button request.

"Seriously wake up." The next time was followed by a more substantial boot to his ribs. Drew looked up to see Harley towering over him with an amused look on his face. Drew sat up making a big show of rubbing his side.

"Good morning to you too. What's up?" Drew was mostly interested in hitting the pee hole then trying to figure out where the coffee smell was coming from. He caught himself looking around for LeBron and Yue. Remembering belatedly that they weren't in this trailer put him in an even worse mood than getting kicked awake had.

"We've got company outside. I need you awake and ready to fight in about ten minutes. Take a piss, grab some coffee, then lock and load and meet up by the back door. You good?" Harley asked.

Drew nodded and stood up while stretching. He'd ended up sleeping on a yoga pad on the floor with his duffle bag of supplies for a pillow. Harley had already walked away to enlist a few other expendables in the early morning surger hunt. Drew stood in a short queue before getting the opportunity to pee in the stinking hole. With the threat of the surgers trying to get in he'd have hated to be a girl first thing that morning. It must be pretty scary planting yourself on that seat knowing a surger could shove his hand right up the hole at any time.

In less than ten minutes he was squatting by the back-door sipping steaming hot coffee out of a tiny Styrofoam cup. A few other guys were gathered around getting their weapons ready while they chatted. Drew was still feeling antisocial towards everyone here. He kept his head down and waited for Harley to tell him what he was supposed to do. Harley walked over a few minutes later holding a laptop in his ridiculously large hands. Drew sat up attentively as Harley flipped the laptop around. He carefully set it on top of a cart so they could all see it.

"There's a handful of infected bouncing around between the trucks. We're going to clear them out then escort the drivers to their cabs. The laptop is showing the view from the back of vardo one. I've been watching and I've counted eight surgers total so not horrible. Keep your cool and you'll be safely bored in here again in no time." Harley made sure everyone had seen the laptop screen then popped open the back door.

They went out the door in the order they'd been lined up in the truck. Drew waited nervously for his turn. His mind scrambling through all the different situations he could find himself in. He hoped none of them were as bad as the previous day when he'd been forced to kill a woman that he'd thought he might end up being friends with. The hairless couple had been interesting if nothing else. Drew was thinking of shaving his off just to keep the infected from being able to grab him by it. Shoving all that noise to the back of his mind he climbed quickly out of the truck and took his place with the others.

A nice breeze was blowing off the lake ruffling their hair as they all stood there. The infected were pounding away on vardo number one based on the noise coming from that direction. Harley jumped to the ground last. He had a shotgun in each hand and two more hanging off his right shoulder. He took the lead position and walked quietly around the edge of the truck. The infected were lined up neatly along the lead truck. Their backs facing the armed gunmen who quickly spread out and waited for Harley to kick off the shooting gallery.

Harley fired a salvo into the back of the infected across from him. Taking their cue from their leader everyone else opened up as well. The surgers spun around but weren't fast enough to attack the gypsy firing line behind them. Two surgers no one had noticed were on the top of the trailer. They'd been up there scraping at the roof trying to find a way in. They could sense there were uninfected humans in the trailer. They just couldn't figure out a way to get at them. Both of the surgers kicked off the top of the trailers to rocket headfirst towards the firing line.

One of the surgers aimed too high and smashed headfirst into the side of the trailer breaking its neck. The other one smashed into the man next to Drew hard enough to make him hit the trailer with the back of his head and go instantly unconscious. The unconscious man and the surger disappeared in a tangle of arms and legs under the trailer. Drew dropped to his knee and spun around to help. Seeing that the surger was already gnawing on the guy's arm and that two more surgers were crawling under the trailer towards them Drew yelled for help and started shooting.

Then it was quiet. They formed up in a circle in between the trucks with guns pointing outwards and slowly revolved looking for any more of the infected. When none showed up after about five minutes Harley called it clear. They hustled back to their trailer where Charani was standing in the open gap with her pistol dangling from her hand again. The drivers were standing there ready to get going. Anybody who could drive one of the trucks good was considered too valuable to go out on surger clearing duty. Harley pulled Drew to the side.

"The guy who got wasted next to you was the escort for the vardo two driver. Now you're the escort for the vardo two driver. His name's Emilio. If he dies, it's on you." Harley turned and climbed in the back of the truck as the drivers were crawling out. Drew didn't have to ask which one was Emilio. A man covered in tattoos with a gigantic bushy beard hanging down to an impressive beer gut was already running to the front of the truck they were riding in. The small framed Hispanic man staring at Drew must be Emilio.

"We going to stand here until one of these things eats us or we going to get the hell out of here." Emilio asked. He wasn't looking forward to having to break in another escort. It took a special kind of person to sit in the front of the cab as surgers were leaping at you from every direction.

Drew didn't bother answering. He just jogged to the other truck with Emilio following close behind. He kept his eyes open and his neck on a swivel. Once Emilio was in, he jogged around to the passenger side and climbed up into his seat. Emilio had the big rig fired up and ready to roll before Drew had his door shut all the way. Once the lead truck pulled out Emilio followed right behind. It suddenly occurred to Drew that Yue wouldn't know where to find him. Then he remembered she hadn't come back yet. Consigned to be worried all day about his siblings he grumpily put his head back on the seat and took in the sights. It was a lot riskier up here than in the back, but it was also a million times more scenic. The smell was way better too.

Drew could appreciate now why the truck drivers were so celebrated. The three eighteen wheelers blew down the tiny park roads like it was nothing. Emilio taking turns with ease that Drew himself would've slowed down for when driving a pickup truck. Forget about driving the massive machine Emilio was at the helm of.

Being the middle vehicle in the convoy came with some perks. The best perk being that the first truck took the brunt of the surger action head on. They had some jump at them as well, but Emilio stuck so close to the first truck that the ones coming from the side were normally caught flatfooted and swept aside by the long poles they had sticking out at multiple angles. The poles broke frequently on impact. One of the things done during that free time every night was replacing the long wooden poles. They had a ton of the poles since they were what was used to setup their circus tents.

"Where to today?" Drew asked Emilio after they'd ridden in silence for a good hour.

"The next bit of nowhere. Some place in South Carolina the boss did a gig for some politicians at a few years ago. On top of it being in the middle of nowhere he thinks it had diesel too. It's a solid five hours from here so you might want to sit back and relax. We're taking mostly back roads through the woods so unless somebody tries to ambush us it should be a boring day."

"I'm a huge fan of boring days." Drew said. Emilio smiled and nodded his agreement to that sentiment.

The drive was as scenic as it was monotonous. The route had been selected since it avoided all the major cities and towns. They cruised down backroads occasionally having to stop to clear trees and branches off the road. One time they had to setup a winch to pull a car off to the side of the road. All of that slowed them to the point that the five-hour trip took over ten hours. By the time they pulled up to the small, paved road leading to their destination it was close to dusk.

The escorts were ordered to get out and clear the cheap metal gate blocking the road. Drew jumped out to join the others in unwrapping the metal wire holding the large bar down over the road. There was a pad lock on a thick chain that one of them took care of easily with a large pair of bolt cutters. Once they had the bar out of the way they ran and jumped back in their respective trucks.

Drew read the big sign half hidden by weeds that warned they were trespassing on federal property. There was a lot of verbiage under that but in big bold letters was a warning they could be shot. Considering it was the end of the world and everything Drew wasn't too concerned with the various fines posted on the board. Getting shot would suck no matter if it was pre or post apocalypse.

They'd driven another half mile when they came to a stop again. The order came down to assist with another fence they needed to get through. Drew hopped out again and ran around to where the first truck was stopped. This next fence was much newer looking. There was no padlock and chain holding this one. Hardened steel bars were reinforced by additional steel bars cross horizontally. The gate was at least twenty feet tall and connected on both sides to a fence of approximately the same height. The three of them were staring at it wondering if maybe the winch would work on it when the gate slid open smoothly by itself.

Not wanting to look a gift horse in the mouth they moved off to the side jumping in their respective trucks as they drove through the gate. They drove to the end of the road where the diesel pumps Blaze remembered were indeed sitting on the edge of a small airstrip. There was a hangar at one end of the airstrip with the doors on it shut tight. Other than that, there were multiple large grass covered mounds scattered around. A door opened in the front of one of the mounds and a man in a suit walked out. He was flanked on both sides by tough looking men in camouflage.

Drew happened to look over to the left. He saw at least twenty men in camouflage on that side of the truck rapidly encircling them. He pointed that out to Emilio who got on the radio and blasted that news out. A few seconds later the response went out to hold tight but be ready to fight. Not that it was going to do them any good against that many well-armed enemies. They couldn't even escape unless these guys opted to open the gate for them.

Vardo number one opened up and Blaze emerged with Yue behind him and a few others. Drew held back on his urge to wave at Yue. No matter what other opinions he had of Blaze the guy was smart enough to have brought Yue out when talking was going to be critical. Looking at the large number of men with automatic weapons all around them Drew hoped they actually got a chance to talk.

Drew leaned forward but couldn't hear what was being said between Blaze and the well-dressed man below. Whatever was discussed must have worked out because an unworried looking Blaze put his radio to his lips and announced that everyone could come out. Extremely outgunned everyone slowly emerged from the trucks. The soldiers still had their weapons where they could get to them easily but weren't actively pointing them at the trucks anymore. That was a step in the right direction.

Drew hopped down from his seat and walked over to see Yue. She smiled nervously and hugged him. She put her lips close to his ear when she hugged him.

"The suit is full of it. Don't trust him. You can trust Blaze." She dropped the hug and went back to focusing on what was being discussed between Blaze and the suit.

LeBron wandered over and gave Drew a quick bro hug before turning to try and focus on the discussion as well. The suit was congratulating them on making it this far. He raised his voice to let them know that they'd managed to stumble on a base supporting the continuation of the United States. They happened to need men who could escort supplies across the country. It was kismet. Drew saw a few of the clan who identified way too strongly with their fake gypsy roots getting excited about the mention of it being fate that'd brought them there. The guy was reading his audience and working to manipulate them. Drew started getting a bad feeling about this.

Dusk was coming on strong, so the man in the suit insisted they all go inside. The men and women would be sent to separate barracks. There was some visible angst about being split up, but Blaze told everyone to chill out. Yue gave them each a hug before walking away. She admonished them both to 'Stay Frosty' before leaving. That was some slang she'd picked up hanging around with their dad's old cop buddies. Plenty of them had served in the military first. It meant to stay on your toes. It did nothing to assuage Drew's feeling that this was all a really bad idea.

In the men's barracks they were served ice cold beer and hot pizza. They were allowed to keep their weapons. The man in the suit introduced himself as Special Agent Leander with the Department for the Continuation of the United States. He welcomed them all to the hospitality of the United States government. He told them they'd be working hard to earn their place here but that they didn't have to worry any longer about not having a place to call home. He excused himself and left as the party was just getting going.

Chapter 36: The Gift Horse was a Trojan

Drew woke up the next morning with a headache he didn't think was fair given that he'd only had two beers with his pizza. He stood up off the olive-green cot he'd been sleeping on to look for the bathroom. Something felt off. He patted his body and looked frantically all around the cot he'd been sleeping on. Around him he saw a few others doing the same thing. Most of the men looked to still be asleep. A lot of them had crashed right on the floor.

"Don't bother. They took our weapons. I'm guessing the beer was spiked. That was so stupid." Drew turned around to see Blaze standing there. The man looked like he had a world class hangover. That could probably be attributed to being roofied the night before.

"What do we do?" Drew said. The act of speaking made his head vibrate painfully.

Before Blaze could answer Special Agent Leander walked in. He was flanked by soldiers with guns again. He made a bee line for Blaze. A few more camouflaged men came in and stood against the walls with their weapons in their hands. They were no longer even bothering to pretend to be friendly. Leander stopped about five feet from Blaze.

"I'm going to say this once. This base serves as a logistical element of the United States continuation forces for the southeast. We really are looking for truck drivers and labor. You'll agree to do that for us. The missions you'll be sent on may be on the verge of suicidal. If you ever want to see your women again, you'll carry the missions out successfully. We flew all the women to another base last night. You'll be provided with appropriate weapons when sent out on missions. Otherwise, you'll not be issued a weapon until it's decided you're trustworthy. You'll live here and we'll feed you when you're not out on supply runs. You'll do as ordered as soon as you're ordered. Is all of that understood?"

Blaze looked around helplessly. Several of the men who'd woken up had wives or girlfriends that'd been taken. Everyone who'd been with the clan for a while felt like they were part of a family. Blaze knew they had a few guys who wouldn't care if they never saw the women again or not. Those men would value the security of a home base though. At least until something better came along. He nodded his understanding to Leander.

"You're doing the right thing. Trust me this will all work out for the best." Leander patted Blaze on the shoulder like he was a child then turned to leave. Harley was standing directly in his path. There was no need for Harley to have a weapon to look intimidating as hell. Drew knew he wouldn't want to be on the receiving end of that icy glare.

"The girls get hurt I'll hunt you down and rip your face off." Harley said in a tone that left no doubt he was serious. He didn't move out of the special agent's way. Leander had to backtrack and step over a cot to leave. He'd lost that smug look he'd had on his face. He looked more like a dog running out with its tail between its legs than like someone who'd just pulled off a slick one as he exited the barracks.

"Now what. We've got to get Yue back." LeBron said.

"We will. We'll kill all these pikers once they tell us where the girls got sent. Then we'll go get them and we'll kill anybody that gets in our way." Blaze said viciously. The man who'd looked so lost a few minutes before was gone. In their place was a leader that Drew knew he could follow. He remembered Yue telling him he could trust Blaze. For now, he would. At least until they'd gotten Yue back.

Authors Note:

Thank you so much for embarking on this journey with me. I hope you've enjoyed it so far and are looking forward to finding out what comes next! The start of a new series is the start of a new series of relationships for me. I get requests periodically to go back and add an epilogue to a series. I'd love to be able to easily step back into those worlds again, but I fear when I do, I'll lose track of the other characters I'm on a different journey with.

The relationship between author and character means at some point you really start seeing everything from the different characters points of view. When confronted with the same challenge, I know Drew, LeBron or Yue would each approach it from a different angle. Staying true to those nuances is what breathes life into the different characters. It takes them from a two-dimensional concept to a three-dimensional construct.

One of my favorite parts of this series was that it didn't start out like a normal zombie book or movie. The characters didn't just wake up one morning and the whole world had gone to hell. It did so gradually. How do they survive when all the gas pumps have already been drained and the store shelves already cleared off? It adds a whole new element to the story telling.

I hope you've enjoyed this new beginning. I write it as I see it happening, but I can see a whole new kind of society rising up to rule in this new normal. Whether it can hold itself together or not remains to be seen. The government had to be ruthless to survive but can it maintain that ruthlessness without sacrificing all of its humanity? I guess we'll find out.

Also, if you happen to be reading my other Zombies series and saw that we'd welcomed a new baby boy to the world his name's Brayden and him and his mom are doing awesome!

If you enjoyed this book, please leave a positive review!

Other Books by RS Merritt

Zombies!

Need more Zombies? Check out the Zournal series:

The Zournal Series

Looking for something a little different? Try the Son of the Keeper Series.

Son of the Keeper

Printed in Great Britain
by Amazon